PACT OF THE KEEPS:

CLIFFSHADE

KEEP:

DARK RESURGENCE

**THE THIRD BOOK IN
"THE PACT OF THE KEEPS"
SERIES**

AUTHORS: BK STAPLES & THEO MOON

Copyright

Copyright @ 2022 by
Bk Staples/Theo Moon

ISBN: 979-8-9995169-0-9

Printed in the United States of America

Published by Staples/Moon Books LLC.

DEDICATION

This book is dedicated to one of our biggest fans who sadly passed away before she could read our third book. We are sure that she will hear the words as each of you read them. Love and gratitude Susan S. rest now and be at peace.

ACKNOWLEDGMENTS

RD Shull (Gavin Brokinhorn) assisted in the editing, continuity, and character development.

Brian Lee (Shamash) was also a tremendous help with early editing and constant re-reading and ideas. Also, our systems and communications coordinator.

Janet (Paladin Sargent Owl) assisted in proof reading, character development, and editing.

Each person behind the characters gave us the backstory or history. We then incorporated it into the story and tried to capture each personality.

Introduction

A story about an eclectic family of friends' survival. Their trials and tribulations. Their fight to rid the continent of Alahora of a recent rash of dangerous enemies and monsters. They are a variety of races and beliefs, with their family histories being equally exciting and, in some cases, unimaginable to most.

Book 1: Blackwing Keep, an introduction to the friends of the realm and the ensuing chaos they must face as a team.

Book 2: Darkwing Keep, the friends are faced with the daunting task of saving Lord Darkwing in a fight against the Cloud Giants.

Book 3: Cliffshade Keep, we hope you enjoy the teams' latest endeavors and fights for the safety of the realm.

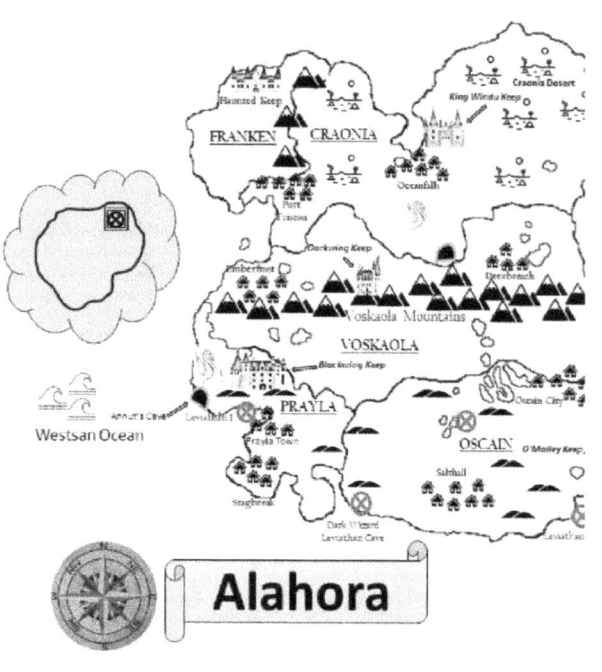

Alahora

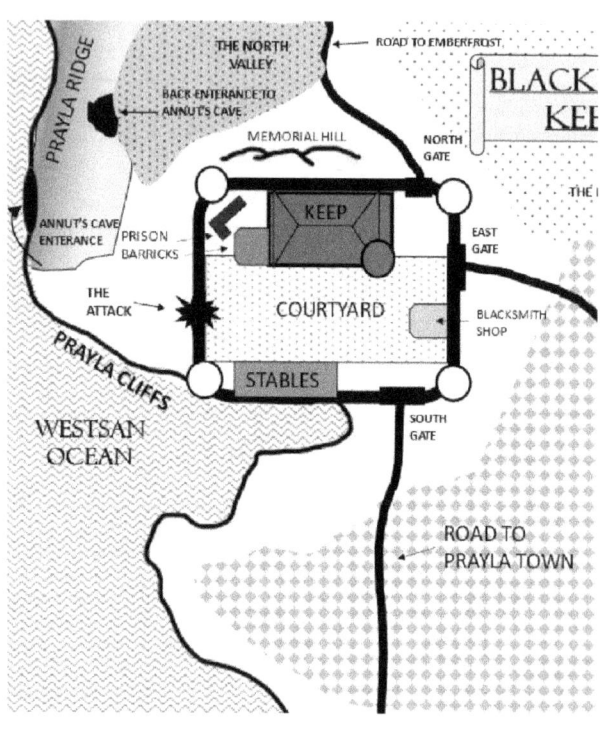

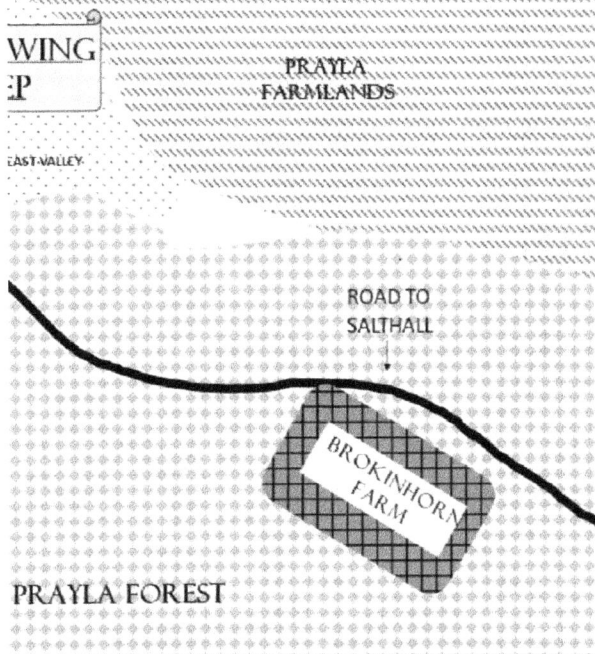

WING
EP

EAST VALLEY

PRAYLA
FARMLANDS

ROAD TO
SALTHALL

BROKINHORN
FARM

PRAYLA FOREST

Table of Contents

Prologue

Letter from a Childhood Friend

A drop of perspiration glides from her forehead and down her cheek as she sits down in her study chair. She stays bent over and rests her elbows on her knees. The droplet makes its way down her jawline to the tip of her chin and then falls to the floor. The dust on the old stone floor consumes the droplet leaving a dark wet oval. In the silence of her own company, Akita can't help but think about the Magma Amulet and then the Cloud Giant King not to mention all the tragedies that her and the team have gone through over the last six months.

Before another drop of sweat can fall from her face, she uses the back of her sleeve to wipe her brow. She takes a deep breath, and the odor of sweat and stagnant air fills her nostrils. She mutters to herself under her breath, "I need a bath and this room needs airing out."

Akita walks to the window directly across from her and pushes open the leaded glass doors. A small breeze wafts by carrying the scents of the Keep and the hillside. She can smell the freshly baked bread from the kitchens below, and the sweet smell of the blooming flowers on the hillside. There is just the faintest bit of the ocean's saltiness in the breeze.

She pulls off her chainmail vest and pulls the hair clasp from her hair. The chainmail thuds to the floor beneath her as her long black hair falls to her shoulders. The melee combat training exercises made her extra sweaty today and she is looking forward to being free of the pungent smelling training gear. She heads back to the chair to get her boots off.

Akita's eye catches the sunset sky painted with bright yellows, oranges, pinks, purples, and blues. Wispy clouds slowly streak through the sky as they slowly float to the south. The beautiful backdrop enhances the view of the cemetery where Rogue and Rani, as well as several of her soldiers, are laid to rest. It is a bittersweet moment for her, alone with her thoughts.

Before she can take her boots off, she sees a thick letter on the desk beside her. Excitement bubbles up in her chest as she sees an old familiar seal. It is a circle with a flame in the center that she had made for her childhood friend, Storm Fireheart. Akita picks up the envelope and quickly breaks the seal. Again, she speaks in a whisper to herself, "What has it been 5 or more years?" She pulls out the folded parchments and begins to read.

Akita,

I just heard the tragic news about Uncle Edmond. I will never forget the kindness he showed when he took me and my mother in. He always treated me like part of the family and then took care of me when my mom passed. I wish I had been home with you both. My friend, I know this is not easy on you. My heart is melting that nothing could be done to save him, and my anger is hot as a fire that the Dark Wizards did this to him.

The rumors over here are that you are fighting those Dark Wizards and other evil creatures. I have always said that I would help you no matter what, so I have decided that it is time I return to Alahora. After I mail this letter, I will book a passage to Prayla. I have learned all I can here and there is war brewing due to the tyrant King of Castilian. He sees everyone from Alahora as a spy or a traitor. I have spent months eluding the Castilian Inquisitors. Omoth is not safe unless you submit to the Crown and pledge allegiance.

So, you are probably wondering what I have been up to all these years and why I haven't written?

As you know I traveled to Omoth to learn more about my ancestral magic, find my strength as a young Wizard, and see more of the world. It took a few months, but I found a Master Wizard who knew my family's ancestral magic and was willing and able to teach me. While I was training with him, we were able to trace my family tree. Apparently, in Omoth the Firehearts were known as a clan of Fire-Whisperers. We could speak to the fire as if it was alive. This mixed with our fire magic allowed my ancestors to create pets out of pure fire. Could you imagine me with a cat of pure fire? I would have made it chase those boys that were mean to us when we were little. I can picture the smile on your face right now.

Everything was going well until the Wizard that was teaching me met with an untimely death by a ferocious Unicorn. Not all beautiful creatures are nice. I describe you as an example all the time. There's that smile again!

Akita, I went through some hard times after that. I had no teacher, no money, and no place to live.

I went to the city and tried to put on shows with my fire magic to get money. That didn't last long when they discovered I was Alahoran. I was tossed outside the gates to fend for myself. I decided then that I was a smart woman, and I could take care of myself. I grew up running around in the forest with you so I should be able to survive on my own in Omoth's forests.

For days I traveled west, and up into a mountain range, then I stumbled upon an old temple in the mists that were hugging the ridge, so it was like walking through fog. As I moved closer the huge temple revealed itself and I could see that it was built into the mountainside. You would have loved it, all dark, gloomy, and mysterious.

In all my training with the Master Wizard, I had only learned to create bugs out of fire, so I created a small swarm of fire bugs to light my way into the temple. So much for fire cats.

With that said I entered this magnificent old building with its ancient architecture. Yes, it was overgrown with forest plants and vines, just how you like them. I found a corner to set up my camp so I would be out of the elements and started to have a look around. The first few days I explored all the upper levels of the temple, but didn't find anything other than an old gold ring buried in rubble from where one of the rooms' roof caved in.

So, the next day I headed to the lower levels. Which, at first, was interesting, with living quarters on one level, storage on another, but on the third level down there was a locked room with a big iron door. I wondered what was behind the door. Can we say I should have walked out then? As you will know curiosity got the best of me, and I used my fire powers to open the door by melting the hinges. This of course caused the door to fall forward onto the floor and disturb years of dust. Between the dust and lack of light I couldn't see beyond the frame of the door, so I sent a swarm of fire bugs to go in and light up the room. Still, I saw nothing to be concerned about and it seemed to be an empty room.

As I walked into the dimly lit room, darkness swallowed the fire bugs and then me. I don't know what happened next because I woke up the next morning on the floor. I was sweating like I had a bad fever, and my fire bugs were gone. I felt my way along the walls until I reached daylight again. I felt horrible. I felt weak and cold. I sat by the remains of my campfire and tried to light it, but I couldn't make any fire. I tried to make more fire bugs, but I couldn't even make one. I began to panic and tried every spell I knew, but nothing worked. I no longer had any magic!

Some time has passed since that day. I still don't know exactly what happened in that room, but I know that I was changed. It's hard to explain in writing. I will tell you when I see you at Blackwing Keep.

Love, Storm

Akita puts the letter on her desk and gazes out the window. It is now getting dark, so stars are starting to twinkle in the sky. With a snap of her fingers, she creates a flame to light the candles in the room. She thinks to herself how lost she would be without her magic; it would be devastating. Storm must feel lost and empty without it. How long before she gets home? She estimates a week or two depending on where she sent the mail from. She starts to feel helpless that she can't even help Storm get home.

Akita heads to her bathing room and as she takes her clothes off, she takes a moment to heat the water already in the tub with a touch. After lowering herself into the piping hot water, she stretches out and memories play in her head of the adventures she had with Storm growing up. The trouble they got into for doing un-lady like things, like climbing trees, exploring alone and other things only boys should do. She smiles to herself and tries to relax. As she continues to soak in the hot water, she can't help but think about the danger Storm was in and possibly could still be in just trying to get home. She knows that she needs to be patient and await Storm's arrival, but she can't stand feeling powerless when it comes to her friends.

Chapter 1

The Proposal

Ishvet and Vivian stand on the balcony of Elderwolf Keep at sunset which has become their usual routine of late. Ishvet holds Vivian in his arms loosely, her back to his chest, as they look over the Keep and further out, to the lake. Ishvet rests his chin on top of Vivian's head, and he can smell the faint scent of Lilac in her golden blonde hair. He straightens his posture and squeezes his arms around her a little tighter, "Viv, I have really enjoyed these last three months here with you."

Vivian leans her head back and turns it slightly to the right to see Ishvet's face, "It has been great, hasn't it? It's a lot slower pace here than at Blackwing Keep."

Ishvet slightly chuckles, "That's for sure, and I have a lot less injuries here."

Vivian smiles and tilts her head back down and stares out over the Keep again, "Well, if you keep training with my platoon, Captain Dub, you may get those injuries that you miss."

Ishvet scoffs at Vivian's insinuation, "I only took my eyes off of him for a second. I didn't even know he could lunge forward like that. Plus, I didn't really get hurt. He just knocked the breath out of me."

Vivian shakes her head back and forth and lets out a slight exasperation, "Ish, when are you going to learn that us Paladins have the ability to use Radiant magic with our fighting?"

Ishvet squeezes a little harder with his arms around Vivian in a playful way, "Well it's not fair. Real warriors use their blades and fists. None of this 'Bright lights and glowing shields' malarkey."

Vivian sharply turns in place inside Ishvet's arms and looks up to him with a scowl, "REAL WARRIORS! Sir Ishvet Bluescale you better choose your next words wisely or this little 'light maker' is going to kick your butt!"

Ishvet looks down to Vivian's face as she is speaking to him through gritted teeth. His eyes get wide, and his mouth hangs slightly open and only a faint "Ah" can be heard from him.

The silence lasts for about thirty seconds before Vivian smiles and starts laughing, "Maybe you will think about who you are speaking of next time, huh?, maybe?"

Ishvet hugs her and pulls her close. In an apologetic tone he whispers, "Yes, you're right Viv, I know you could kick my butt. You're my little light maker and are the greatest warrior."

Vivian turns back around to stare into the colorful and darkening sky, "Apology accepted and you're right."

Ishvet stands there for a few seconds and sways a little with Vivian in his arms before changing the subject, "I do kind of miss the excitement of Blackwing Keep. I wonder what kind of trouble Akita is getting herself into right now?"

Vivian puts her arms on top of Ishvet's in front of her, "I'm sure Wulf is looking out for her. However, getting back to your training with Captain Dub, what had you distracted during training?"

Ishvet sighs and then takes a deep breath, he can smell the lilac from Vivian's hair again, "I was remembering a story my mother told me when I was really little about a fierce Dragon Warrior. She said that this warrior was the hero of a war with the Giants. I was trying to remember the details of the story, because of all the secrets we have uncovered in the past six months, I am starting to think that it wasn't just a bedtime story. She told me that this warrior lead all of the Water Dragons into battle against the Sea Giants to recover a powerful weapon from them. With all that we know now I think that my mother was that warrior. The pieces started falling into place when Annut told me about my mother being a Dragon and then being reborn into a Bahamut Dragonkin.

In the story my mother told me, the warrior was the only one to survive the war and that the Sea Giants were wiped out. She also said that the weapon was hidden until the warrior fell in love with a Prince and gave it to him to keep his realm safe. Now we know that my mother was a Water Dragon and that she was alive back then and my father was the Prince of Cliffshade when they met. What if she gave him the Sea Amulet? That would explain the power he possesses now. When I was growing up, I heard stories of how he was prone to magic, but nothing on the scale of what we have been told that he can do today. This makes me think that he has the Amulet which would put all of us in a lot of danger now that King Cirus is gone and not directing him."

Vivian has a chill run down her back as Ishvet recounts the story to her, "How can we be certain that he has the Sea Amulet? Furthermore, how do we fight that power now that the Magma Amulet is destroyed? Ish, if what your saying is true, then we need to let Akita and the others at Blackwing Keep know that King Carthon could strike at any time."

Ishvet steps back from Vivian and turns her around to look directly into her eyes. He could see a glimmer of fear on her face. He takes her by both hands and clears his throat, "Viv, I have also been thinking about something else. Because of all the battles with the Dark Wizards and Giants, and whatever else may come in the future, I don't want to waste any more time feeling like I have regrets, or I have missed the chance for something special."

Ishvet reaches into his right pocket and pulls out a small object and then grabs Vivian's left hand again. He slowly bends down on one knee and looks up to her face. He can see a puzzled look on her face that begins to wash away as the realization of what he is doing pushes forward, "Vivian, I had Ghod make this before we left the Keep, because I knew even back then what I wanted."

Ishvet opens up his right hand with his palm up to reveal a silver ring. It is intricately carved with a Griffin on one side and a Lamassu on the other. On the crown are two stones, a blue sapphire, and a white opal. The sapphire represents Ishvet and the opal to represents Vivian, both stones encircled by a figure eight.

Vivian's eyes get brighter and a smile forms on her face. She lets go of Ishvet's left hand touches the ring on the palm of his right hand, "Ish, I know what you are doing. You know what I am going to say."

Ishvet interrupts Vivian, "Let me ask you first before you say anything, I had this all planned out, I spoke to your father, your Griffin Zara, and even Captain Dub. They have all given me their blessing, so Vivian Elderwolf will you do me the honor of becoming my life-long partner and protector, by becoming my wife?"

Vivian snatches the ring out of Ishvet's palm and slips it on her finger, then holds her hand up so she can see it better, "Yes, yes, yes!"

Ishvet stands up and embraces Vivian. She snuggles to his chest then looks up as he leans down to kiss her. She then pushes him back and points to the door of the balcony, "Okay that's enough, you have messages to send. Tell Akita that she has a wedding to plan. Most of our friends are there so it makes sense to have it there, plus it's where we met. Ish, don't forget to tell her about the Amulet either."

Ishvet swings around and heads to the door, as he opens it Vivian rushes through, "Wait! Where are you going Viv?"

Vivian doesn't stop as she hollers back to him, "To tell everyone of course, and to show off my gorgeous ring."

Ishvet chuckles and shakes his head as he watches Vivian rush out of the room door. He says under his breath playfully, "What have I gotten myself into?"

Meh-Kola lands on the rooftop closest to the Keep walls in Cliffshade to not alert anyone to her presence. The rooftop is several feet above the wall and gives a direct view of the south side of the Castle within. The walls are in disrepair and the Castle appears to have missing windows and vines growing all over it.

Similarly, the town of Cliffside is in shambles. None of the houses or businesses have seen a fresh coat of paint for years and many structures are boarded up completely. Trash lies in the cobblestone streets and wagons sit scattered and broken next to dark alleyways. Meh-Kola can smell the scent of several people, but she doesn't actually see anyone in any of the homes.

She rests for a long while on the rooftop to regain her strength. It has been a tiresome three-day flight from Blackwing Keep to Cliffshade Keep. She had to keep to the shadows and cover her tracks to make sure that no one knew that she was traveling to the east. Akita specifically told her to keep everyone in the dark about her mission.

Akita told her that she needed to get to Cliffshade as quickly as possible, because Ishvet believed that King Carthon had the Sea Amulet and the first place that they should look is Carthon's Keep. Akita also specified that if Carthon wasn't there that Meh-Kola should look for clues as to where the Dark Wizards may be hiding and report back immediately with any information.

After a good hour of observation, Meh-Kola blinks from the rooftop to the top of the wall and detects a strange smell. She starts to work out what is going on in this place in her head, ["This One smells something odd in the air. It is metallic and rotten like sulfur. This One knows this type of magic, but what is it hiding?"]

Meh-Kola drops down to the untended garden below the wall. All the trees and bushes appear to be dead, and all the garden sculptures are decaying and broken. She heads towards the Keep and passes a large water fountain that appears to be dried up and the three-tiered basins are cracked, however, she can hear the sound of running water.

Everything is starting to click into place in her mind, ["One understands exactly what is going on now. Powerful spells conceal what is the truth of this place. One knows how to get past the spells, but should One do so, not knowing what is on the other side?']

Meh-Kola adjusts her Blink magic to teleport through the magical veil that conceals the Keep. She does it in such a way that she will teleport to the exact same spot and not move any closer to the Keep. This way she can try to keep herself hidden. When she arrives on the other side of the magical barrier she is met with lush foliage, flowering trees, and a magnificent fountain. However, she also hears footsteps in the distance, so she blinks into a nearby bush for cover.

A few seconds after she blinks, a man in a dark robe, walks by as if on guard duty. She can tell that he is a Dark Wizard because she knows him. He is the bumbling idiot she met in the Pigeon Perch Inn when she delivered the Dragon Key Stone that she stole from King Windu's vault. She knows that she could take him down in a matter of a few seconds, but that may alert others.

Meh-Kola stays hidden until the oaf passes and enters a side door of the south side of the Keep. As he is closing the door behind himself, she blinks through the door frame to a dark corner of the interior room. She sits silent and motionless so that he doesn't know she is there. Now she plans her next move, ["One can smell strong magic below. There must be stairs somewhere close. One must be very careful because the powers here are very strong and One does not want to be a fried Fenton. One will stay in the darkest corners and only listen and watch."]

Meh-Kola blinks down a long hallway to another dark corner passing by many painted portraits and expensive looking antiques. At her new vantage point, she can see a Great Hall with three staircases. There are two on the outside of the room going up to the next floor and a wide one going down in the middle of them to a lower floor. She spots a large bookcase at the bottom of the stairs going down that she can hide beside. She blinks to the bookshelf just as a door opens up, further down the next flight of stairs. Seeing her opportunity, she blinks right next to the door as the person walks by. Once they pass, she blinks to a corner next to the door on the other side. Meh-Kola scans the room quickly and sees a table with chairs around it and blinks underneath it immediately. Now that she feels safely hidden for the moment she can observe where she is.

The room is a large rectangle with a large stone wall to her back and in front there is a balcony that runs the entire length of the room. Around her are tables covered with papers and relics. The smell of the strong magic is almost overwhelming now. She thinks that she must be very close to the source. There is a table directly next to the balcony that has crates in front of it and she can see an opening behind them. She blinks behind them and is amazed by what she can see from the balcony.

The balcony railing spindles are just wide enough for Meh-Kola to pop her head through. She looks out into the large cavern before her. It must be at least fifty feet from the floor below. The stairs from the balcony zigzag to the bottom and men in dark robes are walking up and down on both sides, at the bottom of the stairs is another open area with tables and large floor candelabras to light the tabletops. There are more relics and parchments strewn on them too. Beyond the table area is a large circular structure. It appears to be an enormous vat. There is a staircase running up the wall of the vat to the top. Around the whole circumference is a walkway and inside is a glowing liquid. Above the vat is a pulley system like you find on a cargo ship, with wheels and thick ropes.

Meh-Kola can see twelve cloaked figures involved in various tasks around the vat and five more on the stairs to the balcony. On top of the vat there is one person, but they are not wearing dark robes. They are knelt on one knee, and they have their right hand in the glowing liquid. When she adjusts her eyes, she can see they are clasping an object with their left hand that is hanging from their neck. This person's left hand is glowing a bright blue color.

She hears the man on the walkway yell to the robed figures below and she recognizes his voice. However, to confirm her suspicion she needs to see his face. She needs to get to a different vantage point further in the cavern. She looks all around to find a good spot, ["One can blink to the pulley above the vat, but if it gives way, One will get that glowing goo all over Ones nice fur. One will have to find a better spot to go to. Ah, One sees it now. There is a chandelier on the other side of the cavern. No one will see one way up there."]

Meh-Kola blinks to the chandelier at the far end of the cavern and she can now see the man's face, ["One's suspicions were correct. It is King

Carthon on the walkway and the object he is clasping must be the Sea Amulet. One must get out of here quickly and tell Akita, but One also wants to know what he is doing with that vat."]

As Meh-Kola finishes her thought, King Carthon announces to all the Dark Wizards around him that his pet will be ready in a matter of days and that everyone in the Sanctum should prepare for the awakening. As he speaks a large dark shadow as big as the vat moves around in the glowing liquid. All the Dark Wizards cheer and clap for the announcement and their leader's accomplishment. King Carthon stands and reaches out his hand to hush them and when they are quiet, he continues by stating that "Those Blackwing Keep fools will never know what has hit them."

Meh-Kola feels a shiver in her wings. She hears his words and sees the Amulet around his neck at the same time, ["One sees the Sea Amulet and hears his declaration. One must leave now. One doesn't know what he already has in place to attack Blackwing Keep. One fears for One's new friends."]

Meh-Kola retraces her steps to the outside of Cliffshade Keep and adjusts her Blink Magic to get outside of the magic veil that is concealing the true state of the Keep. Once out Meh-Kola starts her long journey back to Blackwing Keep. She decides that she cannot take a direct route home and should worry about who may see her traveling west as she must ensure that she makes it back to the Keep with this information.

CHAPTER 2

LET'S CATCH UP

Akita is with Shamash and Ixenvorlux going over reports. Over the past few months, the team has been working on plans to go up against King Carthon. The decision was made to intensify training and expand the army, while searching for clues and researching Cliffshade Keep.

With a concerned look, Akita asks Shamash, "How is General Ambrose doing with all this new training?"

Shamash answers, "He thinks it is good and that it should have happened years ago. I also believe he is lost and feeling useless as he can only teach military discipline now and, well, it's a different discipline than your team is teaching them. Oh, they still line up and march, with the proper uniforms, but he's lost."

Akita replies, "So maybe we should approach him with retiring? Promote Olek and find two Lieutenants to help Olek, as we are getting more and more soldiers every day. Maybe there is a job we can give General Ambrose that he is better suited for now."

Shamash states, "That would probably be a good idea. So, you know I have been training Ixen to do my job. Teaching her the history and everything I can about how the Keep runs, taxes, supplies, the various jobs around the Keep, and getting her ready to take my place someday."

Akita smiles at Ixenvorlux, "That would be perfect if you are up to all this. In the meantime, Shamash having a second pair of hands and another brain working on things isn't a bad thing."

Ixenvorlux answers, "I love that I can participate and help. I am learning a lot and let's face it, I need a trade for my life besides healing."

Shamash retorts, "Hey now! I'm not retiring yet, but I might like to travel a bit before I am too old, that is once the Dark Wizards are gone, as I want to keep my Dragonkin parts."

Ixenvorlux and Akita laugh at his statement. Akita states, "Wulf has become my right hand and second brain as well. With everything going on it can be a challenge to keep up. I am also very thankful for the team and what they are doing for the Keep."

There is a knock at the door and Alican the messenger walks in.

Shamash grabs a gold piece, "Alican, how are you and your mom this week?"

Alican bows, "We are doing just fine, sir. I have this message for Lady Blackwing from Ishvet Bluescale."

Akita takes the message, "Thank you, Alican. Tell your mom I said 'Hello' when you see her tonight. Give me just a minute to see if I need to send a reply."

Akita opens the message and reads.

Akita,

Vivian and I will be returning to Blackwing Keep with the Earl Jarkon and others of her family and Court. We would like Vicar to officiate our wedding at Blackwing Keep. I know you are now giddy and giggling so we will see you in less than a week.

Your Friend Ishvet.

P.S. I have a feeling the Sea Amulet is with King Carthon, which is extremely troubling. Talk to you more when we get there.

Akita starts laughing and grabs paper and quill, to jot down a quick message. She then thinks twice about it and decides to send a Seeking Stone message. "Alican, thank you so much but we will send a message from our Seeking Stone, as nothing else will get there before they leave." Turning to Shamash, "We have a wedding to prepare for. Vivian and Ishvet are going to be here in less than a week." She does not mention his added comment. They will have to discuss this at dinner with the team.

Akita jogs out to the courtyard and amplifies her voice for everyone in the Keep to hear. "I need all the team at dinner, for a meeting, including Greta and Quinn. Yes, that means you too, Ghod." Akita then heads to the study, to send her message to Ishvet. She is so excited she can barely contain herself.

It's been several hours now, and Akita finds herself pacing the length of the main table in the Dining Hall, not so much as pacing, more like dancing. A closed mouth grin from ear to ear won't go away as her friends enter and find a seat for dinner.

Quinn and Greta find themselves standing to the side wondering what they should do. Akita exuberantly motions for them to have a seat at the table, as she continues to prance.

She looks up to see everyone seated except Ghod who comes sauntering in the door with a fork in one hand and a table knife in the other. "I'm famished, any chance we can eat while we talk or is it talk and then eat? I always think better on a full stomach."

Everyone spins to look at Ghod, as Akita stops dead in her tracks. "I suppose we can do it your way, as I am sure everyone is hungry after a hard day of training, and apparently making their own silverware. Never mind, have a seat." She looks at Quinn, "Run and tell them to serve dinner now, but return to your seat tonight because you and Greta are essential to the conversation."

Ghod scoffs at Akita, "My lady, as Ordyn can attest a Greatsword Fighter is ready for anything, anywhere, anytime. Besides, the dainty utensils around here barely hold a nibble of food." He holds up a fork that looks like a serving fork, with his sword engraved on the handle, "This is a fork for a Half-Orc."

Ordyn bursts out laughing, "Quite right Ghod! I may have to commission you to make some for me."

Akita stomps her foot at the "My Lady" reference and then smiles at her friends.

As Quinn runs to the kitchen door and then returns and takes her seat, Akita turns to the group. She looks around the table noting mentally that everyone is here. A huge smile is frozen on her face, and she cannot stop fidgeting with her hands. It is obvious she is excited about something.

Darkwing blurts out, "Let me guess we have to eat fast because the last two eggs are hatching." Everyone starts laughing yet again.

Akita starts to make a witty remark to him, but the staff enter the room with dinner plates and platters of food. She taps her foot and waits as patiently as she can. Quinn, noticing her mood, quickly prepares a plate for Akita, to move things along faster.

As the staff leave the room, Akita retorts, "Darkwing, if the last two eggs were hatching, none of us would be eating now..." she takes a deep breath, starts giggling and cannot keep her composure at all, "Ishvet and Vivian are getting married." Akita starts dancing around in a circle at the head of the table, "They will be here in less than a week. We have so much to do. The Keep's grounds need cleaned and set up for a huge party, food needs to be planned, and decorations will have to be made for the courtyard. Isn't this wonderful!"

Ghod chuckles while chewing on a large sausage. Bits fly out of his mouth onto the table, and he continues to stare at his plate of food, "You called us here for that? I thought someone died again. I swear you ladies get excited over the smallest things. I've known that Ishvet was going to ask Vivian to marry him for months." He takes a big gulp of ale to help swallow the sausage, lets out a small burp, then wipes his mouth on the sleeve of his blacksmithing shirt, "I made the ring for him before he left."

There is a moment of silence that quickly becomes noticed by Ghod. He stops mid bite of a heaping spoonful of mashed potatoes and looks up from his plate. Everyone at the table is staring him down. He pulls the spoon from his mouth slowly and swallows the hot potatoes, "What? Why is everyone staring at me?"

Akita shakes her head and everyone at the table starts laughing, "Ghod, sometimes you are as dense as that anvil you beat on!" Everyone laughs a little harder, "You didn't think to let us know? How could you keep that a secret? You know what, never mind, it's not important now. I want everyone to pitch in and help with the wedding preparations." Then changing to a playful tone of sarcasm directed at Ghod, "After us 'overly excited ladies' get the plans made, I will let you know what your duties are."

Darkwing laughs and points at Ghod, "Oooh! You are in trouble now. Akita is going to singe the eyebrows off your mask."

Ghod looks back and forth from one side of the table to the other rapidly, "uh… uh… I didn't mean anything by it… I swear…. Umm…uh…okay I'm being quiet now."

Greenbean laughs for a second then clears her throat, "Akita anything that the tavern can do, don't hesitate to ask. It's for our friends after all."

Akita turns to Greenbean and smiles, "That's very kind Greenbean, we will definitely need your Magic Bean refreshments at the reception." She then turns to the rest of the group and then finally sits down in the chair that she couldn't keep herself in previously, "Okay now, let's begin with the updates of the state of the Keep. Wulf, let's begin with you and a report of the warlock training."

Wulf smiles and stands up to give his report, "Well, since we got back from the fight with the Cloud Giant King, we have been training several intermediate level magic users to strengthen and control their spells. Akita and I have three students that have excelled in Fire Magic and are on their way to expert level wielding. Quinn here, is among the three."

Akita adds with a tone of pride, "Yes Quinn is doing great! She will rival me very soon. I've also sent a message to my old teacher Void Roasten. He should arrive in two weeks to help with the advanced training."

Quinn smiles and then blushes. She starts to feel embarrassed and looks down at the floor, "Akita, please, you are embarrassing me."

Akita smiles even bigger, "Okay I'll stop, but it is true." She takes a short pause then looks to Gavin who is sitting to the left of Ghod at the end of the table, "Gavin, you're up. How has your training been going since we got back?"

Gavin starts to stand to give his report then he sees Akita start to put up her hand and shake her head no. He sits back in his seat, "Since the addition of Skip and Meh-Kola to the team, we have all kinds of bases covered. We've grouped up to train everyone we can in the Keep to use daggers and in survival training in the forest. Skip is givin the lessons in archery. Meh-Kola is learnin them how to sneak around and I am helpin with the survival and animal trainin. We have a few fellers that have a knack for earth magic, so Skip and I have been practicin with them. We'll have a few extra Rangers runnin round in no time."

Skip sits forward in his seat, "Yes Lady Blackwing... um I mean Akita. We are helping where we can, and it seems to be paying off. Lord Darkwing helps with the archery when he is not training with the magic fighters. Uh, Meh-Kola do you have anything to add?"

Meh-Kola stops mid lick of her paw and looks up then around the table, "One is trying to teach stealth, but no one has my blink ability, so it is hard. One sees many people getting quieter when they move around the Keep."

Akita nods her head in agreement and then looks at Ordyn, "Ordyn, how is the swordsmanship coming with the troops? Does your team have everything they need?"

Ordyn nods in agreement, "Yes things are going well. With the help of Ghod, we have better weapons for the troops. Also, Greenbean has been working with a special team of soldiers to hone their skills with ward rings and swords. She has the most experience in that regard. Olek has taken on the added responsibility of training all the fighters in the use of shields. As we don't have a Paladin at the Keep right now, we had to ask Fab Ulous to teach some basic Radiant magic to the shield team. They are learning how to imbue their weapons and to create shields of light. I think he has been calling them his 'Light Brigade'." Ordyn stops and looks at Fab Ulous with a raised eyebrow for confirmation.

Fab Ulous smiles and nods and Ordyn clears his throat, "In the last three months we have seen many soldiers and Keep Guard rise to the rank of expert in their respective class fighting styles. Besides a few black eyes and small cuts and scrapes, training has been going well. Luckily, we have plenty of healers on hand just itching for a chance to fix someone up." After he finishes his last sentence, he looks over to Vicar, who is smiling a toothy Dragonkin smile.

Akita looks over to Vicar also and can't help to smile and think, ["It's so funny to see a Dragonkin smile. It's almost deceiving with all those sharp teeth showing."] She snaps from her fleeting thought and looks back to Ordyn, "Thanks Ordyn, it sounds like we are going to have the best army and Keep Guard in all of

Alahora thanks to you, Lieutenant Olek, Greenbean, and Ghod. Fab Ulous thank you so much for stepping in to help the… what was it?... The Light Brigade? I'm sure Vivian will be impressed with your teachings when she gets back."

Vicar stops smiling when Mandrake jabs an elbow into his left ribs, "Ow, what?... oh! It's my turn." Vicar clears his throat and furls his brow at Mandrake then looks back to Akita, "Since Shamash has had his hands full of Keep business and pulling up his trousers. I have taken on a few students to teach the nuances of healing. Several people in the Keep and in Prayla have some natural healing abilities that I have been helping to develop. Most of them are more suited for infirmary duties. However, we have found a few that will do well in a battle situation. Quinn has a knack for fire and healing apparently. She is my top student also."

Mandrake leans forward and looks around Vicar to see Quinn who is trying to shrink into her chair, "Quinn, there is no reason to be embarrassed about working hard to get good at something, or three things in your case."

Quinn looks a little startled and then a bit confused. Her pupils look up, and to the right as she imaginarily counts what she is working to become good at. Before she can finish counting Mandrake interrupts.

With a giggle Mandrake blurts out, "Fire Magic, Healing Magic, and Cooking Magic!"

Quinn smiles and mouths the words "Thank You" to Mandrake.

Akita giggles and smiles while looking at Quinn, "You get any better and you'll be taking my place soon."

Quinn shakes her head rapidly in a motion to say no, not me. Everyone gives a short laugh and then returns their attention to Akita.

Akita pauses and stares forward with a blank expression for a moment. In her head she is organizing what she wants to say next. She looks up to the ceiling and hums a few notes, "Okay everyone, we have a few staffing changes coming in the near future and I want you all to be aware of them. We all will need time to get used to the transitions. First, General Ambrose will be moving up to my Chief Tactical Advisor and General Olek will be promoted to the head of the

Army. My beloved friend and advisor Shamash wants to travel before he gets any older, so his sister and my friend, Ixenvorlux will take over his duties as the Blackwing Keep Cleric and Healer. So, let's give a big round of applause for these three promotions and Shamash's sabbatical."

Everyone claps and stares at Shamash and General Ambrose who are seated behind Akita. Akita turns and walks around her chair and gives each one a hug. Then she walks over to the left side of the table and bends down to hug Ixenvorlux. She then returns to the head of the table and the clapping dies off, "In other news, we have several precious additions to the Keep. Momma Alure's eggs have hatched and are growing very fast. Almost as fast as Annut's Dragonlings. That reminds me, there are still two eggs left to hatch. Annut assures me that they will hatch when they are ready. Of course, I'm a worrier, so I'm hoping that everything is okay with them."

Akita stops and looks at Mandrake and her eyes get big like she just remembered something, "Mandrake, I almost forgot." Then she explains to the team, "Mandrake has been spending all his free time in the library and has been to several towns' Historians to find out all he can about Cliffshade Keep, King Carthon, King Windu, and the Amulets of Power. We haven't had any solid leads yet. Tomorrow he will travel to Durmond Dwarven Hearth Home under the Voskaola Mountains with Darkwing to look through their ancient tomes to find as much information as possible. We will need every tool that we possibly can have before we go up against the two tyrants."

Akita starts to sit and then jumps up, "Greta, Shamash, and Advisor Ambrose, I received a letter last night from Storm Fireheart. She received word about Uncle Edmond and is coming home. I fear that something bad has befallen her, but we won't know until she gets here." Akita looks around the room, "For those that don't know, Storm Fireheart is my Keep Sister. Her mother worked here when she was growing up. Sadly, she was orphaned, but Uncle Edmond took her under his wing. She and I were inseparable. I am not sure when she will arrive here from Omoth, but it has been a long time since she went out on her own."

Akita sits down and starts to finish her meal and the rest of the team starts to have side conversations about all the announcements. She finishes the last of her meal and gets up and walks around to Meh-Kola. Akita bends down and whispers in to Meh-Kola's ear, "Let me talk to you over by the hearth."

Meh-Kola blinks to the hearth and waves to Akita. Akita stands back up from the now empty chair and looks towards the hearth. She sees Meh-Kola waving at her. Akita mumbles under her breath, "That is just not fair. I wish I could blink to and fro."

Akita makes her way to Meh-Kola and sits on the hearth next to the small, winged cat. Then she leans down so that she doesn't have to speak very loudly, "Meh-Kola, I have a very special mission for you. I would like you to leave as soon as you can for Cliffshade Keep. Ishvet believes that King Carthon possesses the Sea Amulet. We don't know exactly where the King is, but I believe that his Keep is a good starting point to find him. I want you to be as stealthy as you possibly can and try to find him there and if he isn't there, find a clue to where he is. Tell no one and by seen be no one. Can you please do that for me?"

Meh-Kola sits silently for half a minute on her hind legs and a front paw scratching her chin, the other under her elbow. She looks up to Akita,

"One would normally get paid very well for a dangerous mission like this. However, One will give you a discount since we are friends now." Meh-Kola meows a slight giggle.

After she finishes her laughter and sees that Akita is not laughing along, "Okay, okay, One will do it as favor… this time. It will take One several days to get there. One can only blink so far at a time. As soon as One knows something, One will come back to report. One will not send a message. There are spies everywhere that can intercept them."

Before Akita can say anything, Meh-Kola blinks out of sight. Akita is slightly startled by the act but then regains her composure. She walks back to the table as she sees several of the team making their way out of the Dining Hall. She meets up with Wulf and asks him if he would like to go for a fly over the valley. Wulf agrees and they make their way to the courtyard and take flight.

As evening turns into twilight, Sham, Scotch and Ben are making the trip up to check on the eggs and make sure there is enough livestock for the Dragons. However, at this point the Dragons are doing their own hunting and fishing in the area. Ben heads up the stairs to the caverns to check on the last two eggs. As he walks in, he hears a crack and jumps. Annut sticks her head in the cavern from her cave and sees Ben just staring at the crack in the egg.

As Sham and Scotch walk into the cave Martyn lands on the ledge.

Darkwing calls out to Sham, "What's going on? Granit told me I should come to him."

Sham replies, "Oh, it's just feeding time."

Darkwing nods, "Akita isn't here is she?"

Sham shakes his head, "Nope, not yet, although you never know when she is coming up here."

Darkwing stops and looks down the hill, "Something is happening in the cave. I was told to stay here by Granit who is obviously listening in to his mother's conversation or he sees something of importance."

Akita's intuition tells her it is time for her and Wulf to get back to the Keep. They land outside of the tower doors right next to Shamash and Ixenvorlux. Shamash says hello to them both. Akita starts to reply but is stopped mid-sentence as Annut enters Akita's mind, "Akita, you might want to gather those that do not have a hatchling yet but are worthy to be chosen. Ben is frozen in place because he was here when one cracked. It's kind of funny, I don't think he knows I am watching. Also, Darkwing is here on the ledge.

Akita jumps up startling Shamash and Ixenvorlux. "One or both of the last two eggs are hatching. Meet at the stables if you want to go up there."

Shamash politely declines, "I have plenty to do here, but Ixen, go as you could easily be chosen as well."

Akita goes running through the courtyard looking for anyone and everyone. Then she amplifies her voice, "Team, meet me at the stables."

Akita announces, "We have a crack. Ben Sham, and Scotch are up there, so is Darkwing. Those that want to join us Hunter and Warrior will bring you up." Akita and Wulf take off as the Wyverns land.

Akita lands then goes over and hugs Martyn, then looks to Darkwing who is just standing there grinning. "Granit told me I needed to be here."

Hunter and Warrior land so that Ixenvorlux, Mandrake, and Vicar can dismount. Gavin comes running up the stairs and runs face first into Martyn. "OOF! Sorry, Martyn. Sorry, I was huntin in the area. I noticed people arrivin. I take it they are hatchin?"

Everyone laughs and starts heading into the cavern to find Ben, Sham, and Scotch.

As they come around the corner, Ben is kneeling in front of a green hatchling with deep red horns and ridges. Ben is crying as he looks up to Akita, "Zold says he chose me. He chose me. I am nothing, no one and he chose me."

Akita looks at the other egg which is cracking as well. She kneels down to Ben, "You were never 'nothing' and 'no one'. You were and are Ben, a friend to animals, keeper of your grandfather and a hard worker. You take care of him, and we will start getting you trained up as a soldier."

Ben forgets himself and hugs Akita sobbing. Akita and the others just smile.

The other egg cracks again leaving only the back half of the body in a shell. The little dark blue hatchling with gold horns and ridges, starts swinging its hind end against the cave wall to break the rest. It starts stumbling around the room as if looking for someone. When it spots Annut he leaps towards her for a nuzzle. Akita giggles at the mother and child snuggle.

The little blue hatching spins around and looks at Akita, then to Mandrake and so on around the group gathered to see the two new hatchlings.

Akita looks to Annut and states out loud, "Is this one confused?"

Annut nods, and says to everyone in their minds, "She likes the Blue Dragonkin because he looks like her. She knows he has a flying horse. She also knows she can't choose you because she says you are my Chosen." Annut shakes her head and does a Dragon laugh.

Akita looks down at the blue hatchling, "This is your life decision. We will work with it and the chosen will do what is right."

Several look at Akita and then nod as they start to understand what Akita was alluding to.

The little hatching stares at Akita for a moment, then stands up tall and walks straight to Mandrake. Mandrake bends down to hug the little wonder standing in front of him.

Mandrake smiles, "Hello and nice to meet you Elsbeth, welcome to the Blackbrew family."

Mandrake looks up towards Darkwing with a huge grin on his face, "Well Darkwing, I guess we will have to postpone our trip now."

Darkwing smiles and nods back. "That's okay, the Voskaola Mountains aren't going anywhere anytime soon. I definitely understand strengthening your bond with the little girl. Granit wouldn't have let me go if he had just hatched."

CHAPTER 3
WEDDING
PREPARATIONS

The past three days have seen all manner of wagons arrive at Blackwing Keep. Several tradesmen from Prayla are arriving today to begin work on the wedding arch that will be built on the Memorial Hill to the North of the Keep. Akita believes it will be the perfect spot for Ishvet and Vivian to tie the knot. The hill has the Memorial Cemetery at the top and the South facing slope looks over the whole keep.

The whole Keep is pitching in to clean and prepare for the arrival of all the guests for the wedding. The main stable has been refurbished to hold the large number of Griffins that will be arriving. To the east of the Keep large straw beds have been laid out for all the Dragons, Annut, Aphorea, and Thoraxian, to come down from the cave. They will sleep there the night of the reception.

Greta, Quinn, and Akita have transformed the nursery into a grand honeymoon suite for after the wedding. The prison ladies have been making decorations and flower arrangements and the male prisoners, under Greenbeans watchful eyes, have been cleaning as well as decorating the Keep. Darkwing has been working on grand ice sculptures for the reception. All seems to be going to Akita and the ladies' plans. By the end of today they should have almost everything in place for the arrival of the early guests.

The next morning, Wulf quietly walks into Akita's room and puts a fresh mug of coffee on her nightstand. He gently sits on the edge of the bed to watch her sleep for a few more minutes. She has been so busy with what has become a grand production of a wedding. She has barely gotten any sleep or real rest.

As Wulf watches Akita, he starts to see a smile at the corner of her mouth. "Well, good morning my dear. I hope you finally slept well last night."

Akita stretches and rolls over, "Yes, I did and that coffee smells heavenly. I could get used to this." She giggles, as she props up the pillows to sit up.

Coming out of her morning fog, a flash of panic hits her chest, and her heartbeat quickens, and she gets short of breath, "Did something happen with the decorations? Did someone break something?"

Wulf reaches out his hand and takes Akitas left hand and squeezes it. He starts to chuckle and shake his head back and forth, "Calm down, nothing has happened. Gretta and Quinn are taking care of everything. You can rest for a minute."

Akita lets out a large sigh and then smiles, "For a second there I started to panic. I want everything to be perfect for our friend's wedding."

Wulf squeezes Akita's hand again, "It will be lovely no matter what we do because we will all be together again."

Akita looks deeper into Wulf's eyes and scrunches up her nose at him, "When did you become the mushy one?"

Wulf slowly leans over and presses his forehead against hers and playfully says, "I learned it by watching you, you big softy."

As he began to kiss Akita, a loud knock on the door stopped him mid pucker. He gets up from the bed and goes to the door. He looks back at Akita and she nods to let the visitor in. Wulf opens the door to reveal Judas with a handful of letters in his hands.

Akita jumps out of bed, puts her mug back on the nightstand, runs up to him and kneels down and embraces him strongly, "Judas, I'm so glad you are back! I have missed you so much. How's your family doing?"

Judas hugs Akita back and smiles, "Everyone is doing great. I have two new nieces and a new nephew. I am glad to be back at the Keep now. This is my true home. As soon as I got back, Shamash put me to work collecting RSVP'S from the message shop."

Akita stands and looks down at Judas with a huge grin, "I am so glad that you are back. I have needed your ear on several occasions. These months have been too long without you. Your family had to be happy to see you again after all those long years away."

Judas nods as he quickly walks to the desk and places the letters on top. He turns to face them both, "Yes, it was nostalgic to see everyone on the homestead. I needed a short rest after all the issues with the Dark Wizards and Darkwing, but now I'm ready to get back to it. I'll be running back and forth to Prayla on a regular interval to pass on messages and receive responses. If you have anything that needs taken care of, you two just let me know and I'll have it done in a jiffy."

Wulf nods and Akita smiles again, "Thanks Judas, I think I'll get dressed for the day and head down to the Dining Hall. I'm imagining the scent of freshly baked cinnamon rolls and I am hoping that it turns out to be real."

Judas quickly runs out the door and Wulf nods and then leaves shutting the door behind him. Akita takes a deep breath and then gets to dressing. The one thing on her mind at this time is freshly baked cinnamon rolls.

Shamash leaves his office and comes out to the courtyard from the side entrance and sees what appears to be a female Elf, standing in the pathway of the main gate. She is tall and skinny with long white hair and caramel colored skin. She has a small travel bag sitting at her feet and she's wearing a dark blue shirt and brown waistcoat, and black pants. She has on long gloves that go past her elbows and they match her tall riding boots. He hasn't caught a good glimpse of her face, but she doesn't look like she is part of the wedding staff.

The stranger is looking all around, high, and low at the Keep. Her hands are clasped together in front of her sort of like you might see a nervous person doing in an unfamiliar environment. Shamash walks up to the lady and clears his throat, "Excuse me ma'am, can I help you?"

When she turns around to answer him, his eyes get big and bright, "Storm! Is that you?"

Storm perks up and smiles, "Finally a familiar face! Shamash, oh my how are you doing? This place looks so different and there's so many new faces. I was beginning to think that I was at the wrong Keep."

Shamash chuckles a little too exuberantly. "No, no, no, you are in the right place. Akita is going to be very excited that you are here. Gretta already has a room set up for you. Come, Come I'll take you to Akita at once."

As Shamash leads the way to the Dining Hall, he grabs his waist and pulls his pants up, "I believe we will find her at breakfast because Quinn made cinnamon rolls this morning."

Storm giggles, "At least that hasn't changed. I'm famished and Quinn's cinnamon rolls are so scrumptious."

Akita just put a cinnamon morsel in her mouth and glanced towards Shamash as he entered the Dining Hall. She looks down to tear off another piece and stops. Looking up again, she stands so fast her chair falls over behind her, startling everyone. She yells at the top of her lungs, "STORM!!" as she runs across the room almost knocking Shamash over and barreling into Storm.

"Well, Hello to you too!" Storm says while trying to maintain her balance. "Those cinnamon rolls smell heavenly."

Akita stands back looking Storm up and down. "I am so glad you are home. I have missed you so much." Akita guides Storm to the table. "Come have a taste of home. We have so much to talk about."

Wulf picks up Akita's chair, setting it upright and puts a plate with a cinnamon roll down at a chair for Storm. Then pours her a cup of coffee.

Akita smiles at Wulf, "Storm, this is Wulf. He has become very important to the Keep and my sanity as of late. Wulf, this is 'the Storm', my Keep Sister that I have been telling you all about."

Wulf stands and bows, "It is a great honor to meet you, Storm. We are glad to have you back home."

Storm nods as she takes a fork and knife to cut her cinnamon roll to eat it, never removing her gloves. Akita notices this but decides to wait till they are alone to ask any questions.

Wulf looks to the two ladies, "My dear, I will take my leave and meet you at the cave. Choren is wanting my company."

Akita swallows the cinnamon goodness, "We will be there as soon as we get Storm settled in her room."

Storm looks at Akita curiously, "Cave? I don't remember any caves of significance around here. Well, except Annut's cave, and it was always a childhood dare to get close to it."

With a grin on her face, Akita states, "Storm, my dear, a lot has changed in the past several months. I cannot wait to introduce you to everyone and share with you the Keep's grandest secret."

Storms eyes get big, and she swallows a mouthful of cinnamon roll with and audible gulp, "Akita, did you finally kill that nasty Dragon?"

Akita smiles and laughs at the same time, "No, there's so much to share with you and I bet it is the same with you."

Then Akita notices Storm putting meat in her bag. Akita thinking to herself, ["What is going on? What has my poor Storm been through that she feels she has to put meat from the table in her bags. I am going to have to make sure she feels at home again and that anything she needs, she can have, we will take care of her."]

Storm notices Akita watching her. Blushing, Storm looks at Akita. "It's not what you are thinking. I am going to introduce you to my baby, but he is special and not meant to be touched by just anyone. Even I have to be careful in touching him." With that, Storm reaches into her bag and a small green creature crawls up her glove. As Storm brings her arm up, Akita see's what looks like a miniature Wyvern. His scales look like swirls of different shades of green. His bright yellow eyes turn to Storm and then to Akita.

"Oh! Look at you, cutie!" exclaims Akita.

Storm pets the small Wyvern with the other gloved hand. "Yes, he is a cutie, but a deadly one. His name is Visham, and he can talk to me in my mind. His skin is poisonous to the touch. I found him on the verge of death in a cave during my travels. I have worked with him to keep others safe, but let something endanger me, and it usually ends up dead. So, I will keep him with me for his safety and the safety of others."

Akita is fascinated with the small Wyvern. She pulls some leather gloves from her waistband and puts them on, as she moves to sit next to Storm.

Storm shakes her head, "I knew you would want to pet him, but know that those gloves go straight to the fire, and I'll remove them from your hands. I will make you special ones if you want."

As Akita reaches to pet Visham, "Wulf was telling us about little Dragons he is looking for. He calls them Pseudo Dragons because of their size. I wonder if this little guy is related in some way to them. We will make sure you have food for him."

Storm responds, "Thank you. However, there is more. Visham is not always little, he can change to a full-size Wyvern when needed. So, we will need to introduce him to Warrior and Hunter as well as teach them how to be with him."

Akita is visibly intrigued now. "Well, we will need to introduce him to Alura, Ransom, and Drako as well as others. What may be more important is that Alura and Ransom are female Wyverns."

Visham shakes his head and looks to Storm. "Visham says he cannot feel any others like him. He would like to be friends with the Wyverns because he was alone for a long time. He will keep our trust in him to not hurt the others."

Akita rubs under Visham's chin, "You are safe here little one. As my friend, Ishvet, will tell you, I love Dragons of all kinds. He says I am obsessed, but I just love Dragons. Now, Storm, I need to show you the Keep's grandest secret. I would take Visham with us. But first let's get your bag to your room."

On the way out of the Dining Hall they stop at the giant fireplace by the door and Storm removes the gloves for Akita and throws them into the fire. The gloves quickly burst into flames and sizzle.

As they walk through the Keep, Storm sees a few old familiar faces. It feels different to her now. The staff and soldiers seem friendlier and happier, not so stoic as if they are going through motions doing their jobs. She remembers when she was running around with Akita, they just seemed to ignore the girls unless they were getting into trouble. Maybe it's just because she's an adult now but she likes the new feel of her old home.

As they are walking to the hall entrance, a large dark shape fills the doorway, but the sunlight behind the person makes the person look like an ominous shadow. Storm stops dead in her tracks and shrinks back. She grabs her head with her hands and whispers through clenched teeth, "Not here, not now!"

Akita stops and looks at Storm, curious about her reaction and what she said. "Ordyn, you startled us. Storm are you okay?"

Ordyn quickly moves farther into the room, "Oh I am sorry ladies. That was not my intention. I was coming for a snack."

Storm puts down her hands and stands up straight. Feeling a little embarrassed, Storm smiles awkwardly at Akita, "I'm fine, I am just not use to being around so many people."

"Storm, I would like to introduce you to Ordyn. He is a Bahamut Dragonkin. He is family now and a very important to Blackwing Keep." Akita puts an arm round Ordyn's waist with a hug.

Storm cannot help but stare at this extremely tall, winged creature, until she realizes they are staring at her. "Nice to meet you, Ordyn. Forgive me but I have never met a Bahamut Dragonkin, I just had to take it all in for a moment. So much has changed here, I am just trying to get used to it."

With a toothy Dragonkin smile, "It is quite alright, Storm. Wait till you meet the rest of the team."

Akita laughs a little, "We are about to make the rounds, but first we are on our way up to her room to drop off her bags.

Ordyn nods his head to them both and proceeds into the Dining Hall. Akita leads Storm down the hallway to the foyer and up the grand stairs to the residence floor. After passing a few solid wooden doors Akita stops and opens one and lets Storm pass by her into the room first.

Akita closes the door behind them and looks directly at Storm's back until Storm puts her bag on the bed and turns around. Akita stares right into Storm's eyes, "Storm, what is going on? I could sense something was off with you from the moment I hugged you in the Dining Hall. I know that you wrote that you have lost your magic and that a lot has changed since then, but I think there is something else going on. You were never a scared little field mouse when we were younger. What has happened to you?"

Storm backs up until the backs of her legs touch the bed. Then in one fluid motion she sits, and her shoulders deflate, and she looks to the ground, "Akita, I knew coming here was a risk, but I needed to help you. I needed to feel like I could do some good. I have secrets too. My secrets are just a little more personal and to me a little embarrassing."

Akita steps over to a small drawing table and chair, pulling the chair over in front of Storm. She sits down facing Storm and reaches out with her right hand until it's under Storm's chin. She slightly nudges Storm's chin until Storm looks up to Akita's face. Akita can now see several tears running down Storm's face, "Embarrassed? Honey, what is there to be embarrassed about? We are sisters and have always been open and honest with each other. Nothing has changed that. I am here for you, and you are home now. Whatever it is that has you this way, we will figure out together."

Storm looks to Akita's shimmering red face while small tears still fall down her own, "I know Akita, it's just difficult to talk about and I'm not sure where to begin. I guess where I kind of ended in my letter. There's no other way to say this than to just say it. I have a Demon inside me. He ate my magic and replaced it with a different kind.

This Demon is what I found in that locked room in the ruins. His name is Rixan, and we are like one now. He is the reason I have to wear gloves. Anything I touch with my hands will immediately decay. When I said earlier that even I had to be careful with how I handled Visham, it wasn't because he might hurt me. It was because if I touched him without my gloves, it could kill him."

Akita sits like a statue in the chair opposite Storm. Her mouth is slightly agape, and her eyes are opened wide and unblinking. After a short pause she blinks and closes her mouth. She stands straight up like she has been hit by lightning and walks around the chair. She shakes her head as she turns back towards Storm. She begins to speak then stops. She closes her eyes and grabs the back of the chair to lean on while facing Storm. Her mouth begins to open again, and a small stutter can be heard by Storm, "Bbb, bbb, By the Gods that was a lot to take in. Wow I can't even imagine what you have gone through. I have a hundred questions, but the most important right now is, 'Is this Demon, Rixan, a danger to the Keep and everyone here?'."

Storm was caught off guard by Akita's question and she jerks her head to look up to

Akita, "No, we are not a danger to you or the Keep. We have an agreement. I feed him and he lets me control the power. I always keep my gloves on unless I'm bathing so there's no need to worry about me touching anyone."

Akita's face changes from one of concern for her Keep to one of caring for her friend. Her furled brow softens, and her jaw muscles relax. She stares into Storm's face and her pursed lips turn into a slight smile, "Oh my, Storm, I'm so sorry. I did not mean to insinuate that you would do anything like that. I guess I am starting to get some protective instincts over the realm I rule. I trust you totally. Now what was it that you were saying about feeding the Demon?"

Storm slightly relaxes after Akita apologizes and she motions for Akita to sit back down in the chair across from her. Once Akita sits, Storm reaches out with both hands and grabs Akita's hands, "Sis there is nothing to worry about. I am in control of this. Rixan has a taste for corrupt souls. So once a month I seek out an evil creature or Dark Wizard and put my bare hands on them. As their flesh and bones begin to decay, Rixan inhales their corrupt soul. He is satisfied and I can go about my daily life."

Akita thinks for a moment and then squeezes Storm's hands, "I wouldn't normally condone any type of killing of another being, however these Dark Wizards that we are at war with deserve nothing more than to be consumed. Let Rixan know that soon he will have a smorgasbord of Dark Wizards to devour. Until then, please just keep all of this between us for now. I'm sure some on the team might have some strong feelings about all of this."

Storm nods her head in agreement and then they both stand. Akita pulls Storm close and hugs her again. Storm feels a tremendous weight lift off of her as Akita hugs her. Akita backs up and smiles.

Storm smiles back at Akita and then wipes away her tears, "Okay, I am glad that is over now. Shall we go meet your team and uncover this secret of yours?"

Akita motions for Storm to go out of the door, and then follows behind her. They go down the foyer steps and outside though the main doors to the Keep. In a quick motion, Akita grips Storm under the arms and takes flight, taking Storm into the air. Storm lets out a high-pitched scream until she realizes what Akita is doing. Akita can't say anything because she is laughing so hard.

Akita's tail reaches down and wraps around Storm's ankles and pulls her up so that she is horizontal. It is only a few minutes flight to Annut's cave, but it seems like Storm is enjoying the bird's eye view of the Keep and the valley on the way there.

When they reach the cave, Akita lets Storm's ankles go and gently drops her on the cliff part of the back entrance. Akita then lands beside her. Wulf is just inside the cave waiting for both of them.

Storm lets out a gasp as she looks down the cave tunnel past Wulf. Choren, a red and gold Dragonling is standing in the middle of the tunnel. "Oh my! It's beautiful. Akita you never cease to amaze me. Where did you find this beautiful Dragon? And it's a Dragon, right?"

Wulf and Akita are laughing as the Choren turns and leads them down the tunnel. "Yes, it is a real Dragon, and his name is Choren." Wulf explains.

As they walk into the main cave, Storm grabs the wall to steady herself, as she takes in the view of six Dragonlings of various sizes. Then she looks up across the cave she sees Annut's head and shoulders in the room. Looking to Wulf and Akita and back to Annut, in complete shock.

Annut nods her head and does a Dragon laugh and enters Storm's mind, "Welcome to my home, Storm. As with Akita, I watched you grow up in the Keep. I know you have a good heart."

Storm is awe struck as she looks around the room, seeing the many colors and sizes of Dragons just lounging around. Just when she thinks she can say something intelligent Thoraxian walks up behind her. She feels his hot breath on her back as she slowly looks over her shoulder to find an ancient Black Dragon staring down at her.

Storm slowly turns to Akita, "Good thing I have a strong heart, because this guy behind me, breathing down my neck would scare someone to death. Your friend that says your obsessed is absolutely right. I don't know how you accomplished this; it is truly impressive."

Akita and Wulf smile at each other, "Storm, you will also be shocked to find out that each of the Dragonlings have chosen a member of

Blackwing Keep to train with in battle. You see Annut and Blackwing Keep have an agreement. We will give them a home and protect them; they will assist us in protecting the realms."

A voice comes from the cave behind Storm and the big Black Dragon. "Thoraxian, can you move over so I can get in the cave with our Dragon crazy leader?"

Akita folds her arms across her chest, "Hey now Darkwing, I resemble that remark."

Darkwing laughs as he moves out from under Thoraxian's wing. "Well, hello. You must be Storm. I am Lord Skrymir Darkwing, but to my friends and family, I am Darkwing. So, what do you think of Blackwing Keep's gigantic secret?"

Storm smiles at Darkwing, "Nice to meet you, Darkwing. As for this secret, well, Akita has always done things in a big way, but what about cats, dogs or even birds as pets, not that I don't love Dragons as well. This is just, wow, a bit of a shock."

Darkwing looks to Akita with a grin and then to Storm, "Birds, you say, I will have to introduce you to Martyn on our way back to the Keep."

Akita has the giggles as Darkwing mentions his Owl Roc Martyn. "What did you need to see me about, Darkwing?"

Darkwing has moved over to his Dragon, Granit. "Well, nothing really. Granit called me up here because he said I needed to meet the lady that looks like Skip. Obviously, he meant another Meso Elf. You know that if anything is happening at the cave, Granit's nose is right in the middle of it. I don't think he could keep a secret to save his soul." Darkwing has a hand under Granit's head and is rubbing his snout.

Akita makes the rounds hugging each of the Dragonlings. "Well, my tummy is growling, so let's head back to the Keep for lunch. Storm still hasn't seen Greta or Advisor Ambrose yet. They have been looking forward to seeing her again."

As they leave the cave, Storm sees a large white and black creature outside. As her eyes adjust to the sunlight, she realizes that it is a giant Owl. Staring at Martyn, Storm exclaims, "Are you kidding me? Let me guess you have a giant dog and cat too."

While greeting Martyn, Akita says "Well, yes and no. Gavin has a Fox that is the size of a horse.

Blitz is beautiful and extremely fast. Ishvet, had a Lamassu named Rani. She was a large, winged lion who gave her life for us in the heat of battle against the Cloud Giants. It still hurts our hearts. So, you see that we do have Dogs, Cats and Birds."

Storm is dumbfounded again. "Wow, after all I have seen I am wondering, what else you have to show me. Home has changed so much, and I know there is more to see and people to meet."

After putting Visham in her room and feeding him a snack, Storm went to find Akita in the Dining Hall. As she walked into the room, she sees a full table of people with one empty chair next to General, now Advisor Ambrose.

Jogging up behind him, she wraps her arms around him in his chair, "Uncle Ambrose, I have missed you so."

Ambrose starts to turn in his chair, "There is only one other person in this room that can get away with calling me Uncle Ambrose." He stands and embraces Storm in a big hug. "I have missed you too lil one."

Storm stands up straight, "I am not so little anymore, Uncle Ambrose."

Laughing at her indignance, "No, no you are not, and no doubt that you are ten times the trouble you used to be. Like our Akita here, older, wiser, stronger, therefore dangerous. I am glad to have you home my dear."

As Ambrose hugged Storm, they heard a squeal across the room. Everyone turned to look in the direction of the noise to see Greta clasping her hands and smiling at Storm.

Storm turns and runs to Greta, enveloping her in a big hug. "I have missed you so much."

Greta quietly sobbing, "We hadn't heard from you. I thought we lost you and then here you are. I am so happy and grateful." Greta pulls out a hanky and wipes her eyes. "Oh, just look at me being an emotional old fool."

Storm hugs Greta gently again, giving her a chance to compose herself. "Let's go join the others for lunch. I am planning on being here for a long time, so don't you worry anymore."

As everyone is seated at the table, Akita stands and puts a hand on Storm's shoulder. "Everyone, I would like to introduce Storm

Fireheart. She was raised here in the Keep by her mother, until her untimely passing. Then cared for by my Uncle Edmond, Shamash, General Ambrose, and Greta. She and I were raised as sisters. Some would say we were the terrors of the Keep, although it was hard to get away with anything when you have a garrison of soldiers watching your every move." Akita turns and looks at Storm, "We are so happy you are home. The people at this table I trust with my life and the well-being of the Keep. I hope as you get to know them, you will feel the same."

After lunch is served Akita begins again, "I expect Ishvet and Vivian to be here any time. The wedding should be the day after unless they have other ideas. Let's try to get the final touches done today or at least by mid-morning tomorrow." With that she sits down to enjoy her lunch. Mandrake and Vicar start off the introductions, by introducing themselves to Storm. Each of the team members do the same as the usual banter and chit chat begins.

Ghod introduces himself in his usual gruff way, "I am Ghod, not a deity, I am just me. After lunch bring any weapons you have to the Blacksmith, as I wish to inspect them. If I can make improvements, I will. If I need to replace them, I will." With that he nods and goes back to eating.

Storm nods in agreement, then looks at Akita questioningly. Akita nods, "He is amazing with weapons. Trust him."

The team, one by one, fills Akita in on the few last-minute preparations for the wedding.

CHAPTER 4
GRIFFINS AND GOOD FRIENDS

As they finish lunch, Storm seems to be fitting right in with the rest of the team. Everyone is telling stories and having a good laugh. Storm is telling stories from her and Akita's childhood which everyone is quite interested in. The embarrassing information Storm is relaying will most likely be used later to tease Akita.

Annut enters Akita's mind, "Akita, the Griffins are coming. They should be here very soon."

As Akita stands to announce their arrival, the horns of the Keep sound. It is such a rare occurrence that it startles most. Storm jumps because it has been many years since she has heard the horns that announce the arrival of visiting Royalty. Akita leads the way to the courtyard and turns to scan the Northeastern sky.

Annut and Thoraxian land outside of the Keep, so they too can greet the Elderwolf visitors.

Akita sees the sun shining off the golden armor as they fly closer to the Keep. It looks to be a smaller contingent than Earl Jarkon brought with him before. As they get closer, she notices something white sparkle behind them.

Storm notices the white sparkle as well, and blurts out, "Don't tell me that is another Dragon?"

Darkwing chuckles, "Yes, that is one of the oldest Dragons, her name is Aphorea. She fought in the Titan Wars with Thoraxian. Annut was just a Dragonling at the time."

Annut and Thoraxian started a short song of greeting to the Griffins and Aphorea. Where everyone in the Keep has heard the Dragons sing before, Storm is surprised by the Dragons' beautiful song.

Vivian, Ishvet, Captain Dub and Earl Jarkon land in the courtyard, while their contingent of Royal Guard's land in the stables that had been added for them during their last visit.

Akita resists the urge to just run up and hug everyone. Instead, she sticks to protocol and walks up to Earl Jarkon for a formal greeting.

The Earl looks at her fondly but with respect and smiles, "Akita Blackwing, High Duchess of Blackwing Keep. Your uncle has taught you the protocols well."

Akita stands regally in front of the Earl, with a smile and a slight blush. "Earl Jarkon Elderwolf of Stonia, welcome to Blackwing Keep. We have been very busy getting ready for your visit on this joyous occasion."

Earl Jarkon reaches out to Akita and takes her hand. "Yes, this is a joyous occasion. One that will not only join Viv and Ishvet but strengthen our Pact of the Keeps. My daughter and soon to be son-in-law are as much a part of Blackwing Keep as they are of Elderwolf Keep. I guess we will have to reach an agreement as to who visits who on the holidays."

Akita leans in closer to Earl Jarkon and whispers with a slight grin. "I think we will soon have our hands full chasing babies around the Keeps."

Earl Jarkon snaps his head around in surprise and a fearful look covers his face, "Oh! Let's hope we have a little time before that happens." Then his fear turns into a smile as he recognizes that Akita is just teasing him.

Akita steps back and gives a slight bow and then breaks protocol. She lunges forward and hugs Earl Jarkon with a giggle, which the team takes as the signal that the formalities are done. The team descends upon Vivian and Ishvet, surrounding them, and the bombardment of hugs and kisses begins.

Grabbing Storm's arm, Akita pulls her forward to introduce her to the new arrivals. "Ishvet, Vivian, Earl Jarkon, and ummm…, sorry, I guess we have a couple of new introductions today. So, I will start. This is Storm Fireheart, my Keep Sister, who recently returned from a long adventure in Omoth."

Vivian greets Storm with a big smile. "Shamash told me about you when I was healing. I am so glad you have returned home." Gesturing towards her Captain, "This is Captain Dubbin Desail, to me Uncle Dub, but Captain of our Oathbound Paladin Guard that is directly responsible for the safety of Earl Jarkon and myself. We still have not heard the end of comments from leaving him behind last time, only to hear the stories of the Cloud Giants and with the wedding this time, he was not going to be left behind ever again."

Akita greets the Dwarf Paladin facing her. He's the shortest Dwarf she has ever seen, with black hair down the middle of his head and the sides of his head shaved, as well as the typical thick black beard down past his belly and mustache with beads braided into them. "Welcome Captain Dubbin to Blackwing Keep. So glad you are here for this visit. I look forward to showing you our army training grounds later. Now if you will all excuse me, we have another guest to introduce as well."

Ishvet smirks, "Well, let's all follow 'Ms. Dragon Obsessed' to greet the Dragons and Aphorea who has left her lair to honor us as a guest at our wedding." With a big Dragonkin grin, he puts a hand on Akita's shoulder and walks with her and Storm through the main gate. The rest of the team with Earl Jarkon and Captain Dub proceed behind them.

To most sane people the enormity of three full grown Dragons before them would be overwhelming. Around Blackwing Keep it has become commonplace and a reassuring sight.

Many in the Keep see Annut and Thoraxian as the great protectors of Prayla.

Akita brings Storm up to Aphorea and introduces her. Aphorea lowers her head to their eye level and enters both their minds, "It's so good to meet you in person Storm. Akita may have shared with you that I have been a witness to her memories, which included many happy memories with you. I can sense her joy at having you back at the Keep. I can also sense a very old presence within you, child. I would imagine that many others do not know about this so we will speak about it later. Come see me alone in Annut's cave at some point while I am here."

Akita looks over to Storm and can see the flash of fear strike her face. Akita grabs Storm's gloved hand and squeezes while nodding her head in reassurance. Storm then begins to relax and agrees to meet with Aphorea later.

Akita then let's go of Storm's hand and walks up to Aphorea and gives her as big of a hug as her arms will allow. Akita's momentary bliss is shortly interrupted by a tap on her shoulder and Vivian exclaiming while laughing, "Okay Akita, that's enough, it's my turn."

Akita turns her head in surprise and realizes that a line has formed behind her. She steps away from Aphorea and feels a twinge of embarrassment. She shakes it off and starts smiling before walking back to the main gate.

After everyone has had their time with Aphorea and Vivian has introduced her father as well as Captain Dub, they all return to the main Dining Hall for refreshments and to hear Ishvet and Vivian's plans for the wedding.

The afternoon sun pushes against Meh-Kola's back as she flies back to Blackwing Keep as fast as her wings will take her. She stays at tree top level for cover and safety. If she is too high up with the sun at her back, she will be easily spotted. At the tree top level, if she senses anyone, she can dart into the trees and hide.

The journey from Cliffshade Keep is long, even more so when covering her tracks and staying hidden. Meh-Kola dares not to even use her blink ability to gain ground because there are evil forces on the ground that can sense the use of magic. She knows that the information she has gathered while spying on King Carthon is only useful if she can get to Blackwing Keep before King Carthon and his monster get there.

She hopes beyond all hope that she can make it in time. She only rests when she absolutely has to and only for the minimum time that it takes to regain her energy. She calculates that she should be back to the Keep by tomorrow night if she keeps this pace.

Meh-Kola's mind is flooded with the images of what she saw in Cliffshade Keep. The secret underground lair, the huge vat, and the shadow. Even more are the words King Carthon uttered about how the Blackwing Keep fools would never know what hit them.

Ishvet and Vivian stand at the head of the main dining table, with their arms around each other. Everyone is gathered around the table holding a drink and looking towards the couple. Ishvet grins and looks to Vivian and then back up to his friends, "My heart is overflowing with the love I feel from all of you. Viv and I are so happy to be back at Blackwing Keep. The very place where we first met. Thank you Ghod for calling upon your friend to come help Akita. I'm not one for long speeches so I will just get past the mushy stuff and to the itinerary. Viv and I have spoken with Vicar and have decided that we would like to have small intimate ceremony with all our friends on Memorial Hill tomorrow afternoon. Then the day after we will have the ceremony for all the dignitaries that have been invited."

Akita walks towards the couple and hugs them, "That's a great idea! We will get everything ready for tomorrow afternoon then. However, tonight we have other things to do. Vivian will be coming with us ladies, and Ishvet, Ordyn has something planned for you boys."

Ordyn laughs with a slightly sinister tone, "Oh yes I do and it's going to be unforgettable."

Vivian takes her arm from around Ishvet and points her finger at Ordyn and with a playfully stern tone says, "Ordyn, Ish better come back to me in one piece and still faithful!"

Ordyn shrinks back and he begins to trip on his words, "Uh, uh, Vivian… it's not like that… I didn't hire any dancing ladies or anything like that…I…I…will just shut up now."

Akita grabs ahold of Vivian and laughs and pulls her towards the kitchen, "Don't worry Viv, we will be up to way more bad things than the boys are going to be. Come on, we have to get you ready for the Cronian Desert Dancers I hired."

Ishvet reaches back for Vivian as Akita whisks her away. His mouth is agape and there's a blank expression on his face. Vivian looks back at him as she's pushed into the kitchen doors by Akita, Storm, and Quinn. He can see the same expression that he is feeling on his own face. Then he feels several arms surround him and pull him towards the Dining Hall entrance. He can only think that he is going to be in big trouble by the morning for sure.

Akita wakes on the floor next to her bed with the sound of hammers hitting anvils in her head. As she begins to become more lucid, she realizes that it is someone knocking on her chamber's door and not actually hammers and anvils in her head. She looks around through squinting eyes and sees Quinn passed out in her study chair, Vivian on the bed in a full set of Paladin Armor helmet and all.

Vivian's blonde hair flowing out of the bottom of the helmet is the only thing revealing her identity. Akita starts to try to remember why Vivian is in full armor, but the knocking snaps her from that train of thought.

Akita slowly stands and makes her way to the door. She turns the knob and cracks the door open just enough to see who is knocking. At first, she doesn't see anyone on the other side, but then she hears Judas say, "Down here Akita." Akita looks down to see Judas' smiling face, "Judas, why are you knocking so hard?"

Judas keeps smiling, "I just knocked like normal Akita. Did you have too much to drink last night?"

Akita shakes her head and rubs her face with her hands, "Maybe, so. I can't remember at this moment. What's going on?"

Judas sticks his hand through the gap between the door and doorframe holding a small bundle of letters, "Here these came for you yesterday. I have just heard the news about the ceremonies from Shamash, so I'm headed back to Prayla to send out the new invitations with the correct date and time on them."

Akita takes the bundle of letters and nods her head to Judas. He takes that as his cue to leave and turns around. She shuts the door and then looks at the room and the state it is in. There are chalices all over and large empty decanters on almost every table. She then notices that someone is missing, "Storm, where are you?"

There's no response from anywhere in the room. She walks over to Quinn who is still passed out in the chair. She slowly grabs her shoulder and shakes it.

Quinn awakens and looks up with a startle, "What!... I said no cinnamon in the stew! Are you a daft goblin or something?"

Akita tries to giggle at Quinn's odd statement but only a quiet ugh comes out of her mouth, "Honey, I don't think you are in the kitchen today."

Quinn snaps out of her fog and sits upright in the chair, "Oh, I guess not. What was in that ale we had last night?"

Akita looks around the room as Quinn starts to get up, "I'm not sure but it packed a punch. Do you have any idea where Storm is?"

Quinn grabs the desk in front of her for stability, "Um, I think I remember her leaving to go see someone, but that was several bottles into the night. Hey, why is Vivian in her armor? Was she fighting someone?"

Akita looks over to the bed where Vivian is laying, "You know, I can't quite remember. I think we better get Vicar to help us with this morning after-fog. Then we might remember what happened last night. I'll go get Vicar and you wake Vivian."

"Ishvet…Ishvet…ISHVET! Could you please get out of my straw pile!"

Ishvet slowly opens his eyes and looks up to see Orien standing over him. As his eyes adjust to the light, he feels Orien's head nuzzle up against his neck, "Okay, okay, I'm getting up. I am guessing I'm not in my bed unless you found a way to fit through the bedroom door."

Orien chuckles at Ishvet's comment, "Nope, you are in my bed and everyone else is asleep in Warrior's corral. He's not too happy that he can't lay down."

Ishvet stands up and looks around the stables as he exits Orien's stall. He sees two pairs of feet protruding from the stall across from him. The rest of their bodies are covered with straw. He walks over and lightly taps the feet with his foot and the two under the straw begin to rustle around.

Soon two people pop up out of the straw. It's Ordyn and Darkwing and they both look very confused. Ishvet chuckles loudly, "I guess a lot of crazy things happened last night. Don't worry boys your secret is safe with me."

Ordyn and Darkwing look at each other and then look down at the straw covering them then back at Ishvet. Ordyn feels all over himself and lets out a sigh of relief, "Thank the Gods I still have all my clothes on, or this would have been awkward."

Darkwing jumps up out of the straw and pats himself all over. You can see the relief enter his face as he realizes that he has all his clothes on too. He looks over to Ordyn, "Wait just a minute, why the heck am I checking my clothes. I would never be naked in a pile of straw. It would be too itchy."

Ordyn snaps his head towards Ishvet and stares at him with a confused look. Then both of them realize what Darkwing just said, and they both break out in a hard laugh. Ordyn gets up out of the straw and walks over to Ishvet, "It must have been some night if we are waking up in the stables."

Ishvet looks around and points to several piles of straw, "I'm assuming that those are the rest of the party goers. Let's get them up then we can discuss how your night of fun ended up with us flying around on our mounts drunk, and Darkwing throwing snowballs for us to avoid."

Ordyn looks down to the ground and swallows loud enough to hear, "Well… it seemed like a good idea at the time, and it wasn't like our mounts were drunk. If I remember right, Ghod said that whoever can dodge the snowballs three times in a row, he will take off his mask. Of course, that started a whole thing of who was the better flyer and then the mounts started saying that they could fly with any drunk fool on their backs. I have my own wings, so I started to argue with myself about if my wings fly me or do I fly them. Now, I'm waking up next to Darkwing in a straw pile."

Ishvet and Darkwing look at each other and walk to the others buried in the straw. They start uncovering their friend's heads, looking for Ghod. Simultaneously they ask, "But did Ghod remove his mask?"

From a distant pile a voice interrupts the two, "Ah, but you see. It will all remain a mystery for those who partook in the ale a little too heavily last night. Some things are just better left to the imagination. Wouldn't you agree Mandrake?"

Mandrake pipes up from another straw pile, "Yes Ghod, I think it was better being left to the imagination. My lips are sealed as to the debauchery that is concealed behind the mask of Ghod."

Gavin groans, "Will y'all be quiet? Do you have to yell so early in the mornin? I think some of ya took this male bondin thing too far. I do wish I could remember seein Ghod's face though. I bet he's hidin some pretty boy face under that mask."

Ishvet stands up and kicks the ground, "Aw Darn, that means I didn't win. Well, I'll see you fellas later. I better get back to the Keep and see how much trouble I'm in with Vivian."

Ordyn looks around and sees that almost everyone is exiting their straw piles, "Go ahead

Ishvet. I'll make sure everyone is accounted for and get them ready for the ceremony. I hope you are not in too much trouble."

About the time Vivian exclaims she can take the full force of one fireball from Akita, in her full armor, Storm decides it's time to go see Aphorea. Her fear and curiosity getting the best of her. She excuses herself and returns to her room, where Visham is waiting for her.

Outside of the Keep, Visham transforms into the full-size version of himself and flies her to Annut's cave entrance. As they land, Storm sees the most terrifying sight in her life, two larger-than-life Dragons with huge mouths full of teeth as big and bigger than herself. They have claws bigger than horses and their paws could crush many men at once. Annut the Fast, a Red Dragon and Aphorea the Bright, a White Dragon, seemingly asleep in the cave.

Aphorea opens one eye looking at Storm, "Welcome Visham and Storm. I have been awaiting your arrival."

Visham lowers himself to lay at the entrance to the cave, as Storm moves closer to Aphorea.

"Forgive me, but this is all so new. When I left here, Annut was the enemy of the realm. Now, not only is she a friend but there are more Dragons than I could imagine being in the world, let alone, living around Blackwing Keep. The Wyvern population has also more than doubled. So, I was already overwhelmed, and then you alluded to my affliction, which only Akita is aware of and no one else."

Aphorea shifts position to get a better look at Storm, "About the Dragons, there are many scattered across the world, but all have been in hiding for centuries. There is another on this continent, but he is too cautious to come visit, shall we say. As for your affliction, the secret is safe with me. I want to offer any assistance you might need in dealing with this affliction."

After a brief pause, Aphorea continues, "As I see it you have two choices, and each has benefits and consequences that you will have to live with. This Demon is attached to your soul, and I have the ability to remove it. However, if I remove it for a better life for you, he will move on to someone else who may not have the moral resolve or the mental ability to restrain him as you do. If the new host becomes deadly and malicious, we cannot just kill that person because the Demon will just keep finding a new host. At this time, we do not have the means to capture and bind him in a temple. I don't know if there is anyone alive that knows a strong binding spell to last the ages. Your other choice is to live with this Demon to protect others, and perfect the powers you have now to your advantage. This does not mean there is no hope of ever being rid of him, it's just a really slim chance at the moment."

Storm sits down in front of Aphorea. She looks down at her fidgeting hands for a long time deep in thought. She knows down deep she would not want to unleash this Demon on anyone else. She knows that with him, she will never have a normal life. If she were to find the love of her life, she could never touch them with her bare hands. She doesn't even want to think about children. But her moral compass is strong, she knows she has to keep this Demon under control. It is her fault that he was set free when she was exploring an unknown temple, so how could she live with herself if it harmed anyone else.

She slowly looks up at Aphorea with a look of determination. "Aphorea, there may come a day when we find a way to safely banish him so that he cannot find another host and hurt anyone. At that time, I will seek you out, but I cannot, in good conscience, have you scatter him to the wind at this time. I could not live with myself, as I know there are too many innocent non-magic people around. Heck, even if there is someone magical, who can say that they could handle him. I still would not give them my burden."

Storm slowly stands and wipes a few tears away. "Thank you Aphorea for giving me the choice and showing me that there might be some hope someday."

Aphorea nods with her big white horned head. "You are a strong woman and like Akita you will do great things for the realm. Have faith in yourself."

Storm climbs onto Visham as he nods acknowledgement to Aphorea. He then turns and drops off the cave ledge, letting the wind catch his wings as he soars out over the ocean before circling back to the Keep.

CHAPTER 5

AN END TO PEACE

The sun shines over the Keep with a warming presence. There is hardly a cloud in the sky and a light breeze from the West tickles the trees into a slow dance. It will be a perfect day for a wedding. Soon everyone will be gathered on Memorial Hill for the ceremony before the official show in the Keep.

Akita walks into the kitchen and hears Quinn barking orders at everyone. Akita can see that Quinn is in a frenzy to get everything done for today's meals and the big official wedding reception for the next day. Akita sneaks up behind Quinn, "Quinn. Relax, everything smells heavenly in here."

Quinn spins around with a start that obliterates the thought she was stuck in, "Oh, good morning. Is there something you want or need Lady Akita?"

Akita looks up and down the tables of food that have been prepared. She bends over and smells the delightful aromas and makes a show of inspecting the delectable dishes being prepared, "I just wanted to see how you were doing? Do you have everything you need? To answer your question, I would like some coffee and cinnamon toast if it's not too much trouble?"

Quinn dries her hands on her apron, "We have everything we need. Lord Darkwing covered all the walls, ceiling, and floor of one of our storerooms with his ice to keep the food cool until tomorrow. That allows us to have many things prepared and waiting. As for cinnamon toast and coffee, how about hot cinnamon rolls and coffee? I will bring them to the Dining Hall in just a few minutes if you like."

With a big smile, "That sounds heavenly, thank you." Akita heads to the Dining Hall, where she finds Vivian and Ishvet seated at the main table.

Akita grabs a chair, "Good morning you two. Are you ready for your big day?"

Vivian smiles as Akita sits down across from her. "Akita, now that the fog of last night has been washed away by Shamash, I just wanted to say that everything you have done is lovely. You have captured the essence of what we are together. Thank you so much." As she gestures to all the decorations in the Dining Hall. "But to answer your question, I think we have been ready for weeks. Now that all the people we care about are in one place, it is time to make it official.

Quinn walks up with Akita's meal. "Thank you, Quinn. Question for you? Is everything prepared for the rehearsal dinner after this afternoon's rehearsal wedding?"

Akita can see Quinn mentally running through a checklist in her head, "Lady Akita, we spent all night getting everything done. As soon as the rehearsal wedding is done, everything will be set up in the main Dining Hall and Sham has everything ready in the courtyard for the friends that cannot fit in the Dining Hall."

Akita laughs a little, "Let's just hope that they can all fit in the Courtyard together without one of our Dragon friends stepping on a smaller friend."

Ishvet and Vivian smile and laugh at the thought of all their creature friends stuffed in the courtyard holding plates and silverware awaiting their turn at the serving tables. They turn their heads and imagine what the other is thinking and start to laugh even more. Akita looks over at them and shakes her head, "You two are something else, barely engaged and already reading each other's minds. You two go on and get ready and I'll see you in a few hours on the hill."

Ishvet gets up and pulls Vivian's chair out a little so she can get up from the table easily and then they make their way out of the Dining Hall. Akita turns to Quinn, "Quinn did you see how Ishvet pulled out Viv's Chair? You don't think there's a bun in the oven, do you?"

Quinn looks towards the door that the pair just exited from and then back down to Akita, "Lady Akita, I think you are having a case of wishful thinking. I'll be in the kitchen if you need anything before the rehearsal."

Akita looks towards the empty doorway and daydreams of a little Dragonkin boy or girl that she can spoil and teach how to get in trouble around the Keep. A big smile overtakes her face as she finishes her coffee and cinnamon roll.

North of the sprawling grounds of the Keep is a large hill. From atop this hill, you can see the Westsan Ocean to the west, the entirety of Blackwing Keep to the south, the valley to the east and all the way to the Voskaola Mountains in the north. Akita spent many hours on that hill as a child reading spell books and adventure novels under a massive Oak Tree. It's the only tree on the hill and it still bares scars from Akita practicing her Fire Magic as a young free-spirited girl. Recently after the loss of several of her soldiers, Rogue, Rani, and Jessa, Akita decided to turn the hill into a memorial and burial site for the soldiers and friends that gave their lives in the pursuit of the Dark Wizards.

Rani was buried right beneath the ancient Oak Tree and today the real marriage ceremony will be held directly in front of Rani's grave. Ishvet and Vivian wouldn't have it any other way than to be able to have all their friends surrounding them as they sealed their life together. That meant the ones that walk on two legs or four, or flew with wings, or have scales, feathers, or fur. No one important to them would be left out if they could be there.

As the sun reaches its peak in the sky, the hill is filled with all their friends. Furthest out from the tree was the three Dragons, Annut-the Fast, Aphorea- the Brilliant, and Thoraxian- the Shadow. Below and in front of them were all the hatchlings and all the Wyverns. Further in were the Roc Owls, Mylar and Martyn, Blitz the fox, and the twins' horses Apothecary and Judgement. All of them were positioned to make an aisle down the middle pointing directly to the trunk of the tree.

On the left side of the aisle Vivian's and Ishvet's Griffins stand with several Griffin Riders, and Captain Dub. Directly across the aisle were Wulf, Gavin, Darkwing, Storm, Mandrake, Fabby, Greenbean, Quinn, Olek, Greta, Ixenvorlux and Shamash. At the foot of Rani's grave, Vicar and Ishvet are standing along with Ordyn as his Best Man, and they are turned facing their friends. Akita flies in as the Matron of Honor, and lands next to Vicar and announces, "They're ready!"

Ghod walks up from behind the tree and pulls out a flute type instrument that has wooden tubes in different sizes. He begins to play a slow melodic song as a Griffin is landing between

Annut and Thoraxian at the beginning of the aisle. The Griffin is carrying Earl Jarkon and Vivian. They both dismount the Griffin and Earl Jarkon takes Vivian's arm. He slowly walks her down the aisle towards Ishvet.

Once they approach Ishvet, Earl Jarkon bows and offers his daughter's arm to the groom. Ishvet takes Vivian's arm, and they turn toward Vicar. Earl Jarkon steps over next to Akita as Vicar looks at the couple, and then out to the crowd of friends and back to the couple as he states, "Today we are here to celebrate love. The love shared between Vivian and Ishvet. All of you are a witness to this love and support it. In these times it is rare to find the kind of love they share. Love that is selfless and pure. From this day on they move forward through the world as partners in that love witnessed by all gathered here. Ishvet, would you like to start?"

Ishvet takes both of Vivian's hands in his as he turns towards her. He looks into her eyes and clears his throat, "I began to give up hope that I would love anyone more than I loved my best friend, Rani. Rani's death felt like my soul was shredded and it laid wounded and bleeding in the depths of my heart. However, as I spent time with you Viv the bleeding stopped, and the wounds began to heal. Your light touched my heart, and your tenderness stitched my soul back together. Today I feel as though our souls are intertwined and I am so excited to spend the rest of my life with you."

Small tears fall down Vivian's cheeks as she closes and then opens her eyes. She squeezes Ishvet's hands and then swallows hard, "Ish, I have loved you since the day you first spoke to me in the Keep courtyard. I saw into your bright shining soul and the conviction you had in helping your friends. After Rani's death I thought that I'd lost you to the despair. I thought that you may never open your heart to anyone again. The only thing I could do was to show you my heart in the hopes that yours would be healed. You were worth the risk to me. Our love grows deeper every moment of the day. I look forward to spending the rest of my life with you."

A loud sniffling sound comes from beside Vicar. Ishvet and Vivian turn their heads and see Ghod slide a handkerchief under his mask to wipe his nose. They also notice the water stains under his eye holes. They both look back at each other and laugh out loud. Ghod exclaims in a higher pitched voice than normal, "What! No! It's not what it looks like. I'm allergic to Oak pollen!"

The whole wedding party starts laughing in unison. Ghod whips his head side to side looking at everyone laughing. He then points up to the branches of the tree, "No seriously I'm allergic to Oak pollen. Orcs don't cry at weddings. I'm not mushy."

His protests go unbelieved as everyone laughs even louder. Then in one quick motion, Annut leaps from her spot to the South side of the hill. When she lands the ground trembles. She has her back to the Keep, and she stretches out her wings. She screams in an urgent sounding voice directly into everyone's mind, "Hold On!"

As everyone else turns their gaze towards her they can see the wall of water rushing at them. The water wall is already past Blackwing Keep and coming up the gentle incline of Memorial Hill. It is so fast that no one really has time to react. The last thing Ishvet sees is Judas braced on Annut's shoulder as the wave hits her outstretched wings.

The water quickly comes from over her wings and from the sides. It hits with the power of a charging bull, and they are all knocked down and sprawled all over the ground for a moment. Then about as quickly as it hit them it recedes from around them. Annut speaks into their minds again, "We are under attack! People are hurt! Take to the air now!"

Annut grabs Akita and launches in the air. As soon as they are off the ground, Annut twist to face the Keep. Akita lets out a blood curdling scream, "Noooooo!" She can see the destruction the wave caused to Blackwing Keep. Everything around the Keep is gone. Only the Keep is still standing, and the grounds are littered with debris from the other buildings and the first floor of the Keep. Then Akita also starts to notice several bodies amongst the debris.

As the wedding party tries to stand, they are knocked back to the ground by the down force of the three full grown Dragons, six various aged dragonlings, and five Wyverns all taking to the air at the same time. Wulf and Gavin are knocked to the ground as they try to fly into the air. Ordyn is pushed sideways across the ground as his wings expand. The Griffin Riders are trying to scramble their way across the wet grass to their Griffins as they are flattened on their faces. Ishvet, Vivian, and Vicar are spared from the downburst by Vivian's quick light shield.

Judas finishes gathering the remainder of the RSVP's from the messenger shop and walks out of the door as he waves goodbye to Alican. As the door closes and the bell rings, he can feel a rumbling in his feet. At first, he doesn't think anything of it. He looks up to the sky and notices the time and thinks, ["Oh no I'm going to be late if I don't get back to the Keep soon."]

After a quick stretch of his legs, he starts running down the road to Blackwing Keep. As he reaches the halfway point to the Keep, he can hear the rumbling that he felt back at the messenger shop. The vibrations are pushing against his back. He stops and turns around and is met with a wall of sea water. It is no more than forty feet away. Instinctively he turns and runs at his top speed towards the Keep.

Judas gains a lead as he heads towards the Keep. He's now about two hundred feet ahead of it, he knows that even if he warns anyone, he comes across they will not have any time to react.

When he makes it to the front gate of the Keep, the gate is open, and two guards are at their post. He yells as loud as he can for them to close the gate, but he knows it will not help. He runs through the courtyard and around the Keep and sees all his friends are on Memorial Hill.

He has lost his lead by going around the Keep and the wall of water has made it to the front gate. The water seems to have gotten faster as it approached the Keep. He sprints up the hill and calls out to Annut in his mind. All he hears back is a grunt and a growl as she leaps and repositions herself between their friends and the water. As soon as she lands, he jumps on her tail and climbs up to her neck holding on tight to her back spines. He can only hang on as the water overtakes them all.

When the wave hit, Thoraxian shielded everyone the best that he could. As soon as the wave dissipated, he gathered the young Dragons and flew with them back to Annut's cave. Once all of them were in, he flew down the coast from the cave mouth to just south of the Keep. That's when a familiar feeling overtakes him. It is the same feeling he had when he was captured by the Dark Wizards. It's an uneasy tingle in the back of his neck. A heavy feeling of a chain wrapping and squeezing his soul.

He knows that King Carthon is near, but he cannot see him yet and that makes it all the more dangerous. He reaches out to everyone left in the Keep and everyone from the wedding party, "King Carthon is here! Be on your guard."

Annut also reaches into everyone's minds, "Judas says that the wave started in Prayla. We need to go help them also."

Thoraxian replies, "Darkwing, Greenbean, Fabby and Olek are going to fly down to Prayla to help the wounded and look for survivors. The rest are going to stay here to do the same. I can hear people calling out that are trapped. It will be easier for us Dragons to move the heavy debris, so Aphorea go with them to Prayla to help please."

Aphorea agrees and takes flight, and catches up with Darkwing on Martyn, Greenbean on Warrior, Fabby on Hunter, and Olek on Ransom.

Meh-Kola arrives at the crossroads just south of Blackwing Keep and is confused as to the landscape she is seeing. Large trees are knocked to the ground and wet, pieces of sawn wood and furniture are strewn along the road as far south and north as she can see, ["One does not know what happened, but it cannot be good. One must get back to the Keep now. One hopes that there is a Keep to go back to."]

She flies north a little further and comes upon the heavy gates of the outer Keep wall and they are knocked down. She looks up and sees Annut flying above with Akita in her paw. She flies up to Akita, "Akita what has happened here?"

Akita looks towards Meh-Kola and tears are streaming down her face, "A huge wave has destroyed our home. Many people are trapped or killed. We have to help anyone we can. Can you blink into the Keep and blink people out that are trapped?"

Meh-Kola's mouth hangs open for a moment in disbelief, "One will help where one can. One does not believe this is the end. One was coming to warn you that King Carthon is planning an attack, but One seems to be too late."

Meh-Kola flies down to the west tower and disappears inside.

Akita asks Annut to land in what is left of the Courtyard to drop her off. There are many large pieces of buildings that they need to check for survivors. She also asks that Annut go to the remains of the barracks and help find any soldiers that are left. Akita can see where the massive gates of the Keep's inner entrance, have knocked big holes in the outer walls, leaving some of the staff and soldiers' quarters bare.

There are walking wounded finding their way to the courtyard, assisting others with more serious injuries out of the Keep itself. A few healers' apprentices are doing their best to heal those they can and make others comfortable while they await the more experienced clerics and healers.

Greta approaches Akita, raising a hand to wipe away a few of Akita's tears. "Akita, everyone in the lower storage areas and dungeons are drowned." Greta takes Akita's hands in hers, "My dear sweet girl, I don't want you to hear this from anyone else. General Ambrose has perished in the wave, as well."

Akita cannot hold it any longer. She lets out a loud cry of anguish and collapses to the ground, shaking and sobbing. She doesn't care who sees at this moment, she doesn't care that she is supposed to put on a strong face as their leader. As she looks up and around the courtyard, she sees four of the soldiers laying the General out next to the others that did not survive. Getting to her feet she stumbles over to him and kneels beside him.

The rest of the wedding party soaked and disheveled walk into the Keep's courtyard. The shock is apparent on their faces as they take in the amount of damage that has been done to Blackwing Keep. Storm runs to Akita's side and falls to her knees next to "Uncle Ambrose". They hold each other and cry. Vicar, Shamash, and Ixenvorlux start attending to the wounded. Wulf and Mandrake join Scotch at the stables, where they find many horses dead or wounded. Ben leads them to Akita's Warhorse, Nightmare, who is also gone. Vivian and Ishvet begin gathering all the survivors in the courtyard.

Drako is helping Annut move heavy debris to the outside of the Keep walls making it easier to attend to the wounded. Ghod walks out of the forge seething with anger as his forges are cold and wet. He also found Bob, his helper, dead from blades that had been whipped around by the force of the wave.

The death and destruction are immense, and Akita can barely stand to look around. Then she hears a familiar voice.

Ordyn starts taking charge, yelling at the top of his lungs, "Right, we have a lot of work to do here. Those that are not wounded or have been healed let's get this mess cleaned up and somewhat livable. Clear as much of the courtyard as you can. Find what you can to build tents and tables." His orders snap people out of their shock and give them purpose for the moment.

Earl Jarkon lands his Griffin near Akita and dismounts. He walks over to her and gently raises her to standing, turning her to him. "Lady Akita, my people, and I are here to help in every way we can. Now you have had a good sob, which shows your people you have feelings. However, this was not a natural occurrence, and we need to think of your people's safety. We will start air patrols around the area. We will send a messenger if we find anything of importance."

A voice from behind Earl Jarkon, pipes up and says, "Sire, I must insist that you leave immediately for Elderwolf Keep. We need to ensure your safety and I will not take any arguments from you. We cannot guarantee when the danger will be over, or if they won't try this again. Now take a few guards with you and leave."

Raising an eyebrow, Earl Jarkon turns to Captain Dub. "Excuse me. I will not just leave our allies in need of help."

Captain Dub folds his chunky arms across his chest. "You will leave and then send back help and supplies from Elderwolf Keep. I'm in charge of keeping you safe, I will remain here in your stead, and we are going to need food as the stores are flooded. You will not be leaving them without help."

Earl Jarkon looks around and then back at Captain Dub, "Very well. I will take one guard with me and send back supplies and troops." Turning back towards Akita, "However, I suggest that you move your people to a safer position as soon as you can. Blackwing Keep is a target for your enemies. Others down the coast may come here seeking help, it would be better if that help was away from your Keep, for now."

Akita seems to stand taller and visibly shake off the anger, fear, and grief for the moment. "You are right of course, Earl Jarkon. As soon as our wounded are healed, we will make our way to Salthall. Thank you for your assistance."

The Earl smiles and thinks to himself, ['She's strong and she will come through this."], as he mounts his Griffin and takes to the skies.

CHAPTER 6
FALL BACK

Akita stands and straightens her clothes. She reaches out to pull Storm to her feet next to her. She amplifies her voice, "Team, come to me for a few minutes." She knows that if King Carthon is around and nobody knows where, she cannot just announce plans out loud.

Ordyn and the team come to stand in front of her. "Ordyn, good idea gathering supplies to repair, but we need to move the people away from the Keep until we know what we are dealing with. Fill wagons with tents, bedding, food, and whatever can be salvaged. We need to move the wounded and civilians to Salthall for now. The Earl will be sending food and help back to us. He has left us Captain Dub and his men, as well. They are on patrol right now. People will have to carry their own clothes and weapons. I would like an accounting of those that have perished."

Mandrake steps forward, "Akita, many of the horses are wounded or dead." She stares at Mandrake.

Her eyes fill with tears again, "Mandrake, is Nightmare, ok?"

Mandrake looks down, "Nightmare did not make it and neither did Fabby's or Greenbean's horses. We need a healer to heal those that can be healed for pulling wagons. Thank the Gods that Judgement and Apothecary were with us, or they may have not survived either."

Akita turns the tears to anger, her skin starts to turn to golden embers, "I want to know what un-natural power caused this so we can stop it. I want King Carthon's head on a pike." Taking a deep breath and sighing. "But what I want most is to save as many as possible, so let's get to it."

Ordyn turns to bark out orders again. Mandrake heads to the stables to get Scotch and Ben for horses and wagons. Ghod begins work on repairing wagons to make the journey to Salthall. Vicar follows to heal the horses and any others that can pull a wagon or carry supplies. Ishvet heads off to find a quill and parchment to make a list of the dead, severely wounded and survivors.

Vivian consoles some of the more shaken Keep residents. Storm helps load supplies and survivors into the patched together wagons. Wulf stays with Akita.

Akita looks to Judas who is helping lay out he dead, "Judas would you please run ahead of everyone to Salthall and let them know what has happened. Tell them that we have wounded coming and that our caravan should be there in about four days."

Judas nods and takes off in a blur out of the East Gate and down the road.

Wulf turns Akita to him, "Walking in the Keep may not be safe, what do you say to flying up to the infirmary and grab as much of the supplies that we can."

Akita takes off at a high rate of speed through the doors and up the stairs. There is standing water in the hall and furniture strewn everywhere. She flies to her room to grab some bags and so does Wulf, and then they meet in the infirmary.

Wulf stops Akita for a moment and just holds her. She melts into his arms and allows herself a moment of grieving. "Akita, I know how strong you are, but this is more than most can handle.

You don't have to shoulder this alone; I am here for you. You know that, right?"

Akita shudders and nods her head against his chest. Then she stands and starts filling bags. "When King Carthon is dead, I'm going to lock myself in my room and have a nervous breakdown for a week. I deserve it and have earned it."

Wulf starts filling bags with potions and powders and chuckles.

Little more than an hour has passed since the wave hit and the team jumped into action. Already wagons are filled, and people are streaming out of the Keep Wall East gate towards Salthall. Skip, and Quinn are guarding the caravan to Salthall. Mylar, Darkwing's Roc Owl, Rogue's Wyvern Drako, and the Twins' enchanted horses Apothecary and Judgement are flying towards Salthall with the most critically wounded. Only a handful of staff and the remaining team are in the courtyard.

As they are standing in small groups coordinating the mass exodus to Salthall, Vivian stiffens then squats into a defensive stance. She raises her mace and slides her shield from her back to her left forearm. A shield of light emanates from her mace and encompasses the whole team.

Ishvet steps behind her and puts a hand on her shoulder, "Viv, what is it?"

Vivian scans the top of the Keep wall to the west and speaks through clenched teeth, "I feel the presence of Dark Magic. It's coming from the west right behind that wall.

Immediately after she stops speaking the ground begins to shake. Ordyn yells to the staff to get out of the courtyard and onto the road. He can sense that something big is coming. The staff drop everything and run out of the courtyard to catch up to the procession of Keep citizens already on the road.

Everyone in the group is looking up towards the top of the wall when Akita and Wulf fly up and land behind them. The shield envelops them as they get near her. Akita moves quickly to Vivian, "Vivian, what's going on? Why is the ground shaking?"

Vivian pushes more magic into her mace and the shield of light becomes bigger. She slightly grunts as she begins to speak, "Akita, he is here. I feel his Dark Magic. I can sense it on the other side of the wall. As for the ground trembling, I can only attribute that to his doing."

Akita kind of gasps and growls at the same time, "Damn it! Not now. Ordyn is everyone out of the Keep?

Ordyn steps closer and speaks quietly, "Yes, I sent the last of the staff to the road. It's just us. I can hear what Vivian is sensing. I think it is coming from further away than just behind the courtyard wall."

Akita looks around the group, "Okay, we can't just sit here and wait for whatever it is to attack us. We need a plan and need more information. Let's see, Vicar, help boost Vivian's shield, Mandrake, Shadow Slip to the back side of the Keep. Wulf fly to the top of the West ramparts and try to get a clear view of what is going on behind the wall. Ishvet, you and Ordyn stay here with Vivian in case there are ground troops. Annut and Thoraxian fly high up into the clouds. Once the two of you are there, contact Aphorea and tell her to meet us in Salthall with her team, after they take the wounded to Stagbreak and do not come back to the Keep. You both are our secret reinforcements if things get out of hand. Storm, you and Visham cover the South gate. Gavin you and Blitz cover the escape of our people. Meh-Kola I want you to blink as quickly and as silently as you can all the way to the ocean cliffs and then report back if you see anything. I'm going to fly straight up and let Captain Dub know what is going on down here and tell Orien and Zora to be ready to swoop down and pick up Ishvet and Vivian. Everyone got it?"

Everyone makes eye contact with Akita and nods in agreement. Akita raises her hand and then swiftly chops the air and the whole team makes their moves. They are all in their position in a matter of a few minutes. Akita reaches Captain Dub and begins to tell him about the ground shaking but is interrupted by Meh-Kola blinking into existence between the two of them.

Meh-Kola seems slightly out of breath and shook, "Akita everyone needs to run now! There is something enormous climbing up the cliff wall just outside the Keep grounds. One does not want to face it. It is a monster. It must be what King Carthon was making in his dungeon."

Akita is startled for a split second and then moves to fly straight down to the courtyard. She yells out as she is flying straight down, "Annut and Thoraxian we are going to need you, get everyone back to the hill. Tell Captain Dub to pull his fliers back to just beyond the Keep."

Halfway down to the ground she can see Annut and Thoraxian speeding to the ground on either side of her. Before they can get any closer there is a huge blast wave that pushes them back. Akita can see a large portion of the west Keep wall go flying to pieces and flames shooting out in all directions.

Vivian's light shield absorbs the blast wave of the wall exploding. Vicar, Ordyn, Ishvet and her are shocked by the power of the explosion. The magnitude was incredible, and smoke and debris is all around them. A large crater begins to appear where the wall was as the smoke blows away. On the other side of the crater is someone riding a huge Owl Roc. As their eyes adjust, they can see that it is King Carthon, and he is inside a large blue sphere.

Annut speaks in all their minds at once and tells them to fall back to the hill. They all start moving out of the courtyard and to the east side of the Keep when they hear King Carthon amplifying his voice and speaking in a mocking tone, "Akita Blackwing are you still alive? Did your home get a little wet? Sorry about your wall, but I figured you might need a storm drain for all that water."

Akita descends to Annut's saddle and with Thoraxian beside them they continue their descent but alter their direction to engage King Carthon from two sides. Once they are upon him Annut and Akita send out searing flames and Thoraxian lands a hard-hitting tail swipe. Thoraxian's tail bounces off the blue sphere and doesn't even leave a scratch. Annut's and Akita's flames surround the blue sphere and then dissipate. The sphere doesn't even have a smudge on it.

Before they can react, something very large emerges from over the cliffside and steps up right behind King Carthon. A gigantic arm slices the air and hits Annut and Thoraxian flinging them though the air to the north of the Keep. Akita holds on as Annut tumbles and fights to upright herself. Thoraxian hits the ground on his feet close to the hill and slides backwards almost one hundred yards leaving huge gouges in the ground from his claws. Annut regains control in the air and flies out from the Keep and around to get a better look at the creature that just swatted at them like they are flies.

Akita yells out, "Annut are you okay? What in Bahamut's name was that?"

Annut speaks to Akita's mind only, "I am fine Akita. I cannot identify this creature, but it is as big as three Dragons and hits even harder than one."

Thoraxian also enters Akita's mind, "I can't believe it. They are supposed to all be dead or sealed away. The power is undeniable though. This creature is some type of Titan."

Akita gasps as she gets a view of the gigantic creature looming over the Keep, "I can't believe what I am seeing. Annut, Thoraxian do we have any chance at defeating this thing?"

Thoraxian speaks up in Akita's mind first, "No, I don't believe we do. Even if Aphorea was here I don't think we would have enough strength."

Annut speaks to Akita's mind while also relaying instructions to anyone else at the Keep and the ones who are at the hill, "He is right Akita. We need to regroup. I am telling everyone now to head for Salthall as quickly as they can. Vivian and Ordyn are trying to hold back Ishvet, and Vicar is trying to calm him. Seeing his father has driven him into a rage. Everyone else is moving back. I have relayed what has happened to the team in Prayla. They say that many have survived and that they are moving the survivors to Stagbreak. They will meet us in Salthall. Thoraxian and I will cover your escape and then meet you on the outskirts of Salthall."

Akita jumps off of Annut's back and flies down to where Ishvet, Vivian, Ordyn and Vicar are. As she lands, she hears King Carthon amplify his voice again.

King Carthon chuckles as Thoraxian's tail hits his Sea Amulet Shell and it bounces off and again when Annut's and Akita's flames engulf him. It didn't even get warm inside. He pets his Roc Owl Hector on the neck and talks calmly to him, "No need to worry boy, nothing can affect us in here. Jessa will be here any moment and then I can see the terror on all their faces. It will be delightful."

He can feel the vibration in the shell as Jessa approaches behind him. It tickles the back of his neck, and the Sea Amulet glows more brightly. He cannot contain his joy when he sees Jessa slap the two Dragons out of the sky. He grabs his abdomen as he laughs aloud. He knows that soon they will run but he is satisfied that he has accomplished his goal of getting some revenge on the Blackwing lady that thwarted his plans with King Cirus.

King Carthon sees Akita dismount Annut and head towards the ground. He decides that this would be the perfect time to reacquaint these old friends. He quicky thinks the spell and amplifies his voice so that all with in a kilometer can hear him, "Akita Blackwing your Keep and its people are lost. Though you did not die as I had wished, I feel like you now understand the powers I possess. I am as powerful as a God, now as a God, I think it is only fitting that I have my own Demi-Titan. I made her from pieces of your past. Though you may not recognize her, she is in there. You left her to the sea and the sea made her powerful. I will allow you to retreat and lick your wounds for now. I have others to visit shortly. Oh, and one last thing, I wouldn't worry yourself with that Pirate woman anymore. I'm sure she is rotting at the bottom of the ocean with her ships and people. I had planned to come see you first, but the opportunity presented itself on our way here."

King Carthon turns Hector towards the sky and flies away at tremendous speed. The blue from the sphere leaves a blue streak in the sky. The colossal monster that was behind him turns and jumps into the ocean. When it lands the water comes up to its chest and then the creature submerges fully. A large riptide expands from its point of entry and waves splash almost all the way up the cliffside by the Keep. The monster's dark shadow can be seen moving beneath the churning water until it turns around the bend to the South.

Ordyn wraps his arm around Ishvet's shoulder and chest from behind to hold him in place. Ishvet is cursing up a storm and is starting to glow blue. Ordyn does not know if he could even hold him if Ishvet got to full power. Vivian is pressing up against Ishvet from the front to hold him back. She knows that seeing his father has him in a rage. Vicar places a hand on the nape of

Ishvet's neck to begin a calming spell and bring him back to his senses.

The intensity of the situation shifts when he sees the large creature rise from the side of the cliff and stand over King Carthon. It becomes even more dire when Annut calls for them to all fall back to the hill. Ishvet is still enraged and has not calmed enough to move at the moment. As Ordyn holds Ishvet in place for Vicar to work his magic, he takes notice of the towering creature.

The creature seems almost fifty feet tall and has a human-esque figure. It has two regular arms and then two lower arms that come out of its ribs. The lower arms appear scaley and where the hands would be there are large Wyvern heads. There does not appear to be any armor or clothing. Instead, the hair from the creature's head flows down and around it's body. The hair is dark red and looks very thick and it wraps around the torso all the way to its shins. The hair covers most of the face of the creature except for the left side. From what he can see the face looks feminine in its features and its eyes are brown.

Ordyn sees Annut, Akita, and Thoraxian make their attack run at King Carthon. He is amazed when the creature moves so quickly and purposefully to swing its arm and knock them all from the sky. He wishes that he could fly up and help, but he doesn't want to see his friend, Ishvet get hurt. He knows that if he were to let go, that Ishvet would run directly for King Carthon and maybe get himself killed.

Much to Ordyn's relief he sees that Annut, Akita, and Thoraxian are okay. That is overshadowed by King Carthon's speech. He proclaims that he has already destroyed O'Malley Keep. This enrages Ordyn now. He can feel his muscles tense even more. Then he hears Akita land behind him, "Calm down Ishvet, we need to protect the people. We are no match for this Demi-Titan. We need to regroup and gather strength. You think I want to leave my home? You don't think I'm madder than a wet hen? Well, let me tell you that I am so mad that I could spit lava right now, but that isn't going to help anyone. Knowing what we are up against and finding a way to fight it has worked for us in the past so that's what we are going to do now. Ordyn, you can let him go now. He's back to normal."

Ordyn looks down at Ishvet and sees that he is no longer glowing blue, "I would have held you forever Ish, but Vivian may have gotten jealous.

Let's go help our people on the road like Akita said."

Ishvet turns and puts an arm around Vivian to hold himself up, "Ordyn, thanks for helping me out. I'm so tired now. Thanks to you also Vicar. I probably would have gotten myself killed running after my father like that. Then Vivian would have been angry with me for eternity. I would hear it from my grave."

Vivian squeezes Ishvet around the waist, "Darn right you would have. I would have come out to your grave everyday just to cuss you out for leaving me all alone."

Vicar chuckles as they all begin walking towards the east gate, "You know Ishvet, they say that only Banshees can wake the dead, but I am betting that they have never met Vivian Elderwolf. So yeah, there is no eternal rest for you."

Akita stops and turns towards Vicar with a look of disbelief on her face, "Really Vicar? In the middle of all this."

CHAPTER 7

SEARCH AND
RESCUE

Darkwing glides over the wave's path of destruction from Prayla to Blackwing Keep. He can't help but to think to himself, ["It's painful to leave everyone behind but there are people in Prayla that need help too. I can't believe that the wave could do so much damage."]

Darkwing signals over to Greenbean and once he has her attention he points down. Below the is where a small farm just on the outskirts of Prayla used to be. All that is left is the house's foundation and the foundations of a few barns. The rest of the ground is wiped bare.

Greenbean shakes her head in disgust looking at the carnage on the ground. Most of the town's debris seems to be caught on the edge of the forest. There are pieces of houses and shops, a few boats, and many bodies of dead livestock. It is a lot to take in. On many occasions she has to close her eyes because she and Warrior pass over a deceased person's body. She keeps repeating in her head, ["Please let there be survivors!"]

Martyn speaks to Darkwing's mind, "Aphorea has made it to what is left of the docks. She said that there are many alive and they are helping others get to safety. She asked that you look on the west side of town for anyone left."

Darkwing gives Martyn a pat on his neck as an acknowledgement. Martyn then turns to the southwest to reach that part of town. As they start to turn, Greenbean yells over to Darkwing, "Darkwing I'm headed to the schoolhouse to see if everyone is okay or needs help. I'll meet everyone in the town square when we are done. Aphorea has just relayed that Fabby is to go on to Stagbreak and set up an area for the wounded to arrive."

Olek and Ransom fly close to Darkwing and hear Greenbean. Olek adds, "I'm going to the market district to help who ever I can. I'll meet you three in the town square as soon as I can."

Darkwing looks back and forth and nods his head in agreement. As they peel off in their separate directions, Prayla comes into view. There are still many houses left standing. From the air it looks like mostly the docks and the west side of the town were affected by the force of the wave. The rest of the town only looks like it had flooding.

Olek makes it to the open-air market area of the town first. It is on the east side, so not much damage is visible. Most of the various booths have been pushed up against buildings creating a large open space where he and Ransom can land.

Ransom lands and tells Olek that he doesn't hear anyone screaming for help. Olek gets down and walks towards some buildings that he is familiar with from his time visiting the market. He calls out to anyone that might hear. An older couple calls back to him from a two-story balcony. They say they are okay and that they believe that everyone in the area made their way to the town square. They recount the event saying that water rushed at them down the streets and all the market booths floated away. The people at the market were able to swim away or cling on to something to avoid the same fate as the booths.

Olek checked on a few more people and heard the same tale. A small bit of relief crept into his mind. He knows it was bad, but it was not as bad as it could have been. He walks back to Ransom, and they take flight towards the town square.

Greenbean sees Olek and Ransom land about three blocks from the schoolhouse. They must have found a spot in the open-air market that Ransom could fit. Fabby and Hunter are out of sight, so they are well on their way to Stagbreak. Darkwing is also out of sight, so he must have found a place for Martyn to land on the west side. She is having a more difficult time finding a place for Warrior to land.

As Greenbean reaches the schoolhouse she can see that there are people walking around and children are with them. She has Warrior fly low over the school and the children wave up at them. She believes that for the most part that the people in this area fared well. She decided to head over to the west side of town to help Darkwing.

Darkwing flies over the path of the wave that flattened that part of the town. Many small homes are wrecked. If his memory serves him right, there was a small clinic in this part of town that Ouch, and Magrath ran. Martyn lands in the middle of the street close to where the clinic was. There is a two-story pile of debris and only one person sifting through it. At first Darkwing doesn't recognize Ahha. He is covered in blood and debris. None the less he is furiously digging in the pile. Darkwing climbs the pile and moves next to Ahha, "Ahha, are you okay? You're covered in blood and dirt."

Ahha doesn't look up and just keeps digging. Finally, after moving a few more boards, he speaks in a faint voice, "They are under here somewhere. I have to find them. They might be hurt."

Darkwing calls down to Martyn, "Martyn can you get some of these big beams and fly them away?"

Martyn flies up and clasps a big beam and flaps his wings harder to lift it off the pile. He flies a short distance and drops it and then comes back for another one. When he lifts the next one the pile starts to shift, and a void opens up to the lower floor. Martyn tells Darkwing in his mind that he has found an opening.

Darkwing grabs Ahha's arm and leads him to the void in the pile. They both look down inside. It is too dark to see any detail, so Darkwing creates a blue flame ball and sends it to the bottom of the void. He sees it at the same time as Ahha. Ouch and Magrath are holding each other and lying motionless on the floor. They must have drowned after being trapped under the debris.

Ahha drops to his knees and cries out a long guttural "No". Darkwing picks him up and Martyn comes over to them. Ahha becomes limp as Darkwing tries to get him on Martyn's saddle. Darkwing can see that he has passed out. He lays Ahha over the saddle on his stomach and tells Martyn to fly Ahha to the town square so that he can get some medical help.

Martyn flies towards the town square and passes Greenbean flying toward Darkwing. Martyn tells Greenbean in her mind that Ouch and Magrath are dead. Greenbean thanks him for the news and continues to where Darkwing is. With many buildings gone it is easier for Warrior to land. Warrior lands and Greenbean gets down and climbs the pile of debris to where Darkwing is.

Greenbean's voice warbles a bit in the beginning, then becomes normal, "So more of our friends have perished at the hands of this lunatic. Darkwing are you okay?"

Darkwing looks back at Greenbean and shakes his head in the negative, "I am sick to my stomach from all the pain we have gone through. I can't take any more friends dying. I don't even want to know who perished at Blackwing Keep. Let's continue to search these ruins. Hopefully, we find someone we can help."

Greenbean puts her arm around Darkwing's shoulders. She gives him a squeeze and speaks in a more determined tone, "We will end this soon. He can't elude us forever. On a more promising note, it looks like most of the town and its people survived. From what I can deduce, King Carthon just needed a place to get the wave on land. Prayla happened to be in his way. He wasn't trying to destroy the town otherwise it wouldn't be here. The majority of them are lucky. We should be able to clear the debris and find anyone who might be alive or bodies in less than an hour with Warrior's help. So come on and steel yourself. We are going to need your help."

Darkwing stands a little taller and takes a deep breath, "Your right, let's get this done and get back to Blackwing Keep."

Greenbean, Warrior, and Darkwing sift through the piles of broken wood and toppled stone. They find two more bodies, but no one trapped. They take the bodies to the town square for identification and then return to get Ouch and Magrath. Prayla will keep their bodies until Akita is made aware and she can decide what to do for their funeral services.

As they finish dropping off Ouch and Magrath's bodies, Olek arrives at the square. He reports that almost everyone in the town made it through the ordeal unharmed or with only minor injuries. Twelve citizens unfortunately lost their lives, the four that they found and eight more that Aphorea discovered at the docks.

They start to feel some relief until Aphorea calls to them in their heads, "King Carthon has attacked the Keep. He had some gigantic creature with him. Akita has ordered that everyone meet on the road Salthall as soon as we can. We are fortunate that the town faired so well. We won't have any injured people to move to Stagbreak. So, mount up and head directly for the road to Salthall. Do not go to Blackwing Keep. Fabby can still hear me. He is also headed to Salthall from his position."

Olek, Greenbean, and Darkwing all mount up and fly directly towards the road to Salthall. The flight will only take a few hours. Hopefully, they can find the caravan of survivors on the road before anything else happens.

King Carthon looks over the courtyard and can see Ishvet and all the others gathered together. He knows that Jessa could destroy them in an instant. However, he was here to send a message. In his mind the message was delivered with a flair that only he could provide.

The Sea Amulet combined with his innate magic has produced amazing results. He can use water as a weapon, as a shield, and cause it to explode. Creating the Demi-Titan was just a step in the greater plan. Before today, the greatest force in Alahora was Dragons. After today it is Jessa the Demi-Titan, which is under his control.

Carthon amplifies his voice, "Akita Blackwing, your Keep and its people are lost. Though you did not die as I had wished, I feel like you now understand the powers I possess. I am as powerful as a God, now as a God, I think it is only fitting that I have my own Demi-Titan. I made her from pieces of your past. Though you may not recognize her, she is in there. You left her to the sea and the sea made her powerful. I will allow you to retreat and lick your wounds for now. I have others to visit shortly. Oh, and one last thing, I wouldn't worry yourself with that Pirate woman anymore. I'm sure she is rotting at the bottom of the ocean with her ships and people. I had planned to come see you first, but the opportunity presented itself on our way here."

As he finishes his speech, he notices something odd about Ishvet. He is glowing blue. It's the same type of blue aura that the Sea Amulet emits. He begins to think to himself. ["What kind of power does Ishvet have? Did it come from his mother? What secrets died with her that I should have known. I need to get back to the Keep and research this."]

He pats Hector on the neck, "Come on boy let's get back to the Keep."

As Hector turns to fly away, he grabs the Sea Amulet and connects with Jessa's mind, "Jessa return home, you have done well. They will think twice before they approach you again."

With the added power of the Sea Amulet, getting back to Cliffshade Keep takes very little time. It will take Jessa at least six hours with her following the Southern coast. That will give him enough time to review reports from spies that were in charge of watching Ashonia, Ishvet's mother.

An hour later he and Hector approach the Keep. The concealment spell is still holding and the whole area looks abandoned. Hector flies to the upper balcony of the main tower and holds his position. Carthon holds out his left hand and a rift opens before them. Hector flies in and lands on the balcony that is on the other side of the illusion.

As soon as they land, they are greeted by his Steward Volaern. Carthon hops down from Hector's back, turns and pats Hector. The huge owl cocks his head back and hoots. Volaern approaches and tosses a dead rabbit in the air. Hector catches it in his beak and flies off. Volaern then greets King Carthon, "Sire, was your mission a success?"

King Carthon stops mid stride and looks at Volaern with a raised eyebrow, "I do hope you are joking Volaern."

Steward Volaern chuckles as he opens the balcony doors that lead to King Carthon's chamber, "Of course Sire! There is no one that is a match for your power. Everything you do is successful."

King Carthon walks into the doorway and begins to snicker aloud, "I got a two for one, Volaern. You should have seen it. I knew that Jessa and the Amulet together were going to be powerful, but I really didn't comprehend the magnitude until I saw it with my own eyes. On our way to Blackwing Keep we came upon O'Malley Keep. I knew that she helped them get to King Cirus' Island. So, I thought a small test of Jessa's power was in order. I told Jessa to push as much water as she could toward O'Malley Keep and then I would direct it to destroy the ships at the dock. She pushed so much water that the wave was taller than the whole damn Keep. The only thing that I could do was to make sure that it hit directly on the Keep towers."

Volaern smiles from ear to ear revealing a whole set of rotten and broken teeth, "Sire, did you see the ships sink?"

Carthon makes his way to his desk and sits in the desk chair and looks back at Volaern. He has a bright gleam in his eyes, "They weren't just sunk, they were flown apart. The wave crushed them into pieces. It was glorious!"

Volaern sits in the chair opposite of King Carthon and then scoots forward to be closer. He is getting excited and is hanging on every word, "What happened next Sire? Did the pirate women die? Did the Keep collapse?"

King Carthon shakes his head and puts up a hand to stop Volaern from speaking, "Hold on, hold on. I haven't got to the best part yet. When the wave hit the Keep it blasted in through the doors and windows. This pushed everything and everyone inside out through the other side. I saw people and beds and all kinds of things shooting out of every hole the water could escape through. Alas, I did not see the Pirate woman. As soon as the water dissipated, I moved on to Prayla."

Volaern moves in even closer and is on the edge of his seat, "I wager that they got the surprise of their lives when that huge wave plowed through the town."

Carthon chuckles a little then clears his throat, "Move back Volaern I can smell your rancid breath. Get up and get me some wine and then I'll finish the story."

Volaern hops up and fetches the wine for King Carthon. He sits the goblet down and returns to the chair, but he sits all the way back this time, "My apologies Sire."

Carthon raises an eyebrow again and a face of disgust forms, "You know, we may be ruthless and unforgiving, but that is no excuse to let your hygiene falter. Make sure you have that taken care of next time you are in my presence, or I may have to have Jessa send a wave of sea water into your mouth. That would surely blow your tonsils out."

Volaern quickly covers his mouth with his hand and his eyes get wide. He shakes his head in acknowledgement. King Carthon continues, "Umm, where was I? Oh yes, the town of Prayla. Again, I had Jessa create a huge wave, but this time I wanted to exert more control over the water. I exerted a little too much control, because instead of destroying the whole town it just cut a path like a knife through a melon. However, I was able to make the wave move faster and faster as it approached Blackwing Keep. It hit with a force that I had never seen. The Keep wall crumbled in an instant and the outlying buildings were torn asunder. At the last moment I saw that there were Dragons behind the Keep, so I pushed the wave towards them. Even as powerful as it was it did not kill any of them. All the rest of Akita's team seemed to survive too. I waited by the sea cliffs so that Jessa could climb up and give them the shock of their lives. That's when I had the idea to use my magic in conjunction with the Sea Amulet's. Then sent a water ball towards the west wall and heated the water so quickly that it exploded. The explosion tore right through the stone wall, and I could see the courtyard. It was amazing."

King Carthon stops with a smile on his face and takes a long sip of his wine. Volaern starts to lean forward but thinks better of it and leans back into his chair. King Carthon doesn't speak for a moment to build the anticipation and anxiety in Volaern.

Finally, King Carthon clears his throat and begins to speak. Volaern lets out an audible sigh of relief when Carthon resumes speaking. Carthon's tone changes to more disappointed than excited, "Unfortunately, most of Akita's team survived. The positive though is that I was attacked by two Dragons and didn't even get a scratch. When Jessa made it over the cliff, she batted them both away with one swipe. That was a spectacle. On another note, my son was there.

He was protecting all of them just like usual. This time though I saw something from him that I hadn't seen since his mother. He was glowing blue. Not just any kind of blue either. It was the same blue as the Sea Amulet. There appear to be some secrets that I still need to learn before we proceed to the next step in my plans. I want you to contact our spies in Salthall and have them find out as much as they can about my son. I am going to find some old journals of Ashonia's and see if there is anything I can learn about this power my son appears to have."

Volaern stands and quickly makes his way out of the chamber door. King Carthon sits back in his chair and sips his wine again. He begins thinking to himself, ["Ashonia, what did you give Ishvet that you never told me about? Did you give him something that could rivel the power of the Amulet?"]

CHAPTER 8

BACK TO O'MALLEY KEEP

Grace O'Malley received a message from Alican on the docks of Prayla, just as the team returned from their battle with the Cloud Giant King. The message urged her to return to her Keep as fast as the winds could carry her ship.

A few days later the ship glides into its birthing and is tied to the dock. Grace sees her second-in-command waiting for her. The look on his face says she will be kicking some butts and taking names later. Her crew knows by the look on her face to get the gangplank down fast.

As Grace walks down the gangplank, Thom looks at his feet. He knows she is going to be raging mad when he reports his findings to her. "Thom, what was so urgent that you needed me back so fast?"

Taking his hat off and wringing it in his hands, he looks up at her. "Captain O'Malley, we need to do some house cleaning. I found a spy in our midst and then a group of bandits tried to break into the Keep and rescue him. The bandits were dispatched to the Gods, but we still have the spy."

Grace clenches her fists and growls. ["How dare that wanna be King send spies to her Keep."] "Take me to him. Now!"

Thom leads the way to the cave by the ship that takes them to the dungeons of the Keep. He knows she wants the fastest route and going along the beach and through the Keep will just irritate her more. "Captain O'Malley, I have tried to get information from this scallywag, but to no avail. He has taken everything I have done to him as if nothing were happening to him. He looks like hell though. I don't think he's drugged because he wouldn't remember what he needed to spy on us for, so I think someone put a spell on him."

Grace smacks Thom hard, "Just shut your trap. How did this spy get in here to begin with? Who brought this mess to my Keep? I want them brought to me. They are probably a spy as well."

As they enter the dungeon, she sees the spy in a dank, small cell, shackled to the wall. He is a filthy mess, and his own blood is splattered on his chest and dripping from his mouth. She is wondering if he is even still alive, until she hears him moan when the torch is lit.

As he lifts his head to see who is going to torture him this time, he sees Captain Grace and an ice-cold fear runs through his body. His eyes go wide. This was not supposed to happen; she was supposed to still be at Blackwing Keep. How much time has passed?

As his head lifts, Grace notices a chain around the prisoner's neck. "Thom, why is that chain still on him? Here you are worried he has a spell of protection, and I am thinking he has an enchanted necklace on. Get in there and get that off of him." She is screaming at the top of her lungs. "I leave the Keep for a few weeks and you cannot do your job while I am gone. Maybe you get the cell next to him."

As Thom tries to take the necklace, the prisoner attempts to bite him. With his other hand he smacks the prisoner and grabs the necklace, breaking the chain as he pulls it off the prisoner. The look of pure fear crosses the prisoners' face.

The prisoner starts whimpering as Grace moves to the cell door. "This can go one of two ways, you gutless wonder. You can answer my questions and live as my servant or not answer my questions and die. So, who sent you here and when?"

The prisoner sags against the wall, "My life is forfeit anyway. Without the necklace I will die in a few hours. So, none of it matters." He sighs and starts to weep. "King Carthon sent me here to see if you were working with the Blackwing lady, when he found out you were the one that brought her to King Cirus' Island. You were gone when I got here and I only recently found out where you were, so I even failed at being a servant under him. I failed everyone, even my family because he imprisoned me."

Grace snarls, "Cry me a river, life is never fair. What can you tell me about his Keep? What his plans are for Blackwing Keep and the Realm? And maybe I will give you back the necklace." Thom looks at Grace in complete shock from a dark corner of the cell.

The prisoner looks up at her trying to judge if he can trust her words, because her reputation is one of a cold-hearted scoundrel. He decides he has nothing to lose. "I can draw you the Keep layout and mark key areas. I can mark the entrance to the new dungeon, but not of the dungeon because only his most trusted are allowed down there. All I ever did was clean his chamber pot and taste test his food for poison." He watches her facial expressions to see if that is enough. "Oh, and the Keep has a spell on it. Unless you know how to enter, it looks like the town and Keep is in ruins."

Grace stares at the man for several minutes thinking, ["Do I do this the 'Akita way', or do I maintain my old ways that have always worked for me. If I am going to make this change in my life, I will apply a little of 'Akita's ways' to see how it works for me."] Snapping out of her thoughts, "Thom, tie the necklace back on him, but if I find he's lying about anything, we remove it and let him die a slow agonizing death." Looking at the prisoner, "Do I make myself clear?"

The prisoner nods vigorously, "I have no allegiance to him or anyone else."

Grace turns to Thom, "Get him a table and chair, paper and writing instruments. Get him a chamber pot and unshackle him. Set a guard outside the cell. Bring him a decent meal twice a day." Looking back to the prisoner, "You have six days to draw a detailed map of the Keep and the surrounding area. You have this time only because I have other matters to deal with. Do not fail me."

Grace starts to turn away and then looks back, "One last thing. Who let you into my Keep?"

The prisoner looks down again, "No one really. I snuck in with a group of your men and blended in until someone finally realized they didn't know who I was or where I belonged. I am a farmer, so I don't know anything about spying or not getting caught, obviously."

Grace wastes no time in getting her Keep in order to her liking again. She punishes all of the guards for not catching this spy before he entered the Keep. She makes it clear that if this ever happens again, the officers will find their heads on pikes. She punishes Thom as well, putting him in a cell for a month and replacing him with one of the few women in the Keep that is not just a maid or cook. Jacklyn is a Greatsword Fighter and a formidable foe, with more brains than Thom, apparently, as she was the one that caught the spy.

Grace starts preparing for more bandits and the possibility of Dark Wizards attacking her Keep. She has all the men training, doubles the watch, brings in supplies for a couple of months, and starts building stables so she can acquire flyers of her own. All of this takes more time than she would like.

While all the preparation is going on, she notices that there haven't been any more bandit attacks. Her own spies have no word on the Dark Wizards of the area planning an attack. In fact, her spies have noticed that the camps have been abandoned. This, to her, makes no sense unless they are focusing all their attention on Blackwing Keep. Still, she is going to be prepared because she is sure word has traveled around the Realm of her helping Blackwing Keep.

As the days turn to weeks and weeks into months since leaving Prayla, a growing madness has started to overtake her. She knows that some sort of Dark Magic is at play, but she cannot find the source. She is seeing things that are not there, hearing people who are long dead, and feeling an overwhelming sense of dread all the time. She has forbidden anyone in the Keep from mentioning it. As the sickness is getting worse, Grace begins to pull away from everyone and orders that no one is to leave the Keep and no one is allowed to enter. Grace won't even accept any messages or let anyone send any. She shuts the Keep off from the whole of Alahora.

Grace has sequestered herself to her room. She is not eating and barely sleeping. Jacklyn has tried many times to bring her to her senses. Jacklyn has caught her yelling at nothing, cowering in corners of her room and speaking of everything being lost. However, Jacklyn cannot find what is causing this psychotic break. Grace is so paranoid that she barely even lets Jacklyn in to see her. The paranoia has led to the dungeons being full of her own men and Thom has not been released from his thirty-day punishment.

Finally, Jacklyn has had enough. For months now she has been running the Keep and fortifying things for a mad woman. There is no end in sight for Grace's illness. The men will not put up with much more of this nonsense out of their leader. If

Grace can't snap out of it and take the lead like she has in the past, then she doesn't deserve to remain the leader.

The last three months have been the worst. Grace has ordered that some odd rules be followed with the threat of death. Everyone in the Keep has to wear a veil on their face. Large bowls of water have to be placed under the windows to catch evil spirits. The most heinous has to be that all citizens of the Keep be questioned daily about being spies. Most of the time there is an element of torture.

At last, the time has come for Jacklyn and the officers that are left to take matters into their own hands. They climb the stairs to Graces room and try to get her to come out peacefully. She refuses and is adamant that a large beast is hunting her. They have no other choice but to break down her door. Jacklyn starts swinging her Greatsword at the door. After two hacks she can hear bells ringing in the distance. The ringing is coming from the docks. Jacklyn stops and thinks to herself. ["That's odd, the bells only ring when an enemy ship is attacking."]

That's when the huge wave comes pushing into the Keep from the south. Jacklyn and the other two officers have no time to react. They are pressed against the walls and churned out the window of the hallway. The water then busts down Grace's door and blasts her in the face…everything goes black for her.

She slowly wakes up lying in a puddle of water. At first, she wonders if she had peed herself at some point in the night. Her body aches, as she blinks her eyes to clear her vision. She carefully tries to roll over but finds her left arm broken. Gritting her teeth, she struggles to get herself up with her right arm, only to find her right leg seems to be broken, as well. She wipes her face with her forearm and looks around the area. She feels as light as a feather and lightheaded, like a huge weight has been lifted off her shoulders. Grace is confused because she remembers nothing and has no idea why she has broken bones, and the sun is shining through the roof of her room while she is sitting in a puddle. Her room is destroyed with furniture strewn everywhere. There are heavy dressers toppled and a chair hanging out the window.

She drags herself to her bed, which is on its side, moaning and groaning with pain as she drags her leg on the ground with her one good arm and pushing with her one good leg. She must find something in the room to splint her leg and arm. Looking at the bed she hopes she can pull the slats off the bottom and use the sheet to make a splint.

She reaches for her sword but it's not with her. ["Where the hell is my cutlass? Why would I be unarmed in the middle of the day?"] She finds her stiletto still in her boot sheath. She uses it as a tool to pry one end of a slat away from the bottom of the bed and then the other. She loosens one more slat for her arm. Reaching for the edge of her sheets she tries to pull it over the back of the bed; however, it seems to be pinned under the edge of her huge king size heavy oak bed frame. She takes a minute to rest because she is going to have to drag herself around the bed to get the pieces she needs.

It took her about an hour to get good tight splints on her arm and leg. There is nothing in the room she can use as a crutch, so she pulls herself out onto the veranda. The pain is excruciating, but she knows she has some potted trees outside.

As she slides through the doors, she sees King Carthon flying away from her Keep, laughing. The white-hot anger she feels at that moment and rush of adrenaline, allows her to pull herself up to a standing position leaning against the door frame. She cannot believe what she is seeing, so she hops on one leg across to the railing and almost collapses in pain. Raising her head, she gazes out over the docks. She lets out a roaring scream of anger, so loud nearby birds take flight.

The Sea Horse is at the bottom of the bay and all that can be seen is the crow's nest on the middle mast of the ship. The docks are destroyed and the grounds around the Keep are flooded. Looking down she sees bodies of her crew and horses strewn everywhere. All that she has worked for is gone.

Grace slumps to the ground and cries. ["Am I the only one left? Is there no one here to help me with my leg and arm?'] Feeling angry again, she says out loud to the wind, "Enjoy this while you can King Carthon, because I am coming for you, and I will kill you. I will laugh as the light goes out of your eyes; you are a murdering maniac."

A woman begins to regain consciousness and opens her eyes to complete darkness. An immense weight is pushing down on her making it difficult to breathe. She can feel another person to the side of her, but they feel cold and lifeless. Her legs are completely pinned but her arms have some range of movement. She reaches up in the darkness and her fingertips meet an obscured barrier that is smooth and feels like wood. She presses up with what little strength she has, and the object doesn't move in the slightest.

She begins to panic as she feels her body begin to sink in the mud underneath her. Her breath becomes labored and thin before she passes out again. Her last thought is, ["I'm gonna die here and I don't even know where I am."]

Chapter 9

The First Nights Retreat

The sun is beginning to set and the sky behind Akita, Wulf, Mandrake, Vicar, Ishvet, Vivian and Ordyn is a fiery red. They have almost caught up with the temporary campsite of survivors and soldiers. The entire flight from Blackwing Keep, no one has said a word. Everyone still seems in shock, and nobody wants to be the first to acknowledge the enormity of what has happened to their home. They seem to be running on instinct at this point and only focused on reaching the survivor's camp. As they get closer to the camp Akita points to a clearing where they can land and dismount.

Ishvet gets off of Orien and Vivian slides off of Zora then starts walking towards Akita and Wulf. Akita looks to the couple that should be married right now. "Ishvet, Vivian, I am so sorry this happened on your special day. I wanted so bad for this to be the most special day of your lives. I think I made Wulf nuts with details." Akita sighs and her shoulders slump. Wulf puts a reassuring arm around her.

Ishvet turns to Akita, "Akita stop it! Don't waste one more tear on things you have no control over. This is all on Carthon. He is the bad guy here. Viv and I knew the dangers when we joined you. We are not sad, we are angry. We want justice for you and the realm."

Vivian moves closer to Ishvet and slides a hand around his waist, "Akita, he is right, don't go down that chasm of despair. Use the hurt to steady your resolve. Only one person is to blame and that is King Carthon. That's where you set your sights."

Akita feels defeated after the events of the day. She knows Ishvet is right, that everything from the death of her uncle to the kidnapping of Darkwing, the death of Rani, Rogue's demise, and now the destruction of Blackwing Keep, with so many dead, has been orchestrated by King Carthon. It doesn't make it any easier to manage emotionally at the moment. She is also kicking herself for not searching more for Jessa. She was obviously not dead, and the Dark Wizards found her. Now the Jessa they did know is gone forever. Now she is doing the bidding for a man, she normally would be trying to destroy.

Akita looks to Wulf with tears still streaming down her face, "Wulf I know that they are right, but I can't bear this enormous loss of the people I loved so much."

Wulf looks her in the eyes and cups her face with his right hand, "Akita, you are not alone. You do not have to bear this sorrow alone. We are all here with you and share it equally. There will be time for grieving, but that is not today. Today is a day for us to reach in the depths of our souls and pull up a strength that we did not even know we had. We use that strength to protect our people and to bring justice to those that prey on the innocent."

Akita nuzzles her face in Wulf's hand and takes a deep breath and gives a slight smile. She stands up taller and looks at the faces around her with admiration. She grabs Wulf's hand that's on her face and gently pulls it to her side, "Wulf, where did that come from? It's like a whole new you. I needed that. I'm finding the strength for myself, all of you and our people. Together we can bear sadness and together we can overcome any obstacle. Even when that obstacle is a fifty-foot abomination that used to be my friend."

Vicar steps forward and grabs Akita's free hand, "Akita, I agree with everyone, especially Wulf. This realm needs to see a strong leader that will stand up for her people."

Mandrake walks up next to Vicar and finishes the train of thought, "One that will show compassion and strength. You are that leader to us; you always have been. Now go show it to them." Mandrake points the camp.

As they walk into camp, Akita feels defiant. Defiant in the face of adversity. She looks at all the people around the fires and makeshift tents and shares a compassionate smile. No words are exchanged, but the people understand that she is there for them. They immediately feel some of the weight of their grief lifted. It is as if the entirety of the camp takes a collective deep breath and becomes focused in the moment.

Shamash and Ixenvorlux join them around the fire next to a tent that Gavin erected for Akita. Akita begins to ask about the injured, Meh-Kola blinks in right next to her, startling everyone.

Meh-Kola looks around confused, "Wait, what did One miss?"

Ishvet leans down and whispers to Meh-Kola with a tone of sarcasm, "You missed Akita finding her inner strength is all, nothing really important at all."

Meh-Kola looks up at Ishvet with a disgruntled look, "This One always misses the good stuff."

Akita goes back to listening to reports of the wounded and the account of supplies from Shamash. Then is shortly interrupted by the sound of large wings flapping in the air. Akita looks up at the same time as everyone else around the fire and the camp sees that the rescue party has found the camp and are beginning to land.

Aphorea, Warrior, Hunter, and Martyn land with the other mounts. Greenbean, Fabby, Darkwing and Olek dismount and make their way over to the fire to talk to Akita. Captain Dub has also made his way to the camp from the opposite direction and joins the group. He bows to Akita and takes a seat on a freshly sawn log by the fire.

Greenbean sits next to Akita, "Well my friend, Prayla is, for the most part, ok. Only part of the town was destroyed. Unfortunately, our friends, Magrath and Ouch drowned in their clinic. Ahha seems to be ok, but we left him with the healers. He was destroyed emotionally when he passed out on Darkwing. As for the survivors, their message to you is, we will rebuild. They want you and your team to rid the Realm of evil. They will help you rebuild the Keep as well. The people of Stagbreak and all the surrounding towns have pledged to help too. Aphorea was an inspiration to them, of course, because up to this point, they have only seen Annut and heard rumors of others. She soothed their worries and minds while we were there."

Akita looks towards Aphorea with a smile. "That is truly heartening news. This evening, we will make announcements and I will make sure everyone knows the towns and cities are supporting us. We are awaiting supplies from Elderwolf Keep in a day or two. We will allow the injured to heal in a camp outside of Salthall. Then we will move northeast to the Dragon Temple. Annut and Thoraxian are going to gather all Dragons and Wyverns there, yes, even the young ones. O'Malley's Keep was attacked also, but we won't know how bad until we go there. Her ship is gone, according to King Carthon. Once we get to Salthall, Wulf and I will go search for survivors."

Meh-Kola interrupts, "One is hoping you are done talking about what has happened and are now ready to hear, what One has found. It was terrifying to see, and One wasn't able to get back fast enough to warn you. So now, One wants you to know what One saw, to prepare you for the days to come."

Everyone looks surprised at Meh-Kola and then to Akita. Akita shrugs, "I had a thought that maybe Meh-Kola could spy around Cliffshade Keep. I sent her on a mission to find out what King Carthon was up to. So, Meh-Kola, tell us what you found."

Meh-Kola lays down tucking her paws under her chest and folds her wigs against her back, wrapping her tail around her side. "One will tell the short version. One used her skills to get to Cliffshade Keep without being detected by unwanted eyes and ears. One came upon a Keep that looked as if no one had lived there for years. The town around the Keep looked abandoned and unlived in. One could smell people there and could sense strong magic, and One was able to blink through the magic. This revealed that the Keep and the town were as they should be. One blinked inside the garden doors through the Keep. Except that it was full of apprentice and higher Dark Wizards, it seemed normal. One blinked through a door to the dungeons. One heard strange noise that only a Fenton would hear and followed that through the maze of hallways and rooms. One came to a huge cavern with a gigantic vat. King Carthon was climbing to the top, so One wanted to get closer. One blinked to a chandelier near him and above the vat. He had something or someone in the vat and he threw in two Wyverns, then did a spell. One knew from his words that he was creating a monster. One also noticed an Amulet in his hand, that One believes is the missing Sea Amulet. One saw the sea blue green shining light as he did his spell. One stealthily left the Keep and flew back to Blackwing Keep, but One was too late. The wave had already hit, and the monster was already out causing destruction. It has occurred to One that he could easily create more of those monsters if he so chooses. The only question is how many he can control with that Amulet around his neck. One wonders what it would take to drain him of power before he had to rest and was too weak to fight. One is too curious for One's own good sometimes."

Akita just stares at Meh-Kola for several seconds. She doesn't know what to say. She is just trying to process in her head what Meh-Kola just told them all.

Ishvet looks to Vivian, "We have to get in that Keep and destroy the underground lab, even if it means destroying the Keep and town. We cannot allow this to go on much longer. We are going to have to take the fight to him." Then turning to Meh-Kola, "Do you think you can get us through the barrier when its time?

Meh-Kola shakes her head no, "One won't be able to get you all through at once. One can tell the other wizards how to destroy it all together."

Akita grits her teeth, "That's where we will make our justice felt. Right there at his home. First, we have to get our people to safety. Second, we need to build an army to take on the Titan and his amulet. The only way I know how to do that is with another amulet. I think we need to see if we can get the help of the Frost Giant Princess. We are going to need at least one of the two last amulets."

Skip looks to Akita, "Keep your head up High Lady Akita Blackwing of Blackwing Keep. None of this is your fault. I will head to Salthall and send a message to the Princess, but this time I will add your name and Skrymir's name. I am sure the news of a Demi-Titan will bring the Frost Giants to help. This is different than fighting another Giant. I will ask them to meet us at the Dragon Temple. I will leave in the morning."

Akita looks up at Skip, "You tell Dutch that you are representing me, and we need it sent so that it finds her wherever she is fast." Akita looks at the rest of the team, "We need a way to move the soldiers and injured faster. A slow walk to Salthall and then to Elderwolf Keep will leave us vulnerable for too long. Any suggestions? Keep in mind we had to leave the cages due to the attack and our hasty retreat."

Olek speaks up, "Our biggest issue will be the horses that are pulling the wagons. I think we can use the tarps to make slings that we can attach to the Dragon and Wyvern claws for the supplies and people. Can the Dragons and Wyverns grab the wagons without crushing them?"

Vicar clears his throat, "The horses can be calmed long enough to carry a few at a time in the tarps. If necessary, we can do the same with anyone who is nervous about flying."

Akita nods her head, "Olek and Vicar, please organize it in the morning. If we need to, we can get more tarps or gear from Salthall to optimize the travel to Elderwolf. However right now I think we all need some sleep. Everyone find somewhere to bunk down. Aphorea will keep watch. Gavin and Skip will you take the first watch with her?"

Gavin springs up from behind Skip, "Sure Akita, good choice on having the Hunters keep watch. Ole Skip and me can see things that others can't."

Vicar jumps up and scares the hell out of Akita, "Stop! Don't let anyone move! Ishvet and Vivian come stand right here in front of me. We are not ending this day without you two being married."

Ishvet and Vivian look at each other briefly, they both get up and stand in front of Vicar. Vicar clears his throat and begins where he left off before being interrupted by the giant wave. Akita decides it would be good for the whole camp to hear this, so she says a small spell and it amplifies Vicar's voice to the camp.

Ishvet takes Vivian by the hands, and they turn towards each other. Vicar places a hand on their shoulders and asks the usual questions of a marriage vow. Vicar asks if he may say a few words. Ishvet looks over with joy and tears in his eyes and nods yes.

Vicar clears his throat again and begins, "This may not be the most opportune time to have a wedding after such a tragic day. However, it may be the right time for two to become one. Each of us here are carrying a burden that may at the time be too much to bear. When you are able to share that burden with someone that cares for you, the load becomes lighter and the more people that you can share it with the better. Vivian and Ishvet are entering a moment in their lives where they are able to share whatever hardship may come, with each other. It is the same for all the delights of life. They come to share those equally. Let their union be an example of how two becoming one makes you stronger. Together they will be able to overcome anything that is put before them. Just as all of us coming together will make us stronger against the forces of evil that wish to destroy us. Let us end this day in a joyful moment and sleep easier knowing that you do not carry your burdens alone. We are now one in the fight against evil and Vivian and Ishvet are now one in marriage. Good night, all."

Akita dispels the amplification of Vicar's voice and then runs up and embraces both Vivian and Ishvet in her arms squeezing them very tight. She whispers into their ears, "I'm so glad it's finally official. We all needed to see this completed. I love you both so very much."

Akita wakes up to the sounds of pans clanging, the smell of coffee and freshly cooked quiche that Quinn has thrown together over open fires. A bit of frustration enters her mind, ["Am I the only one still in bed? Why did they not wake me up?"]

She quickly steps out of her tent to see everyone sitting around the fire stuffing their faces with Quinn's undoubtedly awesome breakfast. "Was no one going to wake me up for this feast and to get things rolling for the day?"

Wulf, quickly sets his plate down, rushing to Akita's side. "My dear, you were sleeping so soundly and peacefully finally, that we decided to give you more time to rest. Come sit down as Quinn has outdone herself on minimal supplies."

Akita allows herself to be led to the fire, only because the food and coffee smell so good and her tummy is grumbling, "Still, I should be up and ready with the rest of you and not being treated any differently. With that said, Quinn this smells heavenly, thank you." After taking a bite of the quiche, all you hear is a moan of delight.

Olek stands, "The rest of us will leave you four, Ishvet, Vivian, Akita and Wulf, to eat in peace and get this walking wounded group of survivors to the Salthall area today."

Akita nods, "As soon as I finish this meal, I will take Aphorea and Skip to Salthall. I want to check on the injured we sent ahead and send the other mounts back to help you. I will find tonight's campsite and have supplies waiting."

Akita finishes eating and calls to Aphorea to let her know the plan. Aphorea agrees and is waiting for Akita and Skip on the road. They both mount Aphorea and start the hour-long flight to Salthall. If all goes right, the first of the caravan should arrive by mount no more than a few hours later. By the early evening everyone should be at the campsite outside of Salthall.

CHAPTER 10

SALTHALL CAMP

As Akita lands Aphorea just outside of Salthall, she sees the Mayor of Salthall coming towards her, with a few council members and Judas. In a field to the north, she can see Mylar, Drako, and the twins' horses. The horse's enchanted wings have worn off. She is glad to see that they are safe.

Akita and Skip dismount Aphorea. Skip runs past the procession and into the town gates. Akita approaches the mayor, "Mayor Finn, I am assuming that Judas told you all that has happened to Blackwing Keep? I hope you have supplies ready for the survivors. We will need to make camp outside the town since we have some large mounts."

The mayor looks up at Aphorea making a mental realization that a gigantic white Dragon is staring at him.

The mayor shudders, then looks down at his feet. "Lady Blackwing, I wish we could be of more help. With that said, you need to know that O'Malley Keep has been destroyed. O'Malley's ship is at the bottom of the bay." He sighs and his shoulders sag. "We have not found any survivors yet. It did take us a while to get there, so I suppose some could have wandered away. However, I would ask that you do not linger here too long, as this evil is following you, due to your provoking the Dark Wizards."

Akita reaches and lifts the mayor's head. She looks him in the eyes for several seconds. "I understand your fear, as Prayla has been attacked as well. However, the damage was not as bad as we feared. Prayla and Stagbreak are working to tend the injured and clean up the mess. We need to stay here just a couple of days to allow our soldiers to heal and the rest of our team to catch up to us." Akita watches his resigned reaction. "The Dragons will warn us if any of the Dark Wizards should decide to move into this area. Know that we have to move to the northeast to face this foe."

The mayor can see in Akita's eyes the concern she has for everyone involved. She has obviously made sure everyone affected is being taken care of. "Lady Blackwing, I would never deny your people the healing they need. I can see you fully understand my concern."

Akita smiles, "Oh yes, I do understand. Tomorrow, Elderwolf Keep will be arriving with food and supplies that should help us until we are on the road again."

The mayor nods, "Whatever you need Lady Blackwing, we will be happy to help." With that he bows before heading back to town, councilmen in tow.

Akita looks to Judas, "We need to send Mylar and Drako to meet up with the caravan. They need to take some very large tarps with them. We are moving everyone here to cut down on travel time. I'm going to head to the clinic to check on the wounded. Can you please see to the tarps and send Mylar and Drako?"

Judas nods, "You have someone waiting for you in the clinic that has been helping. He wants to help with the Dark Wizards too. I'm sure you'll know exactly who I am talking about when you reach the clinic."

Judas runs back into the town and Akita follows at a bit of a slower pace. She heads for the main clinic to check on her people.

Akita walks into the clinic and spots a tall man in robes bent over one of the kitchen staff from Blackwing Keep. As soon as she sees him, she knows that it is Void Roasten, her teacher and friend.

Akita draws in a surprised deep breath, "Void! I am so glad to see that you had not headed to the Keep yet."

Void looks over his shoulder, "Actually, I was on my way down the road when I ran into your emissary Judas. He told me what had happened and that the injured were being flown here. I knew you would follow soon, so I came back to help the healers."

Akita smiles, "Thank you for your help. How are they?"

Void gestures to the patient before him, "This young lady will be just fine by tomorrow. Her bones have been mended, her lungs are healed from the salt water and her liver is repaired, we are letting her rest because the intensive magic to repair her bones has left her exhausted. It is the same for the two soldiers in the next room. I believe they can return to their ranks anytime now. The fourth, however, was lost by the time she got here. I believe she was a maid in the keep."

Akita slowly nods, "I see. Well, we will be staying nearby, so the three survivors can rejoin us tomorrow. I will leave money for someone to bring them to us."

Akita speaks to the lady from the kitchen, "Tomorrow, Celia, if you would like you can come with the soldiers to the camp. Quinn would really appreciate your help. But, if you would like to go to Prayla and help them as they rebuild and start working on Blackwing Keep, I will pay for your transport. The decision is yours, as I know it has been a traumatic twenty-four hours."

Celia's eyes get wide, "Thank you so much, Lady Blackwing. Pardon me, but I didn't even think you knew my name. I believe you are headed to rid us of the evil Dark Wizards. Although I would really like to help rebuild, my heart says Quinn needs me to help keep you all healthy for battle. I believe I will do my part in that battle. You have been good to all of us and deserve whatever support we can give."

Akita smiles, "I try to know everyone's name, but it is a challenge. What I do know is that Quinn speaks highly of you. Your skills and loyalty are always greatly appreciated. Get some rest until tomorrow, as there is no use sleeping on the ground until then. When you get to camp, seek out Quinn and Storm."

Akita makes her way to the two soldiers in the next room. "Good day, gentlemen. How are you feeling?"

The two jump up and stand at attention. "We are good Lady Blackwing." One of the men states. "We are ready to rejoin you in the battle against the Dark Wizards.

Akita smiles, "As you were men. This is your healing time. Tomorrow a wagon will take you both and Celia to our camp. You are to find General Olek so he can bring you up to speed and assign your duties." Looking at the soldier who had been talking. "You are Sergeant Gideon Trek, am I correct?" And you are Sergeant Marshall Luck?"

Then men answer at the same time, "Yes, Ma'am, Lady Blackwing."

Akita nods to them both, "I will let General Olek know to expect you. Thank you for your service and loyalty." She turns to leave the room.

Sergeant Marshall Luck speaks up, "Lady Blackwing it is an honor to be in your service. We will see you tomorrow."

Akita steps out of the room looking for Void Roasten. She finds him awaiting her at the door.

Void holds an arm out for Akita, "I have taken care of their transportation and the bill for their healing." Chuckling, "They gave you a discount because I helped them and showed them a couple new healing methods."

Akita takes Void's arm, "Well done, my friend. How do you feel about meeting an Ancient Dragon? Aphorea would love to meet you."

Void comes to an abrupt stop, "Wait! You are a companion to the fabled Aphorea the Bright? The Ice Dragon of the Titan wars? I had heard you had a dragon in your company, but I thought she was red. Aphorea is white."

Akita pulls on Voids arm, "Oh, just wait my friend. You will be meeting several dragons that are our friends. You are right; Annut the Fast is red, Aphorea the Bright is white, and Thoraxian the Shadow is black. They have helped us in our fight against the Dark Wizards."

Void's mouth slowly opens and only breath comes out then a slight stutter, "Ah, ah, you have got to be kidding me! This is a treat for sure!" Akita shakes her head, giggles, and pushes Void down the road.

Akita and Void walk out the west gate of Salthall and can see that people are preparing to receive the survivors in the large meadow at the city limits. They walk over to where Aphorea landed earlier, and Akita introduces Void to her. Akita can see a look of shock flash over Void's face as Aphorea begins speaking to him in his head.

Akita smiles and puts a hand on Void's shoulder, "I'm going to speak to the horses and Judas and let them know what is going on. You to have a nice conversation."

Void smiles and nods his head. Akita has never really seen such a glow in his face as he has now. She turns and starts walking towards the horses and Judas when she sees Judas point to the western sky. Akita turns and can see the first wave of survivors being flown into the campsite. Akita is touched when she hears the townsfolk start clapping and cheering as the Wyverns and other flying mounts drop off people and supplies in the field.

Storm lands in the field on Visham close to Akita. She dismounts and runs to Akita and gives her a big hug. As they hug, Visham shrinks back down to pocket size and makes his way to Storm. He crawls up her leg and back and perches on her shoulder.

Akita releases her embrace and grabs Storm by the shoulders, 'Where have you been? I haven't seen you since we left the Keep, and I didn't see you in the camp last night."

Storm immediately looks down to her feet and takes a deep breath, well, I had to go off on my own for a while to feed Rixan. It had been a while, and he was getting very hard to contain. So, I went a little north of where you camped the first night and found a small band of bandits. I let him get his fill and then slept there for the night. We will be okay for a few weeks now, but if needed, he can feed on any Dark Wizard we come across in a moment's notice."

Akita smiles and reaches out and lifts Storms chin, "Hon, you have nothing to be ashamed of. This is your reality and I accept you the way you are now. Plus, Rixan will come in handy when we finally face the Dark Wizards."

They both turn when they hear Vicar and Wulf chuckling as they approach. When Vicar and Wulf get close, they stop chuckling and have almost a guilty look on their faces. Akita turns to Storm, "There's always a joke in everything for them."

Wulf turns to Vicar and smiles then looks back at Akita and Storm, "Ladies, we were merely pointing out the obvious. You two standing together makes us imagine a firestorm. One that would never quell if we were to get on your bad side.

Akita points a finger at both of them and starts to laugh, "You best believe it!"

Storm joins in the laughter and forgets herself for a moment, "That's right boys you don't want this demon to come out of me because you'll just be puddles on the ground". She then quickly raises a hand to cover her mouth and her eyes get big as she gasps.

Akita snaps her head to the right and looks at Storm realizing what she just said. Vicar and Wulf stop laughing abruptly and then looks at each other with a confused look on their face. Then, they slowly look towards Storm.

Storm begins to speak but Akita interrupts, "The mayor confirmed what Carthon said. He did destroy O'Malley Keep."

Wulf shakes his head in disbelief, "That's awful. Did they find any survivors? However, before you say anything, I do have some good news. We were able to carry more than we thought at one time and the flight didn't take as long as we assumed it would. Everyone is at the campsite now and are hard at work."

Akita looks to Wulf, "Grace hasn't been found. Since everyone is here now, I want to take Hunter and Warrior to O'Malley's Keep. If she is alive, we have to find her. She was only attacked because she helped us in our campaign against the Cloud Giants, Dark Wizards, and rescuing Skrymir."

Wulf nods, "I will get them. Let's go find our friend."

Vicar steps forward, "Akita, I am going with you, because if she is hurt, I can heal her enough for travel."

Akita smiles just a little, "Thank you, Vicar. Yes, if we find anyone, we will need your exceptional skills." She thinks for a moment and spots Gavin in the distance. "Let's have Gavin and Blitz on the ground and following the road from Salthall to the Keep. Who knows where the wave might have left a survivor or two?"

Vicar agrees, "I will go explain it to Gavin and meet you at Warrior."

As Akita turns to walk to Aphorea, she looks up and is startled. A shimmering wet blue Dragon is headed to their camp and yet the mounts don't seem to be afraid. Aphorea isn't even alarmed, although she is walking to the nearest clearing. The Blue Dragon hovers over the camp for a minute lowering himself towards the ground, but not quite landing. Akita can see in his claws a mass amount of fresh fish wiggling and squirming. The visiting dragon tries to lightly drop the fish to the ground and then flies over to Aphorea.

The Blue Dragon has the attention of most of the camp. Gavin, Wulf, and Vicar are headed in the same direction of Akita. Even Storm cannot help but be in awe of, yet another Dragon and her curiosity sends her walking towards it.

Aphorea turns slightly to Akita, and speaks to everyone in camp, "Akita Blackwing, I would like to introduce you to Rethu the Fierce. He is the one that sent Annut the message from Gavin to send help for Alura. He has come out of hiding to bring us fish, but only because he knew we were all here and in need."

Akita looks up at the beautiful fierce Blue Dragon, "It is wonderful to finally meet you and see you. We all thank you so much for the fish you have brought. It will help feed the troops and heal the wounded. So, you know you are welcome to stay, you are welcome to join us, as Thoraxian killed the only Dark Wizard that had mastered the Dragon Control incantation. My team and I put an end to the other Dark Wizard that was attempting to do the same to Annut. We understand if you

still have fears, but you are welcome with us."
Akita then introduces Storm, Wulf, Gavin, and
Vicar.

Rethu looks around the camp at all of the
people and the array of mounts. He then lands
next to Aphorea and in a deep gravelly voice
speaks to the minds of all in the camp, "Akita
Blackwing, you and your people give me hope for
the Dragon race. I will think over your offer to
join the fight, but I have lived in solitude and in
fear for hundreds of years. If some of your people
would offer themselves as a snack, I may be
convinced to stay a while."

Akita looks quickly to Aphorea and then back
to Rethu, "Um, Um, I don't think…".

Rethu begins laughing hysterically in
everyone's head interrupting Akita, "I am only
kidding my young Duchess. I only eat fish. I will
stay tonight, but I cannot be away from the water
for too long.

Akita and everyone let out a sigh of relief and
begin to laugh. Akita approaches Rethu and he
lowers his head. Akita rubs his snout, "I didn't
know Dragons had such a sense of humor. You
would fit in quite well, if you decided to stay. I

wish I could stay and converse with you, however my concerns cause me to have to leave for the moment. Hopefully, you will be here when I return so that we may speak further."

Rethu nods his enormous head in Akita's arms. She releases and goes to meet with Wulf, Vicar, Hunter, and Warrior.

Akita climbs up to Warrior's shoulders and reaches down to Vicar. "Climb on up Vicar."

Wulf and Hunter walk up to Warrior as Vicar gets seated. Vicar looks around, "Good thing I am not afraid of heights. I apologize in advance for holding on too tight, Akita." She laughs as Warrior takes off with Hunter. Blitz and Gavin take off in a dead run through the town, and out the other side, and down the road towards O'Malley Keep.

In no time Hunter and Warrior are flying slowly over the bay towards the Keep. Akita's last glance down, they had left Gavin behind, as it will take him much longer to get to the bay.

Wulf points down at the Sea Horse and shakes his head. They can only see the top of the main mast and a bit of the crow's nest. What really catches their attention is the Keep itself. It took a lot of damage and is barely standing. Portions of walls are missing, and the roof has many holes in it. There are still pools of standing water on the grounds.

Warrior and Hunter land as gently as they can a little way behind the Keep. Akita and Wulf take flight and turn to look at Vicar. "So, I suppose you want me to fly again on my own. I can see it would be safer, but it has been months now."

Akita looks at Vicar, "Firstly, Mandrake isn't here to mess with you. Secondly, we will help you if you need it. Furthermore, you are a big strong Dragonkin, you got this."

Wulf and Akita hold out their hands to steady Vicar as he stands and spreads the rarely used wings. Vicar lifts into the air, "Maybe I should do this more often. I could get to the wounded faster and boost others power sooner."

Akita starts flying forward, "And assist in search and rescue missions easier."

As they fly over the roof of the Keep to the veranda that looks over the bay, Akita sees drag marks through the muck from someone to the railing and back into a room. Lowering herself down, she tests to see if the roof top will hold her as she slowly flies into the room. Wulf and Vicar follow her.

The room has been destroyed. A large canopy bed has been thrown on its side. Dressers are on their face and sides with clothes strewn everywhere. There is a pile of blankets near the bed that seems to be shaking and moving.

Warrior says to Akita, "I believe Grace is barely alive somewhere near you. I can barely hear her angry thoughts about her dying in an undignified manner."

Akita gives the blankets another look and then kneels down beside them as she spreads them and moves them away from whatever is wrapped in them.

With a gasp, Akita calls out, "Vicar, I have found her. She's burning up. By the Gods, she must have been here this whole time, alone with no food or water." Akita sits at Grace's head and use her leg as a pillow, gently stroking her hair, as Vicar examines her.

Vicar immediately starts reducing the fever as he feels for broken bones. Finding the broken arm that has been crudely splinted, he gently starts it on the mend. She had set it pretty good for being by herself. He moves down and finds no ribs broken or any abdominal cuts.

Wulf brings over the canteen for Grace. "I will go look for other survivors, although I don't believe we will find any unless they are on this level of the Keep."

Grace starts to stir and moan, as she opens her eyes. "Akita? You came for me. Am I dreaming?"

Akita shushes Grace, "Of course we came to find you after we heard your Keep was destroyed. Now lay still while Vicar heals you." Akita looks to Vicar for some sign of good news.

Vicar looks to Akita and then at Grace, "I have stabilized her leg, but we need salves and things we have at the camp. Between all the Clerics we might be able to save the leg. She has been here well over a week, and I am surprised she is alive at all. The decaying skin sickness has taken a good hold of her. We need to get her back to camp. I will hold her in my arms on Warrior."

Akita nods, "I will strap you in and ride back with Wulf, but if you need me, I will fly over to you. I think this is best. Let me find Wulf and we will be off."

Warrior says to Akita, "Gavin still hasn't reached the Keep. He will meet us back at camp as soon as he can."

As the Wyverns take off, there is a loud crack from the direction of the Keep. Warrior and Hunter start to move away from the keep and there is another loud snap. Akita, Wulf, and Vicar turn slightly to look back, just as the Keep starts to crumble. It seems to fall in slow motion one wall and floor at a time. Rock breaking apart at the mortar, until finally Grace's suite falls straight to the widening hole. Akita feels a twinge of pain as her ancestral home, that she was born in, disappears entirely like it was smoke and hadn't stood for hundreds of years. Akita is thankful that Grace is out cold and didn't witness the end of O'Malley Keep.

Blitz and Gavin come upon debris from O'Malley Keep almost a half a mile inland and to the northwest of the Keep. Tall pine trees are striped and broken, some are pushed to the ground with the root ball exposed. There are pieces of furniture, linens, and chunks of the Keep strewn all around. Gavin is sure that this was the furthest reach of the wave. Unfortunately, there are also bodies mangled and bloated scattered amongst the debris that litters the once lush forest floor.

Gavin hops off Blitz to examine a body of a young man, "Blitz I don't reckon that anyone was able to survive this. Let's check all around just case there was a miracle."

Blitz yips in agreement and begins running from body to body. Gavin uses his Detect Life spell. Its range is only one hundred feet so he must cast it every ten minutes to be sure he hasn't missed anyone that could be under a pile of trees or debris.

No more than thirty minutes into the search Blitz alerts Gavin that he has found something. Gavin runs quickly to Blitz. Blitz tells Gavin that he hears something breathing really ragged underneath the pile of debris.

Blitz grabs several branches in his mouth and pulls them away and Gavin uses his Entangled Roots spell to move a large armoire off of several bodies.

Two bodies are ripe with decay and laying on a third body that is partially submerged in mud. Only this person's head is above the mud and the stench is horrendous, as decaying bodies are the worst smell ever. While holding their breath, Gavin and Blitz push the bloated bodies off of the third, trying to not hurt the one trapped below them. As the second awful body rolls away, there is an audible gasp as if someone is taking in air.

Gavin shakes his head and looks at Blitz, "Looker there Blitz, there's a genuine miracle if I ever did see one. Go ahead and gently start digging out the rest of their body."

Gavin reaches to this belt and unhooks a waterskin. He uncaps it and begins to slowly pour water on the person's face. The water reveals some skin under all the filth and the person's eyes start to open. Gavin gently pulls open their mouth and gives them a sip of water.

In no time Blitz has uncovered this person's body and Gavin can now see the form of a women.

Gavin slowly picks her up and lays her over Blitz' back and climbs on behind her. Blitz takes off like the wind. Dusk has arrived and Gavin wants to get back to the camp before nightfall.

Gavin see's the glow of Salthall growing before them, and says to Blitz, "Hey Blitz, tell Warrior about the lady here and ask for blankets, female clothin and many buckets of water to be brought to the edge of camp."

Blitz growls, "I am going to need a bath after this. If she wasn't behind my nose, you would have had to find another way back. She smells like one of the piles you leave behind a tree in the morning."

Gavin laughs, "Well that's why I havin you send a message ahead. I'm right here on top of her and I'm thinkin that after this I may never be able to smell anything good ever again."

As they reach the edge of camp, Ixen and a few healers are waiting for them. They have blankets and items with them, but Gavin sees no buckets of water. "Ixen, dear, we are going to need to douse her in lots of water and get these clothes off her before you will be able to get close to her. She was buried under a few dead bodies for days."

Ixen gets a surprised look on her Dragonkin face. "Oh my, this poor girl. Akita gave us clothes; soldiers should be right here with water. Let's lay her down on the grass until they get here."

Gavin carefully dismounts and carries the woman over to Ixen and gently lays her on the ground.

Blitz shakes vigorously, "I will be back."

Gavin replies, "Stay down river of the camp please." He sees Blitz turn and run into the forest to the south of the camp, where the river runs.

Ixen looks at Gavin with a look of disgust, "We need to wash you too."

Akita walks up taking in the situation. "Oh my, what is causing this stench? It's so bad." As she looks over the woman and Gavin, "Warrior, would you please tell Wulf we need more buckets of water."

Gavin explains to Akita how he found the woman. "She has to have been layin there for days. She only had a small opening to get air by.

So, she was basically just goin to lay there and starve to death in the mud."

A few soldiers walk up, and Akita directs them to gently pour the water over the woman lying on the ground. "Try to get as much of the grime off as possible."

Wulf flies up with two buckets of water, seeing that the woman is being taken care of, he dumps one of the buckets over Gavin's head.

Gavin gasps, "Hey now! What was that for?"

Wulf laughs, "My friend, the Dragons can smell you all the way over there, so I helped you to start washing the stench off." Wulf walks up as if he is going to hand him the other bucket but quickly tips it up and pours it down his chest. "Go get changed, we will get her cleaned up and bring her to the fires."

Gavin, at first is ready to fight, but sees the humor in it and decides to get Wulf back at another time. Smiling to himself, "Yeah, I should do that. I'll be back in a few. Even Blitz just took off to clean up."

Akita starts to generate some body heat to warm the small area around the woman, as the soldiers hold up blankets to make a private spot for Ixen, Akita and the woman. As they remove some of the woman's clothes, they find more lacerations and bruises. One of the other healers brings another bucket of water into the makeshift dressing room and slowly and gently starts to pour it over the woman.

As they start to redress the woman in warm and clean clothes, the woman starts to wake up. One healer holds up a cup of water telling the woman to drink slowly. She blinks a few times, then looks from the healer to Ixen and finally lands on Akita. In a scratchy whisper, "I… know… of… you… but I can't remember."

Akita smiles, "I am Lady Akita Blackwing. Don't you worry about anything; we will get you back to health. Can you tell me your name?"

The woman looks down at her hands, "I think… I am Jacklyn, but I can't remember much else, other than lots of water."

Akita takes Jacklyn's hand, "Well once Ixen is done healing you, we will take you to the fires and get you food. Your rescuer, Gavin, will be glad to see you are ok."

Everyone is slowly gathering around the fire. Gavin is talking to Jacklyn as she eats. He knows she is Elven, but her porcelain white skin and white hair is mystifying, and he cannot place ever seeing or hearing of anyone quite like this. Akita and Wulf are discussing camp business and their plans for the next day.

Darkwing, Storm, Shamash, and Vicar join the conversation. Shamash kneels in front of Akita. "Our friend Grace is in critical condition. Our healers and Clerics are the best in the lands, but no one can stop the decaying disease once it has set in over a period of days." Shamash pauses to judge everyone's emotions, but mostly Akita's, as she has become close to Grace. "We need to remove the leg from the knee down before it starts to grow up her thigh. Vicar and I have done this several times in our lives with great success, but there is always a chance of failure. Someone needs to talk to Grace and let her know this is the only way to save her life."

Akita visibly slumps, staring into the fire. A single tear running down her cheek. She will not lose another to the Gods. Akita slowly nods, "I will talk to Grace and make her understand."

Ghod, who has been sitting quietly to the side eating stew, states in a quiet but strong voice, "Find me the trunk of a white tree, like a Poplar tree. I will build her a peg leg that will be elegant and serviceable."

Akita smiles at Ghod, "Thank you, my friend."

The team gathers around Grace, which confuses her. "Well, hello, all. I don't know if I should be happy, you are here, or scared?"

Akita sits on the stool next to the cot. "We are all very glad that we found you in time to get you some healing and we weren't too late. How are you feeling?"

Grace moves to sit up better. "My arm is healed thanks to these guys. My head isn't fuzzy anymore, and I think I had been cursed or a spell over me because the last few months I don't remember. I no longer feel like a boulder is on my back. My leg on the other hand is in a lot of pain and looks nasty."

Akita looks at the team then back to Grace, "Did you have someone in your ranks named Jacklyn? She's Elven with white hair. She also cannot seem to remember anything."

Grace replies, "Did she live? I had made her my second in command after the previous guy let a spy of King Carthon's in my Keep."

Akita nods, "Yes, Gavin found her, and she is healing by the fire. We have found no one else."

Grace laughs, "Anyone else would have run off, happy to be free of me. Most owed me something and were working it off. If she owed me anything, I cannot remember so she is now free too."

Akita smiles, "Well sounds like you are turning over a new leaf for a new life. We need to talk about your life. Unfortunately, we did not find you soon enough for the best Clerics in the land to save your leg. They need to remove it from the knee down or you will die. We would like to keep you around for years to come, but we want your agreement to remove the decaying part of the leg. Most don't get this choice, as the limb is removed while they are unconscious as an emergency procedure."

Grace stares at Akita, then looks at each person around her. Each one gives a slight nod. "This is what I was afraid of. How am I supposed to live and fight missing part of my leg? I am damaged goods. Who will take me seriously in command of a ship?"

Ghod steps up, "I am going to create a white peg leg for you. I will create a new sword for you to wield with the new balance you will have to learn. This is not your end, as being a good leader is how you command, what you say, your beliefs and your honor. It has little to do with anything else, and your reputation as a fighter proceeds you."

Grace looks to Akita who smiles and then back to this masked man they call Ghod, "Why would you do this for me? All I have ever wanted was to be respected and that eluded me. Then Akita comes to power, and she shows me kindness, which I was not expecting. She did not talk down to me or try to rule over me but allowed me to help in the ways I could. I took a chance and found she showed me respect. I still cannot fathom what changed. Now I am a Captain without a ship, and I have no port to call home."

Ghod moves closer, "I want revenge for the destruction brought upon the Keeps. Do you want revenge or to just roll over and let them win?"

Akita chimes in before Grace can answer. "You are a good person deep down inside. I know you have had to fight for everything you built. I know you want to fight to get it back."

A tear slides down Grace's cheek, "Thank you all. When do they want to do this?" More tears start to fall, "And if anyone ever says they saw me cry, I will deny it to the grave and haunt you forever."

Everyone laughs, but Vicar speaks up, "We need to do this as soon as possible, but we will wait till morning so that you can have a good meal for extra strength."

Akita amplifies her voice for all to hear, "I am sure everyone wants to know the plans from here. Tomorrow Elderwolf Keep should be here with extra supplies. The Clerics have healed all, save our two newest guests. Soon we will prepare to move northeast to an undisclosed location where we will rebuild our strength. Every one of you is an important piece in our plan. We will need all of you to once and for all rid this realm of

Evil. Know this, that the people of Prayla and Stagbreak are going to start rebuilding Prayla and Blackwing Keep. This was their pledge to us, allowing us to take on this evil threat." She then stops the amplification.

Akita looks back to the group standing around her and Grace, "Let's do what we do best. Investigate, plan, and dispel this last threat to our Realm. And you, Grace, just concentrate on healing."

CHAPTER 11

SECRET GLADE

Early the next morning before the sun has even started to rise, Wulf shakes Akita awake in her tent. He holds her shoulder and whispers, "Akita there is something we have to do before we go up north."

Akita slowly opens her eyes and looks around the tent, "Wulf, is that you? It's still dark here. What has happened that you're waking me up?"

Wulf chuckles softly, "Akita, we have something to do. Meet me outside the tent in five minutes with your traveling gear. Aphorea knows what is going on and will let everyone know in the morning that we are on a mission."

Akita slowly pushes herself up and stands to start getting herself ready for Wulf's mysterious mission. She grabs her pack and a thick vest, a waterskin, a bag of rations, and her sword and steps out of the tent.

Wulf is standing there with about the same amount of gear. He leans in close to whisper in her ear, "Okay you are just going to have to trust me and follow me closely. We are going to fly straight up from here then turn to the east. I don't know exactly where we are going or how long it will take, but the way will be shown to me when we are close."

Akita nods and crouches a little to begin the ascent into the sky above the camp. Wulf leaps up first and Akita follows. Several hundred feet in the air Wulf turns to the east and they begin flying in a straight line past Salthall and over the forest.

They fly in this direction for about an hour as the Sun begins to rise before them. Wulf hasn't said a word since they left the camp. Akita can't stand the silence anymore, "Wulf, we are going to have to stop soon to recoup and have a bite to eat."

Wulf looks over to Akita and smiles, "I wondered how long it was going to take for your stomach to persuade you to talk. If the map was correct, we should be approaching a fork in the river. We will land there, and I'll explain everything."

Akita nods and waits for Wulf to point to the place he wants to land. They both land and sit under a large tree for the shade. Wulf pulls out a sack from his pack and opens it. Akita can smell the familiar smell of cinnamon and icing, "Are those Quinn's cinnamon rolls?"

Wulf smiles and then hands one to Akita, "She thought you would be overjoyed to have one for the road. She was able to become fast friends with one of the local bakers in Salthall and she spent all night making these in his shop. Right about now everyone in camp should be waking up to that same smell."

Akita smiles from horn to horn as she takes a huge bite of the sweet pillowy dough. She can't say a word for a few minutes as she savors every crumb of the roll. Wulf takes this opportunity to start explaining why they left the camp.

Wulf takes a deep breath and again reaches into his pack. He retrieves a small ornate box with a hinged lid and a brass clasp on the front. He sets it down on the ground in front of Akita, "Hon, do you remember when I told you that I traveled to Alahora for a specific reason? That my friend and familiar had passed away and I wanted to return his bones to his birthplace."

Akita nods slowly while looking at the box and continuing to devour the cinnamon roll.

Wulf gestures to the box with his hand, "Inside this box are the remains of my friend. He was a very rare type of Pseudo Dragon. He and I grew up together in Omoth. As my magical powers grew, so did his. We were bonded by our souls. When he was killed, a part of my soul died with him, and my magic weakened. That was the only reason that Evad was able to capture me and entomb me in the Leviathan."

Akita finishes her roll and looks intently into Wulf's eyes, "I'm so glad we found you."

Wulf reaches out his hand for hers, "Me too. However, there is more that I haven't told you yet."

Akita takes his hand and squeezes it, "Go on Wulf, I'm here for you."

Wulf squeezes Akita's hand in return, "Just like Annut and the other Dragons, my friend Dojo could speak directly to my mind. However, even after his death, he is still speaking to me. He told me yesterday when we were at O'Malley Keep that we were close to his birthplace and that we must go there as soon as possible. He explained that the glade where his kind lives is only accessible once a year for a week and that time is running out. So, it had to be today, and I wanted to share this journey with you above anyone else. Plus, if I had snuck out of camp in the middle of the night without you knowing, you might have murdered me upon my return."

Akita smiles and lets out a slightly evil giggle, "You're damn right!" She pauses for a second to think, "So you're telling me that even after your friend Dojo passed that he is still able to communicate with you? That's incredible! I imagine that he will lead us to this place he is from once we get close?"

Wulf nods, "Yes, he says that only his bones can reveal the path into the glade. We are to continue east to where the grey rocks meet the valley. When I looked at Olek's maps earlier, I saw that there is a small mountain range on the border between Stonia and Astya. I then asked Ordyn if he had ever been to that area. He said that he had, and he confirmed that the mountains are a grey granite and that there is a valley on the Astya side of the border."

Akita grimaces a bit, "That puts the destination in King Carthon's region. I hope we don't have the pleasure of running into any of his goons when we cross the border."

Wulf nods in agreement, "I think we are clever enough to avoid detection. Plus, we can handle ourselves pretty dang well. Now shall we get back into the air My Lady?"

Wulf stands while putting the box back into his pack and the bows to Akita and reaches out a hand. She playfully knocks his hand away, "My Lady? Don't you start that Wulf Wari!" She then lets out a giggle and leaps into the sky.

The camp begins to come alive as the first rays of the sun touch the tops of the tents. Quinn is already in the middle of the camp with trays of cinnamon rolls. She hands one to anyone that she sees stumbling out of their tent. Ordyn and Olek are at the main soldier's tent looking over maps of Stonia and trying to find the best route to Elderwolf Keep.

Vicar, Void and Shamash have used an entrancement spell on Grace so that she will sleep through the removal of her leg. The actual removal of the leg doesn't take very long, but the closing of the exposed nub and the magic to complete it takes some time and lots of energy. By noon, she is recovering and sleeping peacefully. Vicar predicts that she will have her strength back by this evening.

Ghod has found a suitable chunk of Poplar wood and ha3s begun carving Grace's new peg leg. He has the design in his head and the idea of something special to add. He knows exactly which Dwarven Runestone he wants to add. He believes it will suit her disposition just right.

Gavin is helping Jacklyn around the camp and making sure she has all she needs. He and Storm have been trying to help her with her memory, but so far there are still more holes than memory. They have figured out that she is a Moon Elf, which explains her porcelain skin and white hair, but she cannot currently remember where she comes from.

Vivian and Ishvet are tending to their Griffons, Zora, and Orien. Polishing their armor and combing their feathers. Vivian knows that it is important for Ishvet to build a deeper bond with Orien. They will need to count on each other in the coming days. Ishvet is hesitant to become close to another mount after the death of Rani.

As the morning moves along, Aphorea can hear people asking where Akita and Wulf are. Now that the rest of the team are awake, she decides that this is a good time to let them know what is going on. Aphorea speaks to the team, "Akita and Wulf have left everything in your capable hands while they complete the original mission he came here to do before you all saved him from the Dark Wizard. Apparently, it's in the vicinity. They will catch up to us along the way."

Darkwing walks up to Ordyn and Olek, with Mandrake, "I expect them to come back with more Dragons. I remember Wulf talking about Little Dragons months ago, and Akita got so excited."

Storm also joins the group, "Well, Tall, Dark and Frozen, I think the Dragons and Wyverns are simply fantastic. If you would have told me this was going to happen before I left on my adventure, I don't think I would have left."

Darkwing chuckles, "This statement from the other Dragon obsessed female, and she came with a Wyvern breed even rarer than the ones we have."

Storm sticks her tongue out at Darkwing, "On a serious note. All of you have been friends with Akita for a long time. I have just come back into her life but wanted to ask you about Wulf Wari. Now, before you answer, yes, I can see he's a good man and has been a big help over the past months. I also see a beautiful relationship blooming. Akita deserves that, but what do you all think of Wulf?"

Aphorea interrupts the conversation, "Storm, what you don't know is that Wulf has pledged himself to her through a special bond that was created with the Magma Amulet. He pledged to keep her safe for life, with or without a true relationship. So, you should have no fear. Not that you asked me, but I personally like him."

Ordyn looks to each of the men around the table and back to Storm, "We know your concern is because of your sisterhood relationship with Akita. I believe I can speak for those here at this table, that we have full faith in Wulf Wari. He is a strong Warlock that has shown great friendship and loyalty to us, Akita and Blackwing Keep. Just before making his pledge, he had all of his personal goods shipped to Blackwing Keep. Most importantly, he keeps her calm and grounded, as well as extremely happy through all this adversity."

Storm slowly looks in each of their eyes, "Fair enough. I feel the same way but wanted your opinions as well. Thank you." She looks around again. "By the way, anyone know where Greenbean is?"

Olek smiles and answers, "She is in the clearing over there going through her Greatsword Fighter calisthenics. The funny thing is that every soldier that is not on guard duty is over there watching her and trying to mimic her moves. I believe Ghod is carving the leg for Grace over there as well."

Aphorea then speaks into the minds of Greenbean, Fab Ulous, Darkwing and Vivian, as well as Captain Dubbin, "Before Akita left this morning, she asked that I relay a request from her. She feels that the entire company has exceeded expectations. Even though Earl Jarkon will be arriving soon, she would like a small party to secure the Dragon Temple and prepare it to receive the entire population of Keep survivors and all the Dragons. Captain Dubbin, she knows that you are anxious to return to the service of Earl Jarkon. Keeping that in mind she has asked that you and your soldiers accompany the team as far as Elderwolf Keep so that you may return to your duties. Please meet with Vivian to prepare for the flight."

Vivian turns to Ishvet with a concerned look on her face, "Ish, Akita has a job for me. I'm going to have to leave soon. I'm going to lead the preliminary team to the Dragon Temple."

Ishvet looks over to Vivian with a slight ache and longing, "I understand, you know more about that area than anyone else here. I still don't have to like it. Be safe my love and I'll meet up with you soon."

Greenbean, Fabby, Darkwing, and Captain Dubbin approach Vivian. Vivian turns to them, "Okay everyone, Akita has given us a mission. It's a two-day flight to the Dragon Temple from here. Pack the light, and make sure you have a bedroll. We will be spending tonight under the stars. Darkwing is it okay with Mylar that Greenbean rides on him? Aphorea just told me that Drako has volunteered to take Fabby."

Darkwing nods his head in the affirmative, "Mylar would be happy to take Greenbean. I can have him, and Martyn saddled in less than a half an hour. We can all meet in the field north of the mount area. Captain Dubbin, are you okay with heading back to Elderwolf Keep?"

Captain Dubbin grumbles a little then looks over to Vivian, "Not that I have much choice. Earl Jarkon left me in the charge of Lady Blackwing so I must follow her request. My duty is also to the ruling family of Elderwolf Keep so accompanying Vivian satisfies that. I imagine that we will encounter Earl Jarkon's flying convoy as we head north. He may request that I join him at that time."

Vivian nods her head, "Yes that is quite likely. Father will most likely have almost every Griffon with him as he never does anything slightly. Captain Dub go ahead and get your patrol ready, and we will meet you in the sky."

Captain Dubbin slightly bows and turns to return to his patrol. Darkwing heads over to Mylar and Martyn. Fabby heads over to Drako, and Vivian helps Ishvet finish saddling Zora. In about twenty minutes they are all gathered in the field north of the mount area and are ready to take flight. They can see that Captain Dubbin and his patrol of three Griffon soldiers are already in the air above.

Wulf points to a clearing at the base of some large, jagged rocks just as they pass the border to Astya. They have been flying almost three hours to the east from the river fork. Akita is glad to finally be landing, her wings are tired. As they land, they look around to make sure that no one else is around.

They are at the base of a small mountain range. Save a few patches of evergreen trees, the rocks are varying shades of slate grey. To the east of where they stand is a lush valley. When Wulf touches down, he heads for a large, pointed rock sticking out of the ground at an angle. He touches the rock, and it is warm to the touch from the day's sun.

Akita follows behind and puts a hand on Wulf's back, "Wulf are you sensing something or is Dojo speaking to you?"

Wulf looks back at her, "Both. I can sense an energy in this rock and Dojo is saying that we need to stay here until dusk. That the path will be revealed then."

Akita rubs Wulf's back a little, then turns towards the clearing, "Well this will be as good a spot as any to have a bite to eat before the rest of our journey."

Wulf turns away from the rock and goes over and sits next to Akita on the grey rock floor. Akita unpacks a sack and pulls several small jam sandwiches out of it. She hands one to Wulf and they both take a bite, look at each other, and smile.

Akita starts to giggle a little and Wulf looks at her with a quizzical look. Akita swallows her bite of sandwich, "I was just thinking how wonderful it would be to be stuck in this moment forever. The peace and calm, the birds chirping, you looking at me, the breeze lightly caressing our skin in the setting sunlight, Meh-Kola sitting on a rock behind you."

Akita and Wulf both quickly jump up and turn towards Meh-Kola sitting on a boulder. She is licking her arm and purring. She stops mid lick and looks up at both of them. They can see her eyes look at one of them then the other. Meh-Kola puts her arm down and smiles, "Hello, how are the two of you?"

Akita's mouth hangs open for a few seconds, "Meh-Kola what are you doing here and how did you even know that we left?"

Meh-Kola laughs and states matter-of-factly, "One saw you sneaking out of the camp this morning while One was catching mice in the field. One thought it was strange to see you both flying in the dark. So, One decided to follow you to make sure everything was all right. Then One heard Wulf's story by the river, and One is now excited to see the Pseudo Dragons from Wulf's story. One will take a sandwich if you have an extra."

Akita is stunned and is kind of frozen for a second. Wulf reaches out his hand and gives Meh-Kola his sandwich without even really thinking about it. Meh-Kola takes the sandwich in her paws and starts munching on it. She smiles and says thanks to Wulf. Akita and Wulf just stand and watch Meh-Kola eat the tiny sandwich. When she is done, she hops off the boulder and heads towards the rock Wulf was touching earlier, "So when does One get to see the Pseudo Dragons?"

Finally, Akita and Wulf snap out of their shock. Akita walks over to Meh-Kola and kneels down beside her, "That's entirely up to Wulf. He is the one in charge of this expedition." Akita looks to Wulf, "Wulf do you think it would be okay if Meh-Kola joins us?"

Wulf raises a hand to his forehead and closes his eyes. He stands like this for a few moments then lowers his hand and opens his eyes, "Dojo is saying that it would be fine for you to come along. He says that it will be intriguing to his family to see a creature around the same size as them and they have never met a Fenton before."

Meh-Kola sits on her hind legs and stands up as tall as she can in this seated position, "One believes that they will be in for a treat. One also wonders what kind of good food they will have for One to try."

Wulf chuckles and shakes his head in disbelief, "Meh-Kola are you always hungry?"

Meh-Kola smiles, "Yes, One is always hungry. It takes One lots of energy to look this good all the time."

Akita stands up from Meh-Kola and laughs. Wulf looks up to the sky, "Well, it is just about time for the door to open. The sun is setting behind the mountains."

As the light slowly fades behind the mountains, a small beam of light touches the tip of the large, pointed rock. The face of the rock begins to fade revealing a darkened tunnel. Akita and Wulf gather behind Meh-Kola and look in as far as they can see. Meh-Kola walks up to where the face of the rock once was and puts up a paw. Her paw passes through and across the threshold. She looks back and Akita and Wulf, "One can see much further than both of you in the dark. You will need to make some light."

Akita looks at Wulf and in sync they both raise a hand and snap their fingers. A small ball is fire raises from their hands. They both open their hands, palms up, and the small balls of flame hover in their hands. They both look down to Meh-Kola. Meh-Kola smiles a toothy grin, "One thinks that will do the job."

All three of them make their way down the tunnel in the rock. As they move further in, the face of the rock reappears behind them. They can feel the decline of the tunnel and know that the tunnel is not only going into the mountain range, but deeper in the ground. After about a few hundred yards a faint glow emerges from the darkness and illuminates an open doorway. As they get closer to the door, they can hear water running and smell the scent of the woods.

Akita and Wulf snuff the fireballs in their hands and walk through the doorway with Meh-Kola. As their eyes adjust to the brighter light, they can make out lush greenery, and a tall narrow waterfall in the distance. Directly in front of them is a small, arched bridge that crosses a small creek. They cross the bridge and then walk under a canopy of tree limbs. This opens to a large clearing with a circular ring of small stick-built houses. They look like little cottages that you would find in the countryside around Prayla.

Meh-Kola looks around, "One thinks these houses are just One's size, but One is wondering where all the Pseudo Dragons are?"

Wulf stops walking for a second, then points past the clearing to a path on the other side of the tiny homes. He takes the lead and walks to the path with Meh-Kola and Akita following. Wulf whispers, "He says they are through here."

Once they are through the thick brush, they can see another clearing. In the middle of this clearing is a large rectangle altar, about the size of a coffee table in the Keep, and around it, are about thirty Pseudo Dragons. They are all different colors, but all are about the same size.

An ebony black Pseudo Dragon approaches Wulf and stops in front of him. Wulf stops and then reaches into his backpack. He pulls out the small ornate box that has Dojo's remains in it. He approaches the altar and dumps the contents of the box onto the altar. When he steps back to where Akita and Meh-Kola are, all the Pseudo Dragons begin to vocalize with a harmonic humming.

The remains on the altar begin to glow and swirl in place. The glow intensifies and the Pseudo Dragons song becomes louder. Soon the light becomes blinding and all three of them shield their eyes. All at once the singing stops and the glow ceases. In the place of the glow on the altar is a dark blue Pseudo Dragon. Wulf falls to his knees and reaches out as tears stream down his face, through a tight throat he manages to say, "Dojo!"

CHAPTER 12
PROBLEMS ARISE

Hector lands on the balcony of Cliffshade Keep and King Carthon jumps off of his back. There is no one to meet him which boils his blood to no end. He flings open the balcony doors then turns back to Hector, "Hector you were a good boy today. Go on and go hunting, I do know how you like to swoop down and catch a peasant."

Hector wobbles and shakes his head and with a thrust of his strong feathered wings, he is in the air and flying over the town. King Carthon follows out to the balcony and looks over the town. It looks decayed and abandoned. He grabs ahold of the Sea Amulet around his neck with his right hand and reaches out to the town with his left arm, ["There is no need for this illusion anymore. Our intentions are known throughout the lands."]

The Sea Amulet glows within his hand, and he begins reciting an incantation. Slowly the illusion dissipates, and the true form of the town can be seen by all. The town gleams with freshly painted homes and the market is packed with townsfolk. Everyone in the town is either a Dark Wizard or the family of one. King Carthon grins as the illusion is lifted from the Keep and its grand towers and balconies are revealed.

He then turns and goes back into his room then into the hallway and down the many flights of stairs to the dungeon laboratory. There he is finally greeted by Volaern. King Carthon raises an eyebrow as to scold his inept Advisor. Volaern bows slightly, "Sire I would have been on the balcony to greet you, but we have a problem."

Carthon steps forward, "What problem?"

Volaern points out through the massive wood and iron doors to the bay behind the Keep where the Demi-Titan is, "Look Sire, something is wrong with your creation. She is sinking into the water and is unresponsive."

King Carthon bolts through the small crowd of Wizards at the doors and down the pier closest to the Demi-Titian. He jumps off the pier right onto the water and walks across it to the creature. The Sea Amulet is faintly glowing as it keeps King Carthon above the water. As he gets closer to the Demi-Titan he begins to hear whispers from the amulet. He raises it closer to his ear to hear what the dragon souls contained within are saying. One distinct voice can be heard above the others, "Carthon, the Demi-Titan is losing power. You must recharge it, or it will die. Touch the stone to the creature once more and it will be recharged, however it is not immortal. This is the last time we can renew its strength; the flesh is decaying too much."

King Carthon unclasps the chain around his neck and holds the amulet in his hand. He reaches out and presses it to the flesh of the Demi-Titans chest. The Sea Amulet glows brightly and begins to vibrate in King Carthon's hand. The water around the creature begins to swirl and rise. It envelops the Demi-Titan and King Carthon then begins to glow a bluish green. The water spins faster and faster around them. The demi-Titans mouth opens slowly, and the water funnels itself into the creature's mouth.

King Carthon yells to the creature, "Jessa can you hear me? Wake up!"

Jessa's eyes open and the same glow as the water can be seen in them. Jessa moans as the last of the glowing water enters her mouth. She closes her mouth and looks down at King Carthon then begins to stand up. King Carthon backs away towards the pier as the entirety of Jessa the Demi-Titans body emerges from beneath the sea. When she is fully upright, she flexes her arms in front of her and the two Wyverns attached to her, below her regular arms, roar with strength.

King Carthon makes it back on the pier and heads back to the giant doorway. When he makes his way to Volaern he stops, "Volaern, make sure that she is fed. We need her to keep her strength. I have a feeling that they will be coming for us all soon and she will be our greatest defense against those dragons."

Volaern nods his head, "Yes Sire, right away. May I ask Sire? Who are 'they'?"

King Carthon looks back towards Jessa then back to Volaern, "Everyone, everyone in Alahora. Come find me when you are done down here. We must call our full strength to the Keep."

Vivian is slightly daydreaming as Zora flies through the air. She snaps out of the pleasant thoughts when Captain Dubbin yells out. She looks over to him and can see that he is pointing to in front of them. Vivian looks to the horizon and can see the familiar twinkle of Griffin armor reflecting the sunlight. In a matter of moments, she can make out her father at the head of the platoon. Vivian yells out for everyone to stop.

Earl Jarkon breaks away from the Platoon flanked by two guards and flies over to Vivian and Captain Dubbin. The Platoon stops and hovers behind the Earl. He approaches until his Griffin and Zora are eye to eye, "Vivian, it's so great to see you. What has happened? Why are you heading north?"

Vivian smiles and nods her head, "It's great to see you too, father. We are making our way to the Dragon Temple to prepare for all the survivors of Blackwing Keep and all the Dragons we have in our company at the moment. Captain Dubbin was returning with us as far as Elderwolf Keep."

Captain Dubbin flies in closer to Earl Jarkon and interrupts, "Earl Jarkon, my men and I are ready to join the platoon, if that is your command."

Earl Jarkon puts up a hand to stop Captain Dubbin, "I already know you will not have it any other way. You might as well join the formation.

You can convey suitable landing sites in the survivor's camp to the First Sergeants. We have many cargo platforms to get on the ground."

Captain Dubbin nods his head in affirmation, raises his left hand as a signal to his men and they fly towards the platoon to get in formation. Vivian smiles at her father, "Thank you father, we will make better time now that we do not have to stop at Elderwolf Keep. Just to let you know, when we left the camp, Akita was not there. The great White Dragon Aphorea was looking after things. Do not be startled when she begins giving orders in your head."

Earl Jarkon nods to Vivian, "Good to know. It is a little unsettling to have them speak in our minds. On another subject if I may, a sealed message came for you just as we were leaving the Keep."

Earl Jarkon hands Vivian a small rectangular envelope. He then nods again, and his Griffon turns and flies to the South with the two guards following and the platoon bringing up the rear.

Darkwing flies up to Vivian and has a look of relief on his face, "I am glad that Captain Dubbin is back to his rightful position. I don't know if I could take one more comment about how he shouldn't have left Earl Jarkon's side."

Vivian looks over and laughs briefly, "I definitely understand. He is nothing but duty and insult, but he means well."

Greenbean and Fabby fly close to Vivian and Darkwing and then circle around. Greenbean yells over to them, "We should get going. We don't want to lose the light before we get there."

Vivian nods her head in agreement and puts the message in her saddle bag to read later. She then tells Zora to head out. Darkwing follows and the rest follow them in a loose formation back towards the north.

Wulf opens his arms and Dojo runs to him. Dojo jumps up and Wulf catches him and gives him a big hug. After a few moments Dojo drops down to the ground and Wulf stands back up. Dojo sits on his hind legs with his wings back and his front arms in the air. He enters the minds of Akita and Meh-Kola, "Thank you both for helping Wulf get to this moment. On behalf of myself and my people we also thank you. It is very rare that one of my kind get to be reborn in this manner.

Akita smiles and drops to one knee, "That was spectacular! The singing and you rising from the ashes. I would never have believed it if I hadn't seen it with my own eyes."

Meh-Kola walks up to Dojo and sits in front of him tilting her head and looking him over, "One has seen things like this before. One is happy that One is not the only small one of the team now. One only has one question."

Dojo speaks to all three of them in their heads now, "What does One want to know?"

Meh-Kola turns her head to the side and looks towards Akita, "One wants to ask for Akita how she can get one of you to take home."

Akita's body gets rigid for a second and she reaches up for Wulf, "Meh-Kola, it a little early to ask that. We just met them. We don't know their customs or anything like that." Akita pauses then continues, "However, now that Meh-Kola has brought it up. Do you think anyone would like to join me on our journey?"

Wulf grabs Akita's hand and helps her to stand up, "I knew this was going to happen and I already discussed it with Dojo."

Akita looks at Wulf with a pout and a gleam of disbelief, "What do you mean, 'You knew this was going to happen'. Don't you think I have any self-control when it comes to Dragons and Wyverns?" She looks back and forth from Wulf to Meh-Kola and back to Wulf, "Okay, you both know that I don't, but that doesn't mean that I always get what I want."

Akita huffs a little for effect and all four of them chuckle for a moment. Dojo speaks to all of them when he stops laughing, "Our Chief will allow you to pursue a bond with any Xian that may want to help you in your cause."

Akita looks puzzled and happy all at the same time. "Xian? I've never heard that word before."

Dojo replies in all their heads, "That is who we are. The rest of the world knows us as Pseudo Dragons, but our race is actually called Xian. We were once companions to the Gods. We were created to do good deeds in the world. When the Titans were born, we went into hiding. Their hatred for the world was too much for us to fight against. As the younger races discovered us and our magical abilities, we were hunted and slaughtered. They believed that our bodies could give them more power. Now there are only a handful of Tribes left in the world and we are the only ones left on Alahora."

Meh-Kola shakes her head and looks down at the ground, "One knows this story too well. One's kin has gone through the same thing. We are very few now. One is now sad, and One wants to go back to the camp. One will meet you all there."

Akita is saddened by Dojo and Meh-Kola. She nods her head to Meh-Kola and Meh-Kola blinks away. Dojo reaches out and bats at the place where Meh-Kola was, "She doesn't linger when she decides to go, huh?"

Wulf shakes his head, "No she doesn't. You know she's an assassin and a thief. However, she is so likeable, and she has really grown on me."

Akita kind of snaps out of her sadness and puts a hand on Wulf's shoulder, "Isn't the craziest thing. Deadly in so many ways, but the sweetest and funniest little flying cat you could ever meet."

Dojo starts walking and passes between Wulf's and Akita's legs. He heads through the arch and into the village area of the glade. Akita and Wulf turn and follow him through the thick foliage. They emerge on the other side and are greeted by a handful of other Xian. Dojo stops in front of the others, with Wulf and Akita stopping behind him.

Dojo speaks to all of them collectively, "Everyone these are my friends Wulf and Akita. They have brought back my remains for rebirth. I will leave with them as I am already bonded with Wulf. Akita is fighting against dark forces that threaten Alahora. She asks that she be given the opportunity to see if any of you would like to bond with her and help her in this fight."

Akita is asked to sit on the ground and all the potential candidates surround her. They all begin to sing like they did in the ritual that brought Dojo back to life. The song is different this time and it's directed at Akita. Akita can feel the vibrations from their voices against her body.

Akita's whole body begins to levitate above the ground. She feels herself being pulled to a black Xian like a compass needle to north. Her body swivels and faces the small black Xian then moves forward a few inches. The Xian flies up to chest level with Akita. The black Xian begins to glow white, and a tendril reaches out from the glow towards Akita.

The tendril touches Akitas chest and passes into her. Akita can feel the power surge into her from the Xian. The Xian begins to speak to Akita's mind, "Akita I choose you to bond with. I choose you to empower. I choose to help you in your fight against the dark forces."

Slowly the glow fades away and Akita is back on the ground. The black Xian lands in front of her and all the rest stop singing. The Xian speaks only to Akita, "My name is Sageranta Xulous, but you can call me Sage."

Before Sage can say another word, Akita scoops her up and gives her a tight hug. Akita trembles with excitement. Wulf walks over and puts a hand on her shoulder, "Akita, you may want to let her breathe.

Akita looks up and smiles and then releases Sage. Sage nuzzles Akita's neck and purrs like a cat but much deeper. Then she hops down off of Akita's lap, "I must say my goodbyes before we leave the glade."

Akita nods and then stands up. Wulf starts walking towards the entrance of the tunnel out of the glade and Dojo flies up and lands on his shoulder. As they get to the entrance Akita wonders if Sage would do the same thing. Just as she finishes her thought, Sage lands on her shoulder. They all make their way out of the tunnel and take flight back to the camp at Salthall.

Halfway through the journey to the Dragon Temple Vivian reaches into her saddle bag to read the message her father handed to her. She breaks the seal and unfolds the letter and begins reading it. When she is done, she looks over to Darkwing, "We are going to have to stop at Elderwolf Keep after all. My best friend is very ill, and I need to see him before he passes."

Darkwing nods and pulls on Martyn's reigns a little so that he slows. He then falls back in between Greenbean and Fabby. He tells them what Vivian said and they follow her lead when she turns Zora towards the northwest, directly for Elderwolf Keep.

As the sun begins to set in the West, they approach Elderwolf Keep. They all land at the stables and get off their mounts. Vivian leads them into the keep and shows them where they can wash up and tells them where to go to get some dinner. She then speaks to a guard, and he runs off to get another guard. Vivian tells the group that since she will not be able to take them the rest of the way to the Dragon Temple, she will send a few of her Paladins to show them the way and help with the preparations.

They all understand what it is like to lose a dear friend and do not oppose Vivian's decision. Vivian leaves them and they bunk down for the night in the quarters Elderwolf Keep has provided them. Tomorrow they will make their way to the Dragon Temple and Vivian will join them later.

Vivian goes to her chambers and washes up and then stops by the kitchen to let the staff know that they have three more for dinner and that they will need to provide breakfast for her friends before they leave in the morning. Then she heads back out to the stables and finds Zora, "Zora we need to get to Hornbuckle as fast as you can. Our friend Casheon is dying."

Zora nods and gets in position so Vivian can get on her back. Quickly they are flying through the night sky and over the lake to Hornbuckle. Zora is tired from the long trip to Elderwolf Keep, but the thought that their friend is dying gives her the strength to fly swiftly.

In less than an hour they come to a small village of about twelve buildings. On the far side of the village is a farm with a two-story home just set back from the road. Zora knows the way to Casheon's house and flies practically to the front door of the two-story home. Vivian jumps off Zora and heads to the door. Vivian knocks on the door and doesn't hear anyone moving inside. She moves a few feet over and can see light inside behind a curtained window. She again knocks, but a little firmer, "Casheon, are you in there. Where's the attendant at?"

Vivian hears the lock on the door and the handle rises up. The door opens and a cloaked figure stands in the doorway. The light is behind them so Vivian cannot see their face. Vivian steps forward, "Is Casheon still with us? Can you bring me to him please?"

The cloaked figure takes one step back and Vivian starts to enter the home. Out of the corner of her eye to the right she can see another cloaked figure come out of the darkness. As she turns her head to look at this person approaching, she sees a purple beam of light fly from him and hit Zora.

Zora calls out to Vivian to run, but Vivian doesn't have time to react. Zora falls to the ground and seems unconscious. Vivian takes one step towards Zora and is hit by a flash of light from behind. She hits the ground, and everything begins to fade to black. She hears the cloaked figure behind her call to the other cloaked figure. She hears the words, 'Tie her up' and 'Take her to Windu'.

CHAPTER 13
DRAGON TEMPLE

The Dragon Temple is covered with lush vines and moss, as well as tall trees with long reaching limbs covered in rich green leaves creating a canopy. Hidden under it all is a massive Temple, that has been excavated on the inside by the Dark Wizards, leaving the camouflage foliage covering the outside. The entrance is large enough for a full-grown Dragon to enter and at least ten large Dragons fit in the main entrance hall. There are three very different Dragons engraved on the walls of this room. The next connecting room is even larger but includes two cavernous tunnels that lead under the Temple to a vast maze of caves for the Dragons to live and sleep. The Temple has been in place for thousands of years back to when the Dragon population was immense. The final main hall could hold hundreds of Dragons. The walls in this room depict the History of Dragons beautifully engraved around the entire room and on the ceiling. There are various support pillars in each room that are covered in ancient writings. It has become a long hidden and mostly forgotten relic of Dragon History.

The Dragon Temple will be perfect for the three adult Dragons, six Dragonlings, four Wyverns and other mounts, let alone housing all the survivors.

The camp outside of Salthall is full of activity. Vicar and Shamash check supplies and make a list of items they are running short of. Ixen will go into town to replenish their resources for the battle yet to come. Even with supplies from Elderwolf Keep, they know there will be a great need and want to be prepared. Their only patient, at the moment, is Grace, who is healing from her leg amputation. She is doing a lot of resting and getting used to her new normal way of walking and moving without part of a leg. Jacklyn is assisting Grace just as she would be in O'Malley Keep, but they are building more of a friendship beyond the fact she worked for Grace before.

Gavin and Skip go hunting for the evening meal to supplement the camp's food supplies with fresh meat. Storm and Greta help Quinn take stock of their cooking supplies but are waiting for Earl Jarkon's supplies before deciding if there is anything else they will need.

Ordyn and Ghod help Olek and Ishvet with the preparations for moving the next day. Mandrake and Void gather the magic users to help the soldiers. Everyone is anticipating the arrival of the Griffons from Elderwolf Keep.

Around noon, Ben comes running up to General Olek and stands at attention. He can barely stand still he is so excited.

Smiling, Olek looks to Ben, "What do you have to report young Private Ben?"

Ben points to the sky to the north, "Sir, I saw shining spots in the sky. I believe that they are the Griffons of Elderwolf Keep."

Everyone turns to look to the northern skies. "I believe you are right, Private Ben. That's the way to be aware of your surroundings. If it was an enemy, you might have saved lives by being so alert. Go back to your duties."

Ben salutes, "Sir, yes sir."

Mandrake nods approval, "That boy has come a long way, and he is doing all that he promised Akita. I cannot wait to see what he does once he starts training on his Dragon."

Ordyn turns back to Mandrake, "His grandfather died at Blackwing Keep in the flooding. He is alone in the world now, so I have taken him under my wing so to speak. Guiding him to work hard on his training and come to me if he needs anything. I have been making it a point to check with him daily."

Ghod replies, "I will help keep an eye on him as well. As, I am an orphan."

Ishvet blurts out, "Ghod, I do believe you have a heart under that black mask and leather." Everyone chuckles at Ghod's sudden staunch stance as he stands up straighter and adjusts his sword. Ishvet finishes, "Don't worry you are still a mean ole grump."

Olek looks to the skies again, "The best place for them to land is that clearing over there. It looks like Earl Jarkon brought his entire Griffon army. We should be there when they land."

The sky starts glittering with gold and silver sparkles as the sun glistens off the Griffon armor. The reflective light covers the camp in little lights moving all over the ground and tents, getting everyone's attention, as the Griffons do a fly over to land in the clearing.

Many of the Griffons are carrying cargo platforms and set them down to the side of the clearing before landing in formation behind Earl Jarkon.

General Olek greets Earl Jarkon with a deep bow and then a salute. "Welcome to our camp, Earl Jarkon. Your arrival has been eagerly anticipated. Might I say that was a grand entrance with all the shiny armor lighting up the camp. Akita is away at the moment, but we have already begun preparations for moving the camp tomorrow morning."

The Earl nods, "We passed Vivian on the way here. She let me know the status. Captain Dubbin returned with me and is organizing the supplies. However, I suggest we just load your supplies with those on the cargo platforms for the morning trip. I have brought enough of them and Griffons to transport everyone and the few horses to the Dragon Temple."

General Olek thinks for a moment, "I will have Quinn and Shamash talk to Captain Dubbin to get things moving. Some items will have to wait till morning. Vicar can put a spell on the horses in the morning to keep them calm during the flight. Our soldiers are ready to assist in packing the supplies. Come join us for coffee Earl Jarkon. We were just studying the maps for the Dragon Temple and your firsthand knowledge will be very helpful."

Everyone is sitting around the campfire eating dinner. Cargo platforms are loaded with non-essential items and others will be loaded at first light with tents, the rest of the supplies and horses.

Earl Jarkon admires the Dragons lounging, "If someone told me I would be fighting alongside two of the most ancient, fabled Dragons, let alone Annut the Fast, this time last year, I would have laughed at them and thought them an idiot. But here we are with both Aphorea and Rethu.

Ishvet nods, "I know the feeling. I just find it amusing that we seem to find a new Dragon every few months, that was not thought to be part of this world anymore. Akita seems to be a Dragon magnet." Ishvet sees those across the fire from him start to smile and giggle.

Akita quietly lands behind Ishvet, "Dragon magnet! I like that."

Ishvet turns, "Welcome… Oh geeze. You have another Dragon. Woman, what is it with you and Dragons? Although that one is kinda cute."

Wulf steps up next to Akita pointing at the little Black Dragon on her shoulder. "This is Sage. He is a Xian, otherwise known as a Pseudo Dragon." Pointing to his own shoulder, "This is Dojo. He was the entire reason I came here to Alahora. It's a long story and I will tell it sometime."

Dojo speaks into their minds, in a surprisingly loud growly voice, "Thank you for saving my friend."

Earl Jarkon looks at Akita, "You never cease to amaze me."

Akita smiles, "Well, these li'l guys are as rare, if not rarer than Fenton's. They have been hunted to extinction for the same reason many Dragons and Dragonkin have been hunted."

Darkwing, is awoken to a knock on the door. He stretches as he climbs out of the big four poster bed and hollers, "Coming." As he opens the door, he sees an Elderwolf Elven Lady Paladin standing there.

With a slight bow, "Parden me sir. I am Sergeant Owl Neshaa and am to escort you to breakfast and to the Dragon Temple. Corporals Rose Pearl and Leif Copperbeard are waking your companions."

Darkwing nods "Give me a few minutes to gather my things."

By the time he got back to the door the others had joined Owl and were ready to go.

Sergeant Owl bows again, "Follow me. The cook has put out a good hardy breakfast and packed us all rations for the trip, plus a few extra days. Earl Jarkon and Lady Akita Blackwing should meet us at the Dragon Temple in the next 48 hours."

Greenbean asks, "Has anyone heard from Vivian this morning? She didn't say if she was staying with her friend overnight or coming back to the Keep."

Sergeant Owl shakes her head, "Lady Vivian has not returned to the Keep as of this morning's roll call. Not that she has to answer to anyone, but we do keep an eye on her."

Fabby knows where Greenbean is going with this question. "Could you have someone go to check on her if she doesn't return by early afternoon?"

Sergeant Owl stops, facing the trio, "I will notify my commanding officer of your wishes before we leave the Keep. These are trying times, and we can never be too cautious."

They walk into a beautiful dining hall and are led to a table with huge platters of breakfast dishes and carafes of coffee. The room smells heavenly.

Greenbean takes a sip of coffee, "Sergeant Owl, how long of a flight is it to the Dragon Temple?"

Sergeant Owl looks up from her plate, "We should be there just after mid-day. Our last patrol stated that the temple is habitable, and we will see remnants of the Dark Wizards that were there."

After a full breakfast and idle chit chat, the team is ready to leave. They head to the stables to find their mounts already saddled.

Darkwing feels astonished, "Someone here must have a really special way with animals or there is a corpse somewhere. These Owls don't normally allow just anyone to saddle them."

A stable hand walks out from the tack room. "Your Owls are beautiful creatures much like our Griffons. You just have to show them respect, so I bowed to each one and asked their permission."

Darkwing smiles, "Smart man. Good job." With that, they lead their mounts outside and take off for the Dragon Temple.

The sky is slightly overcast today with a thin layer of clouds just enough to block the sun's rays. There is a nice cool breeze flowing through the treetops just below them. At the moment, the air doesn't smell like rain and there aren't any dark clouds in the distance in any direction.

After a few hours of flying Darkwing starts laughing. He looks over to Greenbean and Fabby. "My friends Annut and Thoraxian are on the way with the younglings. Granit just spoke to me, so they can't be too far away. Greenbean you might be able to reach out to Shemera."

Sergeant Owl drops back next to Darkwing. "Did you say the Dragons will catch up to us?"

Darkwing nods, "They are actually off to the east of us. Some of the Griffons of Elderwolf Keep are used to them, but you might want to reassure your Griffons that they are safe as the Dragons approach. We will probably see Annut and Thoraxian first, with 6 smaller Dragons following them." He stops to listen for a moment. "I was just told that Allura and her younglings are with them."

"I will let the others know. We are just about to our destination." Sergeant Owl replied.

Greenbean had been quiet for a few moments. "Shemera is near and Annut just reached out to me. We should see them any moment now."

At that moment a huge shadow flies over them. As they look up Annut is above them and Thoraxian off to the side. As the two larger Dragons overtake and pass them, they start to see the younglings flying all around them. Rose Pearl and her Griffon are visibly nervous. Fabby flies up next to them and sends a calming spell to the Griffon and the rider.

Annut speaks to the group. "Good to see you again my friends, Darkwing, Greenbean and Fabby. The younglings will be hungry when we get there so we will hunt the area which will also work to secure the temple. Nothing will want to be around the temple once we land."

Thoraxian adds, "When I enter the temple a spell should be activated again, that will work as an alarm. It will alert us to anything not indigenous or Dragon kind that comes close. At least that is what is supposed to happen, but the spell is ancient, and we don't know for sure if it is still active after all these years."

Annut and Thoraxian accelerate forward. They want to see where Dragons can land and enter the Temple. Annut states their observations, "We will have to pull up trees and make an area for Dragons and the Earls army to land. My children stay with our friends."

A few minutes later you see trees being uprooted and set to the side as they clear the area. The two older Dragons are using their skill and experience to clear an area and yet keep the Dragon Temple completely concealed.

Darkwing, Greenbean, Fabby and their Paladin escorts land in the clearing close to the Dragon Temple. They remove the saddles and place them near the entrance so that Drako and the Owl Rocs could go feed with the Dragons.

They turn to the huge main entrance and take their first steps into the most ancient Dragon Temple. As Darkwing lights the torches left by the Dark Wizards with his blue fire, the Dragon carvings on the walls light up.

Darkwing is awestruck, "Akita is going to be so excited to see this, Temple. These carvings are absolutely beautiful."

Fabby asks, "Is that Aphorea? Or another Ice Dragon?"

Thoraxian walks in behind them, "Yes, Fab Ulous, that is Aphorea and on the wall over here is Rethu. The other Dragon is Jaxian, a Water Dragon and father of Ashonia. He would be Ishvet's grandfather. They were and are our leaders before and during the Titan War."

As they head to the inner chamber, Annut walks through the entrance. She stops and makes a brief bow towards each of the images. "I have heard of this Temple, but this is the first time I have ever seen it."

Thoraxian explains to the group that the ramps lead to the main living areas for the Dragons. Each individual cave is a really good size that could house many men at a time with all their gear. He suggests that even though they all join together in the middle that the dragons use the left ramp and caves there while the soldiers and everyone else use the right ramp. He then leads them into the gigantic main hall.

"This room is where the elders and leaders met. The walls are engraved with Dragon history and laws are engraved on the pillars. Maybe after everyone is here, we can have a Dragon history lesson. I am sure it will be enlightening for humankind that thought we were extinct."

Greenbean gazes around the room. "This is absolutely spectacular. I am so glad it survived the ages. There is much to learn here. But we have mounts to take care of and things to organize for our friends. Shall we look at the lower maze of caves."

Fabby looks to Greenbean, "I don't know about anyone else, but can we get some lunch before we start the work. That was a long morning flight."

Sergeant Owl nods to Rose and Leif, who head to set up food and drink just outside the entrance door.

After a quick lunch everyone heads down into the lower levels. The first few sets of caves show evidence of habitation in the recent past. As the team moves farther into the caves, they start seeing dusty webs. The caves need to be swept out, they will need lots of firewood and straw for sleeping pallets. Each cave is large enough for a full-grown dragon to stretch its wings and turn around in.

Looking around, Greenbean observes, "Well, there is plenty of room here. We can put Quinn and her cooks together and one entire cave for cooking, the soldiers can bunk down 10 or more to one cave, we can put the healers in another. I know I feel a breeze, so there must be another entrance or even two." She reaches out to Thoraxian and asks about alternate exits to the cave system.

Thoraxian laughs in their minds, "Yes, there are four exits we are digging out and maintaining camouflage. Can you imagine all those caves full of dragons and only one exit? There are enough caves for many grumpy dragons, it would be disastrous, don't you think."

Fabby giggles, "With the horns, teeth and claws that would be an interesting sight, to say the least. The dragon code would prevent them from killing each other but it doesn't say much about accidently on purpose slashing or biting another. However, these caves offer security and a great fallback point. It is very defensible."

Greenbean turns to Darkwing, "I noticed more torches in each cave. Can we light them all in a few of the caves so we can unload our gear for the night? Let's leave one for Akita and Wulf, as well as one for Ishvet and Vivian, since they are our only couples. We can stake claim on the next two for you guys and I will take one for myself, Grace, and Jacklyn. We can use one for the War Room. Then once everyone gets here, we can worry about the rest. What do you think?"

Thoraxian calls to everyone, "I may be able to help with all the cleaning up and lighting all the braziers. Everyone meet me in the main chamber."

Thoraxian moves to the main chamber, in the center is a large seal carved in the stone floor. A grand Dragon is depicted on the seal with its wings stretched out and a long column of flame emanating from its mouth. Directly above the seal is a hole in the ceiling the same shape and diameter as the seal. Thoraxian tells everyone that at noon and midnight a shaft of light will hit the seal and it will be the exact same size as the seal. That's how they kept track of time back then.

Thoraxian then tells everyone to move back. He looks around to make sure everyone is out of the way then blows fire directly on the giant seal. The seal begins to glow from the intense heat of the Dragon fire. Then the glow starts to radiate to the closest columns. The glow rises up the columns and the carved words in the ancient Dragon language begin to glow.

The whole temple begins to vibrate, and a huge gust of wind blows through the main chamber. All the braziers in the main chamber light at once, and the wind blows all the dirt, webs, and old plant materials off the walls, ceilings, and floors. Color is restored in the large engravings on the walls and pieces of the temple that were crumbling begin to repair themselves.

Thoraxian speaks to everyone's mind, "The temple awakens from its long slumber. All the barrier spells are reforming, and our helpers will soon return to the temple."

Darkwing looks up at Thoraxian, "What kind of helpers do you mean?"

Thoraxian takes a short pause before answering, "Well, I don't know what to call them in your language. They are about the size of a goat; they have six legs and several eyes."

Darkwing sucks in a huge breath, "If you are talking about, what I think you are talking about, then Akita is going to be in for a hell of a shock."

Thoraxian looks towards the main entrance, "I think I hear some of them coming now. They will be of great help. They are strong and can help with all kinds of tasks."

A high-pitched scream comes from the main entrance where the Paladins set up lunch earlier. Then the sound of weapons hitting shields can be heard echoing through the halls. Everyone in the main chamber turns and runs towards the entrance.

Greenbean pulls her long sword over her shoulder as she sprints past Darkwing and Fabby. As they run up on the three Paladins, they see several odd-looking creatures. The Paladins are clanging their weapons against their shields to warn the creatures off. The creatures continue towards them. As Fabby, Greenbean, and Darkwing get closer, they can make out the features of these unusual creatures.

They are about the size of goats like Thoraxian said and in fact the bottom half of them is almost like a goat or a small pony, but they have two sets of rear legs and one set of front legs. At the front the body of the animal melds into a human-like torso covered in short smooth fur, with two arms and a head. The face is almost human looking except they have four eyes. Two eyes in the same place as any human then one more on each side, right above where the temples would be. Their hair is long and flowing like a horse's mane, and they have an elongated nose and mouth like a sheep.

Darkwing shouts to the Paladins, "Wait, don't harm them. I think these are the helpers that Thoraxian just told us about."

Sergeant Owl tells the other two Paladins to step back. As they move to the side, one of the creatures walks up to Sergeant Owl. All four of its eyes are staring at her. The creature kind of smiles and lets out an odd bleat. Then turns and heads towards the entrance of the temple.

Thoraxian makes his way to the entrance, "Yes, these are the helpers I just told you about. I have told them that you are our guest, and they should treat you as any Dragon. They are like forest children. They can speak aloud, but rarely do. They will mostly bleat like a sheep, which us Dragons can understand. Sergeant Owl, the one that spoke to you said, you are very noisy."

Sergeant Owl looks back at Thoraxian, "Really? They said that with just one bleat. Oh, now I've seen and heard it all. Which also makes me ask the question, 'where have these creatures been hiding?' I have scouted these woods my whole life and I have never come across one."

Thoraxian speaks to everyone, "They only exist when we are here at the Temple. That's why you have never seen one. They are a part of the Temple's magic. Don't worry though, they will do as you ask and not get in your way."

Darkwing looks over to Greenbean, "Greenbean you can put your sword away now. I don't think the goat children are going to need slicing and dicing." Darkwing chuckles, "I thought by the description Thoraxian gave that they were going to be spiders. We all know how Akita absolutely loves spiders. I'm kind of disappointed that they are not spiders. That would have been a sight to behold when Akita saw them."

Fabby laughs with Darkwing, "Yes, that would have been a fiery situation. These creatures are more akin to Centaurs than spiders. Lucky for them."

Greenbean huffs a little, "I don't care what they are. It's a little unnerving to have all those eyes looking at you. Be glad you said something when you did Darkwing. If even one of them had of winked at me, I would have been slicing and dicing these little goat children things."

Annut calls to everyone, "Now that the excitement is over and the Temple has awoken, I believe it's time that we finish preparations for all the soon to be arrivals. Also, I have spoken to our new helpers, they are Lommas. They are all named Lomma. They also have the ability to read minds. They will get or conjure what you need or want." Annut makes a short pause, "Yes, Greenbean, that also includes food and drink. They just said that you are wanting something you call Magic Bean Coffee."

Everyone looks over at Greenbean. Fabby laughs and shakes his head. "We just met some of the most ancient magical creatures of the forest and all you can think about is Magic Bean Coffee?"

Greenbean kind of blushes, "Well. Annut said they could get us anything, and that's something I haven't had for a while."

CHAPTER 14
VANISHED

The effects of the powerful Sleep spell start to wear off and Vivian slowly wakes up. Her head is cloudy, and she feels very tired. She can barely open her eyes. She can sense a Dark Magic residue all over herself and around her. As her body regains its feeling, she can feel herself seated with her arms bound behind the chair she is sitting in. Her eyes try to focus, but there is only black in front of her. She then realizes that she is blindfolded. There are sounds all around her and muffled voices. She begins to wonder, ["Where am I? Does anyone even know I'm gone?"]

She begins to replay the last moments at Casheon's home before she was subdued. She wonders what happened to Zora. Zora would have defended her to the death. She wonders if Zora was put to sleep or worse before they took her away. There is one word that she can remember hearing and it causes her to clench her jaw and boil with anger, "Windu!" She speaks it aloud without even realizing it. However, it is even more jolting in her darkness when he answers back.

King Windu replies in a deep, smooth tone like the slither of a snake, "Vivian my darling. I thought you might never wake."

Two Elderwolf Paladins took off just after lunch to check on Vivian. They are approaching Hornbuckle where Casheon lives, her oldest, closest friend.

As they fly into the little village, they notice a group of people gathered around something white on the ground. Their Griffons let out loud distressed screeches, as they get closer. It is obvious to the Paladins that their Griffons have identified the object.

The people on the ground hear the screech and scatter, when they see two Griffons flying in fast to land near their friend.

The Paladins tell everyone to step back, as their Griffons are agitated and angry. They walk up to Zora, a Griffon everyone knows in the Keep, to find she has passed. As they examine her, they see that she was hit with a killing Dark Magic spell.

The lead Paladin turns to the people gathered around, "Does anyone know what happened here? Do you know where Vivian Elderwolf is?"

A young woman gasps, "Why would Vivian be here today?"

They see an older man walking towards the house. As he draws near, Casheon asks, "Why are you in front of my house?" Looking around he notices Zora lying on the ground. "By the Gods, where is Vivian?"

The lead Paladin raises an eyebrow, "We were hoping you could tell us. We were told she was coming to you because you were near death."

Casheon is shocked, "I am very much alive and well. I had an unusual request for some precious stones that can only be found up North. So, I haven't been at the house for days."

The Paladin in charge steps forward, "Sir, is it a common practice for you to go searching for gems like that? What is it that you do?"

Casheon looks over at Zora, "Actually I make custom Griffon bridles. It is somewhat unusual to ask for these particular stones. The gentleman that asked me to make this bridle was from Elderwolf Keep."

The lead Paladin looks around and leans over to speak to his partner, "I sensed Dark Magic lingering throughout the house. If this friend of Vivian's is telling the truth, I might have an idea about the man he described. We need to get to the Keep now. Earl Jarkon will need to know about this immediately."

The other Paladin speaks softly back to the lead Paladin, "The only problem is that Earl Jarkon isn't at the Keep and he's the only person I would trust with this information. If you are thinking what I am thinking, and someone from the Keep set this up, there may be others that are not as honorable as they want to appear to be. Let's get Zora back to the Keep and then we can decide how to get a message to Earl Jarkon."

The lead Paladin takes flight and his Griffon hovers over Zora's body. The Griffon reaches down with his front arms and embraces Zora's lifeless body. He slowly picks her up and flies up to meet the other Griffon and Paladin. They fly side by side back to Elderwolf Keep.

After a long flight the Survivors with Earl Jarkon and the rest of the team arrive late in the evening at the Dragon Temple. Everyone works together to set up their living spaces and workspaces for defensibility and efficiency. Two Dragons have taken residence at each of the exits with ten soldiers that will rotate standing guard.

Akita, Storm, Earl Jarkon, Ishvet and the rest of the leadership step into the entryway with Aphorea behind them.

Akita inhales deeply, "By the Gods! I knew we were in the presence and graced with the help of Ancient Dragons, but Aphorea you are one of the Royalty Trio of history. That looks like Rethu. I don't know or recognize the third Dragon."

Aphorea answers, "You are correct about two of the Royalty Trio. However, Jaxian was lost during the Titan Wars. He is Ishvet's grandfather, a magnificent Sea Dragon and his mother's, father."

Ishvet turns to gaze at his grandfather and is still amazed that he lived over a thousand years ago. "Speaking of my family, where is my Viv?"

Everyone looks around as Fabby and Greenbean walk in from the central room. Greenbean looks at Ishvet and the Earl, "Actually, we were thinking she would be with you. She left us at Elderwolf Keep in the capable hands of Sergeant Owl, to go check on a friend that was on his death bed. We expected her to get here last night but when she didn't arrive, we assumed she had opted to join you on your way here."

Fabby looks at Greenbean, "I hope the Paladins heeded my advice and checked on her at noon as I suggested to them."

Ishvet, Jarkon and Akita look at each other in confusion.

Earl Jarkon asks, "Do you know which friend was supposed to be on their death bed? I can only think of one, but he would not have called for her, he would have left her a note, as cold as that might sound, he understands her mission at the moment."

Sergeant Owl and one Lomma walk up to the Earl. Sergeant Owl bows to him, "She received a message from Casheon, which she said you delivered to her sir."

At that moment, Captain Dubbin rushes in to the Earl. "Sir, two of our Paladins have asked to speak to you and you alone. It's the damnedest thing, they won't even talk to me, their Captain."

As the Earl hurries out to his men, the Lomma bleats several times to Aphorea. Akita jumps as she had not noticed the little creature when Sergeant Owl came up the ramp.

Aphorea does what is now known as a Dragon chuckle, "While the Earl is talking to his men, let me introduce the Lomma. When the Temple is activated by the Dragons, they come to assist in the upkeep and care of those that reside here. They are magical creatures, they can speak but usually bleat in a language we understand, and they read minds, so they can anticipate your needs and wants. They have been told to treat all here like Dragons, which is important as they will also defend the Temple from all strangers."

Ishvet is getting anxious, "I will have time for niceties once I know where my wife is and that she is safe." He starts walking in the direction of the Earl and is just about knocked down by the

Earl as he comes running in with his men and Captain Dubbin right behind him."

The Earl is winded, his fists clenching, and anger reading all over his face. You can tell it is all he can do to maintain some semblance of restraint.

Captain Dubbin looks just as angry, as he punches his left palm with his right fist, as if he is going to pummel something to death.

Earl Jarkon takes a deep breath, "These men, did as you instructed Fab Ulous, and went to Casheon's home when Vivian did not return to the Keep. Thank you for your forethought on this or we might not have known anything was wrong until much later." Taking another deep breath, "When they arrived at Casheon's home, they found he had not been there for several days, and Zora was lying dead on the doorstep. The home and Zora reeked of Dark Magic."

Ishvet is now clenching his fists and seething in anger. "But what about my wife?" Ishvet asks between clenched teeth.

Jarkon looks to Ishvet, "She was nowhere to be found, so we believe she is alive but that she has been ambushed and kidnapped. The question is, who kidnapped her and where did they take her? Did King Carthon take her to his Keep or is someone else involved?"

Akita, who has remained quiet, is starting a slow flame as her body starts to glow. Ishvet is slowly starting to glow blue. The Lomma bleats again.

Vicar walks up behind them, putting a hand on each shoulder, "Now is the time for calm and planning. You two can slice and dice then roast the culprits to death when we find them."

Ishvet, still gritting his teeth, "My father will die for all his atrocities, but if he has Vivian, I will slowly torture him to death, for my mother and my wife."

Aphorea speaks, as Ordyn, Mandrake, and others join the team, "Leif Copperbeard, would you please join us for a special mission in the main entry of the Temple." Unbeknownst to all, Aphorea had been speaking to certain individuals to assemble in the entry.

Akita, Ishvet and the Earl look at Aphorea confused. Then the Earl says with a tone of disbelief, "No!" As everyone turns to look at the

Earl, Leif Copperbeard walks in behind him. The Paladin visibly turns white and starts to sweat.

Aphorea lowers her head until it is right down in his face. She then speaks to the team only, "As I stated, our little Lomma friends here can read minds as well as being attuned to feelings and emotions. This Paladin has been nervous and in fear of being caught at something since Earl Jarkon arrived. Leif, I suggest you tell us what those fears are now."

Ordyn and Mandrake had been slowly moving around on each side of the Paladin to block him from trying to back out of the room and run. The others also moved to encircle the Paladin, trapping him in place.

Leif stares at the giant toothy mouth and nose in front of him. Meh-kola blinks to existence on Aphorea's nose and begins to examine her own claws on her right paw to convey the threat of harm.

Earl Jarkon in a deep growly voice asks, "Leif, what do you know about Vivian's disappearance? I think you know you have no choice but to talk, as you are surrounded, and the Queen of Ice Dragons is calling you out."

Leif is no small Human Paladin, he has an average masculine build and a chiseled face with a thick moustache, so when he speaks, his voice gets everyone's attention. With an indignant tone and a snarled lip, a comical high-pitched voice emanates, "I do not know anything about anything. These creatures are reading the wrong mind."

Akita walks to the Paladin putting her truth ring on her right pointer finger where it is visible to most. As she puts her hand on his shoulder under his pauldron, "While I am not your ruler, I believe Earl Jarkon will allow me to question you under the circumstances." Akita looks to Earl Jarkon and waits for him to nod before continuing. After a slight bow of his head, she begins again and squeezes his shoulder as she starts to talk, "I am going to ask you some questions. This ring I am wearing will glow a bright green when you are lying. When you tell the truth it will lay dormant." She takes note of his trembling body under her hand.

Akita looks around the room at everyone then fixes her fiery eyes into Leif's fearful eyes, "Did you have something to do with the disappearance of Vivian Elderwolf?

Leif swallows hard and takes a deep breath. In his unusual high-pitched voice, he states, "I had nothing to do with Vivian's disappearance."

A bright glow of green can be seen under the left pauldron of Leif. Akita squeezes his shoulder a little harder, "Leif you are not telling me the truth. Now I am not an advocate of needless violence. However, when it comes to my family, I may tend to bend my principles a bit. I will give you one more chance to answer truthfully. If you don't, then you will have the hand of the Duchess branded on your shoulder for the rest of your life. Can you imagine how excruciating it will be to have my hand heat to the temperature of lava on your shoulder and melt into your flesh? We won't even begin to speak about the smell."

Gavin states, "Yeah, she gave me the hot foot once, for drunken back talk. Trust me, you don't want her fire wrath."

Ishvet shoots Gavin a look that conveys he needs to shut his mouth now.

Leif looks over to his pauldron, "Fine, I do know something about Vivian. I arranged for Casheon to be gone for a few days. I forged a letter to Vivian to get her to come to his house. I didn't know they were going to kill Zora, but they didn't tell me the details. When your Lord asks you to do something, you don't question it."

Akitas head turns abruptly to look at Earl Jarkon. Earl Jarkon's mouth is agape. She sees that everyone is looking at Earl Jarkon. Before she can say anything, Earl Jarkon speaks up, "What are you looking at me for? I'm obviously not who he is talking about."

Leif wriggles under Akita's grip and through clenched teeth he blurts out, "Not that fool, he is no Lord. He has no aspirations beyond his own Keep and daughter. He only cares about his little kingdom. He allows these lesser races to hold positions of power and even marry his daughter. My Lord will wash away his type of filth and make a better realm where we can live in peace without your abominations." Lief looks over to Ishvet with a snarl as he finishes his sentence.

Akita and the rest of the team are shocked for a few seconds. Akita loosens her grip on Leif's shoulder for a second. In that second Leif is able to break free. Akita moves a step back as Ordyn and Mandrake take a step forward to secure Leif.

Leif reaches into his sash and pulls out a tiny vial. He pops it into his mouth and crunches it with his teeth. A purple fume wafts from his mouth as he collapses to the floor. Ordyn and Mandrake reach out, but do not catch his body. Leif's body begins to convulse on the ground.

Meh-Kola blinks in front of Akita at chest level and pushes her back, "Move away Akita, One knows that poison!"

Akita steps back as she hears Leif start making high-pitched squeals of pain. Ordyn and Mandrake back up from the body heeding Meh-Kola's warning.

Leif's body twists and turns on the ground then goes completely limp. Quickly his skin turns necrotic and green then begins to tighten around his bones. Within a few seconds his whole body is a dried-up husk and barely fills up his armor.

Akita regains her footing and walks over to Storm. She gets really close to Storm's ear. "You didn't do that, right?"

Storm looks at Akita with a puzzled look. Then you can see it click in her mind, "Oh! No that wasn't me. He took out a little vial from his sash and drank it before anyone could act." She shakes her head with a little smirk, "But I wish it had been."

Earl Jarkon walks up to the armor and what is left of Leif's body, "What in the Gods was he going on about? Why would he have a suicide poison on his person? Captain Dubbin, do you have any idea?"

Captain Dubbin shakes his head shrugs his shoulders, "Sir, I have no idea. What really concerns me is that he was so high in our ranks, and we didn't know he was working against us. We need to get to the bottom of this as quickly as possible and cut off any information going to the enemy."

Earl Jarkon nods his head in agreement, "I need you to go back to Elderwolf Keep and tell Captain Seeker what has transpired. You and he are the only ones I trust to take on the task of finding traitors in our midst. Only report your findings to me directly, in person."

Captain Dubbin bows and turns, leaving the room. As soon as he is gone Ishvet walks up to Earl Jarkon and is within an inch of their chests touching. Ishvet looks down and is snout to nose with the Earl, "What is going on? How is someone like this in your ranks? We need to figure this out fast. I can sense that Viv is in danger."

Earl Jarkon puts his hands up to ward off the two Paladins coming to restrain Ishvet. He then takes a step back and looks right into Ishvet's eyes, "Ishvet, I assure you, I had no idea that Corporal Copperbeard felt this way. If I had any idea, he would have been decommissioned immediately. We will find her. I promise you that. Captain Dubbin and Captain Seeker will get to the bottom of what is going on at the Keep. I trust them both with my life."

Ishvet huffs but is somewhat satisfied with Earl Jarkon's answer for now. He then turns to Akita, "Okay Akita, what do we do now? I can't stand here and do nothing while Viv is out there somewhere in evil hands and only the Gods know what they are doing to her."

Akita looks around to all the faces of the group. Then she steps up to Ishvet and places a hand on his shoulder, "Ishvet, we have some of the best Rangers, Assassins, Greatsword Warriors, Fighters, Clerics, Wizards and Warlocks of all types. On top of all that, they are your family, and no one fights as strongly as your family does. We are with you for whatever comes.

We will get Viv back, and we will make those responsible pay for what they have done. We just have to be smart about our next move. King Carthon is not the only one that can get information from anywhere on this continent. I know lots of people and I happen to know a little furry friend that can find out things and go places that no one else can. So, rest assured that I am on top of this."

Meh-Kola blinks into the air beside Akita and Ishvet with wings flapping, "One knows you are speaking of One. One will be on One's way as soon as you say to go."

Akita looks at Meh-Kola with a fieriness in her eyes and growls out, "Go!"

Meh-Kola blinks away in an instant. The room is still silent. Before anyone can say anything, the Lommas come into the room and start picking up the pieces of armor and remove Leif's withered body. The group watches as they meticulously clean the area. When they are finished everyone breaks off into groups to discuss the events of the evening.

Aphorea speaks to all in their minds, "My friends, I am very saddened by what has transpired. However, we need more information before we can take any action. The one thing that is certain as of now is that we need to prepare for our offensive against King Carthon. I implore you to concentrate on that for the next few days so that we can be better prepared for what is to come. It has been a long day for most, so all of us need to rest and meet tomorrow with a renewed strength."

"My Lord, several of our spies have reported to me this night. Your son's wife has been successfully captured by Windu. Akita and your son are now at the Dragon Temple with all the people from Blackwing Keep. Unfortunately, Captain O'Malley survived the wave at her Keep."

King Carthon slowly puts down the goblet he was sipping from and looks over to Volaern with an eyebrow raised, "Is that all? Any news of the Dragons?

Volaern slightly bows his head and pauses for a few seconds. He looks up and stammers a few times, "From the last report, they actually have eleven Dragons now, my Lord. However, some are only the size of elephants at the last sighting."

King Carthon grits his teeth and slams his hand on the table. The whole table turns to water and splashes all over the floor and their boots, "Damnit Volaern, see what you made me do! The number of Dragons is supposed to be going down, not up. Are these things breeding like rats?" King Carthon stands up and points to the floor, "Dry this up and have another table brought immediately. Also, the next time you come to report, it better be good news, or you'll be a puddle on the floor just like that table."

Volaern bows and backs out of the room to go get rags to clean up the water. He returns within the minute and gets on his hands and knees to sop up the water. King Carthon walks up beside him and looks down, "With all the reports that we have been getting lately, I am beginning to think that they are building an army to make an offensive move on us. I know I have already called all my wizards to the Keep, but I believe we are going to need more power before this is finished. I want you to send word to all the dark creatures, foul beasts, and devious demons that you can find. We need them here within the week to protect the Keep. Tell them that if they do not help me defeat Akita and her army, that nothing will be in her way to keep her from coming after them next."

Volaern finishes drying the water and stands, "Yes, my Lord, right away. My Lord, will Jessa still be at full strength when they get here?"

King Carthon looks down at the Amulet and grabs it in his hand. He squeezes it and his eyes begin to glow a dark blue, "Yes, she is ready for them. Nothing can take her down now. The Sea Amulet has given her even more power than before. Until the time that she is needed she will be asleep in the harbor." He releases the Amulet from his hand and his eyes return to normal, "On your way out send in Evad's brother, I have a task for him."

Volaern leaves and a moment later, a short wild haired Dark wizard enters the room, "My Lord, you wanted to see me?"

King Carthon looks at him with a scowl, "Did you get shorter since the last time you were here? Never mind, I need you to get the most powerful of us and set up a perimeter around the Keep and harbor. I want the most powerful shields you can create by whatever means necessary. They need to be strong enough to withstand Dragon fire and whatever else they can throw at us. Windu may have some artifacts to help defend the Keep. Go get them from him."

Aevid bows to King Carthon, "Yes, my Lord, I will do as you command. Also, I didn't get shorter. That was my brother Evad. I was the tall one in the family."

Aevid turns and leaves to go gather the most powerful Dark Wizards in the Keep. News of the preparations spreads quickly in the Keep and the whole place is abuzz with whispers and speculations.

CHAPTER 15
SECRET WEAPON

Akita awakens to the smell of fresh coffee and cinnamon rolls. Opening her eyes and stretching she sees the little goat children things in her room, delivering her breakfast, or should she say conjuring her breakfast. [Did she dream of this? Or did they just pick it up out of her brain? She is really going to have to get used to these little guys.] She looks over to Sage and sees that she has a meal conjured in front of her too.

One of the Lommas looks at Akita, in its melodic voice its states, "We are Lommas and no relation to the creatures you call goats. We are far more talented than them. Even though we look like children to you, we are ageless."

Akita smiles, "Duly noted. Thank you for the food, as I have to get ready for a meeting."

Wulf enters their quarters, and more food is conjured into existence. This time it is steak and eggs with hot buttered biscuits. "Wow, this is going to spoil us. I was just thinking about steak and eggs before our meeting."

Akita, Wulf, Mandrake, Olek, Ishvet, Earl Jarkon, Skip, Storm, Darkwing, Fabby, Greenbean, Vicar, Shamash and Gavin meet at the new war table. Laying out maps of the area and the few maps they have of Cliffshade Keep.

Olek asks Ishvet, "Can you mark all the normal entrances and any others that might not be so well known on this map?"

Ishvet takes a quill and marks the main entrance and the service entrance. Then he marks a few sewer tunnels and a spot on the cliff that you can climb up to the top of the Keep wall easily. "I didn't grow up at the Keep. I actually know very little about the layout. With that said, as a kid I explored and found things on my own, outside."

Gavin looking at the map, "I have a suggestion. Skip and I take a couple of days to go scout the Keep. We can check the entrances, see who stands guard where, and figure out where the Dark Magic starts to detect intruders. Remember that it will take two days to get there, two days scouting and two days to come back."

Olek and Ishvet nodded in agreement. Ishvet states, "The more information about the Keep, the better. We do not want to tip them off to our presence though. I do not believe they know where we are, but I know he knows we are coming for him. We want the element of surprise. We need to know where his Demi-Titan monster is in the Keep as well. We need to know if it has any weaknesses that we can use to destroy it."

As Ishvet stops talking, the magical alarm horns start blaring throughout the temple. Aphorea speaks to everyone, "Someone is using magic close to the Temple. Be prepared to defend yourselves." Everyone at the meeting jumps up and starts running up the ramps to the entrance. Akita and the others that can fly take flight immediately. Gavin grabs Skip under the arms carrying him as he flies with the others.

Ishvet throws his hands up in exasperation at the fact that another meeting is interrupted. He begrudgingly follows the rest. Thinking to himself, ["We need Grace, Ghod and Jacklyn there too."] He hears a bleat next to him that startles him, then hears Ghod in the distance yelling that they were on their way. Looking down at the Lomma, that he hadn't even noticed before, "Thank you, I guess."

As Ishvet and Olek are walking fast up the ramp, Olek says, "Who else would know that we are here?

Ishvet responds, "No one that I can think of. However, the Dark wizards used this place for a while and may have come to take it back."

As they get to the top of the ramp, Akita and the team come to an abrupt halt, and everyone lands. There is a huge rift opening. The rift is glowing yellow and white and pulsing as it gets wider. It stretches from the ground to about thirty feet in the air. Whatever is going to come through is probably going to be big. Annut and Thoraxian land close to the rift ready to protect the others from what may come. Aphorea lands in the middle of the group and cuts off the entrance to the temple. Above the trees and the rift Warrior, Hunter, Ransom, and Drako circle to attack from the air. Akita takes point in front of the group and her hands turn into flames. She looks from side to side at her fellow warriors and sees that weapons and magical powers are drawn while they wait to see whom or what comes through.

A loud crackling sound fills the air as two sets of four fingers emerge and clasp the sides of the rift. Slowly the rift widens, and a bright glow backlights a dark figure as it steps through. The rift continues to widen, and six more large dark figures walk out. With a snap the rift closes, and the figures are revealed.

There is an audible gasp from the group when a twenty-five-to-thirty-foot female Giant, followed by six Giant guards carrying their gear are illuminated by the midday sun. The Giantess has long flowing blonde hair pulled back and braided. She has a circlet of gold around her head that has a tear drop diamond that hangs on her forehead. Her blouse has many shades of blue graduating light to dark, from her neck to her hips, with tiny gems around the collar. She is wearing deep blue leggings with knee high white leather boots. To some she has the face of an angel, others are too afraid to pay attention.

Skip yells at the top of his lungs, "Stop!" He runs and jumps in front of Akita and turns towards the group. His arms are stretched out and waving up and down, "Don't attack, I know these Giants!"

Darkwing looks up in disbelief, "Is this the little Princess my ancestor saved from a dire bear years ago?"

Princess Gianna takes a step forward and then kneels to one knee behind Skip. "Greetings Skip, my old friend. I received your messages and decided to help you, even with my father fuming at my disobedience. She then looks at Darkwing, "Yes, if you are descended from Slawomir. I was but a toddler, although, I have no recollection of it. My parents still speak of it when stories are told at the campfires."

Skip looks to Akita and Earl Jarkon. "Princess Gianna this is Lady Akita Blackwing, and Earl Jarkon Elderwolf, they are our leaders in charge. With them is Blackwing's General Olek and the Earls son-in-law, Sir Ishvet Bluescale."

Earl Jarkon then steps forward. "Welcome to the Dragon Temple, Princess Gianna. We are so grateful that you made the trip to aid us in this battle against evil. With that said, we can find you and your men accommodations in the caves below. If they can fit Dragons, I'm sure you all will be comfortable." Pointing to Aphorea. "This is Aphorea the Bright, last of the Ice Dragons from the Titan Wars, on your left and right is

Thoraxian the Shadow, and Annut the Fast. We have six young Dragons, five adult Wyverns and four young Wyverns as well, all residing below."

Princess Gianna stands and looks over the crowd with a big smile, "Wow, you have put together quite a group here."

Aphorea speaks to everyone, "Welcome Princess Gianna. It has been centuries since I have been in the presence of Giants, I lost many friends during the Titan Wars. Like Earl Jarkon said, you are welcome to set up living quarters in the Caves below. The left ramp takes you to the Dragons and Wyverns, while the right ramp is everyone else. Our friends and helpers, the Lommas, will help you settle in with anything you need."

Princess Gianna walks up to Aphorea and bows. "It is a great honor to meet you in person. We also tell stories about the Dragons at our campfires, that includes you, Rethu and Jaxian. I will have to send word to my father, King Iglis Frozenbolt, that his old friend Aphorea is here with me. Thank you for your hospitality."

Akita steps up to Aphorea and the Princess. "Princess Gianna let's get you settled in and then we can reminisce as well as fill you in on the situation. As for the rest of us, let's get back to the war table."

Ghod states, "I will join you in a few minutes, I want to see if one of these Giant soldiers will wrestle me. I'm sure I can take em."

Akita stops in her tracks and turns towards Ghod, "There will be plenty of time for that later. Leave our new guest alone for the time being."

Ghod huffs and looks up at a particularly muscular Giant soldier, "But he's looking at me funny."

Akita cocks her head to one side then looks up to the Giant soldier and then back to Ghod, "Well, he can probably tell that you are part Dwarf."

Ghod's face changes immediately and softens. A slight grin begins in the corners of his mouth and his Half-Orc teeth protrude from his lips. He begins to chuckle, "Hell Akita, to him we are all Dwarfs. But right enough there will be time for that later. I better get back to the forge before it cools down."

Akita laughs and follows Ghod and the rest of the group into the temple. There is a slight tremor in the ground as the Giants follow behind her. Once they are all inside a large circular stone rolls into the opening and secures the temple.

The next day at Annut's request, Ben is out with the three youngest Dragons while they hunt. Including his own Dragon, Zold. He has been instructed to teach them to control their bursts of fire, as well as aiming and directing it precisely at their prey. Ben has challenged them to try to be stealthy. He knows their size and the forest makes this almost impossible, but it's funny watching them try.

At the moment, prey is in the form of deer and a bear every once in a while. Otherwise, it's small creatures that would be a snack. Dragons' eyesight is unique because they have two lenses. One allows them to see heat signatures, useful especially when hunting, and the other allows them to focus in on a target at a great distance or relax to see the surroundings up close.

The younglings are having great fun aiming at the squirrels and rabbits to hone their fire skills and occasionally getting a snack.

Ben says loudly, "Don't get too far away from me." He jogs along to keep up, climbing over branches and rocks. Ben jumps from one bolder and feels the ground under him give way. With the sudden loss of support, he yells as he falls fifty feet to the floor below. He lands on the soft dirt that fell below him and screams as he hears a snap and a shooting pain in his right leg, with searing pain in his right arm. He gasps for air from the fall and his eyesight is blurry but slowly starts to clear.

Granite, Elsbeth and Zold spin around looking for Ben. Zold lets out a roar because he can feel his friend is in pain.

Ben looks up at the opening that he fell through as more dirt and branches fall down around him. He tries to look around the cavern, but the beam of light does nothing to brighten the far sides of the subterranean cave. In the distance, Ben can hear several thuds that displace the air so that it feels like vibration, a weird swishing sound and clicking as if many walking sticks are hitting the rock floor.

Ben calls for Zold, telling him to retrace his steps, and use his heat vision, as he watches the opening above him for Zold's head to peer over.

Out of the corner of his eye he sees movement. Looking in that direction he sees two long spider legs and what look like spider mandibles. He swivels his head and realizes he's in a large Rock Spider nest. There are at least three different sizes of spiders closing in on him and none are smaller than a pony or calf.

Ben screams out loud, "You don't want me, there's not enough of me to go around! Help!! Rock Spiders!!" Then Zold looks down at Ben but knows he cannot just flame the cavern, without killing Ben. Zold tells Granite and Elsbeth to be ready, because these spiders will follow him and Ben out of the cave. Without further warning, Zold drops into the cave trying to gently pick Ben up in his claws. Ben uses his one good arm to hold on to Zold's claw. As they rise a Rock Spider leaps onto Zold's wing. The spider is a full-grown adult with a six-foot diameter leg reach. As it is scrambling to hold onto Zold, when one of its legs pierce the webbing of the wing, causing Zold to tilt to the right from the weight of the spider and growl. Zold snaps his wing out dislodging the spider and throwing it into a wall as he keeps ascending out of the cave in a spiral motion. The spiral motion causes another spider to miss Zold completely.

Elsbeth and Granite had already been yelling for their mother, Annut, to come help them, but they had to act as soon as Zold cleared the cavern opening because several of the larger Rock Spiders gave chase. The two Dragons let loose blasts of Dragon fire into the cavern with such ferocity that Ben could feel the heat on his back as he rose into the sky.

Annut, Vicar, Akita, and Wulf land next to the two Dragons and are amazed at the sight before their eyes. At least sixty Rock Spiders lie in curled up ashy messes and piled on top of each other at the bottom of the cavern.

Annut tells Zold to gently lower himself down so that Wulf and Vicar can grab Ben for immediate healing. Ben almost passes out from the pain, but as Vicar's hand touches his shoulder, he feels instant soothing.

After a quick assessment of young Ben, Vicar pulls a branch out of his arm and closes the wound, healing it completely. "That was easy. The leg will need to be reset and healed. Easier to do in the Temple. I will take him and meet you there. Zold, I will send Shamash to mend your right wing. The three of you did great today."

Akita examines the wing, "Yeah, that's an easy fix for Shamash. Look at it this way, Zold, you have your first battle wound by heroically saving your rider. Let's all get back to the temple."

Granite stomps a foot, "We didn't find dinner!"

Akita laughs, "Granite sometimes that is how life works. However, I am sure if you let a Lomma know you are hungry, they will conjure up fresh meat for you and Elsbeth."

Annut lets her younglings know how proud she is of what they accomplished on this day.

Ordyn and Ghod are coming up to the war table after seeing Ben being brought in by Vicar. They needed to check on his welfare, since the death of his grandfather, they are trying to be there for him. Akita and Wulf join them.

Ishvet looks to Akita, "So what happened now?"

Akita tells them about Ben's fall into a Rock Spider den, about Ben's injuries, Zold's ripped wing, "But most importantly the three young Dragons handled the situation and killed about sixty Rock Spiders with Dragon fire and didn't start a forest fire. So, we are good."

Ishvet folds his arms, "Well good, glad to hear it, but can we get back to the matters at hand now? We need to be looking for Viv. I know Meh-Kola is out gathering information, but we don't know if she will find anything. I want to know if there is anyone that can go into Cliffshade, without being instantly noticed, to get supplies and snoop around for information as well. We don't have any converted Dark Wizards in our midst to play double agent."

The Earl grumbles, "If I can't trust my own army, I sure wouldn't trust someone converted from his side."

Storm asks, "Do you think I could just walk into town? I haven't been around in years. I never lived on this side of the continent, so maybe no one will notice."

Ordyn thinks a minute, "Except that you have no Dark Magic aura to fit in. Akita, could Wulf or Void disguise her?"

Grace hobbles up to the table, "Jacklyn and I can go, as I have been trading in that town for a while."

Mandrake shakes his Dragonkin head, "Jacklyn can, but you most certainly cannot." Seeing the scowl on her face, he holds up a hand before she can snap back at him. "You cannot go my dear because King Destruction thinks he killed you in your Keep. If you go walking into town, he will either try to imprison you, or have you killed outright. The peg leg will tell him that you had significant help to survive, so torture would be in order to find out all he can. It has very little to do with your new leg though."

Akita speaks up, "Grace, do they know Jacklyn as your right-hand person? If not, Storm could go with her as two wandering Dark Wizards."

Grace shakes her head, "No, I always left her to mind the Keep."

Void and Wulf arrive at the table and Void speaks, "I was told you had a question for us."

Akita startles and thinks, ["Aphorea, we need to talk. Your helpers are great and wonderful, but it's spooky how automatically they pass messages along without asking or without us realizing one is near us. Oh, and Quinn wants to cook, so maybe, they could supply the Dragons with food and Quinn with the supplies she needs or wants to cook for us."]

Akita turns to Void and Wulf, "Would either of you know of an illusion spell that would make these ladies seem like they have a Dark Magic aura?"

Void scratches his chin, "Let me think on it while you guys' plan."

Wulf shakes his head and puts his hands up, "Void is the expert when it comes to that type of magic. I better defer to him on this one."

Olek suggests, "Okay so we will use a two-pronged approach. Gavin and Skip will use their special talents to go unseen and find the weaknesses of the Keep while Storm and Jacklyn will gather information from the townsfolk and low-level Dark Wizards."

Gavin asks, "Not that I'm opposed to a two-day ride, but is there any way we can get the

Princess to open a portal near Cliffshade? It would cut two days off our trip. Or is there anyone else that can teleport us like that?"

Skip replies, "I will ask the Princess if she can aid us and get us within a short ride or walk of Cliffshade Keep. I think that will be close enough and yet not too close to alert them. We should have Jacklyn and Storm with us when we go, as to not impose on her too much."

Void addresses Jacklyn and Storm, "Pack your gear and I will meet you at the Princess' quarters with Skip and Gavin. I need to gather some items."

Akita looks around and everyone nods in agreement. Gavin, Skip, Storm, Jacklyn, Skrymir, and Void all make their way down to the caves. The rest stay back at the meeting to finish other discussions.

Wulf asks, "What are we going to do about finding recruits to help us fight this battle? We cannot just send out notices to come to the Dragon Temple. We need to be sure of which side they are on from the minute we meet them. Especially, if we can't trust those in our own ranks at the moment."

Earl Jarkon shakes his head, "I am still shocked and angered about Corporal Copperbeard. How do we know who to trust"?

Akita turns to Jarkon, "It is maddening to find someone you trusted betrayed you. The men that poisoned my uncle had been with him for years, but they decided the Dark Wizards were the way to go. However, on to a more present issue. Corporal Copperbeard was working for King Carthon, and he knew the location of our camp. Who knows who he may have told before killing himself?"

Jarkon looks from Akita to Ishvet, "I don't understand this level of hate that these followers of King Carthon have."

Akita sighs and looks down at the table, "We have to be very careful that we don't become the mirror image of King Carthon. We have to make sure that we are fighting him for the greater good of Alahora and not out of personal revenge. If that is what we are doing, we are no better."

Earl Jarkon furls his brow, "Akita you are right. It is very hard for me to separate the ruler from the father. It has started to become more personal for us that love and know Vivian and all the others King Carthon has hurt in his quest for power."

Vicar weighs in, "We can debate the philosophical differences between King Carthon and us all day long, but that won't get Vivian back or stop his reign of terror on anyone that isn't human. Our actions will tell the truth through compassion and morals.

Mandrake then adds, "Also speaking of the truth, I would like to go to Elderwolf Keep to assist Captain Dubbin in finding the traitors, if any, in our midst. We have several truth rings to use, and we need to clean house so to say before we engage King Carthon."

Akita and Earl Jarkon nod their heads in agreement with Mandrake and Vicar. Akita then looks around the table, "I think that will conclude our meeting today. We all have our individual things to do to prepare for the upcoming battle. We'll meet here again tomorrow. Mandrake go ahead to Elderwolf Keep and take Darkwing with you, he likes to question people."

CHAPTER 16

FORGING AHEAD

Shamash and Ixenvorlux find Akita in the dining cave, sipping on a cup of coffee. Shamash sits down in front of her. "Akita, I would like to let you know that Ben will be back on his feet tomorrow and Zold's wing is almost healed as well. We had to remove all the fine poisonous hairs that stuck in her wing from the spider before we could heal it.

Akita swallows and nods, "That is very good to hear. I made light of it when we found them but as we all know this was a very dangerous situation. That is not just my fear of spiders talking either. Rock Spiders are one of the worst."

Shamash laughs, "Yes, my dear, I have to agree with you. Now on another subject. There is one object that we saved from the Keep's Study, the Seeking Shard. I don't know how it survived, but I didn't leave it. Now that we are settled, I have set it up in the war room. I believe it will help us with the recruiting and other issues."

"Wow" exclaims Akita. "That is extremely good news. I had forgotten all about the Seeking Shard. This just made our lives a ton easier for getting the word out. We will have to let Darkwing know when he comes back, as he may want to contact Stan at Darkwing Keep."

Ghod comes into the mess hall to grab a cup of coffee and runs into Akita, Shamash, and Ixenvorlux sitting around a small table. He had just been thinking that he wanted to see Akita to tell her about his secret project and how the Lommas had helped him. He walks over, sits down, and starts talking without being aware of what they were already discussing.

Ghod clears his throat, "Akita, do you remember those runestones we found in the Ice Cave forge? I was able to save them after the wave hit. Well, some of them were actually control stones. With a small bit of help from the Lommas and my genius, I was able to create a Golem. Then using my superior thoughts, I was able to get the Lommas to recreate what I was thinking. So just give the word and you will have an army of Golems to fight with us in the end battle. They don't need food, water, tents, or anything else.

Plus, they fight to the very end and no real person gets hurt."

Before Akita can say a word, Ghod downs his whole cup of steaming coffee in one gulp, gets up from the table and leaves the mess hall. Akita looks at Shamash and Ixenvorlux with a perplexed look. Then looks towards the door where Ghod just exited. She looks back to Shamash, "Did he just say what I think he said?"

Shamash starts to stammer, "I… I… think he did, but I can't be for sure because he said it so fast. And, and, and the coffee must be scalding. Is that an Orc thing?"

Akita gets up as she is talking, "I better get down to the forge and see what he has been up to. Mr. Grumpy may have just given us the edge we will need in this fight."

Ixenvorlux giggles, "He didn't sound too grumpy when he was talking about himself just now."

Akita quickly runs out the door and starts yelling down the hall, "Ghod wait a minute! Ghod slow down, I'm coming to see the Golems."

Skip and Gavin are waiting in the large chamber with Princess Gianna when Void, Storm and Jacklyn arrive. Skip explained the situation to the Princess, and she agreed to send them to the outskirts of Cliffshade. She has only to open the rift with the Earth and Frost amulets to send them on their way.

Void takes one last look at Storm and Jacklyn. He has illusioned them with the look and aura of low-level Dark Wizards. They are in dark purple robes with golden sashes and their faces are transformed into less definable features. Void does a detect magic spell on them both, "Reveal your powers to me." He invokes while holding out his hand.

A light violet glow appears around Jacklyn. Storm also starts to glow, but the aura is much darker and is mixed with green hues. Storm notices the difference and begins to get nervous.

She looks back and forth to Jacklyn and Void, "I don't understand? Did something go wrong with the spell?"

Void motions for Jacklyn to go over next to Skip and then he steps close to Storm, "Storm I have seen this before. I know what you have in you. You seem to be in control so I will not alert the others. You should have told me so that I could adjust the illusion. It is too late now. Just don't get close to any really powerful Dark Wizards and you should be okay. They will be able to sense the demon's power and try to take it for themselves."

Storm swallows hard and takes a deep breath, "Thanks Void, I'm glad it was you that discovered this and not Wulf. I have a pact with the demon, and it will stay at bay until it's needed. Akita knows, so please don't think that you must keep this from her. I guess we should be going now."

The chamber starts to fill with yellow light and a crackling sound through the air. The rift starts too slowly open. The scent of pines wafts through the opening and light filters through the trees from the mid-afternoon sun shines into the room. The princess looks down at the travelers, "I can only hold it open for so long, where are your horses?"

At that moment, Apothecary and Judgement, Mandrake's, and Vicar's horses come trotting into the chamber led by one of the Lommas. Skip turns to Gavin and says, "Well what are you waiting for youngin? Let's jump these horses through the rift."

Gavin smiles a toothy grin and jumps upon Judgments back, "Vicar did say that they ride like the wind."

Both Skip and Gavin on horseback jump through the rift and Storm and Jacklyn take their turn passing through on foot to the other side. Before they enter Visham climbs out from under the collar of Storms cloak to take in the sight. Once they are all through, the princess closes the rift, and the smell of fresh pines dissipates. Void bows to the princess and leaves the chamber.

The first place Meh-Kola thinks to go is a small inn on the outskirts of Dragon Rest. If any guild members are working in the area, they usually end up there. With her blinking ability she is there in no time and is able to scout it out and wait until the cover of darkness to sneak in. She hasn't decided if she wants her presence known yet.

Meh-Kola stays unseen as she sneaks into the rafters of the old inn. Her first observation is no obvious Dark Wizards at any table. However, she feels Dark Magic in the room. It's coming from a man at a corner table, sitting with another who is known as a mercenary leader. At another table across the room is a familiar face. She decides to make herself known to him.

She blinks to right beside him, on the opposite side of where the two men of interest are sitting. They won't be able to see her from where they are, but she can still talk to her friend, "Runt, what are you doing in this area?"

Runt doesn't move a muscle when Meh-Kola blinks into existence beside him. This speaks to his never-surprised personality. He slightly looks down at Meh-Kola, "I could ask you the same thing."

Meh-Kola slightly purrs, "One did say that one is like the wind. One gets from place to place very fast. One wants you to know that the Dark Wizards are going down fast so you might want to get all your gold from them while you can."

Runt slightly smiles, "It will be good to see them gone. They give us assassins a bad name. They never kill quietly or for gold. It's always you're a lizard or you're a demon. It will be nice to get back to just killing for money."

Meh-Kola laughs a little, "You are right Runt. One's business has brought One to the area and One thought you may be able to help One out with a direction."

Runt raises an eyebrow and looks down at Meh-Kola, "Again you want information for free? Word in the Guild is that you were hired by a Duchess as a lap cat. There wouldn't be any truth to that would there?"

Meh-Kola starts to growl, "One would have you watch what you say. I am still the best assassin in Alahora. One only wants you to tell One what you know about the Earl's daughter being kidnapped."

Runt smiles crookedly and puts a hand up, "Okay, okay, I just wanted to see if you still had some fire in you. You're in luck. I do happen to know something about the kidnapping. I was approached by that feller over there in the corner with the mercenary leader Jax. He offered me a whole bag of gems to set up the snatch. I told him no in the end but not before he gave me the rundown of the operation and who wanted it done."

Meh-Kola's wings start to shake with excitement, "Really! How much will it cost One to get that information?"

Runt is silent for a few seconds then he takes a gulp of his ale. He sets the mug down on the table and leans closer to Meh-Kola, "Two deaths in the Inn right now."

Meh-Kola's eyes get big with surprise, "Two deaths right here, right now? Whose deaths, and why?"

Runt smiles again, "The two over in the corner. The same person that wanted the Earl's daughter kidnapped, wants these two dead. He hired me to tie up their loose ends. However, I'm quite comfortable in my seat and you happen to be here wanting information. My job gets done, you get your information, and I don't have to get out of my chair. Does that satisfy you?"

Meh-Kola hesitates for a second to think about Runt's proposition, "Okay, One will do it, but One needs the name first. Plus, One happened to bring One's signature poison with One. Just one drop and they'll be dead."

Runt leans in even closer to Meh-Kola and whispers to her, "King Windu."

Meh-Kola blinks immediately to the rafters above the two men in the corner. She takes a small glass vial out of her pouch and removes the stopper. She tips the vial to the side and lets one drop of the liquid fall into each of the men's mugs. She then blinks to a tree outside of the Inn. She thinks to herself, ["One has to let Akita know this information without Ishvet hearing. He might do something crazy."] The silence of the night is shattered by the agonizing screams of the two men in the Inn as she starts her journey back to the Temple.

Ishvet heads to the top of the temple to look at the night sky. There is not a cloud in the sky and the moon is big and bright. He takes in a big breath of the crisp night air and exhales slowly. He can only think of one thing, ["Vivan why did this have to happen to us and now? It doesn't seem right that our life together has started out in such a rocky way. We should be here together under the stars enjoying life. Not you being held captive and me preparing for war."]

In Ishvet's mind a response starts, ["Don't lose hope young one. I am sorry to intrude, but I was drawn to such pain and anguish. I too have lost the ones I loved so I can feel your pain. I have faith that you will soon be united with Vivian."]

Out of the corner of his eye Ishvet sees Aphorea crawl onto the roof of the temple and lay down beside him. She is cold to the touch, but he can feel a warmth radiate from her. He can only imagine the atrocities that she has lived through having been in the Titan wars and then the slaughter of her kind from the newer races.

Aphorea continues, "When I was young, I was full of life and love. The day the Titans came that all changed. In that day I lost my mother and my mate to the Titan Rovolax. It snatched them out of the sky right in front of me. My heart was torn into pieces, and it took me a long time to let myself open up to anyone again. I learned a valuable lesson in the centuries that followed and that is, we only have this moment and when that moment is gone all we have is the next. You have this moment right now to be strong for Vivian and the people around you. Live in it."

Ishvet is quiet for a moment and then replies, "Aphorea you are right. All we have is this moment and the next isn't promised to us. It is just hard feeling helpless. What do I do?"

Aphorea gets up and walks down the ramp to the lower floor and heads into the temple. She stops halfway in and turns to look at Ishvet, "You prepare for the next moment."

Ishvet shakes his head in a playful way, "Thanks for the wise advice. I guess there is an answer in that somewhere."

He goes to the edge of the roof and looks back up to the sky. The stars are twinkling and shining high above him. He thinks about what Aphorea said and how he can do what she implied. Then it sinks in. He needs to prepare for the next moment. He needs to take his talent to the next level. Since the destruction of Blackwing Keep he hasn't had a chance to train his blue streak ability any further. Now is the time to hone it so that when the next moment comes, he will be ready.

Akita walks into the main hall to help Quinn begin setting up the dining area for a special dinner that she has prepared. Akita has been annoyed by the Lommas ways of instantly making a thought happen, but tonight she needs their assistance. She begins formulating her thoughts. Instantly a Lomma walks up to her, and she looks down and begins her requests, "We need a long table to seat sixteen people. I need another table for the Princess and her guards, with giant size place settings. Once Quinn brings up her dishes, duplicate them on the Princess' table in a size more fitting a Giant. Set all of this up in the middle of the room so that the Griffons, Dragons, Wyverns and all our creature friends can join around us. Please cast an amplification spell from the main table to the Giant's table so they can be part of the conversations. Oh, one more thing, please set up a table with ale off to the side and keep the giants mugs filled as they wish."

The Lomma nods to Akita and turns to fulfill the request. Eight more Lommas arrive in the Main Hall. Magic begins to flow from their hands and all that Akita has requested begins to emerge from the floor. Table and chairs made of the finest mahogany seem to grow from the stone floors. Dishes and goblets then rise from the tabletops.

The larger table and chairs dwarf the regular sized ones in seconds. The final touch is the floating candles and the softest of rugs appearing out of thin air. Quinn walks up to the table and signals for the Lommas to transport all the food that she has fixed into the dining room from the makeshift galley. The food transported for the Giants is enlarged as it hits the table. It is incredible to see a chicken leg become the size of an ostrich leg in a snap.

Akita then speaks to Annut, "Annut would you have our team, that is still here, the Princess, her guards, all of the Griffons, Dragons Wyverns, and other animal friends join us here in the main hall? Include Ben and Scotch in that invite."

Annut speaks to everyone that she needs to, including all the furred, scaled, and feathered friends. Soon all that can be heard is wings and hooves. They all land and or congregate in the outer ring of the Main Hall. As soon as they are settled the team and Giants arrive at the elegant tables and are seated. Large bins of food appear in front of the Dragons and the rest so that everyone will be full by night's end.

As the Princess enters the great hall, she looks around the room. "Lady Blackwing, I am honored to be invited to this dinner, but am impressed to see that you could accommodate our needs."

Akita nods, "You are our guest and just as much a part of this war as anyone. That and the Lommas are little wonders." Akita looks around the room, "Everyone please enjoy Quinn's wonderful food."

As everyone takes their places, Akita moves to the foot of the smaller table, so that she is facing the princess. Wulf, with Dojo, sits by her right side and Sage crawls up onto her shoulder. Ishvet sits to her left and then Earl Jarkon, Ixen, Shamash, General Olek, and Ghod. On the other side next to Wulf is Vicar, Greenbean, Fab Ulous, Grace, Void and Ordyn, with Ben and Scotch at the far end of the table almost under the Giants table.

Akita looks round the room, "My friends it has been a very long time since we have been able to dine and just enjoy each other's company. I do have a few things to talk about, so fill your mouths and enjoy. The aroma in this room is scrumptious, as it looks and smells that Quinn has outdone herself." She looks up to the Princess and her guards, "Can you hear me without my having to yell?"

Princess Gianna smiles, "I suspect this is another intervention of the Lommas. Yes, we can hear you and it is nice to be able to have a conversation like this."

Akita is pleased, "My friends, I know Greenbean and Fabby have been working with our soldiers and magic users. Olek has kept the guards on patrol to keep us safe, as we plan our next steps. In short, everyone has been preparing us for battle in their own ways. Darkwing, Mandrake and Captain Dubbin are investigating at Elderwolf Keep, and we should have word soon on their progress. Meh-Kola is using her talents to find out where Vivian is, so we can go rescue her and set things right. Gavin and Skip are investigating the area round Cliffshade Keep. Jacklyn and Storm are in disguise in the town seeing what information they can glean from the town's folk. And last, but not least, Ghod has been inventing in his usually unusual way."

Akita looks at Ghod who is too interested in food to speak and then continues, "Ghod has come up with a brilliant idea to distract the Dark Wizards." She pauses and Ghod finally looks up and smiles. He then gets back to gnawing on a chicken leg.

Akita shakes her head, "Well, we won't let brilliance get in the way of your stomach Ghod. I will tell your story while you eat. Ghod found a way to use the rune stones that we found in Aphorea's ice cave to give sentience to stone and iron golems. There were only a few of these special stones that we found. However, the Lommas are able to make more stones and are also able to duplicate Ghod's work with the Golems."

Akita again pauses and waits for Ghod to look up. He becomes aware of the silence and finally looks up. He nods his head in agreement before shoving a whole potato in his mouth. Akita starts again, "They have already started to make many copies of each, the runestones and the golems. I have asked for one hundred. They are resistant to magic, but not physical attacks. They will be on the front lines when we attack the Keep. This will keep a majority of the Dark Wizards and whatever foul beasts occupied while we go directly for the Demi-Titan and King Carthon. This will hopefully reduce the number of fatalities of our and Earl Jarkon's men."

General Olek smacks Ghod on the back in congratulations. Ghod immediately lets out a deafening belch that echoes in the great chamber. Everyone stops in mid bite or chew and looks at

Ghod. If red could be seen through his mask, or for that matter on a half-orc's face, he would have been a tomato. Akita gasps and covers her mouth. She looks from Ghod to the princess to see if she is appalled.

The princess looks at Akita and smiles then says, "Everyone, it is a natural process. I am not offended at all. In fact, I would like to thank Ghod for removing the shock everyone may have felt."

Akita is confused for a second at to what the Princess means and then it hits her with great force when the Princess lets out a belch four times as loud as Ghod's and with even more power that several of the floating candles are blown out immediately.

Akita kind of drops back into her seat in disbelief. Wulf takes her hand and then lets out a mild burp then looks to Akita, "If you can't best them, then join them. Several belches can be heard echoing around the Main Hall and several laughs and chuckles. Akita covers her mouth and joins in the activity.

Annut speaks to all of them, "My friends in the Dragon culture it is a compliment to the Gods to belch in thanks for the food that was provided.

The trouble with Dragons is that very quickly a belch can turn into a friend, or the temple being set on fire. So, if the young Dragons will please restrain themselves until they are outside and flying."

Princess Gianna looks around the room, "Since that is out of the way, please do not take what I am about to say as an insult in any way. My father wondered how you all were going to beat this Demi-Titan and a Dark Wizard. Yes, he knows about the Cloud Giants, but he chalked that up to pure luck and the Magma Amulet. With all that said, in the short time I have been here, watching and listening, I believe he would be in awe of you. The strength, determination, loyalty, and skills you all bring together is amazing. I will have to send word to him, that his thoughts and assumptions were wrong. Just like you don't judge a book by its cover, size does not seem to matter either." She looks to Akita, "Once you know where Vivian is, you come find me with your team that is going to rescue her, and we will open a portal to get you there fast and save time."

Akita smiles and nods, "That would be greatly appreciated, as time is not something we have a lot of." Looking back at the table, "Does anyone have anything else to add?" When there is no reply, she looks to the Griffons, Dragons, and Wyverns, "Do any of you have anything would like to say?"

Granit cannot help himself, he speaks in everyone's mind, "All I know is I want to burn those that destroyed our home."

Everyone breaks out laughing. Ordyn and Olek yell "Agreed!"

Akita now looks to Aphorea, Annut Rethu and Thoraxian, "Aphorea do any of you have anything to add?"

Rethu speaks up, "I had lost hope of a day in the future when I would be free to fly the skies of Alahora again. Thank you for giving this Ancient Dragon hope again."

Ghod finally stands, "I want everyone to know that the Golems will only take orders from General Olek. That is how I had the Lommas configure the Runestones. Also, is there any dessert?"

CHAPTER 17
VIVIAN

Vivian has been held captive by King Windu for three days now. She has been kept in a small room with no windows, a small cot and a private nook with a toilet and a sink. The whole area seems to be blanketed by some Dark magic that stifles her abilities. There are always two guards in front of her door, and she hasn't seen King Windu since she first woke up.

He didn't have much to say when they were face to face other than he was on the side of King Carthon and that he would be rich beyond measure for turning her over to King Carthon. He then sent her to her cell to wait. She was only guessing that it had been three days.

On the evening of the third day the guards opened the door and ordered her to the dining hall. As she steps out the guard has her put her hands out and he places imbued cuffs around her wrists. He tells her that they wouldn't want her to try any of her power in an attempt to escape. As soon as the cuffs are on, she can feel her energy drain.

She is seated next to the head of the table and told to wait for King Windu. Moments later King Windu comes sauntering into the Dining Hall holding a very familiar object. He sits and places the flute on the table, "Vivian, do you remember this?" He points to the flute.

He continues in his low smooth voice, "I had you and your friends get this from the Wind Temple. It is very precious to me now that I have figured out its secrets. Do you want to know what it can do? Do want to know why King Cirus had it so well guarded?"

Vivian stays silent for a moment then clenches her jaw, "No, not really, but I am guessing you are going to tell me anyway."

King Windu chuckles, "Yes, you are right. Theres that indignant tone that I remember from you. You and your leader are very much alike. Soon you will both be put in your places, and I will be delighted."

King Windu picks up the flute and smiles, "This not actually a flute. It sounds horrible if you try to play it. I spent months having the best musicians in the land try to play a simple tune on it. None even came close to getting a pleasant note to come out of it. Then in a fit of rage one day I threw the flute against the wall. To my surprise a small scroll fell out of the end. On that scroll was the spell to awaken the flute. Well, it is more of a wand than a flute. It only performs one singular specific type of magic. That is the reason that I do not go anywhere without it now."

Vivian is a bit intrigued but doesn't want to show it to King Windu so she uses a sarcastic tone to see if she can bait him into telling her more, "I'm so happy for you. Another self-proclaimed King with a magical toy. Do you envy King Carthon that much that you are trying to be just like him?"

King Windu's facial expression changes in an instance. He grumbles and furls his brow. In an unnaturally quick motion, he hefts his mass out of his chair and whips the flute around in the air. A powerful gust of wind slams against Vivan and blows her out of her chair and against the wall behind her. The force knocks the breath out of her and the chair she was sitting in is rendered into pieces. The force of the wind holds her in place on the wall several feet above the ground then dissipates. She slides down the wall onto her feet but quickly crumbles to her knees and catches herself with her cuffed hands.

King Windu rushes to her and bends over to whisper in her ear, "I am nothing like that deluded fool. I know it is folly to try to erase a race from the world. I only care about me continuing on and with this flute I can protect myself from even the most powerful of magics. I am sorry that I became so angry. All will be moot soon. You will soon be in the hands of Carthon, and I am sure even you can imagine what your fate will be." He then motions to the guards as he stands back up, "Take her back to the room. The Dark Wizards will be here to collect her tomorrow."

Shamash can be heard before he is seen as he runs to Akita's chamber. He is huffing loudly and the gold chain around his neck can be heard clanging against the top button of his shirt. He enters the doorway of the chamber and stops to pull up his pants that were sliding down from his running.

He takes a deep breath and points at Akita who is already out of bed and grabbing her shadow sword, "Ah… Ah… Akita. Come quick, (deep breath) Meh-Kola is back, and she says she will only speak with you. (another deep breath) She is in my room."

Akita grabs a robe off the bed and runs past Shamash, "Stay here, I'll inform you later."

She gets to Shamash's room and Meh-Kola is sitting on her haunches on Shamash's bed waiting for Akita. Akita looks around the room and sees that the room is empty. She goes up to the bed and then gets down on her knees. She gets close to Meh-Kola so she can speak softly, "Tell me you found something."

Meh-Kola nods her head, "One wanted to tell you alone so that Ishvet won't hear. One found out where Vivian is being held from an old guild friend. Vivian is being held by King Windu at his palace. One thinks he is holding her for King Carthon. One knows that all need to go quick to get Vivian before King Carthon gets her."

Akita swiftly reaches out and grabs Meh-Kola and gives her a tight hug. Akita then pulls back and looks at the furry little creature, "Thank you so much Meh-Kola! I'll get the others and meet you in the Giant Princess' chamber. We are going to need her help. Don't worry I'll make sure

Ishvet doesn't hear about it until we have Vivian safely back here."

Akita then gets up and runs out of the room, down the hallway and stops at Greenbean's room. Greenbean meets her at the door and Akita tells her what is going on. Then Akita moves down to Grace's room, then to Quinn's room and finally back to hers to prepare for a fight.

Within half an hour Akita is in Princess Gianna's room with Meh-Kola, Greenbean, Quinn, and Grace. They are all geared up and waiting for the princess to open a portal to King Windu's Palace.

Akita walks up to the Princess and puts a hand on her hand. The Princess kneels down, and Akita reiterates the plan, "Okay, after you open the portal we are going to run through and take them by surprise. So, make sure to close it quickly behind me. Give us one hour to get Vivian and deal with King Windu. Open up the portal at that time and in the same spot and we will jump back through. If Ishvet finds out after we leave under no circumstances let him follow us to King Windu's."

Princess Gianna nods, "Don't worry young Akita, I will make sure I get you back and that Ishvet stays here. Are you ready?"

Akita looks to her sisters in arms, "Yes, we are ready. Open it up.

Princess Gianna clasps the two amulets around her neck and holds her free hand out in front of her. A crackling fills the air, and a thin golden line appears in front of the crew. It slowly widens until it is about four feet wide and about ten feet tall. Meh-Kola blinks through first and takes out a guard standing outside of the room that the rift is opening into. Greenbean and Quinn follow, and Akita and Grace quickly fall in behind. As soon as they are through the rift closes.

It has been a few hours since they all stepped through the rift into the small clearing. Skip and Gavin immediately started to set up camp. Storm and Jacklyn gathered some firewood and went out as far as the main road to see if there was anyone traveling to Cliffside. They saw several processions of wagons and Dark Wizards on horseback heading to the town gates.

After getting back to camp they all decide to head into town as the sun starts to set. Storm and Jacklyn will try to find out some information in Cliffside and Skip and Gavin will split up and use their skills to uncover any weaknesses in Cliffshade Keeps defenses.

Just after dusk, Storm and Jacklyn step out of the wooded area about a quarter mile from town. Skip and Gavin departed quickly and are nowhere to be seen. Soon they are on the main road into town. They can see no one in front of them or behind them, as they make their way to the town gates.

As the gate comes into view, Jacklyn notices more guards than usual. "Let me do the talking. They have more than doubled the guard. It does me no good to find anyone I know, because of the disguise, but I might know who I can coerce if need be."

Storm nods, "I will follow your lead. Let's just hope they are not suspicious of two female Elven Dark Wizards coming into town for supplies?"

Jacklyn lowers her voice, "Just act angry and uninterested and we should be fine."

A large guard with a long Polearm steps up to them as they reach the gate, "Where are you two going in Cliffside? Are you here for the recruitment or are you here for something else?"

Jacklyn looks the guard straight in the eyes and furls her brow, "We're here to eat and get supplies. Move aside you're slowing us down."

Storm steps up and gets in the guard's face, "Have you ever been a pile of ash? Let us through or you'll answer that question as yes next time!"

A second guard steps up, "Ladies there's no need for that. We are just required to ask. Just know security is in place to keep out spies, obviously you both are Dark Wizards, so have a good time in Cliffside. Might I suggest my wife's bistro for your lunch, just up the road."

Storm replies, "Does she serve eel eggs? If she doesn't, she won't have our business."

The guard begins to stammer. Storm grabs Jacklyn by the arm and pulls her around the first guard, "That's what I thought. We'll be on our way now."

Proceeding through the gate, she whispers to Jacklyn, "That was too fun. We are definitely not going anywhere near his wife's bistro."

Jacklyn leans over to Storm and whispers, "I thought you might have overdone it, but that worked pretty well."

Storm just looks over to Jacklyn and smiles a satisfied grin.

As they head down the now cobblestone street, the buildings on both sides are two- and three-story mudbrick and wood, with crude tile roofs. Only the street lanterns can be seen further ahead on the main road to Cliffshade Keep. They imagine that homes closer to the Keep are grand estates of Dark Wizards that are strong enough to be personal guard of King Carthon.

As they observe the townspeople going about their evening with trades and sales of homemade goods, they move further into the town to a small tavern with a half-way decent outdoor patio. They sit down at a table to await service.

A young woman in a short dress and a too tight blouse saunters up to the table. She has a thick layer of red wax on her lips and bright purple eye powder around her eyes. Her hair is blonde and curly and teased out by six inches all around her face. She seems very put out because Jacklyn and Storm sat down. She is obviously more interested in who is walking by and noticing her rather than serving customers.

Finally, after a pause and a dirty look, "What's your order? I ain't got all day.". Stopping abruptly as she sees a good-looking young dark Wizard walking past. In a high-pitched voice, "Hi, Hansel, you coming by later?"

The Dark Wizards barely looks over to the server and keeps on walking. The server huffs, "Well, he must not have heard me, anyway… you twos gonna order or what?"

Storm looks to the waitress, "Soup and bread, and we are in a hurry."

Jacklyn nods and looks at the server, "Yes, quick and simple just like you."

The waitress glares at them and marches off to get their order. As she gets to the door, another young Dark Wizard is walking by. Flipping her hair and swinging her hips, "Hi! Sturm!" she says in a bright voice. He too ignores her and walks on by. Clenching her fists and stomping her feet she lets out a huff of frustration, and marches into the tavern.

Jacklyn whispers to Storm, "Can you believe that hussy? Looks like the men around here have her number. She is drama, trouble, and lazy. She is trying way too hard.

The waitress comes back out with the ale and bread, just plopping them down on the table, and stomps off again. A few minutes later she appears with the two bowls of soup, almost dropping them down on the table. "Anything else?"

Storm shoos her away with a wave of her hand to show her that she is as unimportant as she is acting like they are.

After a mediocre meal they head down the street and see a well-kept specialty shop. The sign on the door says, "MADAM SUZIE'S SHOP OF CURIOSITIES".

Jacklyn stops and points to the shop, "For some reason I have a memory of this place."

Storm thinks for a minute. "Well, maybe we should stop in and act like we are shopping. Plus, the shop owner may have some good information."

Jacklyn concurs, "I feel like I have been here before. Hopefully, these illusions hide any familiarity."

As they step through the door, they find a spacious shop with many shelves and tables cluttered with all kinds of candles, dried animal parts and jars of powders and liquids. In the back of the shop is a round table with a dark tablecloth and a crystal ball on a small gold stand. Behind the crystal ball is a handsome older woman with a colorful headwrap and an equally as colorful dress that seems to have many layers of sheer fabric.

The woman behind the table doesn't speak. She gestures with her hands for the two ladies to sit. As Jacklyn and Storm walk towards the table two wooden chairs appear from nothing in front of the table.

Storm looks over to Jacklyn with a nervous expression. Jacklyn nods back to her to give the okay to sit. They sit in the newly formed chairs and stare at the woman across from them. The woman leans in close to the crystal ball and her reflection can be seen in the crystal ball, but it is upside down.

The woman smiles and in a smooth warm voice she greets them, "Hello ladies, I'm Madam Suzie, knower of the unknown, temptress of fate, and brewer of concoctions. I saw that you would enter my shop today. I have been waiting for you."

Jacklyn tenses up and a cold chill runs up and down her back. Through gritted teeth she asks, "Did you really?"

Storms interrupts and grabs Jacklyn's hand, "Wait, do you say that to everyone that comes into your shop? I've seen charlatans on the streets be more convincing."

Madam Suzie puts her hands on the crystal ball and closes her eyes, "Theres no need to lie to me Storm Fireheart. I can sense the companion that you bring here with you. No, I don't mean you Jacklyn Moondancer of the Lunais Clan or little Visham."

Storm is stunned and in awe. Rixan writhes inside Storm and bellows to make Madam Suzie stop. Storm instinctively reaches up and covers her ears to no avail. She blurts out, "Rixan quiet!"

Jacklyn is confused as to how Madam Suzie knows her last name and she doesn't even remember it. A sense of dread comes over her but instantly calms down as she feels Madam Suzie grab her hand from across the table. Madam Suzie hushes them, "Please don't be frightened. No harm will come from me. All four of you are safe in here."

Jacklyn pulls her hand away, "What do you mean all four of us? There is just the two of us and Visham."

Storm clears her throat to get Jacklyn's attention, "Jacklyn, I have a demon inside me. His name is Rixan and Madam Suzie can sense him. He can feel her power and is frightened by it. I didn't mean to keep it a secret, but Aphorea and Akita have asked me to keep it quiet."

Again, Jacklyn is stunned and almost at a loss for words. Then she remembers Void talking to Storm before they went through the rift and wonders if it was about the Demon. She turns towards Storm, "Did Void discover your secret before we left?"

Storm closes her eyes and looks down at the table. In a soft voice she replies, "Yes. He warned me about the danger it posed by keeping the secret from him. He said it might put the mission in jeopardy."

Madam Suzie stands and reaches out over the table, "He was right. Stand and take my hands."

Storm and Jacklyn stand and clasp each other's hands and reach out and grab Madam Suzie's hands. They can feel a jolt of power surge from Madam Suzie into them and connect where they are holding each other's hands. Visions start to appear in the crystal ball. First is a scene of a group of Dark Wizards surrounding the both of them. Then it fades into a scene of Rixan emerging from Storm in a dark alleyway. The final vision in the crystal ball is Storm on Visham flying at dawn.

Madam Suzie releases their hands and Jacklyn and Storm fall back into their chairs. Madam Suzie makes a tsking sound with her tongue, "Jeopardy it seems is coming your way tonight."

When the sun retreats behind the forest Skip and Gavin go in opposite directions. Gavin heads North through the forest to get to the most exposed side of Cliffshade Keep. Skip heads south around Cliffside to get down to the coast and docks.

Gavin conceals himself until he gets to the northern woods on the opposite side of the main road from Darkforest. He can see a very tall pine tree at the edge and decides that it will be a good perch to observe from. He climbs the tree like he has known it all his life and the branches at the top bend into a makeshift bench for him to sit on comfortably.

Gavin starts mentally reaching out to the animals around him. He senses a warren of bunnies and fox den nearby, but he's really looking for some flying help. Joining minds with the smaller birds can be a challenge, but he coaxes it into being his eyes. He enters a deep meditation and melds with the bird.

The sparrow he has connected with gives the feeling of uneasiness being so close to the Keep. It shows Gavin images of its friends being zapped out of the sky as sport for the Dark Wizards in the Keep. However, Gavin is able to convey the importance to the small bird of how he needs to see around the castle.

Gavin has the bird fly to the north side and look around. The first obstacle is a very tall and thick wall protecting this side of the castle. The wall goes all the way from Cliffside, around the castle of the Keep and then to the cliffs that drop one hundred feet straight down into the ocean. The bird follows the wall around and Gavin takes notice of several high windows and balconies on the castle's north side but really no points of entry for anyone on foot.

After the wall ends at the cliff, there is a rocky coastline with jagged rocks and outcroppings. There is no way to get a boat safely to the Keep from the north without the danger of sinking or being seen. He wonders if an aerial attack by the Griffons might be the best course of action for the northern side of the Keep.

Time passes quickly when he is in this state and it is now becoming too dark to see much detail except the lantern light coming from the windows of the castle. He releases his connection to the sparrow and wakes from his meditation. Soon he will need to meet back at the clearing with the others so they can make their journey back to the Dragon Temple.

Skip makes his way south along the road to the outskirts of Cliffside. The town has a tall wall surrounding it so he can use it as cover until he makes his way to the shoreline. The smell of the salt spray tells him that he is getting closer, and the caw of seagulls gives him an idea of how he can see without being seen.

Where the wall of the town ends there is a sheer cliff with several staircases going down affixed to the cliff face. He won't need the stairs because he has his enchanted rope with him. He ties the rope to a small tree and throws it over the cliff then begins to shimmy down. Once down to the bottom he can see the entirety of the Cliffshade docks, and several ships moored.

On this side of the docks is a thin shoreline with several big boulders. He quickly hides behind one and begins reaching out with his mind to a seagull. He finds on atop the mast of the ship closest to where he is. He exerts little effort to control the mind of the bird. Once he is locked in, he takes flight.

He can see several sailors on the ships drinking and having a good time in the cool night air. Closer to the cliff he can see guards patrolling the docks. Directly below the Keep of Cliffshade is an inlet covered by two enormous wood and iron gates. They are big enough for the biggest ship he has ever seen to sail right in. He now understands what Meh-Kola was describing to the team.

He knows that any assault against those doors would be difficult even if the Dragons were busting them down. He will need to find another way that soldiers could sneak in. He flies the seagull higher and over the bay. He can see a large shadow on the seabed of the bay. From what he can make out, it appears to be the Demi-Titan Jessa. It is not moving much, and he wonders if it is gathering strength.

As the bird moves closer to the large doors, he can see an eight-foot round opening between the dock stairs and the doors. With the birds' senses he can smell that it is some kind of drainage system for the town and Keep. He has the seagull land right at the opening. There are no bars or doors covering it. He can sense something that feels like Grizzels inside. They are tiny, thin, and dirty beings with long pointy ears, long arms, and hands with sharp claws. They are only two feet tall but are lightning fast and will swarm their victims in groups. They are going to have to be careful because Grizzels are cunning and dangerous.

Grizzels are blood thirsty as well as armed with ragtag armor pieces and weapons from their victims. They are smarter than the dozen or so Trolls that seem to be camped around the walls of the city. Trolls are simply big green lummoxes', see it, smash it, and eat it, beings. They do have fires for cooking and warmth but can live without fire. They carry big clubs, crude daggers and furs that are barely better than rags. However, they can still squeeze a person to death or crush their heads to mush with their bare hands. Both are formidable dark creatures on their own but being influenced by the Dark Wizards makes them double the trouble.

He knows that there are more than Grizzels inside he can hear the familiar clicking of the Rock spiders that are lurking in the drainage tunnels as well. He can only sense smaller creatures like rats and bugs besides the Grizzels, and Rock spiders. He is sure that they will be helping the Dark Wizards fight in the upcoming battle and would pose a danger to anyone entering the Keep this way.

He takes in as much detail as he can the rest of the night so he can report back to the team. Soon the sun will be coming up and he needs to meet the others back at the clearing in the woods before they make their way back to the Dragon Temple. He releases the seagull using his concealment ability and makes his way back to the rope. He knows that no one has seen it because it blends in with the rock of the cliff. In fact, it blends in with anything that it is in front of or laying on.

In very little time he is to the road by the wall. He can hear a commotion just inside the town walls. Several people are running out of the main gate. One of them is Jacklyn. He is surprised that she is running but even more surprised that her disguise is gone. He catches up to her and grabs her by the arm, "I'll conceal us so we can reach the forest undetected. I can sense that Gavin is close to us but can't sense Storm. What happened?"

Jacklyn shakes her head back and forth, "Wait until we are back at camp, and I'll tell you everything while we pack up and get back to the Dragon Temple as quickly as possible. I think they are going to be searching for us at first light."

The room completely darkens as the rift closes behind them. Meh-Kola immediately tells them that she has subdued a guard that was in the hallway. Akita moves to the door and looks out into the hallway and can see both ways. There are candles on the wall about every six feet.

She stops in the doorway and keeps the others from stepping into the candlelight. Meh-Kola is hovering by her head. She turns to Meh-Kola and whispers, "Go ahead and try to find us a way that we won't get detected and find Vivian."

In a blink Meh-Kola is gone and Akita steps further into the dark room. She gently snaps her fingers, and a small flame appears on her pointer finger. The small flame illuminates all their faces. Quinn looks very nervous. Akita reaches out her free hand and places it on Quinn's shoulder. She can feel her tense body sort of relax. Akita whispers to her, "It's okay Quinn, we are all on edge. We are going to find Vivian. This is your first time on a mission, isn't it?"

Quinn doesn't dare speak for fear that she will be too loud and alert someone to their location. She nods her head in affirmation. Then gives a slightly nervous smile. Greenbean reaches over and grabs Quinn's hand, "Don't worry, I've seen your fighting ability. You can take on anything." Quinn smiles fully now and relaxes a little bit more.

They sit in silence for the next few minutes until Meh-kola pops back into the room. Akita turns towards the door and the others huddle behind her to hear what Meh-Kola has to report. Meh-kola lands on the ground and everyone kneels down around her.

Meh-Kola starts talking in her normal volume of voice and she can see everyone jump in fear. She puts a paw up to calm them down, "One can speak this loudly. There is no one around this area. The only guard is dead. One has seen Vivian. One told her to be ready. She is down the hall from the dining room. One knows how to get there, but One sees a problem."

Akita asks, "What's the problem?"

Meh-Kola starts again, "King Windu is in the dining room with ten of his guards. Once we get to the dining room we will have to fight. One will go directly to Vivian and get her out of her cell. One will take Greenbean's extra short sword to her, so she can fight too."

Grace scoots closer to Meh-Kola and speaks through gritted teeth, "I want Windu for myself. I have a score to settle with him. I'm telling you right now Akita, no one can get in my way. He or I will die this night."

Akita can see and hear the determination that Grace has. She disagrees with letting Grace take him on by herself but knows that she shouldn't stop her. She grabs Graces knee, "Okay, but if he hurts you, I personally will make him a pile of ashes on the floor."

Grace nods in agreement and feels both Greenbean's and Quinn's hands on her back. Thay all stand back up and Greenbean gives Meh-Kola her short sword. Meh-Kola takes it and put it in her special pouch. Then Greenbean draws her great sword to get ready for the upcoming fight. Grace follows suit and draws her enchanted cutlass. Akita starts producing a concentrated fireball in her right palm and Quinn conjures a flame sword in her right hand.

Meh-Kola can see that they are all ready, "One will blink to Vivian. You take the left hallway to the corner then straight into the dining room. When One hears fighting, One will come with Vivian."

Meh-Kola blinks away and the rest start down the hallway. When they get to the corner of the hallway, they can hear King Windu talking to his guards. They rush along the wall and almost jump into the open. Greenbean grunts and the guards snap around and look at her for a second trying to understand what is going on. Before they can even move, Akita throws her fireball at the closest guards' feet.

The fireball explodes and flings two guards over the long dining table. Greenbean and Quinn rush in and start slashing at the guards that are still upright. Grace pushes past them and heads straight for King Windu. Akita watches Grace slide past a few wild slashes from the guard's sword. An instant thought flashes through her mind, ["Wow, Grace really took to her peg leg."].

Quinn puts down two guards, and Greenbean puts down three as Vivian hurries into the dining room. They can hear her yelling something in a panicked voice but can't quite make it out.

Akita rushes to Vivian and Grace comes into striking distance of King Windu. He stood up in front of his grand oversized dining chair. Grace lunges for Windu as she hears Vivian.

Vivian yells out as she enters the room, "Stop he has the flute!"

Akita finally comprehends what Vivian is saying as she sees Grace lunge towards King Windu. Akita isn't quick enough to get to them or to throw a fireball at King Windu.

King Windu stands silently in front of his chair as Grace lunges at him. He raises his hand with the flute and points it at Grace. A blast of wind slams against Grace and blows her up against the wall behind her. With a flick of King Windu's wrist, the wind cuts into Grace's body and the stone wall she is pressed up against. In a mere few seconds Grace is cut into pieces and they fall to the floor.

Akita launches a fireball towards King Windu. It engulfs him in fire. The fire swirls around him then dissipates. He is untouched by the fire. He seems to me protected by a shell of wind.

Meh-Kola tries to blink beside King Windu to slice open his throat but is bounced away by the wind shell. Vivian tries to blast him with a wave of pure light, but it also bounces away. Greenbean slices at him but again the slice is deflected by the shell.

King Windu walks over to where Grace lays dead. He shakes his head in disgust, "Grace O'Malley is no more. At least she died fighting. Which of you will be next? Come Meh-Kola use your tricks and try to get me. No? Okay How about you kitchen wench? Do you want to try your fire sword? Akita what do you have to combat me? You have already wasted the Magma Amulet on King Cirus so that can't help you here. Even Vivian's pure light cannot penetrate my wind barrier.

Akita screams at the top of her lungs in anguish. If the rest of the Keep wasn't awake, they are now. She growls, "Windu how could you! You are a monster and an illegitimate King. I will find a way to avenge Grace. In fact, I have a way right now. Meh-Kola now!"

Meh-Kola blinks to Akita's shoulder then both of them blink away.

King Windu starts to chuckle, "Blinking around isn't going to help you Akita Black… ugh…wing."

A black sword slowly emerges from the front of King Windu's chest. The blade is almost smoke and seems to be in some sort of dual state of existence. The protruding blade stops then swiftly recedes into his chest. King Windu is gasping and clasps at his chest wound, "How… No… can't… Damn you…"

King Windu falls to his knees and then face first to the floor. The flute hits the floor and bounces then rolls over to the wall. Vivian grabs it and throws it into the air towards Akita and Akita swings her enchanted smoke sword and it slices the flute in half. The two pieces hit the floor and the magic that was inside visibly leaves the flute in a whisp of blue.

Quinn projects a column of flame at it and the wood is reduced to ashes. Greenbean walks up to the ashes and crushes them under her boot. Vivian runs up to Akita and hugs her. Tears are streaming down her face. Akita grabs her and starts to cry too. Quinn and Greenbean surround them and put a hand on Vivian's back.

Through tears and sobs Vivian tries to speak, "I never wanted this to happen. I never wanted anyone to lose their life to save mine. How will I ever live with this guilt?"

Akita pulls back from Vivian and sheaths her sword. She then puts her hands on Vivans shoulders, "Viv you stop that right now! This was not your fault! Grace was going after Windu whether it was to save you or not. She knew the risks; she just didn't know that he would be able to use such a powerful item on her. We will mourn her when we get back to the Temple. We need to get back to the rift and out of here before the rest of the guards get here. Greenbean and Quinn will you please grab that tablecloth over there and wrap up Grace. We have to take her back with us. I'm not leaving her here."

Greenbean and Quinn wrap up Grace and Meh-Kola blinks her to the storeroom to await the rift. By the time the others get to the room, the rift has reappeared. Meh-Kola blinks the body through the rift into the Princess' room. Akita, Greenbean, and Quinn walk through the rift behind Meh-Kola.

Ishvet is waiting next to the Princess. He doesn't see Vivian but sees Meh-Kola with what appears to be a body. He yells out and runs over to Graces body, falling to his knees. Akita runs over to him and pulls him up before he can uncover Grace, "No, Ishvet! That's not Vivian. She is fine."

Akita turns Ishvet's body towards the rift as Vivian comes through. He jumps up and grabs hold of her. Tears are welling up in everyone's eyes. Ishvet is telling Vivian how much he loves her as the rift closes behind them. Shamash runs into the Princess' room and sees the body on the ground. He stops next to Akita and puts an arm around her.

He speaks with a labored breath, "Annut just let all of us know that Grace has been killed. Please tell me that you did away with King Windu."

Akita turns and hugs Shamash and then sees Wulf race into the doorway. She rushes to Wulf and buries her face in his neck and sobs, "It's happened again, we have to bury another of our friends and I'm so frightened that she won't be the last. I can't bear it. Please take me back to the room. I need to have a breakdown in a hot bath."

CHAPTER 18

RIXAN REVEALED

Theres a loud bang on Madam Suzie's shop door. So loud that it startles Jacklyn and Storm from their fugue. Madam Suzie knows that it is the Keep Guards and jumps up from her chair. Jacklyn and Storm do the same.

Madam Suzie opens the curtain behind her and motions for them to go through. As Storm passes, she points to the back, "There is a door to the back alley. Go out the door and turn right towards the center of town. You should be able to make it to the gate from there."

Storm hesitates, "Will we see you again?"

Madam Suzie pauses for a second, "I will see you soon. We will fight together. Now go before they break the door down!"

The ladies hurry through the storeroom to the back door and fling it open. Stepping out into the alleyway and closing the door behind themselves. It is pitch black, but they know to turn right. They take two steps to the right then the alley fills with light.

In front of them is a short man in a dark robe and two guards. The short man has an orb of light hovering above him. They swiftly turn around and see four more guards to the left. The ladies are trapped. They turn back to the short man.

Jacklyn steps in front of Storm and towards the short man, "Let us through."

The short man giggles, "No, there will be none of that until we see who you are."

The orb of light gets brighter and reveals both of them and the face of the short man. Jacklyn gasps and takes a step back, "I know you. You are Aevid Chaos the Dark Wizard and left hand to King Carthon. I don't know how I know that, but I do."

Storm grabs Jacklyn by the hand, "Whatever Madam Suzie did must have given your memory back."

Jacklyn squeezes Storms hand, "I think you are right. Images are flooding my mind, and I can remember the wave now."

Aevid steps closer, "Well I don't know you. Who do you report to? What guild do you belong to?"

Storm tries to think of something quickly that will get them out of this situation, but nothing comes to mind. Then she can feel a familiar unpleasant feeling. Like she is being ripped apart from the inside out. She reaches out and pushes Jacklyn to the ground.

Jacklyn looks up at Storm wondering why she pushed her to the ground when they were trying to get away. Then she can see that Storm is in some kind of pain. Her face is twisting, and she is groaning. Jacklyn can also see that Storm is growing taller and wider. Her robe is starting to split down the back and across the sleeves. She is turning into something else.

Rixan takes over Storms body and begins changing it to his likeness. In less than a minute she is invisible with his transformation into a dark green, thin, muscular demon. He is covered in pustules and oozing green mucus. He is eight-foot—tall and has razor sharp teeth behind decaying tattered lips. His eyes glow a putrid yellow.

When Aevid sees this creature towering over him he starts to shake in his robes. He sends a defensive knockback spell at the creature, but the creature deflects it to the side like a fly. Rixan takes a step forward and Aevid is stuck in place. The two guards beside him turned and run down the alley. Before Rixan can even turn around, he can hear the other guards run down the other side of the alley.

Rixan turns to Jacklyn, in a guttural deep and wet voice he speaks to her, "Run back to where we started."

Jacklyn hops up onto her feet and begins to run down the alley. She knows this is her chance to get out of town. She looks back and can see Visham on Rixan's shoulder. She is relieved that the little creature is okay.

Aevid is still frozen scared in place. He tries another more powerful spell and again it is brushed away by Rixan. Instead Rixan steps forward and is almost over Aevid. Aevid stares up and is trembling, "Uh…. Uh… never mind. You can go now. I don't need to know who you are."

He turns to run out of the alleyway but can feel a tug on his robe. Rixan had reached out and grabbed the robe with one finger, keeping Aevid in place. Aevid tries with all his might to break free but can't move or get his robe off.

Rixan leans down until his head is directly over Aevid. Drool and mucus drip down onto the hood of Aevid's robe. Rixan slightly growls, "Where do you think you are going little man? You wanted to hurt us. Now you shall nourish me."

The sound of water being poured onto brick starts to echo down the alley. Aevid can hear it too and wonders where that sound is coming from. Then he feels the warm sensation on his own leg, and he then knows that he has wet himself. At first, he feels embarrassment then he returns to fear.

Rixan is still directly over Aevid, and mucus and saliva are still dripping on Aevid. Aevid hears a new sound and is able to turn his head slightly to the left. On the wall next to him he can see the shadows cast by his light orb. He can see Rixan standing over him by the shadow cast. The noise is growing louder, and it sounds like a hundred knuckles being cracked. It echoes just like when he urinated on himself and the ground.

The shadow begins to change shape over Aevid's shadow. What he can make out to be the creature's mouth is opening wider and wider. Soon it will be bigger than Aevid is wide. Before Aevid can think another thought the shadow envelopes him. Aevid is instantly killed and melted in Rixan's mouth like a sugary confection. Rixan swallows and absorbs all of Aevid's power and soul.

The alleyway is pitch dark now and no one can see as Storm returns to herself. She knows that the guards will return and probably bring more Dark Wizards with them. She asks Visham to change into a full-grown Wyvern as she runs out the alleyway into the dim lights of the street lanterns.

Visham enlarges and lowers down for Storm to get on his back. She pats his neck and tells him to make for the Temple. As they fly over the city walls, they can see that Jacklyn has made it out and is running in the direction of the clearing. When they are past the forest, they can see the beginning of the sunrise on their right over the ocean. Storm hopes that the others will make it back to the Dragon Temple safely.

King Carthon hears the sounds of guards running in the hallway towards his room. He doesn't sleep anymore so it doesn't wake him. He hears an angry squall from Hector who was sleeping on the balcony. King Carthon gets up and walks towards Hector, "Now, now my friend I can't have you eating my guards because they woke you from your slumber. I will punish them and make sure they don't make noise in the future."

Hector shakes his feathers and puts his face under his wing as King Carthon heads to the door. As the guard's approach, Carthon flings open the door and points at the guards. They freeze in mid stride. Carthon used a delay time spell on them. They can still see and hear but can't move a muscle. King Carthon approaches them, "If you are not coming to report an attack from Lady Blackwing and her merry misfits, I may have to turn you into fish and feed you to Hector. He is quite unhappy that you have clambered through the halls in the most noisily of fashion waking him from his pleasant dreams." He walks to the back of them and stays silent for a moment, "You know you can still feel pain when you are in this state."

King Carthon holds his hand up with the palm facing the two guards. Muffled screams of pain start to be heard from them as Carthon inflicts a pain spell on them. The delay time spell dissipates, and the guards fall to the floor. Their swords and armor hit the stone blocks with a loud clanging. They try to catch themselves before any more noise is made.

They look up at King Carthon and can see the disdain on his face. He walks past them back into his room, "Come along you buffoons, I don't have all night."

The guards quickly stand with as little noise as possible and make their way to King Carthon. They both bow and in unison whisper, "Sorry your Highness, we won't do it again your Highness. Please forgive us."

Carthon hasn't sat down yet, so he quickly turns to the guards, "Which of you has the most knowledge of what you are about to tell me?"

The guard on the left raises his hand, "I saw it with my own eyes Sire."

Without hesitation, King Carthon raises his arm and flicks his wrist and the guard on the right is transfigured into a fish. The guards' clothes, armor and sword fall to the ground covering the flopping fish beneath them. Carthon motions to the other guard to pick up the fish out of the pile and toss it to Hector. The guard is trembling as he riffles through the clothes and grabs ahold of the fish that was his friend and tosses it towards Hector.

Hector smelled the fish before he saw it and popped his head up from under his wing. He stretched forward and took the fish into his beak and then tossed into the air with a flip of his head, the fish flipped up and went straight down Hector's gullet. Hector then looked over at the other guard and squalled. The guard jumped back in fear but quickly composed himself. Hector returned his head to under his wing.

Carthon sits in his drawing room chair and motions for the guard to give his information. The guard steps up to the table, "Sire there has been an incident in Cliffside tonight. I was guarding Aevid tonight when he sensed an odd kind of magic. He pinpointed the location of the magic at Madam Suzie's shop. We went to investigate and saw two low level Wizards with her. We cut them off from escaping out the back into the alley but that is where things went wrong. One of the Wizards turned into a monster and ate Wizard Aevid whole. I saw the whole thing with my own eyes."

Carthon sits back in his chair and ponders what the guard has just told him. A mix of anger and joy fill his mind. He is definitely angry that someone was able to defeat Aevid so easily but a joy to him that the little pain in the behind is gone. He sits forward a little, "Can you describe the two women that you saw at Madam Suzie's?"

The guard stops and thinks for a few seconds, "They were dressed as Wizards, and both looked to be human from what I could see. Then the one transformed into some big creature like a Demon and then went back to a lady. The lady it transformed back into looked a lot different than before she transformed."

King Carthon raises his hand for the guard to stop talking, "So she looked one way before she changed and then another. That means that she is either a shapeshifter or she had an illusion spell on her. That, however, doesn't explain the Demon that ate Aevid. Go and get Madam Suzie and bring her to me."

The guard bows and then turns abruptly and slowly makes his way down the hall to the stairs, being very careful not to make any noise. He heads down the stairs and to the town to get Madam Suzie.

Madam Suzie sits at her table with four guards around her. Two behind her blocking the storeroom door and two in front of her. She is quite perturbed that these men are muddying her floor and looking through her wares. They have been here for about an hour now and are constantly asking her about the two women that she had in her shop.

She refuses to answer any questions and that only makes the guards angrier. They threaten to break everything in her shop if she doesn't cooperate. Still, she says nothing as glass shatters and wood splinters around her. Before long a few other guards enter the shop and are all telling their version of what happened to Aevid and how if they had been there, they could have saved him.

The murmur is broken by a guard rushing through the front door, sweating, and panting. He yells to the highest-ranking guard that King Carthon wants to see Madam Suzie immediately.

The guard Captain orders the other guards to escort Madam Suzie to the Keep. They all surround her and walk her up to the Keep and then only the guard that Carthon ordered to get her takes her the rest of the way to King Carthon's chamber.

Madam Suzie thinks it's all a grand spectacle. All these guards for a little old fortune teller. However, she is somewhat curious to meet King Carthon since his change to the darkness.

King Carthon waits for them with the door to his chamber open. When they enter, he motions for Madam Suzie to sit across from him at his table and waves away the guard. She sits and stares at him and he does the same to her.

He lays the Sea Amulet down on the table in front of Madam Suzie but closer to himself. He points to the Amulet, "This will glow when you lie to me, but we both know that you won't lie. You will speak in riddles like you always have since I was a child visiting your shop. Let's try to make this as painless for me as we can and just be plain with me."

Madam Suzie glances at the Sea Amulet then back to King Carthon and looks directly into his eyes, "I remember a little boy that was so curious and innocent. I can't see him in your eyes anymore. Did the darkness devour him like the Demon devoured poor little Aevid?"

Carthon huffs, "That little runt got what he deserved. I couldn't care less about him. There will be another to take his spot in no time. I'm more interested in this Demon you mentioned and the two women that were with you in your shop tonight. Are they affiliated with Akita Blackwing?"

Madam Suzie slightly smiles, "Oh you should be interested in the Demon. It has a part to play in your future. As for the two ladies, I am positive that you will see them again in the near future and they will be accompanying Lady Akita Blackwing."

Carthon furls his brow and sort of grits his teeth, "Always telling me just the edge of the truth and future. Never the whole story. I should have you executed for conspiring with the enemy. However, I know how your type of magic works and I would be cursed and haunted for the rest of my days by your unrelenting spirit. So just tell me one more thing before I send you back to your shop. When is Akita coming to engage me?"

Madam Suzie closes her eyes and reaches her hand across the table, palm up. King Carthon reaches out his hand and grabs hers. She begins to mutter a string of words that he can't understand. She abruptly stops and opens her eyes, "I see the full moon in the sky and three days of rain proceeding it. The time is closer than you think. I see stone and fire beating at your gates. I hear screams of Dragons and Demons echoing in your halls. The time is closer than you think."

She lets go of his hand and he sits back in his chair. She could see the slightest tinge of fear on his face. She knows that he is trying to hide it from her. She stands and bows to him then makes her way out of the chamber.

King Carthon watches her leave. When she is gone, he jumps up and closes the door then hurries back to the table. He picks up the Sea Amulet and holds it in his hands. He squeezes it between his hands, and it glows and pulses. He brings it close to his face, "You told me that I would be unstoppable. You said that I would have all the power I needed to beat Akita and her friends. Now this soothsayer alludes to my destruction. Tell me what I need to do to ensure my victory."

King Carthon begins to hear the whispers of the Dragon souls within the Sea Amulet. Only he can hear them. They are directly in his head. He listens to what they tell him and a big smile gleams across his face. When they stop, he runs to the door and calls for Volaern, his second in command.

Volaern rushes in and King Carthon explains all that has transpired this night. He also explains what the Amulet has told him and how they can defend themselves against the Dragons. He then asks Volaern when the next full moon is. Volaern stops and thinks and tells him that it will be in two weeks. They now know when Akita will attack the Keep.

Storm and Visham see the Temple just ahead of them. They have been flying the whole day to reach the Temple. She is so exhausted but needs to get to Akita before she can sleep. As Storm slides off Visham, the Lommas appear and conjure a meal for him. ["Visham, you eat and relax. Find me with Akita or in our room when you are finished. We have been very busy."]

Storm asks a Lomma to have Akita come to her quarters, as she heads down the walkway. Akita steps out of her quarters and beckons Storm to follow her. Storm notices Akita's red eyes as if she has been crying. As they walk into the room, Wulf is sitting at a table.

Storm takes a deep breath. "Akita, what has happened? You look like you have been crying for days."

Wulf looks to Akita and then to Storm, "Akita, Meh-Kola, Greenbean, Quinn and Grace went to rescue Vivian." Storm looks at him in shock. "Don't worry, Vivian is back safe but there was a casualty. Grace was killed by King Windu. Needless to say, Akita sliced and diced him so he will never manipulate or hurt anyone again. King Carthon just lost his major rich puppet, as well."

Storm walks up to Akita, wrapping her in a big hug. "I am so, so sorry about your friend Grace. I know you have a lot on your mind. I wish I had been there to help you."

Akita looks Storm in the eyes. "You my dear were where I needed you to be. Grace was dead set for revenge against King Windu, no matter what anyone said to reason with her. She knew he was the reason for her Keep and ship being destroyed. He told King Carthon who helped us get Darkwing back."

Storm shakes her head, "I get it. I really do but someday when this isn't so fresh in your mind you will have to tell me about it. However, not to sound insensitive, we have other things to discuss."

Wulf turns to Storm, "Good, give her something else to think about."

Storm sits down next to Wulf keeping his attention. "I have a secret that only Akita knows about, but as soon as Jacklyn gets back everyone is going to know. So, as I discuss what just happened in Cliffside, I need you to listen with an open mind, so that you understand."

Wulf states, "Storm, you are family. We will work through whatever this is as a family."

Storm catches her breath and wipes away a tear. "Akita, please sit down." After Akita sits, Storm continues. "Jacklyn and I were visiting various shops in town. We were having nonchalant conversations with anyone that would talk. Everyone is preparing and putting supplies away for the big battle. With that said, most are not excited to be having a war to begin with. I would say the average town person has no love for King Carthon and his plans."

"So, we went into a little store called, 'MADAM SUZIE'S SHOP OF CURIOSITIES'. Madam Suzie is this cute older lady with a brilliant smile and welcoming personality. What she showed us in her crystal ball was not what I was expecting. She knew we were in disguise and not who we said we were. We believe she unlocked Jacklyn's memory, but we only had seconds to discuss it. Madam Suzie showed me what was going to happen not even 20 minutes later. As we were about to ask her questions, the guards were pounding on the door. Madam Suzie hustled us out the back door to evade the guards. Unfortunately, Evad's twin brother was waiting for us with guards surrounding us."

Storm pauses to take a deep breath, looks to Akita, "Rixan made his presence known. The guards ran and Aevid stood frozen in spot. Rixan looked at Jacklyn and told her to run so that he would not hurt her. Aevid tried to throw spells at Rixan, but they were just batted away. Rixan might really be of help to us during the battle. Aevid will never be a danger to anyone again. As soon as I came back to myself, Visham transformed, and we flew off." Storm lowers her head.

Wulf looks to Akita, "As soon as she came back to herself? Please explain."

Akita then tells him about Storms travels and her affliction with the Demon that resides inside her.

Storm looks up at Wulf, "I can control him, but we were in danger of being caught, and he came out to save us. For instance, I kept him under wraps with that Paladin Lief. Anyway, I saw Jacklyn running to the rendezvous point to meet up with Skip and Gavin, as I flew over. I am sure the guards have already notified King Carthon about the events."

Akita states, "With Aevid out of the picture, that is one less major Dark Wizard to deal with. I will send Annut and Thoraxian to bring Gavin, Skip, and Jacklyn back with the horses. That will speed up things." Looking to Storm, "We will be having a meeting when everyone is back. I will explain your situation, and how it benefits us at the moment. I believe Jacklyn will be able to help as Rixan saved her too. We need to get a message to Mandrake, Darkwing and Captain Dubbin to come back to the Temple."

Visham flies into the room and lands on Storm's shoulder. As he gets settled, he lets out a little burp. Storm jerks her head around and looks at him. She then looks back towards Akita and Wulf, "Visham says excuse me and that he is grateful that Rixan was there tonight because otherwise they would have been captured by Aevid."

Akita agrees, looks fondly at Visham, "Yes, and I'm thankful that you were there to get Storm back to us so quickly. You're such a good little deadly poisonous, but sometimes big Wyvern. And you Storm, you go get some sleep. Skip, Gavin, and Jacklyn will be back by late tonight. Annut and Thoraxian are already on their way to search for them."

Storm nods and then yawns, "Yea I could really use some sleep. So, when do you think we will have this meeting about Rixan?"

Akita pauses and thinks for a second, "When everybody is back, we will meet in the Great Hall and just tell everyone at once. Don't worry Storm, I know everyone, and they are going to be supportive of your affliction. There may be questions so just be prepared to be open and honest about everything and it will all be okay. Now go, it's late and you need to recover. We'll all be here when you wake up."

Storm turns and goes out the door then comes back in, "Um, Akita this is my room."

Akita looks around at the room and then to Wulf, "By the Gods! You are right! I have just been a mess since last night. We will go so you can rest. Come on Wulf, let's go."

Wulf gets up and follows Akita to the door then pauses at Storm before exiting, "I knew this was your room, but sometimes you just can't stop her until she has finished her thoughts. I'll look after her and help her get back on track. Have a good sleep. We'll see you for breakfast."

Mandrake, Darkwing, and Captain Dubbin arrive back at the Temple at first light. They flew all night to get back to the Temple after they received a message from Aphorea for them to come back. Fortunately, they had already started preparing to move the Griffon army to the Dragon

Temple for staging. There was already a large area cleared just outside the Temple for the Griffons and their riders to set up camp and with the help of the Dragons and Lommas, the whole area is concealed by the forest canopy.

Darkwing makes his way in first to the Great Hall, "Hello, is anyone awake yet?"

A deep voice echoes from the set of tables set up in the middle of the room, "Hello, I'm here."

Darkwing takes the steps up to the dais and sees Ghod eating breakfast by himself and two Lommas conjuring food to the table. He walks up and sits down next to Ghod and then Mandrake and Captain Dubbin follow suit. Darkwing looks around at the food, "Hello Ghod, Are you the only one up?

Ghod swallows his mouth full of food then answers, "Yup, I don't sleep much and just come in here to eat and get way from the forge for a moment. You guys can just tell the Lommas what you want, and they'll make it for you. Also, Grace is dead."

Mandrake almost chokes on his hot coffee and splatters fly all over the table, "Wait! What?"

Ghod takes a bite of oatmeal and swallows, "Yup, they went to rescue Vivian at Windu's place and he killed Grace, but they got Vivian back home safe, which is really good because I was tired of seeing Ishvet mope around the Temple."

Darkwing stares at Ghod in disbelief, "Uh, I don't know if this is really 'over breakfast talk', maybe we should go talk to Akita."

Captain Dubbin agrees with a nod, "Yes and I should report to Earl Jarkon. I also need to speak to the Lommas about feeding the troops and Griffons in the new courtyard."

Mandrake finishes a jellyroll and takes another sip of coffee as he gets up from the table, "I also need to go speak to Vicar."

Ghod looks around as the table is again empty, "Was it something I said? Ah, who knows. Okay Mr. Lomma, another bowl of oatmeal please and this time could you add some of those sweet grubs that I like so much."

Akita's voice can be heard coming from the common dining hall as the returning team make their way through the caverns.

Darkwing looks to the others, "I bet we find them all here." As he turns into the dining hall. "Yep, Ghod was just being Ghod, eating alone. That was probably his fifth bowl of oatmeal and didn't know the others were awake. That man can put away the food."

Ghod walks up behind them, "Seventh, but who's counting. Pardon me." Ghod then pushes through then into the Dining Hall, "I heard Quinn made cinnamon rolls, I'll have four."

They can see that Akita is sitting at the bigger of the dining tables with Wulf, Storm, Ishvet, and Vivian. Darkwing waves to Vivian as Akita turns to look towards the door. They hurry over to the table and Akita jumps up and hugs them both. Then they move around the table and hug Vivian.

Darkwing comes back around to Akita and hugs her again and speaks softly, "Ghod just told us what happened. I'm so sorry to hear it. At least Vivian is safe now and I'm sure she won't be out of Ishvet's sight ever again. "

Akita takes a deep breath, "Yes, it was awful. I'm going to go over everything tonight when the others get back from Cliffshade. So how did your guy's mission go? Hopefully better than ours."

Mandrake responds, "It went well actually. We pushed everyone hard and found nothing of note. Those we questioned were shocked and some were even insulted about the questioning. However, it all worked out in the end. When we got your message as soon as Aphorea was in range to speak to us. It took us all day to get everyone ready and then flew through the night to get here this morning."

Akita replies with a tired voice. "Storm had some excitement in Cliffside and flew back on Visham, so now we are just waiting on Annut and Thoraxian to find and return with Jacklyn, Skip, Gavin, and the horses. I've just been a mess since we returned from Windu's palace."

Wulf looks to the guys, "She is having a rough time at the moment, but she will be fine tonight."

Darkwing holds Akitas shoulder, "She is remarkable in the ability to be resilient. I am positive that she will get back to herself in no time."

Mandrake agrees and then looks around the Dining Room, "I'm sure Vicar could help you to relax, but I don't see him. Do you know where he is?"

Ishvet speaks up, "He is working on some projects and has been taking his meals in his room. I'm sure that's where you will find him."

Akita goes back to sit down at the table, "You are welcome to join us for breakfast or you can go rest and have a bite to eat when you get up. Also, you might think about washing up as I can smell Griffon all over you."

Darkwing sniffs his arm, "I hadn't noticed until just now." He looks at Mandrake, "Yea maybe we should go clean up and then join them later."

Mandrake sniffs the air and shakes his head, "Yes I do believe some soap and water are in order."

They both make their way out of the dining room to their rooms. Akita and the others finish breakfast and go over inventories of supplies and make notes about what they will need in the upcoming battle. Later in the afternoon Akita sits down with Princess Gianna and has a long conversation about the Earth and Frost Amulets. Earl Jarkon meets them both later and goes over plans and gives an update on the army's status so that Akita has as much information as possible before the big meeting tonight.

The sun has just set as Annut and Thoraxian return to the temple with Jacklyn, Skip, and Gavin and the two horses. Almost everyone in the temple is starting to gather in the main hall. The Lommas have turned one side into seating for the armies and staff with stone benches and tables. On the other side of the Hall large stone platforms have been raised for each kind of mount, creature, and Dragon. In the middle of the room is the raised dais with the leadership and Princess Gianna and her soldiers.

Annut and Thoraxian are the last to enter the Hall following Jacklyn, Skip, and Gavin. They all take their places at the main table and the Dragons take their places with the young Dragons. Lommas begin to conjure food for everyone as soon as everyone is seated. Akita has asked that libations be held off until the meeting has concluded.

Akita looks around from the end of the main table and can see that everyone is here now. She reaches over and grabs Wulf's hand and squeezes it. She takes a deep breath and stands slowly, dreading having to tell everyone about the terrible events that occurred two nights ago. She begins to shake a little and Wulf squeezes her hand back.

Akita starts to speak, and her voice is amplified throughout the Main Hall, "We used to meet like this in the evenings at Blackwing Keep giving updates and discussing the matters at hand. I feel it's time we start to do that again." With a deep sigh, she looks around the room, "First, let us all welcome Vivian home." Applause, squawking, and roaring fill the Hall.

"Greenbean, Meh-Kola, Quinn, Grace, and I left here under great secrecy with the help of the Princess. Unfortunately, King Windu had a powerful weapon to use against us. A Magical flute, the very one we stole from King Cirus while we were rescuing Darkwing. Grace was determined to engage King Windu because he had betrayed her many times in the past, including to

King Carthon. He used the power of the flute's wind to dispatch her attack and she was killed as a result."

Looking around the room, "nobody is to blame here except King Windu. Any one of us would have given our lives to bring Vivian home. She is family and that is what family is all about."

Akita looks to Jacklyn, Skip and Gavin and can see the shock on their faces. She then walks behind them and put a hand on their shoulders, "I know that some of you are hearing this news for the first time tonight. I understand the shock. I still can't believe it myself and I was there."

Akita can see that Storm was right about Jacklyn having her memories back, because of the physical change and the tears rolling down Jacklyn's cheeks. "Jacklyn, Storm told us about Madam Suzie. Normally my next question would be, how much can you remember? Now I can see by the way that you have reacted that everything has come back. I want you to know that she died with honor and dignity, fighting those who were doing evil in our lands."

Akita clenches her hand on Jacklyn's shoulder, "As a team we were able to defeat King

Windu and destroy the magical Flute. We brought Vivian back to Ishvet and we've brought Grace's body back with us for a proper service."

She squats down next to Jacklyn's chair and Jacklyn turns to face her. Akita grabs her hands and looks in her eyes, "You are part of our family and team. You were a part of Grace's family and team. We want to honor her as we have others. Think about it and let me know how best we can do that. The choice is yours as her closest friend all these years."

Jacklyn nods, responding with a shaky voice, "It is an easy choice. She once told me, if this ever came to pass, that she wanted her ashes spread out over O'Malley Keep and the Bay."

Akita takes a deep breath, "You and I will see that it is done." She then looks to Ghod, "When this is over I would also like a marker in our honored cemetery."

Ghod gives a wry smile, "Already working on it, Akita. The marker will have the likeness of the Sea Horse at the top, being held up by her peg leg. Her name is written in the sails. She will be remembered."

It takes Akita a minute to stop staring at Ghod and get back to the meeting. Wulf walks up and puts an arm around her, which snaps her back to the moment.

Ishvet stands, "I want to thank you ladies for rescuing my Viv. I still feel like I should have been the one to rescue her. It could have been me in Grace's place and Vivian would have been widowed. I understand why you did what you did, and my family will forever be in your debt."

Clearing her throat, "Ok on to the next subject. As you know we sent Jacklyn and Storm into the town of Cliffside, as well as Skip and Gavin to do some surveillance of the area around the Keep. We will get to Gavin and Skip in a bit, as their information will be very valuable to the attack. However, I need to explain what happened to Jacklyn and Storm."

Akita feels Jacklyn's hands stiffen. Looking at her eye-to-eye Akita gives a gentle nod and stands back up. "When Storm came home to Blackwing Keep a few months ago, I noticed some things had changed with her. Storm is a Fire Wizard from an ancient line, which is why she left us to begin with. She wanted to find and learn from those like her, as well as learn her family history. Well, we all know that unexpected things can happen on these pilgrimages."

Akita smiles at Storm, "When we were children, we got up to all kinds of mischief that girls of our status shouldn't. We were always in trouble. Natural curiosity and intrigue followed us into adulthood. While exploring a temple ruin on the east coast of Omoth, her curiosity got the best of her."

Akita walks back to her place at the table and sits. She motions to Storm to stand. Storm slowly rises and looks around, "Akita is right. I did let my curiosity get the best of me. I was having a terrible time in Omoth after my teacher was killed. I had no money or family there. The city I was closest to ran me out because of my magic and I was alone and scared. I retreated into the forest and came upon an ancient temple. It was a beautiful place and I decided to set up camp there."

"As I explored the temple, I came across a sealed chamber with a large iron door and writing in a language I didn't know. I could feel something beyond the door that beckoned to me. I melted the hinges on the door and stepped beyond the threshold. I lost consciousness and awoke to having none of my powers, and a new entity residing within me. Over time I and the entity reached a symbiotic relationship. He even helped me save Visham's life."

"The major drawback is I can never touch anyone with my bare hands for the risk of killing them. His name is Rixan, and he is a Pestilence Demon. He requires life essence to stay subdued. I have made the rule of only allowing him to feed on bad people, like Dark Wizards and bandits. Occasionally a Troll or Ogre."

Looking to Akita, "I told Akita about what had happened on the day that I arrived at Blackwing Keep. We thought it best to keep my affliction a secret until the time was right to tell everyone. The events in Cliffside have made it apparent that the time to share is now. This brings me to mine and Jacklyn's mission."

"Our task was to gather information from the townsfolk about the Dark Wizards and King Carthon. The only person we came across that seemed willing to speak to us was the purveyor of a Curiosity shop. Her name is Madam Suzie, and she is a Mystic. She was able to see through our disguises and she even knew stuff about Jacklyn and myself that even we didn't know. She somehow unlocked all of Jacklyn's memories and she told me my future."

"She saw that we were going to be surrounded be the city guards and that I would be flying at sunset. All that we saw in her crystal ball came true. A powerful Dark Wizard was able to sense Rixan's power within me and that lead him to the Curiosity shop. Jacklyn and I tried to escape through the back alley, but we were trapped by the Dark Wizard and the guards. Rixan knew his existence was in danger and protected me from the Dark Wizard. He transformed me into his true form and devoured the Dark Wizard."

"Jacklyn was able to escape after the guards ran in fear and I was able to escape because of Visham. He enlarged and we flew back to the Temple. However, we were able to get some interesting information from Madam Suzie. She told me that we would be fighting against King Carthon together. So that leads me to believe that we have some allies in the town of Cliffside that will join us in the fight."

"I'm sorry that everyone has to find out like this. I assure you that Rixan will only come out when we need him to." Looking directly at Jacklyn now, "Jacklyn, I consider you a sister much like Akita here, so I don't ever want you to fear for your safety. We probably should have told you about Rixan before we left. I was shocked when Void found out about him while checking our disguises. Please forgive me if I scared you or if we scared you."

Jacklyn takes a deep breath and stands up, "If there was one thing, I learned from Grace it is that the most unlikely of people can become your friend and even become your family. Grace was stubborn and bull-headed, quick tempered and even hostile at times. However, as I got to know her, I also saw her generosity and compassion. All the gold that Akita paid her for helping to rescue Darkwing she gave to the orphanage in Salthall."

"Since the day Gavin rescued me, you have all made me feel welcome and like family. I have become close to all of you and see you as family. I'm sure Grace saw it that way too. For that, I thank everyone here. As far as what happened at Cliffside, I am thankful that Rixan revealed himself and saved us. I was scared at first, but then he told me to run and then I knew he was protecting us."

Darkwing finally speaks up, "Ok, enough of all this crying and emotions. We all love each other and all that family stuff but let's get to the important plans so we can destroy those that have brought this all down on us."

Ghod speaks up, "Now there is a sensible thought. This mushy stuff is ruining my mood and my food."

Both Storm and Jacklyn sit down and then Akita stands back up. Akita motions her had towards Skip and Gavin, "Skip, Gavin what do you discover from your time observing Cliffshade Keep?"

Akita sits back down and Skip stands. He looks over to Gavin waves his hand in an upward motion so that Gavin will stand too, "Gavin and I scouted the perimeter of the Keep. I took the South side and Gavin went to the North. I saw the big iron and wood doors that Meh-Kola has described and the inlet under the Keep. I also saw the Demi-Titan under water apparently gathering strength. A total assault against the harbor by ship would be inadvisable. The only weakness that I saw was a large drainage pipe that only someone on foot could enter, and then only two soldiers wide."

Skip shakes his head, "Even that way would be dangerous. I sensed Grizzels and Rock Spiders inside.

Gavin chimes in, "We also have Trolls camped outside the town walls to consider too. We do have a way'n from the North side, but only by air. There are many large balconies that Griffons could land'n to get soldiers into the Keep. A ground fight wouldn't be good cuz the walls are too tall."

Akita stands, "Thanks everyone for putting yourself in danger to bring us back all this information. As all can see we have a familiar face back in the temple that has been absent for a while. I sent Judas to find us some allies in the West. I am happy to report that he was able to find the clan Durmond of Dwarven Hearth Home in the Voskaola Mountains to help us in the fight against the Dark Wizards. Fifty of their best warriors will be on the front lines with us."

Akita nods to Judas and smiles, "Does anyone else have anything to report? She looks around the room at all the soldiers and then the mounts and Dragons.

As she begins to sit, Princess Gianna clears her throat to get Akitas attention. Akita looks up and nods her head. Gianna looks over to Vicar, "We have run into some problems that Vicar and I have a solution for. The Lommas magic will only last for one day outside of the Temple. That means that Ghod's Golems could crumble before the army makes it to Cliffshade Keep. Vicar has shown me how he and Fab Ulous can amplify others' magic. His solution is that they will amplify the magic of the Amulets so that I can make multiple rifts and get everyone directly to the Keep at once and immediately. This will give us the advantage of surprise."

Akita smiles and mouths a thank you to Princess Gianna and looks around the table, "This is great news! We will be in and out before King Carthon even knows what hit him. Let's make sure we have all our plans ironed out before we make our move. I want all leadership in the War Room tomorrow evening. We will get prepared then let everyone know what their role is going to be. I'd like to have a small service for Grace in the morning. We'll give her a proper send off and then we can scatter her ashes after the battle."

Ghod stands up and wipes his mouth, "My Lady, I have something to add." You can almost see the sheepish grin under his mask.

Then Ghod bows and steps back from the table and goes and stands by Akita. Akita steps close to him and whispers with a smile, "I'll get you for that Ghod."

He chuckles and then begins again, "Back at Blackwing Keep when Akita became the Dutchess, I made her a pendent. A pendent that represented her love for Dragons and the unity of our team. It has become a symbol for Blackwing Keep and all who work together to defeat the darkness. I felt like we should all be unified in this upcoming battle. I have made everybody a pendent to represent that we are one unified army."

Ghod holds up the small pendent. The gold reflects the candlelight and glints. It is a circle with a flying dragon in the middle. The Dragon is breathing fire and it's very detailed. Ghod admires his work then reaches into his vest and pulls out another pendent that is about six times the size of the original. Ghod holds it up towards Princess Gianna, "See Giant Princess I have made one for you and each of your guards that is the right size."

Princess Gianna slightly bows and smiles while she stays seated. Ghod bows back and then hands the giant-sized pendant to Akita, it is very heavy, and Akita almost loses her balance when Ghod hands it to her. Ghod then turns and hurries back to his seat. Akita just shakes her head and places the pendant on the table.

Akita regains her composure and then reaches up and clasps the pendant that she is wearing, "Thank you Ghod, that was very thoughtful. We will meet King Carthon on the battlefield as one unified army. Now that all that is settled everyone can enjoy their meals and the Lommas can now serve wine and ale. I want everyone to have fun tonight and try to forget what is about to come."

CHAPTER 19

GRACE

The night was pretty tame compared to some of the nights of drinking at Blackwing Keep. Most of the leadership went to bed early and allowed the soldiers to have a bit of fun and blow off some steam. Akita and Jacklyn got up early in the morning to start preparing for Grace's service. After breakfast they spoke with the Lommas and Annut to arrange the place and time.

Akita asks the Lommas for a tall task of pushing the forest back from the main entrance. To make enough room for all the Dragons, Wyverns, Griffons, Owl Rocs, and Horses. She asked for a stone circle in the ground with a large rectangular stone block big enough for Grace's body. In front she wanted a small, raised area for Vicar to give the eulogy and for anyone to speak about Grace.

Jacklyn asked for water to be around the stone circle with a miniature Sea Horse sailing around. She also requested a small ornate urn to hold Graces ashes. Her last request was that Grace be wrapped in gold colored silk and that a Tricorn be placed on top of her.

The Lommas agreed to all the requests and went to work immediately. In less than an hour they had the outside of the Temple rearranged and the forest pushed back. Annut spoke to everyone and asked them to meet outside for the service just before lunch.

Sunshine fills the newly cleared area in front of the Temple. The area seems to stretch for a half mile on both sides of the entrance and the same in front. As requested, there is a small stone stage with a podium for Vicar to give the eulogy and about a Dragons length behind him is a three-foot-wide moat that surrounds a large circular patio. In the middle of the patio is a six foot by three-foot block of stone that is raised three feet from the ground to the top.

Atop the stone block is Graces body wrapped from head to toe in golden silk. A large ornate Tricorn hat lays on her chest and a large frilly white feather sticks up from one of the sides of the hat. In the moat that surrounds her is an exact replica of the Sea Horse, Graces flag ship. It is slowly sailing around the patio.

Jacklyn walks out and sees the ship and immediately begins to tear up. Vivian walks up behind her and wraps her arm around her. Jacklyn turns and embraces Vivian, "I don't know how they did it. They must have pulled it straight out of my mind. It looks exactly like the Sea Horse, even down to the barnacles on the hull."

Vivian hugs Jacklyn tightly and begins to lead her to the chairs that the Lommas set up for the two-legged mourners to sit in, "From what Ishvet has told me, they can conjure up just about anything you can think of. We are really lucky that they came back to the Temple after the Dragons returned."

Jacklyn and Vivian take their seats in the front row next to Akita, Wulf, and Ishvet. Ordyn, Shamash, Darkwing and Ghod sit directly behind them, and Olek, Fabby, Mandrake, Skip, and Gavin sit behind them. On the other side of the isle are Earl Jarkon, Captain Dubbin, Greenbean, Judas, Storm, Void, Ixenvorlux, and Quinn. Further back is Greta, Scotch, Ben, and several other staff.

The Dragons, Wyverns and other mounts fan out in a semicircle behind the seating area with the smaller mounts in front of the Dragons. Annut lands behind the patio with Grace's body. Vicar steps up to the podium and looks around to see if everyone has arrived.

Vicar clears his throat and asks if everyone can hear him. Thoraxian speaks into his mind and says that they can. Vicar then looks at Akita and takes a deep breath, "Captain Grace Dawn O'Malley by all descriptions was a pirate. People on the open sea feared her. She was known to be ruthless and unforgiving. She had ambitions to start her own Port and Keep and she obtained that goal by purchasing Akita's Mother's family Keep."

"Akita was so mad that her uncle sold it, that she traveled the whole day to confront Grace and have a fist fight with her. Neither one of them would say who won, only that it ended in laughter. From then on Akita only spoke highly of Grace."

"Years later, when Akita and the team needed sea going transportation, she thought of Grace. Grace was well known for her fleet of ships. She and Akita formed a fast friendship and Grace agreed to ferry them for a small fortune.

Soon Grace became invested in the rescue of Darkwing and put her ship and her crew in harm's way to secure him. This adventure with Akita and the team changed Grace forever. She gave up piracy and turned to the betterment of the people around her. We even learned from Jacklyn that Grace gave all the gold she made from helping to rescue Darkwing to the orphanage in Salthall."

"Grace became close to all of us at Blackwing Keep and because of that connection she was targeted by King Carthon. She met this challenge, like most things, head on. She believed in the cause and that Alahora could be at peace with the Dark Wizards gone. For this reason, King Carthon released the Demi-Titan upon O'Malley Keep, destroying the Keep and her fleet of ships."

"Anyone that got to really know Grace, fell in love with her quick wit and twisted sense of humor. She was loyal to her friends and ultimately gave her life to protect her friend. Per her wishes we will commit her body to fire and scatter her ashes over the remains of O'Malley Keep and Bay. Annut would you please use your Dragon Fire to release her mortal ties to this realm?"

Annut rises to a standing position and spreads her wings fully. A column of flame shoots from her mouth and engulfs Grace's body. Within seconds there is only a pile of ash. The Dragons in the rear begin to sing their melancholy song. It is deep and full, resonating through everyone in front of them. Many stare ahead in deep contemplation and others allow the tears to flow down their faces. Slowly, over the next half an hour, everyone goes back to their duties.

The Lommas collect Grace's ashes in a beautiful urn for Jacklyn. They begin to clean up the area and return to normal. By midafternoon, the forest is back in place like nothing had even happened. However, no one will soon forget the touching service for Grace O'Malley.

Rain has been falling for two days at Cliffshade Keep. Tomorrow night will be the full moon. Last minute preparations are finishing, and all the Dark Wizards and vile creatures are gathered within the wall of the Keep. The Demi-Titan, Jessa, is at full strength and awaiting orders in the bay.

King Carthon has many of the Dark Wizards positioned around the Keep producing barriers to protect from aerial assault. Giant bats fly above the Keep and fifty Trolls patrol the perimeter. All the Grizzles and Rock Spiders gather in the Courtyard. The legion of Centaurs should be at the Keep by midday.

Volaern comes into Carthon's chamber with another Dark Wizard, "Sire, I would like to introduce you to Grand Wizard Waxmen. He was the one that secured the allegiance of the Centaurs. His power is way higher than Evad or Aevid ever dreamed of having. Would you like him to stay at your side and protect you from harm?"

King Carthon glares at Volaern, "Why do you think that I need someone to protect me? I am the most powerful Wizard to ever live. I am eternal. I am enduring, I don't need anyone to protect me from Akita and her misfits. I could destroy them all at once with the Sea Amulet. Tell you what I do want you to do Waxmen, go down to the docks and protect my Demi-Titan. I don't want anyone near her until the time is right."

Waxmen bows then stands, "Master Carthon, I will protect the Demi-Titan until my last breath."

Carthon looks to Volaern with disdain, "See that is how you respond to your superiors. You do as you are told and that's it. Both of you leave me. Volaern make sure the scouts are reporting in. I want to know the second that Akita Blackwing is spotted heading this way."

Volaern slightly bows, "Yes Sire I will do as you ask."

Carthon smiles and waves his hand at Volaern and Waxmen to leave the room. After they exit, King Carthon goes over to Hector. He pats Hector on the head, "Hector when the fighting starts, I want you to stay by my side all the time. I couldn't bear the thought of losing you. You are the only one I trust."

Hector coos and shakes his feathers then rubs his head against King Carthon's side. Carthon then returns to his table and pours a glass of wine. He sits and thinks about the things that Madam Suzie said as he sips from his glass. He wonders if there is any force that could actually defeat him.

Madam Suzie moves through the shadows and under the cover of the rain to get to the old bookstore on the outskirts of town. She enters through the backdoor which opens into a large storeroom. There are about twenty other townsfolk in the room. A lean man with a large moustache approaches her, "Suzie, we are ready to go."

Suzie looks around the room at all the faces, "It is almost time for the festivities to start. Von and Isriale will protect the group with their barrier magic. Hoyt and Koller will use their fire magic if anyone tries to stop us. We only need to get out of the main gate and go half a mile into the woods. That's where Storm will be exiting the rift."

Suzie turns and opens the back door, "Okay the town guards are on high alert. Everyone, move with haste. Our distraction will be when my shop catches fire."

Madam Suzie looks down the alleyway towards her shop and can see the orange glow of the fire. Soon bells are ringing, and shadows of guards go running by. She makes her way down the alley to the main street. She motions for the others to follow and runs out into the street. The

Main Gate is unguarded. They all run through and towards the woods.

Princess Gianna stands on the top of the Dragon Temple and looks over the East side down to the forest area. She can see the Stone Golems lined up in formation along with General Olek. They all appear to be ready to move out. She then turns to the North and looks over the side of the Temple to the clearing where all the mounted Griffons are located. They too are in formation with Captain Dubbin and Earl Jarkon at the front.

She speaks to Aphorea to let her know that the others are ready and waiting. Aphorea lets her know that the Dragons are receiving their last pieces of armor from the Lommas. Akita and the team make their way up to the top of the Temple and stand with the Giant guards. After a short wait, the Dragons start flying out of the Temple and landing the large flat roof. Aphorea lands on next to the Princess and her guards.

Akita admires the newly conjured armor that Aphorea is wearing. It is glossy white with blue banding. The head piece covers her horns and bends over her snout. There are interlocking pieces all down her neck to the tip of her tail and full chest and abdomen protection. She even has armor on her legs and claws. Akita thinks that it is stunning. Especially how the moonlight glistens on it.

Aphorea reminds everyone that the Lommas magic will only last for a day outside the range of the Temple. That will mean that the armor will fade and that the Stone Golems will turn to dust tomorrow night. So, they will need to make this battle swift and precise. If the battle goes on too long, they will be more vulnerable to attack without the armor.

Hunter and Warrior land close to Akita and start talking at the same time, "Look mom shiny metal."

Akita turns and goes to them. She gives each one a hug around the neck, "Okay, you both stay safe. Be smart and don't get hurt. I love you."

They both nuzzle her and agree to be safe. Akita then makes her way back to Wulf and the others. When she gets back, Vicar and Fabby break from the group and approach Princess Gianna.

Fabby looks up and smiles at the Princess, "We will only have one attempt at amplifying the magic of the Amulets. When Vicar and I start, you will have to open all the rifts as quickly as possible. We don't know how long we will be able to help before we will need to recuperate."

Akita sees that Fabby and Vicar are in place, so she gives the signal to the team to mount up. Akita and Wulf head for Aphorea, Darkwing gets on Mylar, Ghod gets on Hunter, Ordyn climbs up onto Thoraxian, Quinn and Jacklyn get on Annut, Judas gets on Warrior, Mandrake gets on Ransom, Ixenvorlux gets on Drako, Void gets on Rethu, Vivian and Ishvet are on Shemera and Addrit, and Storm gets on Visham. Gavin has Blitz stay at the Temple to keep guard since it will be easier to get around the battlefield on a winged mount.

The younger Dragons are almost fully grown now. However, Annut and Thoraxian believe that they will be faster without riders. They tell them to stay close to them since this will be their first battle. Alure and her children will be staying at the Temple at this time. The Blackwing soldiers are all gathered in the Main Hall waiting for the rift to open.

Princess Gianna kneels down and removes the Earth and Frost Amulets from around her neck. She clenches them with one in each hand then holds out her fists in front of both Fabby and Vicar. They both lay their hands on Princess Gianna's fist. They begin the spells as Gianna concentrates on opening the rifts.

A large glowing seam appears in front of her, and then another in front of Olek and the Golems, and Earl Jarkon and the Griffons. A smaller one appears in the Main Hall in front of the Keep soldiers and the freshly arrived Dwarven fighters.

Storm can hear someone calling her behind the seam that has opened on the roof. She and Visham walk up to the seam as it starts opening up. As soon as it is wide enough Madam Suzie walks through with the other townsfolk onto the rooftop of the Temple. Storm hops down off of Visham and runs over to Madam Suzie to give her a big hug. All the townsfolk bunch up behind

Madam Suzie and grab each other in fear. This is their first-time seeing dragons and Giants.

Madam Suzie turns to them, "It's okay, they are our allies."

Akita flies over and land beside them, "Madam Suzie I presume?"

Madam Suzie nods, "Yes, Lady Blackwing. Do you have someplace for the townsfolk to stay? We don't want to be anywhere near the Keep when you guys' attack."

Akita stops and thinks of a Lomma, and one appears in front of her, "Could you please take these people down to the Main Hall and get them food and someplace to rest their heads."

The Lomma reaches out its hand to one of the townsfolk and then starts leading it to the stairwell into the Temple. Madam Suzie stops at Storm, "Storm I know I said that we would fight King Carthon together, but the visions have changed. I see that we are meant to be here and that we will help with the wounded when you return. I also know that I am supposed to tell you that the town is evacuated of all the people that are not loyal to King Carthon. Lastly, I see you becoming yourself again on this night."

Storm reaches out and hugs Madam Suzie again then goes back to Visham. Akita takes flight and lands on Aphorea's back. She then gives the word for everyone to begin entering the fully opened rifts.

Everyone makes it through the rifts into the designated areas just as it stops raining at Cliffshade Keep. The Dragons, Wyverns, Griffons, and Owl Roc stay in flight. The ground troops make their way into the woods. Finally, Fabby, Vicar and Princess Gianna walk through the rift and all the rifts close simultaneously.

Princess Gianna and the ground troops are in the clearing that Skip and the others made camp while surveilling the Keep. She tells the ground troops to move to the side and she uses the Earth Amulet to create a flat and wide path directly to the gates of Cliffside.

Aphorea and Akita start to make their first run at the town with all the Dragons and Wyverns following behind. Captain Dubbin and Earl Jarkon take the platoon of Griffons North around the town and make for the backside of the Keep. The Blackwing Keep soldiers follow behind the Princess and her guards towards the town. The fifty Dwarven Fighters head to the South of the town down to the docks to make their way into the drainage tunnel. General Olek takes the stone Golems to the North of the town to where the walls of the town and the Keep meet. They are hopeful that they can break through to the other side.

As the Dragons get close to the town, the bells of a church start ringing, which means that their presence is known. Akita directs Aphorea to dive and take out the church steeple. Behind them the others begin to dive and blow Dragon and Wyvern fire on the northside of town.

King Carthon hears the bells of the small cathedral in the town, and he can feel the Keep slightly shaking. He knows that the time has come. He goes to the West balcony and can see the orange glow of fire from the town. He orders Volaern to make sure that the barrier over the Keep is reinforced.

Volaern runs out of the room and yells through the halls of the Keep, "Reinforce the barrier. It needs to withstand Dragon Fire."

King Carthon then holds the Sea Amulet and sends his thoughts to the Demi-Titan, "Be Vigilant Jessa, if you see anyone at the docks, destroy them."

There is no answer from the Demi-Titan. She moves through the bay closer to the iron and wood gates by the dock. She begins to survey the dock area and the doors. Even with the torches along the dock, the moonlight, and her enhanced eyesight nothing can be seen moving along the docks or shore.

King Carthon looks out over the town again just as a blast of fire hits the barrier in front of him. The fire spreads across the barrier and dissipates. Then a blast of Frost breath hits the barrier and frost spreads out then melts off the barrier.

He can see a big white Dragon and a just as large red Dragon flying back and forth in front of him. On the White Dragon he can see armor and two riders. Both are Demonan and he is sure that one of them is Akita Blackwing. The White Dragon hovers in front of the balcony for a moment and the front rider reaches out and points at him. Then the Dragons fly off back towards the town.

Aphorea crushes the tower of the church with her back claws and then flies up over the South side of town. She looks back as the fire from the Dragons and Wyverns engulf the North side. Below Guards can be seen running up the main road to the walls of the Keep. However, they are not being let in the gate.

Annut contacts Akita and Aphorea to tell them that she sees King Carthon on the balcony directly ahead of her. Aphorea whips around and flies directly towards Annut. Annut with Quinn and Jacklyn on her back head towards King Carthon and blast fire at him, but it hits an invisible wall before reaching him. Aphorea sees this and tries her frost breath, and the same thing happens.

Akita tells Aphorea to come to eye level of King Carthon. Aphorea does and hovers in place. Akita can see King Carthon standing on the balcony with his Owl Roc beside him. She knows she can't get to him, so she just points at him to let him know that she is coming for him.

Princess Gianna, her six guards, Vicar and Fabby, and the Blackwing Keep soldiers follow the path towards the town walls. As they reach the gates, they can hear large footsteps running towards them and the skittering sound of Rock Spiders. They look to both sides and can see several Trolls and hundreds of Rock Spiders headed towards them.

Princess Gianna stops in her tracks and allows the soldiers to proceed ahead and engage the Trolls and Spiders. The soldiers use their pikes to stab at the Trolls and some use their swords to slash at the Rock Spiders. Others use their ward rings to stop boulders from hitting their fellow soldiers. Several Spiders are dispatched immediately, but some of the Trolls are able to take out some packs of soldiers.

Fabby and Vicar team up against a particular nasty looking Toll. Vicar looks over to Fabby, "Well it's been a while since I actually used my sword in a fight. Hopefully I remember how."

Fabby laughs, "Well if you could remember how to fly again after all those years, I'm sure it will come back to you. You slice him up and I'll inflict enough pain to bring him to his knees."

Vicar unsheathes his sword and runs towards the Troll. The Troll swings a huge hammer at Vicar and Vicar is able slide to the side as it hits the ground. He turns with his sword raised and brings it down on the Trolls wrist. The troll's hand falls to the ground along with the giant hammer. Fabby inflicts his pain ability on the Troll and the Troll falls to the ground as it yells out and grabs the stump where its hand was. Vicar does a spin with his sword stretched outward. He hits the Troll right beneath the chin and the Troll's large ugly head goes rolling down its own chest.

Fabby laughs and shakes his head as he looks at Vicar, "What was that? That spin you did. You are a lot more agile than I thought you would be for your age."

Vicar laughs with Fabby, "I don't know where that came from. I guess I have been watching Greenbean too much."

In a quick motion, Fabby leaps in front of Vicar and puts up a ward just as boulder hurdles towards them. The boulder hits the ward and falls to the ground. Fabby is knocked to the ground.

Vicar rushes over and begins to help him up as the boulder begins moving. It sprouts legs and its head pops up. It is a Rock Spider.

Vicar pulls Fabby back across the ground away from the spider. Fabby throws an inflict pain spell at it. The spider is unaffected by the spell. It keeps coming towards them. It gets within a foot of Fabby's legs when a huge foot comes from above and steps on the spider.

One of the Giant Guards is standing on the Spider keeping it from moving. He turns to Fabby and Vicar, "You both need to run to Princess Gianna. I'll keep this one from getting you both."

Fabby gets up and turns toward Princess Gianna. They start making their way back to where she is at. They can see flashes of light coming from her position as she uses the Earth and Frost Amulet. Walls of ice and stone are raised in lowered to keep back the masses of Rock Spiders and to immobilize the Trolls.

When they reach Princess Gianna, they can hear the deep guttural roar of one of the Giant guards. He is being overwhelmed by a large group of Rock Spiders. Their sharp claws pierce his body and armor. Within seconds, the large Frost Giant is dead and falls to the ground.

Princess Gianna tries desperately to freeze and crush the Rock Spiders but is unable to stop them fast enough. She cries out in anguish then notices that another of her guards is being overwhelmed to the left. She begins to use the Frost Amulet to freeze the spiders but then hears another guard yelling that the line has been broken.

Two exceptionally large Trolls and about twenty Rock Spiders break through a group of soldiers and head straight for the Princess. Fabby and Vicar jump in front of her and prepare to engage the Trolls and spiders. Gianna creates a wall in front of them of ice and stones, but the Trolls runs at full speed and break through it.

The Spiders scamper through the opening made by the Trolls. Fabby uses wards to deflect their attacks and Vicar swings his sword at their legs. The last two Giant guards come to protect Gianna and start fighting with the Trolls. As the guards hold the Trolls, Gianna creates several ice spikes in the air and hurls them at the Trolls. They find their mark and impale the Trolls' chests and abdomens.

Fabby and Vicar are still fighting the spiders as they hear wings above. They look up and see Thoraxian, Ransom, and Warrior swooping down and blasting fire on the Rock Spiders. The spiders begin to scream and panic. Some shrivel up and roll on their backs while others run back through the opening in the wall while on fire.

Ransom and Warrior land on each side of Fabby and Vicar. Fabby gets on Warrior with Judas and Vicar get on Ransom with Mandrake. They take off and get above the fighting. Thoraxian hovers above and speaks to Princess Gianna, "It's going to get very hot very fast. If you are able to make a wall of ice, I would do so."

Princess Gianna yells to her guards to gather up the remaining Blackwing Keep soldiers and get behind her. The soldiers that hear her start running to get behind her. The guards scoop up the other soldiers that didn't hear or are too wounded to run. When all of them are behind Gianna she creates a thick ice shell around all of them.

Thoraxian, Warrior, Ransom, who are now joined by Granite, Shemera, Addrit, and Zold begin spewing Dragon and Wyvern fire on all the Trolls and Rock Spiders around the Princess and the soldiers. There are screams and yells that can be heard for miles coming from the Trolls and Spiders. Many drop dead instantly and others run the other way. Further back from the main area of fighting, the other Trolls and Rock spiders see the fire rain down. They panic and run from the battlefield towards the Western woods.

After all the Trolls and Rock Spiders are either dead or have fled, the Wyverns and Dragons land next to the ice shell. Princess Gianna retracts the ice shell and begins to thank the aerial saviors. One lone soldier runs out from the group and heads straight for Zold.

Zold runs to the soldier. He leans his neck down to the ground and the soldier hugs him. The young Dragon speaks to the soldier, "Ben, I am glad you are safe. I was scared that I would lose you to those nasty spiders. I knew how to take care of them because of the time that you fell into their den."

Ben continues to hug Zold tightly, "Zold, I was scared too. We were overwhelmed by their sheer numbers. I'm so glad you all came to save us."

Thoraxian speaks to Ben's mind, "You'll have to thank Darkwing. He is high in the sky watching what is going on down on the ground and coordinating where we should go."

Ben lets go of Zold's neck and looks over to Thoraxian, "I will thank him as soon as I can. We still need to get to the Keep. Thanks to you and the others, we are able to get into the town."

Princess Gianna huffs loudly, "I can't believe that we have lost so many already. Three of my guards are dead and at least fifty soldiers. We have underestimated the force that King Carthon could raise. We need to regroup. Plus, Aphorea just told me that the Keep is protected by a barrier of powerful Dark magic."

Darkwing flies high on Mylar above the town of Cliffside. He has a full panoramic view of the town and the Keep. He can see that Griffons to the right of himself, the Dragons, and Wyverns to the left in the air, and directly below him are Princess Gianna and the soldiers from Blackwing Keep. He cannot see the Dwarves on the South side of the town walls. He hopes that means that no one else can see them as they make their way to the docks.

Annut relays a message to him that the Keep has a barrier around it that fire and frost cannot penetrate. She then lets him know that they are commencing to burning the rest of the town. Then he sees that Annut, Elisbeth, Granite, Shemera, Addrit, and Zold are burning the buildings closest to the Keep and Thoraxian, Choren, Ransom, Drako, Hunter, and Warrior begin to torch the buildings close to the outer wall.

The fighting starts to become intense below him and he is saddened as he can see soldiers fall to the Trolls and Rock Spiders. He is hopeful that they can persist until he sees a Frost Giant become overrun and killed by a swarm of Rock Spiders. He can then see the masses break through the defensive line and head towards Princess Gianna. Darkwing calls out for Thoraxian to help the Princess, Fabby, and Vicar.

From the North he gets message from Orien that they are not having any luck getting to the balconies because of the barrier and for the moment they are just protecting Olek and the Golems from attacks from above.

Darkwing looks to the North but cannot see the hundred Golems because of the high walls. He, however, can see that a dark cloud is moving towards the Griffons. He wonders what it could be and if he should be concerned. He asks Mylar to use his keen Owl eyes to decern what the dark cloud could be.

Mylar focuses his eyes, "Master, they are big Bats with sharp claws and teeth. They even have armor like they Lommas gave me."

Darkwing reaches out to Orien, "You have giant Bats coming your way! Let Earl Jarkon know immediately!"

Darkwing then reaches out to Aphorea. "Aphorea, the Griffons are being attacked by giant Bats on the North side of the Keep Can you and Rethu help them?"

Aphorea relays the message to Rethu and Akita, then flies to the North side of the Keep. Darkwing can see intense fighting from the Griffons. When Aphorea and Rethu arrive, he can see spouts of frost and water in several directions. Then Bats catch on fire, which must be the work of Akita, Wulf, and Void.

He feels that the Griffons are being looked over well by Akita and them, so he turns his attention to the Princess again. The ground below him is covered in fire and there are dead Rock Spider and Trolls all over the battlefield. The soldiers and Giants are in some kind of ice shield.

He and Mylar fly a little more to the South to get a better look at the docks area. The first thing he sees is the Demi-Titan in the bay. She is luminescent from the moonlight and the power of the Sea Amulet. The water around her heaves as she moves in the bay.

He asks Mylar to look for the Dwarves. Mylar searches along the town wall. He finally spots one of the Dwarves as they begin to descend over the cliff. Mylar lets Darkwing know and Darkwing relays the information to the others.

CHAPTER 20
FINAL BATTLE

Aphorea receives a message from Darkwing that there are giant Bats headed for the Griffons. She then tells Rethu and Akita what is going on. They all race over the town and up to the North. The Bats have engaged the mounted Griffons by the time that they reached them.

Aphorea tries freezing some with her frost breath, but it doesn't slow them down much because they have really thick fur. She then has Rethu spew his Water Breath at them so she can freeze that around them. At the same time Akita and Wulf are sending fireballs at them as Void uses a shock spell to knock them out of the sky.

Several Griffon riders are knocked off of their mounts and have fallen to their death. The Griffons were unable to swoop down and save their riders because the Bats are holding them back by their wings. The Bats have bloodied many Griffons to the point that they had to land.

More and more Bats seem to be coming for them. Earl Jarkon yells for them to regroup and form a line. The remaining Griffons and Dragons line up across the sky and move forward to meet the Bats head on. They all push through the cloud of Bats with frost, fire, and boiling water from Rethu. Bats begin dropping from the sky. The ones that get through are swiftly dealt with by the riders with their polearms and swords.

Somewhere in the cloud everyone can hear a loud scream of anguish. They soon realize that it is Captain Dubbin. A Bat has pierced his left pauldron and has pulled him off his Griffon. The bat begins to fly away with him.

The Griffon he was riding tries to fight off the Bat but is attacked and killed by three other Bats. Earl Jarkon and Orien fly to Captain Dubbin's defense. As they get to him, a large Bat swoops in and hits Earl Jarkon from the side. Earl Jarkon slumps over onto Orien's neck. Orien can't get Earl Jarkon to respond to his pleas to get up.

Aphorea can hear Orien pleading to Earl Jarkon to get up. Aphorea tells Akita, Wulf, and Void what has happened. Akita and Wulf immediately leap from Aphorea's back and fly to get Captain Dubbin. They reach him in less than a minute and can see Captain Dubbin is stabbing the bat with a dagger. They get on either side of the bat and grab its wings. Akita yells to Wulf to burn them off. Fire starts to emanate from their hands and the Bat's wings singe and catch fire. The bat quickly lets go of Captain Dubbin and he begins to fall. Akita and Wulf fly down and catch him then fly him to the ground.

Captain Dubbin wrenches from their grasp and heads towards Orien and Earl Jarkon who have also landed, "Let go of me. I'm okay! I need to check on the Earl."

Aphorea calls to everyone to tell them that the Earl has been hurt. Shemera and Addrit fly Ishvet and Vivian to Earl Jarkon as quickly as possible. Behind them is Ixenvorlux on Drako and Mandrake and Vicar on Ransom. They reach Earl Jarkon as Captain Dubbin gets him off Orien.

Captain Dubbin lays the Earl on the ground and looks over the Ixen and Mandrake, "Hurry, he's not breathing!"

They both kneel beside the Earl and begin a barrage of healing spells. Trying to heal the gashes in the Earl's neck. Mandrake then stops and grabs Ixen's hands, "Stop Ixen, He is gone. We can heal the body but not the spirit."

Ixen hangs her head in defeat and slowly gets up as Vivian runs to her father's side. Ishvet gets behind her and embraces her from behind. Vivian begins to sob and shudder. Ishvet tries to pull her away, but Vivian stands firm, "Vivian, please, we have to move. It's not safe here. We still have a battle to fight.

Akita walks up and kneels next to Vivian, "I'm going to have Addrit take Earl Jarkon to Princess Gianna. He's going to ask her to open a rift to the temple and he is going to take your father's body back."

Vivian wipes away her tears as Ishvet pulls her up to her feet, "Okay, yes that's a good plan. Thanks Akita."

Akita looks up to Aphorea, "Please have the younger Dragons gather up any wounded soldiers and Griffons and take them back to the Temple when Gianna opens the rift. Tell them to stay at the temple with the wounded. This has become a more dangerous fight than we anticipated."

Aphorea relays the messages to all the young Dragons. Akita then walks over to Wulf, "I was afraid this was going to happen. We need to find a way through this barrier."

Wulf holds Akita for a second, "We will, and we knew that we were going to lose people. That's the nature of war. We just need to keep going and end this before we lose anyone else,"

Akita shakes her head in agreement and starts walking back to Aphorea, "Aphorea can you take me to Gianna? We need to figure out how to get through the barrier."

The Captain of the Dwarven fighters is slim for a Dwarf. He has a charcoal black beard and sky-blue eyes. As he leads the group of fighters along the south wall, he begins to imagine the Grizzles they are going to face in the drainage tunnel. He looks back at his men and knows that some of them won't make it out of the tunnel tonight. Still, he leads them to the cliffs edge that Skip described to them.

They all set their anchors and threw the climbing ropes down. One by one they descend to the beach below. Once they get to the beach, they hug the cliff and stay in its shadow so that the Demi-Titan can't see them. Several guards are walking the docks. Closer to the giant wood and iron gates is a rather menacing looking Centaur.

With hand signals, the Captain lets his men know to stay down, stay single file, and keep weapons sheathed until in the tunnel. As they creep along the cliff face, they freeze when the Demi-Titan looks their way, resuming their trek as it looks away again. The Centaur will soon become a problem because it can see in the darkness.

They come to an outcropping that will expose them in the moonlight and will allow the Centaur to see them from the dock. The Dwarf Captain stops and assesses the situation. He looks back in whispers, "Hess, you will need to make your way to the water, sneak under the dock, and send an arrow directly into the heart of that Centaur. If you miss, we will all be killed by that Demi-Titan."

Hess nods his head in acknowledgment, "Yes, Captain Ruskin. My aim will be true."

The young Dwarf locks a bolt in his crossbow and waits for the Demi-Titan and the Centaur to look the other way. He runs down the slope and under the dock into the water. He slowly moves in the frigid water to line up his shot.

Hess splashes the water to get the Centaurs attention. The Centaur turns in the direction of the noise and a bolt strikes him in the heart. He falls to his knees and rolls over on his side. However, the Centaur is not completely dead. It reaches for its bow and arrow and begins to draw back.

Captain Ruskin steps from behind the out cropping and let's bolt fly from his crossbow. The bolt makes its way to the heart of the Centaurs torso. The Centaur makes a loud cry and becomes limp.

The Demi-Titan hears the cry and moves closer. Waves slap up against the dock and cliffside. The Demi-Titan can see the dead Centaur and knows that an enemy is nearby. She begins smashing the dock and all the ships in the bay, splintered wood and water are flying everywhere.

Captain Ruskin, motions for his men to make for the tunnel entrance. Luckily the barrier doesn't come down this far. It stops at the cliff edge. They all run for the opening and make it inside as the

Demi-Titan notices them. She punches the opening to the drainage tunnel and the cliff around it collapses and the ruble blocks the tunnel.

General Olek directs the Stone Golems to begin bashing the thick stone wall of the North side of the Keep. The control rod that Ghod made relays his instructions to all the Golems at once. The Golems move up to the wall and begin pounding into the stone. The fact that they can actually hit the stone means that the barrier stops where the wall juts out from the Keep.

Several Golems climb onto the shoulders of the front Golems and begin pounding into the stone above them. Large cracks begin to appear in the stone and chips and chunks fall to the ground. The Golems continue to beat the stone as a commotion can be heard above them.

Olek looks up to see the Griffons engaging large bats in the air. He has some of the Golems move into a defensive line around the others in the event that the bats attack them. He then moves inside the line for protection. The Golems continue to beat the stone wall.

He continues to look up and watch the battle unfold between the Griffons and Giant Bats. He is saddened as he sees Griffon riders and Griffon hit the ground in front of him. Olek wants to run to their aid, but he needs to stay with the Golems.

Aphorea enters his mind and alerts him along with the others that Earl Jarkon has been hurt. Soon he sees Orien land in the field several hundred feet away. Then several Wyverns and Aphorea and Rethu. The Dragons and Wyverns surround Orien and Earl Jarkon.

Moments later, Aphorea announces that Earl Jarkon is dead from a wound caused by one of the bats. Then she lets everyone know that the Younger Dragons are taking his body and the wounded soldiers back to the Temple. Olek is astonished at how quickly events can unfold.

The pounding from the Golems stops as he finishes his thoughts. He turns and sees that a large section of the wall has crumbled in. The hole is about twenty golems wide and two Golems tall. He looks beyond the Golems and can see that they have knocked the wall into a large storeroom. He directs the golems to begin entering and to pulverize anyone that they come across.

Golems move into the storeroom and bust through the door in no time. They enter a wide hallway and walk three abreast into a Great Hall. The Hall is filled with about forty Centaurs and maybe six Dark Wizards. The Golems run into the group and begin to fight. Two Golems stay at General Olek's side to protect him.

The Centaurs use arrows at first against the Golems, but they just bounce off. They then try knocking the Golems on their backs with the horse part of their bodies. Several Golems get knocked down. The Dark Wizards move in and use several spells on the immobilized Golems.

One spell finally works and destroys a golem. He tells the other Wizards, and they begin to destroy Golem after Golem. The Spell shatters the stone of the Golems into small pieces. Olek has the Golems turn their attention from the Centaurs to the Wizards. The wizards had to take out one on one, so the Golems essentially overwhelmed them with numbers.

Olek starts to think that Ghod should have made more than one hundred. As the fighting in the Great Hall begins to subside, Olek can see that the Wizards are dead and that only a hand full of Centaurs remains. He can also see that there are only about twenty-five Golems remaining plus his two bodyguards.

He directs the remaining Golems to dispatch the last of the Centaurs. They begin to head for the large horse men, but the Centaurs retreat down a hallway. Olek has the Golems break off pursuit and regroup with him and the bodyguards as he contacts Aphorea. He lets Aphorea know what has happened and that they have a way inside the Keep from the North.

Ishvet and Vivian get on Orien and Captain Dubbin gets on his Griffon. They escort Addrit with Earl Jarkon's body back to Princess Gianna's position. The other young Dragons and the Wyverns meet close by. Aphorea, Thoraxian, Annut, and Rethu take up defensive positions around all of them.

All the riders get off and group up next to the Princess. Princess Gianna opens a rift to the Temple. Addrit goes through with Earl Jarkon's body and is followed by Shemera, Granite, Zold, Elsbeth, Choren carrying the wounded soldiers.

The rift closes and Princess Gianna calls Akita over.

Akita makes her way to Princess Gianna and Gianna kneels to the ground, "Akita, these dark creatures appear to be stronger than we initially thought. You have lost many soldiers and I have lost three of my guards. Not to mention the Earl has been killed. We need to revise our plan. Until we can get through that barrier, we have no hope of ending this quickly."

Akita looks around at everyone. They seem to be waiting for her to answer with a sold plan, but she doesn't really have one. If Dragon Fire and Frost can't penetrate it, she doesn't know what will. She thinks that maybe the power of the amulets will have better luck, but she remembers what happened to the Magma Amulet and is afraid to ask Gianna to risk the Frost or Earth amulet.

Before Akita can answer Aphorea begins to speak into their minds, "Olek and the Golems have breached the North wall where the barrier wasn't to the ground. They engaged many Centaurs and several Dark Wizards. They have them on the run for the moment."

Akita breathes a sigh of relief, "Thank goodness they were able to get through. At least something is going right. Everyone, listen up. We are going to enter the Keep from the North side and face the enemy hand to hand. Get prepared."

Aphorea speaks again, "You all will be on your own until the barrier is down. We will wait out here for your signal."

Ishvet steps forward, "There are several staircases going up to the rooms and only one that I know of that goes down to the dungeons. May I suggest that we break up into teams to cover as many floors as possible."

Akita agrees, "Yes that sounds good. Vivian, Storm, and Ishvet you come with Wulf and me. We will go up the first set of stairs, Skip, Quinn, Gavin, and Jacklyn you go to the next set that lead down to the dungeons., Ghod, Judas, Mandrake, and Vicar you go up the further set of stairs that lead up. Greenbean, Fabby, Ordyn and Darkwing when he gets back down here make your way to the south Courtyard and dispatch the guards out there. Ixen, you stay here with Princess Gianna and heal up the Frost Giant guards."

Annut tells Darkwing to meet them at the breach in the north wall. Everyone else gets on a mount or gets picked up by a Dragon and makes their way over to the breach. The Dragons, Wyverns, Mylar, and Orien drop them off and return to the Princess outside of the town gates.

Meh-Kola watched as the Dwarf fighters made their way down the cliff, killed the Centaur, and ran into the tunnel. She was helpless to do anything when the Demi-Titan smashed the opening and trapped the Dwarfs. Now that the Demi-Titan turned her attention away from the tunnel, Meh-Kola could move in to assess the situation.

Akita asked Meh-Kola to shadow the Dwarves, in the event that they needed help, or if they found a way into the main part of the Keep. She stayed a good distance away and was very impressed with the stealth of the Dwarves. They had been trained well and anyone in that same situation would have been lucky to escape with their lives.

Meh-Kola makes it to the cave-in at the tunnel entrance, "One wonders if everyone is okay beyond the debris. One will blink into the tunnel and check on the stealthy Dwarves."

She blinks into complete darkness beyond the jagged pieces of rock blocking the tunnel exit. Her eyes adjust quickly and can see the Dwarves further down the tunnel. They are not using lanterns, so she wonders how they are making their way in the dark. Meh-Kola decides that they will be safer together, so she blinks next to Captain Ruskin.

Captain Ruskin doesn't even flinch when Meh-Kola blinks right next to him. He just turns and whispers, "Nice of you to join us little one. We may need your help. I can hear the distinct sound of the Grizzles up ahead."

Meh-Kola tilts her head and twists her ear towards the tunnel, "One can hear them. They sound like a swarm of hornets in clanky armor."

The Captain nods his head, "Yup, they are ferocious. You could easily get overwhelmed in seconds by them. Your ability to blink to and fro and being able to see in the dark will help. We are able to see pretty well in the dark too, being a subterranean race and all."

Meh-Kola looks back at the other forty-nine Dwarves and wonders if they are going to be enough to dispatch the horde of Grizzles, "One doesn't know if you have enough Dwarves to take all these Grizzles on. Do you have a plan?

Captain Ruskin smiles a wily smile, "We are going to do what we do best. We're going to hammer them into the ground."

She almost laughs aloud but stops herself. A vision of the Dwarves using oversized hammers to catch mice, runs through her mind, "One likes the sound of that. One can scout ahead and find the best spot to get them."

The Dwarven Captain agrees and Meh-Kola blinks ahead to a larger chamber where several tunnels meet. She is against the ceiling and covered in darkness. There are hundreds of Grizzles in the chamber and a particularly oversized one giving them directions in their native tongue. She blinks back to the Captain and tells him what she has seen.

They decide that the best course of action would be to rush them and catch them off guard.

Captain Ruskin alerts his men to the plan and the message is passed on all the way down the tunnel to the last Dwarf. They prepare and have their war hammers at the ready. Meh-Kola has her claws out and is ready to pounce after she blinks into the chamber. She is going directly for the leader Grizzle.

Captain Ruskin gives the signal, and the Dwarves pour from the tunnel and begin bashing Grizzles left and right. The Grizzles are soon aware of what is happening and begin to turn and fight. Their small swords are very sharp, and they can move very quickly. They are able to sever a few Dwarves from the group and overwhelm them.

Meh-Kola is able to blink within striking distance of the Grizzle leader and claw his throat. Several Grizzles rush to his defense and try stabbing at Meh-Kola. She is able to dodge most, but one sword tears through her right wing and she falls to the ground. The Grizzles begin to swarm her.

As the Grizzles reach Meh-Kola she tries to blink away. However, the pain from the slice in her wing is keeping her from blinking. She thinks that this will be the end of her when she starts hearing loud thuds getting closer. Next to her a large hammer comes down and squashes a Grizzle. Then another to the other side of her. Captain Ruskin is then kneeling beside her and picking her up.

He stands as several Grizzles rush towards him, but he is able to dispatch them all with one swing of his hammer, "Meh-Kola grab onto my cloak at my shoulder."

Meh-Kola grabs onto the cloak and watches the Dwarven Captain smash and bash his way through the Grizzle into an adjacent tunnel. Ten of the Dwarves follow them and the rest guard the entrance to the tunnel behind them. Further down the tunnel she can see light and smell the familiar smell of the dungeon laboratory.

When they get to the end of the tunnel there is an iron gate and beyond is the laboratory. Captain Ruskin sits Meh-Kola down on the ground and bashes the gate open. Meh-Kola hurries into the open and around the corner. The Dwarves quickly run into the laboratory and start to engage the few Dark Wizards that are in the room.

The Dwarves that stayed back to keep the Grizzles from following down the tunnel soon join the Captain and the other ten Dwarves. The Grizzles have all been dealt with and now only these few Dark Wizards remain. The fighting starts to get intense in the Dungeon Laboratory. Spells are flying everywhere, and several Dwarves have already fallen.

Meh-Kola scurries behind a large table and begins riffling through her enchanted bag. She finds a small container of powder and begins sprinkling it on her sliced wing. Her wing begins to mend, and the pain subsides. In no more than a few minutes the wing is completely healed. She begins to Blink around the room using her special set of skills to slice the throats of several Dark Wizards. Saving many Dwarves as result.

Soon the Dark Wizards in the laboratory are all deceased and the Dwarves regroup at the bottom of the staircase. There are only thirty-two Dwarves left out of the fifty. Meh-Kola begins to describe what is above them and how they can get to the main staircase of the Keep.

Captain Ruskin leads the charge up the stairs and follows Meh-Kola's directions to get to the main Staircase. Him and his men arrive just as

Akita and her warriors are dispatching the last Centaur on that floor.

The way that the Keep is designed there is a grand staircase that leads up and then splits to the two wings of the Keep. At the top of the grand staircase are large double doors that lead to the throne room and at the back of that large room are two more sets of stairs that lead to a tower with living quarters and the other to a mezzanine and rooftop gardens. On the first floor to the right of the grand staircase is the hallway that the Dwarven came through from the dungeon Laboratory. To the left, is several hallways that lead to the storge rooms, Dining hall, and Kitchen.

In front of the grand stairs, across the great length of the room is the main entrance to the Keep. Those doors are still sealed by the barrier. Large ornate windows flank the entrance and continue up to the second floor. Above the staircase on either side are walkways that lead to meeting rooms.

Akita looks up and around taking in the magnitude of the Keep. She thinks that the Keep would have been beautiful in its prime, but age and neglect have seen it fall into a state of disrepair. That aside, they will need to search every corner of the Keep to find all the Dark Wizards that are conjuring the barrier.

General Olek has already led the Golems into the Throne room at the top of the stairs. Ordyn, Fabby, Greenbean, and Darkwing have already gone down the hall and out the side door to the courtyard and are fighting the Keep guards and a couple of Dark Wizards. Quinn, Skip, Gavin, and Jacklyn are back in the main room with the others because the Dwarves took care of everyone below.

Ghod, Judas, Mandrake, and Vicar are on the walkways above clearing out the various rooms that surround the staircase. Akita leads everyone else up the grand staircase into the Throne room. There they will break off into groups to search for the remaining Dark Wizards and King Carthon.

CHAPTER 21

CLIFFSHADE KEEP

Ghod walks up to Akita, "The first two floors are cleared. Only five Dark Wizards for us to take care of. I am highly disappointed."

Akita shakes her head, "I'm sure there are more above us. You will get your chance."

As Ghod was beginning to speak, Meh-Kola blinks next to Akita in the air about shoulder level, "Akita, One has found the way to his chambers."

Akita turns to Ghod, "Get everyone in position we will attack from both sides and clear out all the Dark Wizards along the way."

Wulf moves to Akita's side and tightens the strap on her breastplate. She draws her enchanted pact blade in her right hand and produces a fireball in her left palm. She then turns to the group, "Let's go get this tyrant. Olek, leave the Golems in the Throne room and go with Ghod's group up the right set of stairs the rest are with me on the left set of stairs. Meh-Kola says that Carthon is six floors above us and that there are about forty Dark Wizards between here and there."

Darkwing steps up clears his throat, "Don't hesitate to eliminate the Dark Wizards. Ishvet and I hunted them down for many years and we both know that they will not hesitate to eliminate you. Stay in pairs as you clear the floors. If anyone is alone, they will use that to their benefit."

Ishvet agrees, "Yes, Darkwing is right. However, most of these Dark Wizards that you encounter will be channeling the barrier and distracted. Use that to your advantage to strike before they can." Everyone nods or verbally agrees, then they begin going up the stairways.

The two groups make their way up the stairs. On each floor they fan out in pairs and clear the rooms and take out the Dark Wizards that are channeling the barrier. All is going well and beyond a few scrapes and cuts, everyone is in good shape as they make it to the sixth floor. The stairs open up to a great room and the room is filled with about twenty Dark Wizards.

Akita and her group are on one side of the room and Ghod's group is on the other. As soon as they make it to the top of the stairs they are bombarded by offensive spells. The first spell hits Ghod directly in the chest and he is knocked out. Darkwing throws up an ice wall about ten feet in front of them and the rest of the group run out of the stairwell to begin fighting.

Akita and Wulf are the first out of the stairwell on the other side of the room and they send large bursts of flames to cover the rest of the group leaving the stairwell. Vivian and Vicar create shields to deflect the Dark Magic. Fabby rushes to Ghod's side and begins to heal him. Greenbean and Jacklyn begin to engage the Wizards in the forefront with their Great swords and Ward rings. Gavin and Skip step out and begin firing enchanted arrows from their bows.

Several Dark Wizards fall quickly, others that are closer are putting up a good fight. In particular, there are four powerful Dark Wizards engaging Ghod's Group that no one is able to take down. Spells are streaming back and forth, and each side is deflecting the opposing attacks. Finally, in a lull, Darkwing is able to break through and freeze all four of the Dark Wizards.

Quickly the Dwarves run in to smash them with their hammers.

On Akita's side of the room is a very powerful Dark Wizard. He is deflecting all their attacks and coming close to injuring several members of the group. He is even able to crack and dispel the shields that Vivian and Vicar are putting up. Akita and Wulf's fire magic won't even touch him. Meh-Kola tries several times to catch him by surprise but is blasted back to the stairwell each time.

After about twenty minutes of a stalemate with this powerful Dark Wizard, Storm has had enough. She steps up between Akita and Wulf and asks them to cover her as she lets Rixan loose. Akita and Wulf conjure walls of fire and Vivian and Vicar reinforce the flames with shields. Storm lets Rixan transform her body into the visage of the Demon.

Rixan steps through the flame walls and heads directly for the powerful Dark Wizard. The Dark Wizard stops and stares at Rixan, then he begins to chuckle, "So you decide to show yourself finally. I have been waiting twenty years to see you again Rixan, The Putrid. When I imprisoned you in my old temple, I knew I would have to deal with you eventually. So, I learned how to permanently take your power."

Rixan stops in his tracks as he begins to recognize the Dark Wizard before him. In his deep wet voice, he replies, "Waxmen, I wondered if I would encounter you on this continent. Now I will have my chance to exact revenge on you for using me and leaving me locked up in the Fervant Temple twenty years ago."

Grand Master Waxmen begins to recite an ancient incantation as Rixan moves closer to him. When Waxmen finishes, chains grow out of the floor and wrap around Rixan's wrists and ankles. Usually, iron and steel would decay as it touched Rixan, but these conjured chains are not affected. The chains become tight and pull Rixan to the floor.

Waxmen waves his hand, and Rixan is pulled closer to him. Rixan tries to resist but there is nothing he can do. Akita sees what is going on and tells everyone to throw everything they have at the Dark Wizard. However, all of their attacks are deflected or absorbed by some type of magical barrier around Rixan and Waxmen.

Waxmen moves close to Rixan then places his hand on Rixan's head. Puss and fluids squeeze out between his fingers. Waxmen keeps his hand there and begins to speak an ancient language while going into some kind of trance. His body levitates off of the floor a few inches and where his hand meets Rixan's head, it begins to glow a bright yellow.

Rixan writhes beneath Waxmen's hand, seemingly in excruciating pain. Akita and the others can only watch as their attacks are ineffectual. The remaining Dark Wizards can sense that something is not right, and they are scared. They run past Ghod's group, down the stairs and out of sight.

Everyone with magic abilities in the room can feel a pull towards the Dark Wizard and Rixan. It feels like the very air in the room is being sucked to where Waxmen's hand is touching Rixan. Everyone takes a few steps back as Rixan yells out in pain. His decaying skin begins to be absorbed into Waxmen's hand. More and more of his body is pulled in.

Rixan's back begins to split open along his spine and Storm begins to emerge from the split. She has her hand on either side and is pulling herself up and out of Rixan. Storm gets herself free as the last remnants of Rixan are absorbed by Waxmen. She tumbles across the floor almost all the way to Akita and Wulf's feet.

Waxmen's whole body is glowing bright yellow. He seemed empowered by absorbing Rixan. He puts out his hand, palm first and a wave of power pushes everyone in the room onto their backs. They all begin to slide across the floor to the outside walls. After a few seconds the wave subsides, and they start to get back to their feet.

Akita rushes over to Storm and helps her to her feet, "Storm are you alright? What just happened, and where is Visham?"

Storm's voice is hoarse and weak, "I don't know. I can't feel Rixan anymore. Visham is over in the corner of the room."

Akita starts to tear up, "Oh Storm, I think you may be rid of Rixan, but that means you won't be able to touch Visham anymore."

Storm looks over to Visham and then down to her hands. She starts to shake them as they catch fire, "Look Akita! My magic is coming back. I can't believe it after all this time. And you don't have to worry about Visham. It was Rixan that made him that way. He will be back to normal now also."

A blast of power hits Akita and Storm, knocking them apart. Waxmen walks over and looks down at them, "That is all very touching. However, did you forget that we are in the middle of a battle here. I was just about to use all my powers to turn the lot of you into goo."

Storm looks up to Waxmen with defiance in her eyes, "It is your fault that this happened to me, and I lived in shame all these years. I have faith that all of us can defeat you and your sorry excuse for a master."

Waxmen laughs, "My child, no magic can kill me. I am as ancient as the beginnings of my people. We are the first of the Fervant. My power is total. Now it is time for you…"

A blue flash fills the air in front of Akita and Storm. Waxmen stops talking and has a puzzled look on his face. He tries furling his brow, but eyebrows won't move. A trickle of blood runs down his forehead to the tip of his nose. The blood forms a drop at the end then falls to the floor.

Akita grabs Storm and pulls her away from Waxmen, "I know what this means. Scoot back or you'll get messy."

Waxmen grasps his stomach as his guts begins to spill on the floor. He starts to crumple on the floor and his whole-body splits in two from the top of his head to his crotch. Wulf hurries over with a cloak and covers the gruesome sight. Blood oozes out from the cloak forming a pool. Storm and Akita get up and move back even further.

Ishvet is standing on the other side of the room with Bitter Bite in his hand. It is covered in blood, however Ishvet isn't. He looks over to Akita, "Well, I spent all that time perfecting my Blue Streak that I thought I might as well try it on this guy, while he was distracted and contemplating our gooey demise. It worked even better than I thought it would. Sliced him down the middle like a summer tomato."

Storm sits up and calls for Visham. Visham flies over to Storm and lands at her feet and crawls up her leg and up to her shoulder. She pets him with her bare hand. He is delighted that they are both no longer cursed by Rixan.

She looks over to Ishvet, "I believe that your Blue Streak is the only thing that could kill him. Rixan had told me that this Wizard was immune to magic somehow. I only wonder how old this guy really was. Rixan said that the Wizard had siphoned his Demon powers to stay young looking. That's why he was being kept in that chamber in the ancient temple. It's not a surprise that he was drawn to Carthon and the Sea Amulet."

Akita sends her thoughts to Aphorea, "Aphorea, we have eliminated the Dark Wizards that were making the barrier. We fought a particularly nasty Dark Wizard that killed Rixan, but Ishvet sliced and diced him in the end."

Aphorea lets the other Dragons, Wyverns, and Princess Gianna know what has happened in the Keep. Then she asks Akita for direction, "Akita should we begin to engage the Demi-Titan or wait for you to deal with King Carthon?"

After a short pause, Akita responds, "We are going after King Carthon right now. I'm afraid that once we start fighting him, he will send the Demi-Titan after all of you."

Aphorea talks it over with Princess Gianna, "The Princess thinks we should try to keep the Demi-Titan busy while you deal with King Carthon. We will engage from the air while the Princess moves to the docks."

Akita lets the others in the room know what the Dragons, Wyverns, and Giants are going to do. She gives Aphorea one last message, "Let the Gods be with you all."

Princess Gianna and her three guards run through the town to the East side, break through the wall and slide down the cliff to the dock and shore area in the Cliffshade Bay. Aphorea, Thoraxian, Annut, Rethu, with the four Wyverns fly around the Keep and over the bay. The Demi-Titan is standing in the waters of the bay watching the Dragons circle. She is thrashing and roaring in a fit of rage.

Princess Gianna uses the Frost Amulet to begin freezing the water of the bay. Then uses the Earth Amulet to raise small islands as steppingstones for her and the guards to get closer to the Demi-Titan. Aphorea, and Rethu attack the Demi-Titan from the air by swooping in and blasting her with their breath attacks.

Jessa, the Demi-Titan, reaches out and tries to grab at the Dragons with her hands. The second set of appendages that she has below her arms are snake-like with the heads of Wyverns as the hands. One side is an Ice Wyvern, and the other is a Fire Wyvern. They work independently from Jessa. They are shooting fire and ice breath in several directions to keep the Giants away.

Hunter, Warrior, Ransom, and Drako try to attack Jessa's back, but she turns and swings wildly in the air. They are nearly struck but manage to dodge her quick strikes. They fly back around the Keep getting some distance from her. Thoraxian and Annut make a run at Jessa both coming from opposite sides and blasting fire in front of themselves. The fire only scorches Jessa's hair and skin.

Each attack seems less and less effective against Jessa. The Dragons regroup and all four of them fly straight for Jessa and combine their breath attack into one powerful blast. It hits Jessa in the chest and knocks her back. She falls backwards into the sharp stone outcropping and blood can be seen trickling into the Sea.

Aphorea speaks to all the Dragons, Wyverns, and Giants, "It seems she can be injured. The sharp stones have cut her back. Princess Gianna, the Earth Amulet may be your best weapon at the moment."

Princess Gianna agrees and concentrates while holding the Earth Amulet. She imagines massive, pointed stones rising from the bay floor towards the Demi-Titan. Out in the bay, the sharp stones shoot out of the water and pierce Jessa in the side as she stands back up. The stone sticks in her beneath where the Wyvern arms are and blood gushes out of the wound. Jessa screams out with a deafening roar.

The scream is so loud and at first Princess Gianna believes that it is the cause of the explosion that engulfs the top of the Keep. Very quickly she realizes that the explosion came from within the Keep from the top of the main tower. Chunks of stone fall to the ground all around her. The force of the blast pushes the Wyverns in the sky causing them to tumble for a moment before they can right themselves."

Akita turns to everyone, "Okay, get ready. Carthon is beyond that door. He has the Sea Amulet, so he is already way more dangerous than the last Dark Wizard we just faced. Plus, he is very experienced in Dark Magic. I want wards up as we enter, weapons drawn, and spells at the ready. If anything in there moves, blast it and stab it. We take no chances."

Everyone lines up behind Akita and moves to the door. It is a large wide wooden door that can fit two wide at a time. Akita and Wulf open the door and Vivian shields herself and Ishvet as they walk through the doorway. Akita and Wulf follow behind, with Darkwing and Storm behind them. The Dwarves stay behind and watch the stairwells to make sure no one or any creature tries to attack from the back. They also stay to watch over Ghod who is still knocked out.

Mandrake and Vicker step in the doorway, then Ordyn and Greenbean, behind them is Fabby and Void. Once they are all in the next room Skip and Gavin along with Qwinn and Jacklyn move in. The last to enter are Judas and General Olek.

Meh-Kola has already blinked to a corner of the next room.

The room is dark with only a few candles making any light. Meh-Kola lets everyone know that someone is in the room with them. The team spreads out along the back wall of the room. Suddenly all the candles in the room light and everything could be seen.

The room is large and well decorated. Several sofas and small tables line the walls in the center is a larger table with about ten chairs around it. At the head of the table is an older man in a dark robe. He stays seated and offers seats to anyone that wants to sit. No one takes a seat.

Akita steps closer to him, "Who are you? Where is King Carthon?"

The man in the robe lifts his hand and motions to the door behind him, "King Carthon is in the next room waiting for you Lady Blackwing. I am Volaern Holfstead. I am right hand to our King. He has ordered that I do not engage you but allow you the opportunity to surrender and pledge your loyalty to him."

Ishvet lets out an audible laugh. Akita turns and gives him a funny look, "Ishvet, I think he is serious."

Akita then looks at Volaern, "Sir I don't care who you are. We are here to kill your King, not to pledge our loyalty."

Volaern stands up at the end of the table then there is a loud thud, and he falls back into his chair. His eyes are wide then close. His head falls forward until his chin hits his chest. Directly below his chin, in the middle of his chest is a lone arrow buried deep.

Everyone sharply turns to look behind them and can see Gavin with a bow out in front of him. Gavin then reaches back and pulls another arrow from his quiver and nocks it. He notices everyone looking back at him, "Whatcha lookin at me for? Akita said that if we see somethin' move to eliminate it. He stood up so I put him down."

Akita smiles a bit and shakes her head, "Gavin I meant if they were being aggressive. The poor guy just stood up. I guess we won't get any more information out of him."

Gavin looks puzzled, "Well you mighta been more specific Akita. You said take no chances, so I let 'em fly."

Storm walks up to Volaern's body and lifts his head, "Well it doesn't really matter now does it. The right and left hand are dead now, so let's go cut off the head."

As they get close to the door, Carthon's voice echoes through the room, "Are you ready to face your doom Akita Blackwing?"

Before Akita can answer a blast pushes through the door and splinters it, the walls split open, and the roof blows off. Everyone is knocked to the ground and all the furniture is thrown about the room. The force blew the whole top of the Keep off. The only thing above them is the night sky and the full moon.

In the other room stands King Carthon next to Hector. He is holding the Sea Amulet above his head. He looks around and surveys the damage, "I thought we might need a little more room to finish this. Too bad about the Keep, but it can be rebuilt. Akita are you over there?

Akita starts to get up and looks around at everyone on the floor and the level of destruction.

She can feel small cuts on her face and arms from the force of the blast and flying debris. The others are in the same shape and are starting to get up from the floor. As she stands, she can look across and see King Carthon, "It is about time that we finally meet Carthon. You have many deaths to answer for."

Carthon lowers his arm and walks closer to Akita. Only the remains of the wall that was between them separates them. He looks up into the sky and can see the Wyverns, Dragons, and Mylar flying above. They had come to see what the explosion was.

He shakes his head and makes a tsking sound with his tongue, "Akita Blackwing, I have only got started."

King Carthon turns towards the bay and holds out the Sea Amulet. Tendrils of water spring out of the sea and reach up into the sky. They move very quickly and grab Aphorea from the sky. The tendrils wrap around her wings, arms, and legs. She tries to bite at the tendrils but they just reform after being broken. Thoraxian flies to her and tries to burn them away to no effect.

The tendrils move Aphorea closer to Jessa until the Demi-Titan is able to grab Aphorea. Her hands clench Aphorea's wings and the Wyvern arms wrap around Aphorea's torso and begin to squeeze. Aphorea struggles against the Demi-Titans strength. The rest of the Dragons, Wyverns, and Mylar try to free Aphorea with breath attacks and by clawing at her face and arms. Jessa doesn't let loose.

Akita watches helplessly for a moment from the Keep. She tries to fly up, but she is knocked back to the floor by a spell from King Carthon. She cries out for Aphorea, "Carthon stop this at once! Make Jessa let her go!"

Ordyn and Gavin try to fly up and are immediately knocked back down to the floor. Darkwing tries to send large shards of ice towards Jessa, but they are also knocked away. Vicar runs over to Darkwing, "Try again and I'll buff your power. Maybe they will get through then."

Darkwing concentrates his magic to focus it into one large ice shard. Vicar buffs Darkwing's magic and Darkwing lets the shard fly. They watch as it hits King Carthon's knock back spell and slices right through it. It continues flying towards Jessa. Before it can reach her, they are shocked as Aphorea is crushed and killed by Jessa's brute strength.

Jessa lets go of Aphorea and her limp body falls into the ocean at her feet. Ice from Gianna had just reached Jessa and began creeping up her legs, freezing her in place. The Dragons, Wyverns, and Mylar cry out at the sight of Aphorea being killed. They intensify their attacks but are being batted away by the Demi-Titan.

At the Keep, Akita and all the others scream out in disbelief. Horror turns to anger in a flash and Akita flies up and charges at King Carthon. Wulf tries to grab her, but misses. Carthon flicks his wrists and hands in an intentional pattern. A blade of water emanates from the Sea Amulet and heads for Akita. Akita tries to dodge it, but it hits her. It slices off her right wing almost directly where it attaches to her back.

She falls to the ground in pain. Vivian runs in and puts up a shield, while Wulf and Ishvet grab Akita and pull her back into the other room. Vicar runs to Vivian and helps strengthen the shield. Several other water blades came at them, but the shield holds. Akita is fighting Ishvet and Wulf trying to escape their grasp to go after Carthon. Tears are streaming down her face, and she is calling Carthon every bad name she can think of. Storm gets behind Akita and cauterizes the wound on Akitas back. Mandrake then forms ice on it to help with the pain.

Gavin runs into the room that Carthon is in. He thinks that if he gets Akita's wing they will be able to reattach it. He slides across the floor and ends up next to Akita's wing. Carthon holds up his hand and the wing bursts into flames. Gavin grabs at it but it is ash in an instant.

Carthon laughs, "Good try little hunter. The rest of your master will soon be ash along with her wing. Now what to do with you."

The Sea Amulet glows bright. Water begins to move around Gavin and form a sphere. It raises Gavin off the ground and holds him in the air as it is drowning him. Gavin struggles to get free, but he is just swimming in place. He tries to hold his breath, but water is being forced into his lungs.

From the left side Darkwing sends ice shards at Carthon and from the right Skip sends a barrage of enchanted arrows. Carthon is caught off guard and has to dodge to avoid the attacks. Judas runs into the room and catches Gavin as the sphere evaporates. Judas then takes an unconscious Gavin back behind the rest of the group.

Fabby meets Judas in the back of the room and helps Gavin to start breathing again. Vivian and Vicar move back into the other room to shield the entire group. Void moves up and helps with the shielding. Something behind Carthon catches Ishvet's eye.

Hector falls over onto the ground and his wing starts flapping uncontrollably. He starts squawking and calling out for King Carthon. Carthon turns and rushes to him, "Hector, what's wrong? What happened?"

Hector is bleeding all over floor and no longer speaking in Carthon's mind. Carthon can then see the wounds on Hector's body. Arrows are deep in Hector's side. Carthon Shakes Hector, but Hector is gone.

Annut and Thoraxian take aim at King Carthon and swoop down to blast him with fire. The fire engulfs Carthon and catches the furniture and floor on fire, however Carthon isn't touched by it. The Sea Amulet surrounded him with a shield of water and protected him.

Carthon is still holding Hector's head in his lap as he kneels on the ground. His rage is boiling up from his sadness and about to reach the surface. He has only one mission and that is to destroy Akita, the Dragons, and everyone with her.

He slowly stands and a blue sphere surrounds him. The sphere carries him up and away. He gets to about a hundred yards above the Keep and grabs the Sea Amulet. Water begins to swirl around the Keep from the bay. It quickly encompasses the lower floors of the Keep up to where the top floors have been blown off. The lower floors fill, and it forces General Olek to abandon the Golems in the Throne room and join everyone in the King's quarters.

Ordyn sees the water rising and flies above the team. He tells Akita that they need to get out of here before they drown. Akita calls out to the Dragons and Wyverns to come get them and Darkwing calls for Mylar.

One by one the Dragons and Wyverns fly down and pick up all that they can. Darkwing and

Mylar are the last to take off from the Keep as the water submerges the whole Keep. Everyone is flown to the shore where the Princess, Ixen, and the Giant guards are.

The Dragons and Wyverns land on the shore and stay landed while the team gathers to discuss their next move. Ixen runs to Akita's side, "Akita what happened? Where's your wing?"

Akita winces in pain and grabs her shoulder, "Carthon caught me by surprise and then destroyed my wing."

Ixen gasps, "Oh my! We could have healed it back to your body."

Akita waves Ixen off as to stop worrying about her, "It's okay, we've been through worse. Gavin tried to get it, but he almost drowned. Both he and Ghod are out of commission right now. Go to them and see what you can do."

Ixen nods her head and goes over to where Wulf and Ordyn laid Ghod and Gavin on the ground in between Annut and Thoraxian and starts to assess their situation. Ordyn and Wulf walk up to the group to listen in.

Akita growls a bit, "I wish I could get ahold of his scrawny neck and just squeeze until the light went out." She looks over to Wulf, who is giving her a funny look. "What? I can have a sinister imagination with the best of them. I don't care if it is not becoming of a Duchess. He is going to get what is coming to him in the end."

Mandrake steps forward, "While we all would like to destroy King Carthon, the issue is how do we get through his defenses? I haven't seen any point of weakness except for his Owl Roc. We can't use that against him anymore since Skip dispatched the bird. Our next move has to be a united attack on the Demi-Titan. If we get rid of Jessa, he may be easier to deal with."

Princess Gianna exhales loudly, "I have been able to hurt the Demi-Titan with the Earth Amulet and freeze it with the Frost Amulet. The only thing that I haven't tried is to use both Amulet's together. It is the one thing that my Father and Mother warned me about doing."

Fabby clears his throat, "Well, I may be able to use my magic to help with that. I have felt the power from both amulets, and I think that I can keep them from destroying each other. You would be able to use their power together and hopefully destroy Jessa."

Vivian moves quickly to the front of the group and puts up a shield of light just as several spikes of water come down on top of the group. The spike hit the shield and dispersed. Wulf jumps in behind her and helps to add his own magic to the shield. The shield grows until it is covering everyone, the Giants included.

More spikes fly down from King Carthon, but this time towards the Dragons and Wyverns. Annut and Thoraxian are able to blast them with fire before they hit their marks.

Ishvet looks around and points to Vivian, "She won't be able to keep this up all night even with Wulf's help. We need to act fast."

The Princess agrees and moves out from the shield. She can see that the Ice around Jessa's legs is cracking and the shards of earth that she pierced her with are crumbling. She looks over to Fabby, "It has to be now Fab Ulous. She is breaking free."

Jessa starts moving towards the wrecked dock and towards the shore. King Carthon moves beside her at shoulder level and continues to rain down water spikes. Jessa uses her Wyvern arms to spew fire and ice at the team while getting closer and closer. Waves start to crash against the shield and get larger as Jessa moves towards them.

Gianna freezes the waves in front of them and puts up earthen walls to combat the columns of fire and ice. She then kneels to the ground and Fabby steps in front of her. She takes both of the amulets and pushes them together. A blast of light shoots out from the amulets directly in front of them. It condenses into a thick ray of light and destroys the ice and walls in the direct path of the beam.

Fabby reaches up and grabs Gianna's hands. His magic pushes into the amulets and stabilizes the beam. Gianna slowly moves the beam up and towards The Demi-Titan. The beam boils the ocean waters that it touches. Jessa moves closer and the beam hits her leg. Jessa cries out in pain. The beam cuts into Jessa's leg.

Jessa starts to thrash around and tries to use the Ice Wyvern arm to deflect the beam with a blast of ice. It doesn't stop the beam and Gianna slowly moves it up Jessa's body. Suddenly the beam goes completely through Jessa's leg and out the back. Fabby is struggling to keep the beam stable and yells at Gianna to finish Jessa off.

Gianna pulls back really hard, and the beam slices up through Jessa's torso and ends at her shoulder.

Jessa roars and starts to gurgle as blood fills her mouth. Her body splits in two and one half falls backwards into the waters of the bay and the other falls forward towards the shore on top of several wrecked ships and her head lands on the shore. Slowly her eyes dim and she is motionless.

Gianna pulls the two amulets apart and Fabby falls to the ground from exhaustion. The Giant Princess scoops him up and lays him beside Akita and Ordyn under the protection of the shield.

Annut and Thoraxian take flight and begin burning Jessa's body. Hunter, Warrior, Ransom, and Drako fly over and begin burning the body with the others. Slowly Jessa starts turning to ash.

Carthon is astonished that the Giant with the amulets was able to defeat Jessa. He ramps up his attack and moves closer to the group. He tries thinking of other attacks he can use to hurt these people. More waves crash around them, and tendrils of water launch towards them. The shield or the Dragons intercept the attacks time and time again.

The battering from King Carthon becomes worse and the group needs to retreat away from the shoreline. Ordyn picks up Ghod and Wulf picks up Gavin and everyone runs up the coast to a slope they can get up easily and then end up back in front of the town.

Carthon follows from above and continues to try to attack the Dragons and Wyverns with water and Dark Magic attacks. They are able to dodge most of them. Rethu takes a direct attack and is slightly hurt. He has to land behind the group in front of the gates of the town. Mylar lands beside him and Vivian and Wulf put the Sheild back up. Fabby has recovered enough to help this time and even Rethu and Mylar are covered.

Ishvet has had enough and yells to his father, "Enough of this. Come down here and fight us. If you are really as powerful as you think you are then you won't have any problem defeating us."

Carthon can hear Ishvet and hears the challenge in his voice. He yells back as he descends to the ground at the town gate, "Fine, it is about time this is over once and for all. It's time to unleash the full power of the Sea Amulet upon you."

When King Carthon touches the ground the blue bubble he was in dissolves. He steps forward two steps and attacks. A whirlwind of magic springs from his outstretched palm and slams into Vivian's shield. The shield shatters and the force pushes Vivian, Wulf, and Fabby to the ground. Ordyn and Greenbean run towards Carthon with their swords drawn. He knocks them to the ground with a blast of the same type of magic. They are knocked unconscious.

Akita and Storm charge out and move in front of Wulf, Vivian, and Fabby. They use their fire magic to make walls of flames. The Dwarves fan out and guard the sides of the group with their shield and weapons drawn. Vicar and Olek run in and drag Ordyn back to Rethu and Darkwing pulls back Greenbean. The walls of flame give them some protection for a short time, but a counter spell from King Carthon quickly destroys the fire walls.

Carthon takes another step towards them, "Anyone else want to take a run at me? Isn't it obvious that none of you, even your mighty Dragons and Wyverns are no match to my power."

Princess Gianna steps over the group and in front of Akita and Storm, "The power of the amulets was not meant for the likes of you small man. I will not let you hurt any more of my friends."

Gianna raises both arms with an amulet in both hands. A white beam shoots out of the Frost Amulet and a brown beam shoots out of the Earth Amulet. King Carthon raises the Sea Amulet and a blue beam fires out of the Sea Amulet and intercepts both the other beams.

The Princess strains and pushes forward with all her might. Her whole body begins to have whisps of white and brown tendrils swirl around her. She steps closer to Carthon and begins to push his beam backwards. Carthon struggles against the power of the Earth and Frost amulet. He can begin to hear the Dragon souls in the amulet speak to him.

Seven as one voice, "Give us all your power and we will defeat the Giantess."

Carthon pushes forward with all his strength and sends all his power into the Sea Amulet. The other two beams are beaten back for a few seconds. He pushes even harder and gives every ounce of his own innate magical power to the Amulets. He can feel the power in the Amulet start pulsing in his hands and the blue beam become more intense. Suddenly he could feel it crack in his palms. A huge wave of power expands from the Sea Amulet and flattens everyone to the ground. Even the Giant Princess is knocked back on to her rear end. The seven Dragon souls that were contained in the Sea Amulet are visible for a brief moment. They quickly rise in the air then vanish.

Carthon lays on the ground and writhes in pain. The blast hit him especially hard. He holds up his arms and his hands are gone. They were destroyed in the blast. He tries to get up, but he can only get to his knees. He cries out, "No! This can't happen. I'm supposed to rule over all of you. This isn't what I was promised."

There is a flash of blue light and Ishvet is directly in front of King Carthon. Carthon looks up to Ishvet, "Have you come to gloat at your father's defeat? Have you come to tell me that I should have been a better father to you?"

Ishvet looks down at King Carthon with tears in his eyes, "No, I haven't come to do either of those things."

Carthon sees the tears in Ishvet's eyes, "Why would you cry for me then?"

Ishvet uses his left hand to wipe away his tears, "I'm not crying for you. I'm crying for me. I was the one that had to kill his own father." Ishvet looks down to his right hand that is holding the dagger that is in King Carthon's chest.

King Carthon looks at Ishvet's face and sees that Ishvet is staring down at his chest. He looks down and sees the dagger plunged into it. As soon as he sees it, he can feel the pain and the warm sensation starting to engulf his body. He falls to his side onto the ground as Ishvet lets go of the dagger. He watches Ishvet turn and walk away as his sight dims and finally blackens.

CHAPTER 22

RETURNING TO THE TEMPLE

Meh-Kola blinks to Akita's side while hovering and helps Akita to her feet, "Akita it is over. Ishvet has killed King Carthon."

Akita, still a little dazed from the blast of energy shakes her head, "Oh my! Is everyone else, okay?"

Before Meh-Kola can answer, Vicar walks up, "We need to get Ordyn and Greenbean back to the Temple for some rest and healing. Ghod and Gavin are just now coming to."

Akita looks over to Vicar as she stands, "Yes, let's get home." She then turns and looks up to Princess Gianna, "Gianna are you able to open a portal back to the Temple for us?"

Princess Gianna looks around at the team and then over to her guards, "Yes, I'm just a little weak from the fight with King Carthon. I won't be able to hold it open long, so we need to rush in once its open."

Akita nods and walks over to Ishvet. He is still standing over King Carthon's body, "Ishvet, are you okay?"

Ishvet doesn't say anything. He is staring at Carthon's body. Vivian makes her way around Akita and steps next to Ishvet and puts her arm around his waist, "Ish it's time to go. There's nothing for you here."

Ishvet physically shakes off his disorientation in Vivans arm. He slowly turns to Vivian, "I wonder what my mother would have done in this situation? Would she have killed him? Would she have spared his life and then imprison him?

Vivian moves in front of Ishvet and puts her other arm around him. She squeezes him firmly and puts her head on his chest. She searches for words that might console him but can't get anything out.

Thoraxian lands behind Carthon's body and speaks to Ishvet's mind, "Your mother would have done what she needed to do to protect innocent people and the people she loved. She would have done exactly what you did. I know this because I saw her make a similar decision time and time again in the war with the Giants. Every time she had to take a life to save a life, it destroyed her."

Ishvet looks up to Thoraxian with tears still trailing down his face, "I can understand why it destroyed her. As I plunged the dagger in his chest, I thought about everyone he has hurt and killed and then all of my friends and then Vivian. I knew I had to stop him, but I wanted to hesitate. Now, I have to live with the fact that I killed my own father."

Annut lands beside Thoraxian and speaks to both Ishvet and Thoraxian, "Ishvet, he was no father to you. He may have sired you, but he never showed you love or care. To me that is the definition of a father. Today you saved many fathers. You can be proud that you did the right thing in protecting all of us and the realm. So don't give this evil man any more thought."

Ishvet looks over to Annut and starts to smile as he wipes the tears from his face, "Thank you Annut. You are right. I need to focus on what we saved and not what we have lost. We are going to move past this point and make a great future."

He squeezes Vivian in his arms and slightly sways back and forth. She looks up and gives him a smile. She grabs his hand and starts walking back towards the group, pulling him along and away from Carthon's body.

Gianna sees them walking towards her and takes it as a sign that they are ready to leave. She nods to Ishvet as thanks for stopping King Carthon. Gianna then tells everyone to get ready to go through the portal quickly because she will not be able to hold it open long. She grabs the Frost Amulet and begins opening the portal to the Dragon Temple. It slowly opens and gets big enough for the Dragons to get through.

Annut and Thoraxian fly through first followed by the Wyverns. Rethu lands by the portal and waits while Akita and the team start going through. Princess Gianna tells Rethu to go through now that everyone has gone through. He shakes his head and speaks into Gianna's mind, "I can't go back until I recover Aphorea's body. I will bring her back to the Temple as soon as I can. Her bones need to be buried in the Temple as she was an Elder."

Princess Gianna reaches up and puts her hand on Rethu's snout, "Thank you friend. We will prepare for your return and have the Lommas ready the ceremony to lay Aphorea's bones to rest." She then walks through the portal, and it closes behind her.

Captain Dubbin and Blitz sit atop the Temple gazing at the moon and the billions of stars above them. Thin wispy clouds drift by on a light breeze.

Captain Dubbin reaches over and puts a hand on Blitz's neck, "It should be over soon. If they were struggling, Akita would have already called for reinforcements. Do not fret, my friend, we should see a portal soon."

Blitz gently leans into Captain Dubbin's hand and whimpers. He is worried about his friend and master, Gavin.

Captain Dubbin watches as Blitz tracks several shooting stars. He smiles and comments, "My grandad would have said that was a good omen. It is a beautiful night for a victory, as we have lost to many friends to these wicked wizards."

The courtyard is suddenly illuminated with a bright light that grows into the portal they had been waiting for. Blitz stands in anticipation, with his tail doing a slow wag. Luckily, they are farther back from the portal because the first to exit are Annut and Thoraxian followed by all the Wyverns. They fly out and up into the night sky then dive down to the Temple's main entrance.

Next several shadows form in the portal. He sees Akita, Wulf, Vivian and Ishvet step through the portal next. Then Storm, Jacklyn, and Skip, who are helping Ordyn and Greenbean walk. A moment later, Ghod comes sauntering out with his arms raised and opened wide as if he is anticipating some fanfare. He looks around and is slightly confused that there isn't a crowd of cheering people to greet him.

Blitz starts to whimper again, then spots Gavin behind Ghod. He starts prancing, his entire body wriggling and his tail swinging at high speed. He can't stand it anymore and with a gigantic leap from the rooftop to the center of the courtyard, he bumps Ghod to the side and lands on Gavin, knocking him to the ground. Gavin groans from the hit and is slightly dazed from the pounce and is still recovering from being knocked out earlier.

Blitz towers over Gavin looking him in the eyes and sniffing. All smells right with his friend and master. He is so happy, he starts licking

Gavin's face while speaking to him, "You will never leave me behind again. I should have been there to protect you and help. I will talk to Akita too."

Winded, Gavin starts laughing and trying to push the slobbery tongue away from his face. He finally just reaches up around Blitz's neck, pulling him down into a hug. "I missed you too buddy, but I was glad you were safe here. Many were lost and I couldn't bear it if I had lost you. Now I need food and sleep, so could ya let me up."

Blitz steps to the side and lets Gavin up, "I would get you food myself if I had thumbs, but I know the Lommas have huge tables of food set out in the main hall. Go fill your belly and I'll go warm the bed."

Vicar, Mandrake, Judas, Olek, Void, and Quinn walk past Gavin and Blitz followed by Darkwing. Darkwing just shakes his head while looking at the two of them on the ground, "You better make way, Gianna is coming through and I'd hate for her to step in the middle of your reunion."

Gavin gets up, then him and Blitz step aside as Fabby comes out of the portal. Then he can feel the slight tremor in the temple roof as two Giant guards come through followed by Princess Gianna. As she steps out, the portal closes behind her.

All of them make their way down the large set of stairs that lead into the Main Hall. They can see that part of the Hall has been set up with cots, tables, and wounded soldiers are being tended to by Ixen and Shamash. Fabby and Vicar hurry over to both of them to get an update on the wounded and to help where they can.

Vicar assess some of the injured as he walks down the ramp. When he can, he heals the easy breaks and abrasions, then sends the injured to eat and bed.

The rest make their way to the large tables. Large amounts of food are spread about. Lommas' scurry from one end to the other setting down dishes. Along one side of the table sits Greta and Scotch. They both stand and slightly bow as Akita makes her way to her seat. Akita puts up her hand and motions for them to sit back down. She sits down and rests her elbows on the tables and then puts her face in her hands.

Wulf walks up behind her and puts his hand on her back. Sage crawls onto her shoulder and curls up in her neck. She nuzzles Akita for a moment then lays down. Slowly Akita looks up and around the room. A small smile forms on her lips. She looks up to Wulf, "I can't believe that it's over. Now we can get back to our lives and rebuilding Blackwing Keep."

Wulf leans over with Dojo on his shoulder and gives Akita a kiss on her cheek. Dojo stretches his neck and gives Akita a lick on her forehead. Wulf straightens back up, "Yes, it is finally over. And considering the odds that we faced, I would say we did pretty well. It's just terrible that we had to lose so many great friends to obtain victory."

Akita reaches up with her left hand and finds Wulf's hand on her right shoulder. She squeezes his hand, "I can't even think about them yet. It's too hard and I'm too tired to fall apart."

Vicar makes his way through the grid of cots and wounded soldiers. He spots Ben who is holding his right arm and limping, hurrying over to him. "Ben, let me take a look at you."

Ben stops and gives Vicar a small smile, "There are those who need help more than I do. I can wait."

Vicar chuckles, "Yes, you probably could, but this is a perk of having me as your unofficial uncle." Vicar puts his hands on Ben's head doing quick heals of the bruises, mending the hairline fractures of his leg, as well as his broken arm."

Ben shakes his head, "No Sir, you are not unofficial. I look at you, Mandrake, Wulf Darkwing, Ordyn, Olek and, yes even Ghod, as the uncles I never had. I cherish all of you and appreciate your guidance. The best day in my life was when I walked into Lady Akita's camp. If it had not been for her, I would still be begging and stealing to survive, or in jail. The townspeople felt I was more trouble than I was worth. Lady Akita, has no clue, but she is the Aunt I never had."

Vicar gives his best Dragonkin smile, "And now you are one of the heroes of the land, who helped keep evil from their doorsteps. It will be fun to see their reactions the next time you are in Salthall." Giving Ben a final look over, "Go eat and get a good night's sleep. I need to help Shamash at the moment."

Ishvet and Vivian make their way to the makeshift morgue area. She finds her Father's guards surrounding him on a cot. All of their heads are bowed. Ishvet puts his hand on Sargent Owl's shoulder, startling her.

Sargent Owl, in a firm voice calls, "Attention."

Everyone looks up and shifts places for Vivian to be next to her father. Tears start rolling down her face, and she tries to wipe them away furiously.

Sargent Owl kneels beside her, placing a hand on her back. "Duchess Vivian Elderwolf, you cry all you want. I know I am not one of high rank, but I know you need to grieve for your father's loss as we all grieve for him as our leader. You can be tough as nails in front of the masses tomorrow."

Vivian looks over to Sargent Owl with a sad smile, realizing she has been referred to as her father's successor. She bends over and kisses her dad on his forehead, and then states, "In the presence of my father and all of you, Ishvet and I want you to know, I will take up the mantel as is tradition in Elderwolf Keep. Until my return I name Captain Dubbin Diesel as Steward of Elderwolf Keep. Ishvet and I must return with Lady Akita to help rebuild Blackwing Keep."

Vivan turns towards Captain Dubbin, and he catches her gaze. He nods in the affirmative, accepting his new responsibility.

Slowly Vivian bends over and kisses her father's lifeless body on the forehead. She turns back to Captain Dubbin, "Please see that he is buried next to mother in the family cemetery. When I return, we will have a proper ceremony."

Captain Dubbin turns to the guards and begins to direct them on how to handle the body and when to return it to the Keep. He bows slightly to Vivian and makes his way out of the Hall.

An older woman comes up and sits next to Akita and starts filling her plate with fruits and cheeses. She reaches in front of Akita and grabs a saltshaker and shakes some salt on her food. Akita just stares at her and wonders who she is. As soon as she has the thought the older lady stops and looks at her.

The older lady smiles and leans back slightly, "Darling Akita, it is me, Madam Suzie of course."

Akita jumps up and hugs Madam Suzie tight as ever, "It is so great to meet you. Jacklyn and Storm told me how you helped them escape the city."

Madam Suzie shakes her head, "No, no, don't fuss over me. It was the Fates that wrote their escape. I only conveyed the message."

Akita looks around and spots Storm and Jacklyn, "Storm, Jacklyn come over here."

Storm And Jacklyn hear Akita and rush over and see Madam Suzie. Jacklyn leans over and hugs Madam Suzie in her chair and Storm comes around the other side and does the same. Madam Suzie protests slightly at all the attention, "Go on girls, let me be. I need to breathe you know."

They both cease their hugs and pull up chairs next to Madam Suzie. Akita leans in and looks to both Jacklyn and Storm, "You didn't tell me that Madam Suzie was such a beautiful lady."

Storm laughs, "Not only that, but she is also mysterious and powerful too. She knows way too much to be just a fortune teller."

Akita tilts her head to the side, "Is that right? I may have to seek your guidance soon. There are a lot of decisions to be made by me and others of the future of Alahora."

Madam Suzie reaches out her hand and takes Akita's, "I know your questions Akita. There are many obstacles still in front of you, but I see ten times as many joyous moments around them. One joyous moment is coming sooner than you think."

Akita, Jacklyn, and Storm all lean in closer as Madam Suzie's voice gets softer. She looks to all three of the ladies' faces, "One among your lady friends is keeping a secret. Soon there will be crying in Blackwing Keep."

Akita looks puzzled for a second, "Crying? Blackwing Keep? Wait is one of us with child?"

Storm and Jacklyn gasp and jerk back in their chairs. Akita looks to both their faces and then down to their bellies. They both start adamantly denying that they are the ones. Akita looks at Madam Suzie then down to her own belly. Madam Suzie reaches out again and shakes her head in the negative, "No honey it is not any of you. You will know soon enough who it is. When the Keep is finished, the babe will be borne."

Akita sighs in relief, "That's a relief, you've assured me of two things; one, I'm not the one with child and two, that we will rebuild Blackwing Keep."

Madam Suzie chuckles, "I just relay the messages. The last message that I have to pass on is that Blackwing Keep is already being rebuilt by the Dwarves of Hearth Home. They owed your Uncle a great debt and have taken that opportunity to wipe the slate clean, so to speak."

A warm sensation creeps up Akita's back and a sense of peace falls over her, "Wow, I can't believe it. That is great news. I can't wait to get back there."

Madam Suzie stands up and grabs her plate and turns around. She smiles at the ladies, "I need to go see Ishvet now." With that, she trots off towards the infirmary area. Akita watches her walk off then leans back in her chair. All she can do now is imagine what the new Blackwing Keep will look like.

Ishvet and Vivian are walking up to the main dining table when a handsome older lady appears in front of them. She stops and hands them the plate she is carrying. Ishvet takes the plate then looks to the lady's face, "Hello, can I help you?"

Madam Suzie smiles and nods her head, "Of course love, hold this plate for a minute while pass along the will of the Fates. They have much to say."

Vivian realizes what is going on, "Wait, I didn't get a chance to ask your name. I'm Vivian and this is my husband Ishvet."

Madam Suzie smiles again, "I'm Madam Suzie from Cliffside. I have come here on behalf of the townspeople and also in the capacity of my gifts."

Ishvet smiles and bows slightly, "Ah yes, I have heard of you. Jacklyn and Storm told us of what you did for them in Cliffside. It is so nice to meet you."

Vivian smiles and reaches out a hand in greeting, "It is so nice to meet you. Shall we sit at the table and talk while we eat?"

Madam Suzie nods affirmatively, "Yes, but let's go over to the other side of the room away from the big tables. I've already spoken to Akita and what I have to relay to you both is for your ears only."

They make their way over to the area where the staff and guards sat during the feast. When they sit, a Lomma comes up and sets a pitcher of wine at the table and places a plate with roasted chicken and vegetables in front of Vivian and Ishvet. Ishvet thanks the Lomma, and it scurries off out of sight.

Madam Suzie looks at both Vivian and Ishvet with adoring eyes, "I hurt for you both and I envy you at the same time. You both have a love for each other that is so rare in this world. At the same time, you have both experienced such tragedies this night. As I said before, I have come to you both for two very different reasons. First is on behalf of the townspeople of Cliffside. Second is to relay a message from the Fates."

Ishvet looks confused as Madam Suzie mentions the Fates. Vivian squeezes Ishvet's hand so that he stops making an odd face at Madam Suzie. Ishvet snaps out of thought, "The Fates? Do you mean like mystical beings that weave time and fate?"

Madam Suzie nods her head, "Yes Ishvet those are to whom I speak. However, the first issue I must see to is the fate of Cliffside. Almost all of the town was burned to the ground and the

Keep was destroyed, not to mention that all the fishing ships and the docks were wrecked. We have a request for the new ruler of Cliffshade Keep. Please help us to rebuild the city. Most of us have lived there our whole life and would like to see it come back to its former glory.

The Fates have told me that you will not rule over the town or the Keep. They see you at Elderwolf Keep with your family. To that end, the townsfolk ask that you allow us to elect a counsel to oversee Cliffshade Keep and Cliffside."

Ishvet looks over to Vivian, "She is right, I have no aspirations to sit where my father did or to rule over anyone. My only desire is to be where you are, and your place is at Elderwolf Keep."

Vivian shakes her head in agreement, "I know that's what you want, and I want the same." She then looks to Madam Suzie, "Elderwolf Keep will aid in the rebuilding of the town first then allow the counsel to decide what they want to do with the Keep."

Madam Suzie laughs a little, "I knew that was what you were going to say, but it had to be spoken aloud. So on to the last bit of business. The Fates pass on to you a gift. Soon you will have a child. That child will be very special. He will lead the forces of good against the growing evil in Omoth. When he comes of age, he is to be given this blue stone."

Madam Suzie reaches into the pocket of her robe and pulls out a brilliant blue stone. It is flat on one side and convex on the other. The stone is polished to a glassy finish and smooth as silk to the touch. She hands it to Ishvet and once it is in his hand, he begins to see images of his mother in her Dragon form. He starts to gasp, then a tear falls from his right eye.

Vivian looks up at him, "Ishvet what's wrong?"

Ishvet turns to her, "Nothing, it's just that I can feel my Mother in this stone."

Madam Suzie places her hand over the stone and Ishvet's hand, "You are correct. There is a piece of your mother in that stone. She will help guide your son on his journey."

Ishvet places his hand on Madam Suzie's, "Thank you, wait we are having a son! I just realized what you were saying. Vivian, we are having son!"

Vivian smiles a big smile, "Yes Ish, I know. I found out before we left Salthall. I just couldn't bring myself to tell you until all this stuff with King Carthon was over."

Ishvet's voice gets soft and concerned, "You mean that you knew about this, and you went into battle carrying our child? You could have been hurt or killed."

Vivian furls her brow, "That's exactly why I didn't tell you before. You would have tried to stop me from going to Cliffshade. I am no delicate flower, Ish. I am a Paladin of Elderwolf Keep. My Oath is to eradicate evil no matter what the cost and I'm pretty good at it. Plus, I had you by my side, so I knew nothing was going to happen to me. Anyway, it is all over and we are both healthy. My only regret is not being able to tell Daddy about his grandchild before he was killed."

Ishvet melts into his chair and leans over and hugs Vivian. She starts to sob in his arms. Madam Suzie excuses herself from the table and leaves them to their emotional moment.

Before dawn arrives, almost all the team is at the big tables. Everyone is having side conversations when Annut and Thoraxian enter the grand room. The room quickly becomes silent as Annut speaks to all their minds at once, "Everyone here has gone above and beyond their duty to ensure the safety of Alahora. Us remaining Dragons cannot be more grateful to all of you."

Thoraxian speaks next, "I have been around for millennia and have never seen such a camaraderie and devotion as the one you have. Not since the Titan wars have there been better allies to the Dragons. However, not all the races of this realm are as caring, selfless, and hopeful as the lot of you are. That is why we cannot stay in this realm any longer."

Annut begins speaking again with a touch of sadness in her voice, "Thoraxian and I have decided that we must leave and take our children to somewhere safe. This realm isn't safe for our kind, and we cannot take the risk of someone taking control of one of us ever again."

Akita is in shock and tears stream down her face. She grabs ahold of Wulf's hand and the other hand wipes her tears, "Annut, please don't go. We can keep you safe. You will be safe here in the temple."

Annut leans her head down as close as she can get to Akita, "Akita dear, you have shown us a kindness that can never be repaid. I am and will forever be your friend. My children will always love you and your friends and will tell stories of your adventures for hundreds of years to come. I know that you would do everything within your power to see that we are safe, but the risk is too great that a Dark Wizard will try to control one of us again like they did to Thoraxian. That is why we must journey to our Hallovie. Our sacred place. Until now we did not know that it would be possible."

Thoraxian interjects, "With the Earth and Frost Amulets Princess Gianna can open a portal to Hallovie. All the Dragons of this world can retreat and be at peace there."

Akita jumps up and runs over to Annut and hugs her snout. The others start to get up as all the young Dragons come into the Great Hall. Everyone that has been paired to a Dragon runs over to them and shows a gesture of affection. The people that remain at the table all stand and start clapping in support of the Dragons.

Princess Gianna speaks over the applause, and it starts to die down, "I have agreed to help the Dragons on one condition. That they allow all that is left of the Frost Giants to come with them to Hallovie. They have agreed. In two weeks', time, All the Frost Giants will return to the Dragon temple, then my Father and I will open the portal. All of us and the Dragons will leave this world and build our new lives in the next."

Thoraxian speaks up again, "I have called out for all remaining Dragons of this world to travel to this Temple. I have given them one week to arrive. I am sure Akita will be glad to hear that she will have a week to meet all the new Dragons before we depart."

Akita turns and looks up to Thoraxian which a huge grin on her face, "Yes, yes, yes! I can't wait to meet all of them. I am just so sad that you all have to go. It seems like I just met Annut and then the rest of you. We didn't have enough time together."

Annut nudges Akita with her snout, "Akita you have been the best friend I have ever had."

As the Sun comes up over the forest trees, the last of the staff turn into bed. The Temple becomes eerily quiet and still.

Ishvet and Vivian lay in bed next to each other. Ishvet is holding the blue stone that Madam

Suzie gave him. He stares into Vivian's eyes, "I'm having a hard time going to sleep after all that has happened. I can't believe all that has unfolded and everything that is about to happen. Viv, we are going to be parents. This melts my big Dragonkin heart."

Vivian stares back at Ishvet, "Ish we are so lucky. We are lucky to have each other. We are lucky to have all our friends and we are lucky to have this child come into the world. There is no one else I would rather be lucky with than you. Close your eyes and dream of our son."

CHAPTER 23

THE UNION

Wulf wakes to Akita getting dressed for the day. The sun is already high in the air. It seems to be mid-afternoon. Akita is struggling to cover her wing stump with a cape. Wulf comes up behind her and adjusts her cape which startles her. He puts his hands on her shoulders and chuckles.

Wulf then turns her around for a deep kiss. After the kiss, he pulls back and looks her in the eyes, "My dearest, please do not let this battle scar bother you so. You are the strong, smart, leader you have ever been, with the wing or without."

Akita bows her head, "I now know how Grace felt. Granted, I can still walk, but I have lost my gift of flight. Ghod was able to make a suitable replacement for Grace. I cannot fathom a fix for this. I feel lopsided and incomplete."

She reaches back over her shoulder to feel the stump, "Earlier I felt an itch, but when I instinctively went to scratch it, nothing was there.

I was brought to tears. I know that in the big picture, me missing my wing is a small sacrifice. There are more important things to be concerned about. Our Dragon friends are leaving, Blackwing Keep is being rebuilt. We are soon going to have a little baby running around."

Wulf, with a finger under her chin, lifts her head to look her in the eyes. Wulf's voice starts to quiver slightly, "Akita, I think I have loved you from the moment I first saw your face. I was so scared to let my love for you be known in the beginning. When Aphorea asked me to take the oath of your protector, there was no hesitation, no second thoughts. I knew then that I wanted to only be with you."

Wulf takes a deep breath and sends his thoughts to the nearest Lomma to have the team come to their room. He exhales loudly then continues, "When the Magma Amulet exploded, I knew I was free of Aphorea's oath, but I had my own personal oath I made in that same moment to live up to. When your wing was sliced clear, fear pierced through my heart. I thought I was going to lose you, and I couldn't live with that. The wing might be gone but you remain here for me to hold and love." He holds her tight in his arms and watches the door. Thankfully she wanted a long hug, until he saw they were all there.

Wulf reaches into his pocket, and kneels on one knee, "High Duchess Akita Blackwing of Blackwing Keep, I Wulf Wari of Omoth, a humble Warlock, with the permission of your friends and of course Shamash, ask for your hand in marriage. Akita my love, will you take my hand in marriage?" He holds up a ring, that makes her gasp. It is a dragon with a rider, with a diamond in its claws. To Akita it is spectacular.

With tears running down her face and a lump in her throat she manages to get out one word, "Yes!"

Wulf stands, as he places the ring on her finger. To Akita's surprise applause erupts at the door and they are swarmed in hugs.

Akita looks at them all, "You all knew about this?"

Vicar speaks up, "Well, we knew he had asked all of us for our blessing, but it wasn't until the Lommas message did we have a clue when he was going to pop the question. All I have to say is, it's about damn time."

Ghod adds with a cheeky grin, "Agreed, I have had that ring made for a month or so."

Wulf looks at Storm, Greenbean, Jacklyn and Quinn. "Is all ready for the second surprise?"

Vicar raises a Dragonkin eyebrow, "Well maybe it was just the men that didn't know when... Hmmm."

Storm answers, "Yes, now all you men get out of here and let us take care of Akita. Wulf, go to the war room and you guys go with him."

Akita is looking around, wondering what is going on, as the men usher Wulf out of the room.

Akita looks at her bed to see a long white dress with embroidered flames crawling up the hemline and sleeves. On the back of the dress there is a small gold embroidered symbol that would be below her missing wing. She picks up the dress and looks more closely. It is the emblem of the team, a gold circle with a Dragon flying in the middle. There is a fire diamond tiara and necklace. Before her eyes four more dresses show up in varying shades of yellow, orange and red. Vivian is putting on the red dress, with Jacklyn putting on the darker orange dress. When she snaps out of her shock Storm and Greenbean order her out of her clothes and into the white dress. She is like a puppet being dressed for a show.

Once she is dressed, she is ordered to sit down, so that Jacklyn and Vivian can start working on her hair, while Greenbean puts on an orange dress and Storm a bright yellow dress. All of the dresses and accessories are to represent flames leading up to the bride's main dress. Akita is astonished by the idea and the coordination.

They all stand back admiring each other and Akita as Quinn walks up with the final accessory. Quinn smiles, "My Lady Akita, my friend and mentor, we know this is your wedding day, but it is also the marriage of the High Duchess of Blackwing Keep. When you enter the courtyard, your Blackwing House Crest will be seen by all. We also know this is very quick, but Wulf knows you would want the Dragons to be here, and we have only a couple of weeks left." Quinn puts the amulet around Akita's neck and clasps it tight.

Akita has been speechless the entire time, but now wishes she had a full-length mirror. As always, the Lommas provide a large mirror.

Greta walks in and stops dead in her tracks. She then walks up to Akita and pins a broach to her dress. A beautiful fire like cameo broach. "This, my dear is a cameo I have kept for just this day. It was your Mother's and is of your mother. I thought I had lost it when the Keep flooded, but I was able to retrieve it."

As the ladies all line up next to Akita in the mirror, Akita is amazed at the beauty and friendship she sees reflected. She wishes she had a portrait of this moment in time. Of course, the Lommas provide, with a life size portrait popping up in front of them.

Akita jumps, "Wow! Thank you, my little friends."

Greta claps her hands, "Ok, now on to the courtyard. We will take the back way out. The Groom is waiting, the food is in the main hall, and everyone is waiting to see the High Duchess of Blackwing Keep, Lady Akita Blackwing."

As they reach the entry to the courtyard, Akita notices a large marble platform where they had Grace's ceremony. Something huge is wrapped in white silk. She quickly realizes that Rethu has returned and has laid Aphorea's wrapped body on it. Tears begin to fill her eyes. She tries to hold them back as the Wedding Ceremony begins.

Chairs line both sides of the aisle. Friends and staff on both sides. Surrounding the chairs are all the Dragons, Gryphons, Owl Roc's, and Wyverns. The ground is covered with small purple flowers and an intoxicating scent fills the air when anyone walks on them. Above them, the forest canopy has stretched from one side to the other and sunlight peeks through lighting up the wedding altar and the marble platform more brilliantly than the rest of the area.

Vivian starts her walk to Wulf and his best men, Darkwing, Mandrake, Gavin and Ishvet. Vicar is standing front and center next to Wulf, as always. Then Jacklyn followed by Greenbean, with Storm walking last to make her way to the altar.

The men are in their finest black outfits, but Wulf's has embroidered flames to match her dress. It is only fitting as he commands flames like she does. They all look so handsome, and Wulf looks so confident. She cannot see any nervousness in her groom.

She starts her walk, only to be startled to a stop. The Dragons start a beautiful song in her honor. She briefly looks to each of them and smiles. She notices Hunter and Warrior stand to the right of the best men with their wings spread. Sage and Dojo are sitting on Gavin's shoulders.

Akita stops in front of Vicar and then turns to Wulf. Vicar clears his throat and motions for everyone in the chairs area to be seated. He then takes one step closer to the couple and places a hand on the shoulder of each of them.

He looks to both of their faces, "Friends and family we are gathered here today to witness the union of two beautiful souls, both fiery and loyal. High Dutchess Akita Blackwing who we only refer to as Akita, and Wulf Wari. All of us that were close to them could tell that there were sparks between them from the moment that they met. I believe their meeting will become legend for the realm just because of the circumstances in which it unfolded."

"Wulf came to Alahora on a mission to return the bones of his faithful companion, Dojo. Unfortunately, Wulf was captured by the Dark Wizards and imprisoned in a Leviathan. By fate or chance Akita and the team were able to rescue him. He became a part of the family for us almost immediately. For Akita he became a rock and an escape from the stress of ruling and fighting the Dark Wizards."

"Very quickly they formed a bond and through Aphorea, Wulf pledged to protect Akita. They rest of the story leads us to where we are today."

"Wulf, have you come here today with an open heart to embrace Akita for the rest of your days?"

Wulf looks Akita in the eyes and moves a little closer to her, "I have."

Vicar starts again, "Akita, have you also come here today with an open heart to embrace Wulf for the rest of your days?"

Akita squeezes Wulf's hands, "Absolutely yes!"

Vicar smiles and steps back one step, "With that said and the power invested in me by the Dutchess of Blackwing Keep, I decree you both to bound in the love that you share with each other. Your union is now solidified before all your friends and family. You may kiss in a show of affection."

Wulf goes in for a kiss. When his lips meet Akitas he turns and pushes her back so that she is hanging in his arms. Everyone at the ceremony claps and yells in support. Wulf pulls Akita back to her feet and they turn, hand and hand and walk back down the aisle. When they get to the first row of chairs, Wulf tells Akita to sit because there is more to come.

Rethu moves behind the grand marble table that Aphorea's body is upon. He begins speaking into everyone's mind, "Aphorea Brightscale was the most ancient dragon left in this world. Her wisdom and experience were only overshadowed by her love and generosity. She will be missed by all that are here today, and the world is a darker place without her. Us Dragons have a ritual when one of our kind dies. We bring their body back to the Temple and offer its flesh and bone to Bahamut. If he feels that the soul of that Dragon still has purpose on this plain, he may bring it back in a new form."

He looks over to Annut and Thoraxian and motions with his head to take their places. Thoraxian gets on one side of the marble altar and

Annut proceeds to the left. Rethu speaks to Darkwing and has him put up a barrier of cold blue flames between the altar and the guests. It is transparent so that everyone can still see the altar on the other side. Princess Gianna moves behind the seated guests with her remaining guards for some protection. When Rethu gives the cue, Annut and Thoraxian spew flames upon Aphorea's wrapped body.

Rethu spreads his wings and prostrates himself to the ground and begins chanting the offering of Aphorea to Bahamut in the Dragon language. Akita comments to Wulf on how intricate and beautiful the language sounds. When Rethu is finished, only a pile of ash remains on the giant marble altar. He folds his wings back and stands up on all four legs, "I have pleaded to Bahamut to return Aphorea to us, however his godship works in his own mysterious ways. She could have reappeared immediately, or she could return years from now when her soul is needed most in this world, and she may never come back to this world again. The Lommas will now collect Aphorea's ashes, and she will be entombed in the Hall of Dragons which is directly below the Grand Hall."

As everyone begins to leave the sitting area the Dragons begin another audible song, but his time with a tone of sadness. Akita sheds tears for Aphorea and in her head she prays to Bahamut to bring her back. Many others do the same as they return to the Grand Hall for the wedding reception. The Dragons linger at the altar and plan to join the reception later in the evening.

The Grand Hall is decorated with all kinds of streamers and floating balls of fire in several shades of red, orange, and yellow. The large tables in the center of the Hall are all set with fine China and candles, several centerpieces of arranged flowers. In the middle of the team's table is an eight-tier wedding cake that is decorated with an ombre of white to red to represent a flame.

On the side by the stairs to the roof there are four Lommas playing musical instruments. Their songs are soft but joyous. Around the Hall are many Lommas that are carrying pitchers of ale and wine. All the Keep staff, guards, and soldiers are already in the Hall when the Team members start to trickle in. The last to walk in are Akita and

Wulf. When they do, the music stops, and everyone claps until they take their places at the end of the table.

After they sit, Princess Gianna stands and clears her throat to get everyone's attention, "Akita and Wulf you will forever be friends to the Frost Giants even after we have left this realm. I would like to leave you with a gift. I have been working with Ghod, Darkwing, and Void to create an amulet that has some of the power of the Earth Amulet in it. We have succeeded in its creation and present it to you today. May it help you in the moving of small hills and large boulders."

A Lomma brings up an ornately carved box and presents it to Akita. Akita opens the box and finds an amulet with a brown stone in the middle encircled by silver metal work. Akita and Wulf both stand and thank Princess Gianna, Darkwing, Ghod, and Void. Several team members give various gifts of cloaks, jewelry, and baubles. Akita and Wulf love all of them and are astonished that everyone knows the things that they would like.

Quickly the evening turns into late night. Several groups of people have split off to have side conversations and mingle amongst the guests and the mounts. The Dragons come in and are served their dinner along the outside of the Hall. Akita goes over to Annut and Thoraxian to speak to them about the Dragons they expect to arrive at the Temple in the coming days.

Everyone is caught off guard when they begin to hear deep rumbling thunder and can see flashes of lightning. There is an eight-foot hole in the top of the Grand Hall that allows a shaft of sunlight or moonlight to illuminate the seal in the center of the Hall. Everybody turns and looks up at the hole when the lightning and thunder start. Other than a slight drop in temperature nothing seems out of the ordinary, so they all go back to their conversations and the Lomma musicians play a little bit louder to be heard over the occasional thunderclaps.

Akita is speaking to Annut when Meh-Kola blinks next to them. Meh-Kola looks up to Akita with a concerned look on her face, "One feels something is wrong in the air. One can sense something coming."

Before Meh-Kola can say any more, a powerful beam of light shoots down through the hole in the roof to the banquet table below. It hits the wedding cake, and the cake explodes in all directions. Then the beam hits the table and shatters it into splinters. They also fly in all directions. Princess Gianna and her guards quickly dive to the ground as their enormous table is flipped on its side. Annut wraps her wing around Akita and Meh-Kola and Thoraxian moves to shelter the young Dragons. Judas runs and tackles Ghod to the ground as a large shard of the table flies towards Ghod's head. The others take cover where they can.

The beam of light hits the seal that was under the table, and it begins to glow. The air fills with a static charge. The beams become more intense until it is blinding. Then as if someone had snuffed out a candle flame it is gone. It takes several seconds for everyone's eyes to adjust to the dim lighting that the floating flames, candles, and braziers emit.

When they can see again, they see Ordyn in the middle of the seal with someone in his arms. He is down on one knee and holding them as if he had caught them in the midst of falling. Akita rushes over with several of the team coming from other directions. They all get to Ordyn at about the same time.

In his arms is a white Dragonkin lady with shimmery scales that catch the light from the floating flames. The reds, oranges, and yellows dance across her body. She is completely nude. One of the Lommas comes up and produces a robe and Ordyn helps her into it. Then he stands next to the mysterious Dragonkin as everyone around gets their first look.

The Dragonkin looks down at her arms and hand the lifts a foot out of the robe to see it. She then looks up and around at all the faces staring back at her. She touches her throat as she begins to form a word, "Hel… hello."

Ordyn puts his arm around her and looks to Akita, "I think all of our prayers have been answered. Can't you feel it? This is Aphorea!"

Akita gasps in concert with almost everyone around them. Akita runs over and looks the Dragonkin in the eyes. They are light blue and icy. She can sense Aphorea staring back at her. Akita can't contain herself and hugs Aphorea like she hasn't ever been able to. Aphorea hugs her back with just as much pressure. Everyone starts cheering and clapping. Ordyn leads Aphorea over to a chair and has her sit down.

Aphorea sits and seems a little dazed still, but she begins to speak. Her voice is melodic and soft, "Akita, Ordyn, I'm back. Bahamut has sent me back."

Akita drops to her knees and has her hand on Aphorea's lap and Ordyn is standing behind her with his hands on her shoulders. Akita has tears streaming down her face. Wulf comes up behind her and starts rubbing her neck in comfort. Akita starts to laugh, "It's okay honey, I'm just so darn happy that I can't control it."

Aphorea seems to gain all her senses and puts a hand under Akita's chin then lifts her face, "Akita thank you for all that you have done for this realm. It is for that reason that I come with a message to all from mighty Bahamut. I need to be where all can hear me."

Akita stands and Aphorea stands up from the chair. The Lommas have already conjured a small, raised area with a lectern. Aphorea stands behind the lectern and begins to speak, her words fill the Hall, and everyone can hear her, "Thanks to all of you and Rethu's ritual, Bahamut has seen fit to reincarnate me in the form of a Bahamut Dragonkin like my friend Ordyn here. He has tasked me to deliver a message and to bestow a gift. First, he wants all of you to know how proud he is that you have banded together to fight the forces of evil that have threatened his favorite children. Next, he wanted to thank our leader, Akita Blackwing. Akita, please come here and turn your back to me."

Akita cautiously walks up to Aphorea and turns her back. Aphorea places a hand on the stump where Akita's wing was at. Akita feels a warm sensation on the stump and her weight starts to shift. She can feel her posture begin to balance out. Her wing rematerializes just the way it was before King Carthon sliced it off.

Akita steps forward then turns to Aphorea, "Thank you so much! Thank you Bahamut!"

She spreads her wings and flaps them until she is about six inches off the ground. She looks to Wulf, and he nods his head in encouragement. She smiles and takes flight up to the roof of the Hall and flies a few circles before landing back in front of Aphorea. When she lands, she goes straight for Aphorea and gives her another big hug. Aphorea smiles and laughs and hugs her back.

Aphorea begins speaking again, "I thank you all from the bottom of my heart. I am so glad to be back with all of you. I am tired from my journey so I will find an empty room and see what a bed feels like for the first time. I am so excited to have all these new experiences."

Akita walks up to the lectern and tells everyone that she is going to call it a night and that she and Wulf will be back in two days. They will be flying to the Secret Grove this night for their Honeymoon. She really doesn't want to leave but feels that it is important for her and Wulf to get away for a moment. They say their goodbyes and fly from the rooftop to the grove where they met the Pseudo Dragons.

Chapter 24

Saying Goodbye

Akita and Wulf return to the Dragon Temple and see all kinds of wonderous Dragons on the rooftop and down in the Courtyard. Akita is so excited to meet them all that she flies down faster and leaves Wulf behind. She is sure that he will forgive her for leaving him up in the air. She makes her way down to Annut who is standing next to a metallic silver Dragon with gold tipped horns and dark onyx scales down the middle of its back.

Akita lands next to Annut, giving her a hug on the snout, "Annut, who is this amazing Dragon?"

Annut gives her Dragon chuckle, "Akita Blackwing meet Centurion. He has been observing us while slowly making his way here from the other side of our world. As you can guess ducking and dodging the baddies, he did not feel like killing because that would have drawn attention to himself. Such are the stories of most of our brothers and sisters."

Centurion bows his head down to Akita, "How refreshing to not be called pretty or cute. I am a Dragon therefore not pretty or cute, but amazing is a great description. Nice to make your acquaintance, Akita Blackwing, Friend of Dragons." Looking over her shoulder, "I believe the man behind you is Wulf, your life mate."

Wulf steps forward, "Yes, Centurion, that would be me. My lovely wife loves dragons almost, if not more than me. So, seeing all of you here, she raced to meet you. But we have a lifetime together, I will not deny her this chance to mingle with you all."

Centurion makes another observation, "I see you both are bound to our distance cousins."

Akita reaches up and scratches Sages ridges, "Yes, this is Sage and Dojo is Wulf's little buddy. I was honored when Sage chose me on our first visit to their grove." Sage then nuzzles Akita's neck. "But all Dragons are magnificent, fantastic and amazing to me."

Ordyn lands next to Akita and bows to Annut and Centurion, "Akita, our dear Aphorea is requesting you come see her at your earliest convenience."

Centurion responds, "Lady Akita, it is a pleasure to meet you, but I know there are so many more you want to see. I would definitely start with Aphorea."

Akita bows her head to the two Dragons and heads further into the courtyard. She sees Thoraxian surrounded by several Dragons unfamiliar to her. She starts to turn towards them, when Wulf gently guides her to the main hall.

With a hand on her back, Wulf suggests, "Let's see Aphorea first. Thoraxian says he will wait for you."

Akita looks up to Wulf, "There are so many more than we knew of it is a shame, that we finally made things safer for them, but they are leaving us. Don't get me wrong, I understand after a millennia of hiding, torture and murder. That's what we have been fighting to stop. If we had known of more than just Annut, sooner we might have been able to turn it sooner. Someone in our past might have taken up the fight. But, alas, their happiness is all I wish for."

Wulf empathizes with her, "Well dear, I know you have been trying to figure a way to get a few to stay back with us. I know how your mind works. You must talk to as many as possible." Laughing, "I wish you luck."

As they walk into the Hall, they see Aphorea seated in front of two beautiful Dragons. They are white with blue horns and ridges. They are a matching pair. Akita comes to a stop just behind Aphorea. The Twins look at Akita, and nod at her. How is she ever going to tell them apart. She studies them for a few moments, and then notices a few blue scales at the corner of the left eye on one and the right eye on the other. Like birth marks she thinks.

Aphorea stands and turns to Akita, "Akita and Wulf, I hope your couple of days away were enjoyable."

Wulf smiles and Akita smiles, "It was nice to have time with no gloom and doom hanging over our heads."

Aphorea smiles, "That will be a new reality for all of us, for a while anyway." She glances over her left and right shoulders. "I would like to introduce you to my granddaughters. Fenix and

Onix, meet High Duchess Akita Blackwing Wari and her new husband Duke Wulf Wari." Akita makes a mental note that Fenix has the blue scales at the corner of her left eye and Onix's are at the corner of her right eye.

Akita runs up to Fenix and hugs her, then to Onix, "Granddaughters, how wonderful. Fantastic White Twin Dragons, I am at a loss here. But of course, the Granddaughters of Aphorea would be simply gorgeous in their frosty white glossy splendor. The blue hues and tear drop at the corner of each eye, give you your own uniqueness. You are mirror image twins."

Aphorea smiles, "See girls, as Ishvet says she is crazy about Dragons. She already has you figured out by the only thing that is different about each of you. However, Akita, they have good news and disturbing news for us. The disturbing news is just a confirmation of Storm's story about Omoth. The good news I will let them tell you."

Fenix opens up to talk to Akita and Wulf, "My sister and I have come to an important decision. We…"

Onix blurts out with excitement, "… are staying here with our Grandmother and you."

Fenix finishes, "Annut has already given permission for us to use her cave, but one of us will stay with Ishvet and Vivian, to guard over their family and Elderwolf Keep. The other will stay with you and Wulf at Blackwing Keep."

Akita laughs, "This is the best news you could have given me. I was so disappointed that the Dragons were leaving us, but to hear the two of you are staying gives me joy and hope. Thank you so much." With a devious grin, "You know Annut's caves have room for a few more Dragons, maybe others would stay too." She looks to Aphorea, "We need to discuss Omoth for Vicar and Mandrake's sake. Their Father and Queen, heck the entire castle was killed by a potent poison added to their dinner one night. That is how the usurper was able to move in and take control. This was ten plus years ago now. With that said, we are severely diminished in manpower and supplies. We will have to plan well for a continent-to-continent battle and do some research."

Akita looks to Aphorea, "I need to go see some of the other new arrivals. Then I am going to take a few dragons with a few of us to check on Blackwing Keep. We will be back before time to leave."

Aphorea nods, "Safe travels my friend."

Taking Wulf's hand, Akita pulls him towards Thoraxian. As they get closer, she sees a deep forest green dragon with lighter green horns and ridges. Standing next to that Dragon is a Gold Dragon, you would think was made by a sculptor with pure gold.

Thoraxian lowers his head as Akita approaches. As is her way, Akita gives him a big muzzle hug. "Who are our new friends, Thoraxian? Forgive me I'm on Dragon overload and loving every minute of it." She has a big smile as she turns to the two newcomers.

Thoraxian chuckles, "We knew you were going to be in your version of heaven, as more arrived. Rukur and Janda, meet Lady Akita of Blackwing Keep, a friend to all Dragon Kind. It was Akita and her friends that assisted in freeing me from Dark Wizard magic. She is the one who made it possible for Annut's clutch to thrive."

Rukur bows his head towards Akita, she of course takes the opportunity to give him a hug. "Oh, well it is an honor to meet you finally. I have sensed much since your first encounter with

Annut, and she has told me of your accomplishments."

Janda, also bows her head towards Akita, "It is an honor for me as well. You and your companions will live forever in Dragon Lore. We slept and hid for centuries awaiting the right stars to align so that we could travel to our secret sanctuary. You were the catalyst that made that journey possible. I, for one, thank you from the bottom of my heart and Dragon soul."

Akita starts to tear up, "It has been a pure joy to have the Dragons as part of our family. It saddens me that most of you will be leaving, but I do understand the yearning for safety. Just know that any who stay or decide to come back, need only to find me and they will have a home, with love and kindness."

Rukur bows his head again, "Your ways are known to most Dragons. More of us would have traveled to assist in removing the Dark Wizards blight from this land, but know this, each of our homelands has blights of their own. It was not safe to travel. I am not even certain that all who remain will make it here before we depart."

Akita nods in understanding, "We will do our best as time moves forward to rid this world of those blights. Alas, I must take many of my people back to Blackwing Keep before the Dragons depart. Enjoy your stay."

Akita turns to Wulf, "We need to gather those who are not bound to a Dragon and take them back to Blackwing Keep, while the Dragons are here to aide us with transportation."

Wulf agrees, "That is an excellent idea. Then the Wyverns can handle the rest, with Olek organizing a march for our soldiers. I believe Ishvet and Vivian are sending their people home with Captain Dubbin's. They mentioned sending others if we needed assistance getting people back to Blackwing Keep."

As they walk back into the hall, they find most of their team enjoying a meal at one of the tables. Akita sits down with them, "Ghod, Shamash, Ixen, Greta, Sham, all those who are not bound to a Dragon, are heading home today with the help of the Dragons. I need you all to get things ready for our people to come home. Wulf and I will be going with you, but we will return with the Dragons."

Ben looks up, "You're leaving me here for the moment?"

Akita nods, "Yes, Ben. You can stay with Zold until he departs. I know you want to go too. I have felt the same way, but the reality is that this realm is not safe for them any longer. We have a duty to our realm. We have our Wyverns to care for and a Wyvern flying army just like we planned with the Dragons."

Ben nods, but Akita knows his heart is breaking, even if he is in full agreement.

Akita looks back to the others, "I need to speak to Storm and Jacklyn. Olek and Quinn will stay with me here to help get the soldiers back home and keep them fed. The Dwarves are at Blackwing Keep now, rebuilding it, so I am sure camps and kitchens have been set up. Mandrake, Greenbean, Gavin and Fabby will help us with the Wyverns on the return trip." Akita turns back to Ben, "Ben, since Gavin will be taking care of Allura and her younglings, I will need you to help guide Aphorea's granddaughter. I am not sure which one is coming to Blackwing Keep, so why don't you go over and get to know them."

Ben looks over at the two white beauties, "They are staying, but only one is going to Blackwing? Where is the other one going to live?"

Vivian sits down next to him, "She will stay at Elderwolf Keep for the protection my family and my child."

Akita looks around the table, "Ok, so let's be ready to fly in an hour. What you can't carry put in Storm's room and I will have Olek pack it in with the rest of the gear." She looks around at the food on the table, wishing there was a cinnamon roll. Predictably, one pops up on a plate in front of her. "I am going to miss these Lommas, now that I have gotten used to them." Taking a bite as she walks away.

In the courtyard Akita finds Annut and Thoraxian with Rethu, Rukur and Janda. The five dragons have been loaded and are ready for flight.

Annut sees the look on Akita's face, "Yes dear, Rukur and Janda have volunteered to help us get this group back to the Keep. Rukur and I have room for you and Wulf." No more needed to be said as Akita launched onto Rukur's back. Wulf laughs as he lands on Annut.

Akita stares sheepishly at Annut. "I have to ride him at least once, but it's you and me on the way back. The skies are clear, the sun is bright, so let's be off. I am curious to see what has become of our home and our Keep."

All the Dragons laugh, as Rukur states, "Annut you know this one well. She almost makes me want to stay around, but it is time for our kind to depart from here." Then he abruptly launches into the air.

With the wind in her hair and Sage on her shoulder, Akita is exhilarated.

As they near Blackwing Keep, Akita vividly remembers the devastation and destruction that befell her home not too long ago. The walls knocked down, personal possessions floating in flood waters, bodies strewn all over the grounds. Up till now taking down King Carthon and the Dark Wizards had occupied all her thoughts, pushing out any thoughts of what she would return to.

The Dragons make a wide turn as they fly in, giving everyone a Dragon's eye view of Blackwing Keep grounds. All of the debris has been removed. Stables and workshops have been rebuilt. The outer wall is almost complete, but Akita's breath catches when she sees what looks like one hundred Dwarves camped around Blackwing Keep. The forge is up and running at full strength. The actual Keep, although it still needs some work, looks to be getting close to completion.

As the Dragons land on the grassy hillside next to the Keep, all the Dwarves and towns people start to migrate towards them. Prayla's town Mayor Statler leading them, he bows to the Dragons and their passengers as Akita and Wulf land in front of him.

Akita smiles and magnifies her voice, "Mayor Statler, you will be glad to know we succeeded. King Carthon and his Dark Wizards are defeated. Lady Vivian Elderwolf Bluescale and Sir Ishvet Bluescale are returning to Elderwolf Keep but will help us bring the rest of our people home. I also want to introduce High Duke Wulf Wari, my husband. I am now Duchess Akita Blackwing-Wari. We are returning

Shamash and others from my council to assist in your work here at Blackwing Keep. It is time to rebuild our homes, our businesses, and our lands." Akita sees a stout; proud Dwarf join Mayor Statler.

Akita bows, "I understand we have you and the Home Hearth Dwarves to thank for assisting our people with the rebuilding of Blackwing Keep. Your brethren that came to the battle to fight at our side, fought gallantly, assisting in delivering the final blows to the Dark Wizards. They are Heroes of the Realm."

The Dwarves all cheer and pump their tools or weapons in the air.

The Dwarf speaks, "Lady Akita Blackwing-Wari, I am High Master Builder Grunch Chiseler. When news reached us in Home Hearth, we mobilized immediately. Our people cannot forget the kindness of your uncle when our home was threatened by the monstrous Orc Army from the East Voskaola Mountains. He sent aid and men to help us defend our home. Now we can repay that debt by helping to rebuild yours. Many of our Elders send their best wishes but were unable to make the journey. However, there was one Elder that insisted that he be here for your return. Elder

Myles Axiom and a few of his Wizard Apprentices are assisting with the rebuilding and the redesign."

Akita smiles at Grunch and reaches out a hand, "Growing up I had heard the stories of how my Uncle Edmond helped the Home Hearth Dwarves. At the time I was a child and had no real concept of the deed. Now I really understand the concept of alliances and pacts between many different peoples. From the bottom of my heart, I thank you for all your help and aid. Darkwing will be here in a few days with the rest of our people. I know he will be happy to see Myles Axiom again. I am excited to see what Elder Axiom has added to Blackwing Keep."

Grunch slightly bows and takes Akita's hand, "If you will, please follow me I will take you to him."

Akita follows Grunch down the hillside, through the gates and into the courtyard. She sees an older Dwarf with a long white beard and dark blue robes speaking with several younger, muscular dwarves. Grunch leads Akita and Wulf to the older Dwarf. Behind them, Ghod comes through the gate and makes a bee line to the newly rebuilt Backsmith shop. Shamash and Ixenvorlux excuse themselves and head to the infirmary to check on supplies. Greta heads for the Kitchen and Sham goes to the stables to check on the animals. Storm and Jacklyn head over to the tents to see if the Dwarves are in need of any help or supplies.

Grunch stops in front of the older Dwarf, "Elder Axiom, this is the High Duchess Lady Akita Blackwing-Wari and her husband Duke Wulf Blackwing-Wari. She is Duke Edmonds niece."

Elder Axiom turns and smiles at Akita. He bows to both her and Wulf, "It is so good to meet you both. A splendid Keep you have here. I have thoroughly enjoyed overseeing its reconstruction. I do hope that it will be to your liking when we are complete."

Akita looks around in awe at what the Dwarves have accomplished in the months since they arrived, "It looks spectacular Elder Axiom. Grunch mentioned that you have added a few things to the design."

Elder Axiom's lips stretch into a sly smile and a mischievous look flashes over his face, "To right he is. We Dwarves do one thing with flare above all others. We build underground and trough mountains. We heard that you were building a Wyvern army and needed someplace to stable all the beautiful creatures. I didn't want to erect a gigantic building behind the Keep, so we dug down." Elder Axiom grabs a large parchment from the table in front of him and holds it up to Akita.

"As you'll see on these plans, there is now a vast underground stable and tunnels beneath Blackwing Keep. Tunnels so big that the biggest Dragon could walk through. Speaking of which, there is now a tunnel to Annut's cave from the Keep. The Stables open in the back hillside, and you can access them from the cellar of the Keep. Your Wyverns and Dragons will never be far from you."

Joy can be seen twinkling in Akita's eyes, "Wow, I can't even imagine! This is great."

Wulf chuckles, "She will be spending all her time under the Keep instead of in the throne room. I will say that having the Wyverns and Fenix so close in the event that there is trouble will be great."

Akita lunges and gives Elder Axiom a huge hug. He starts laughing and jokingly protests against the show of affection, "Lady Akita please, you might break my old bones."

She releases him and steps back, "I can see why Skrymir Darkwing holds you in such high regard. He will be here next week after the Dragons move on to their secret realm."

Elder Axiom looks confused for a moment, "The Dragons are leaving?"

Akita looks down and speaks softly, "Yes, they are moving on from our world to a safer place along with the Frost Giants. A couple Dragons are staying to look over Blackwing Keep and Elderwolf Keep, but the majority are leaving next week. Wulf and I will be returning to the Dragon Temple with the Dragons tonight."

Elder Axiom shakes his head in disbelief, "Oh that is such a shame. Please ask Annut and the other Dragons to explore the stables before you leave. If you have any suggestions, please let me know. Go now and explore the Keep before you leave."

Akita takes Wulf's hand, and they make their way towards the main doors of the Keep. Two

Dwarven workers rush over and open the doors for them. Akita squeezes Wulf's hand and gasps as she sees the Main Hall for the first time. They both rush in and take in the exquisite architecture of the Hall with its ornate columns and marble floors. The Windows are stained glass depicting Dragons spewing fire and the ceilings have murals of Akita flying on Dragons. Akita whispers under her breath, "I am home."

The flight from home is quite bittersweet for Akita, but she knows that soon she and Wulf will be back to the place she loves so much. For the moment she tries focusing on her last flight with Annut. She leans over the saddle and hugs Annut's neck and begins speaking to her, "I'm going to miss you so much. Before I met you all I could think about was meeting a dragon. Then our paths crossed, now I can't imagine you not in my life. It's going to take me a long time to recover from your leaving."

Annut purrs in Akitas mind, "Akita dear I am also going to miss you. You are the first not of my race that I have ever cared for like a daughter and a friend. Without you I would not have been able to allow my clutch to hatch and feel safe. I wish things could stay the same, but the world is changing around us. I need to take my children somewhere where the forces of evil could not touch them. I know that if you could do the same with your team, that you would. I will never forget you and our friends. We have both lost and gained so much in the last few years."

Akita squeezes Annut's neck and starts to cry. She lets her mind wander to the memories of the moment she entered Annut's cave and the first time she spoke into her mind and flashes of the first time that she flew on Annut's back. To the day that she first touched a Dragon egg and felt the presence of the little one inside. Next to the day that she met Aphorea in the ice cave and Aphorea had Wulf pledge himself to protect her. Then she opens her eyes and tries to take in every detail of where she is now. Her hands rubbing on the rough scales of Annut's neck, the smell of the clouds as they fly through them, the smooth horn of the saddle, and the warmth radiating from Annut's body keeping her warm in the cool night air.

Without warning, Annut makes a sharp dive and Akita has to grab the saddle to stay atop of her. Annut is going almost straight down to the ground. Akita's heart races, "Annut what is going on?"

Annut starts to laugh in Akita's head, "I've always wanted to do that to you. Just to keep you on your toes."

Akita starts to laugh with her, "Well you certainly did."

Annut levels off then starts to climb in the sky to where the other Dragons are flying. As they rejoin them the clouds break, and the moon is in full view. The light shimmers off of the Dragons and creates a beautiful effect in the sky. Akita takes it all in. Soon they will be back at the Dragon Temple, and she doesn't know if she will ever experience something like this again.

The day comes for the Dragons to leave, and Akita doesn't want to get out of bed. Wulf nudges her, "Come on honey, staying in bed will not cause it to not happen."

Akita looks over at him, "A girl can dream, can't she? I was just hoping that by some small chance that this was all a dream and Annut would be in her cave with the little ones, and we could go play in the meadow chasing butterflies."

Wulf smiles at her, "I'll meet you in the Grand Hall for breakfast. Thoraxian has already let me know that the first wave of Giants are in the courtyard and that King Iglis is excited to meet you. He's speaking to Darkwing right now."

She pops out of bed at this news and starts to get dressed. Wulf leaves her to get ready and heads to the Hall for breakfast. She puts on a nice pair of embroidered black pants that end at her shins, a buttoned white blouse, and a deep purple vest with gold filigree. She then twists her hair up into a knot and sticks a long gold pin through it to hold it in place. A glance into the mirror and she realizes that she has forgotten her lapel pin.

Akita goes over to the table and picks up the solid gold pin. A smooth circle with a Dragon in flight, wings spread from one edge of the circle to the other. The Dragon on the pin is a depiction of Annut that Ghod made when they first formed the team at Blackwing Keep just shy of two years ago. She stares at the pin and admires the detail that

Ghod put into the Dragon with all the texture of scales and the jewels for eyes and the delicate gold work for the wings. Her heart swells and her eyes become misty. She bites her lower lip to stop herself from crying. She takes a deep breath and puts the pin on and heads out the door for the Hall to join the others for breakfast.

The main hall is filled with Dragons of all colors and kinds. It reminds her of a tapestry she once saw with all the known types of Dragons. This makes her smile. At the large table in the center are most of the team that remained to send off the Dragons and Giants; General Olek, Quinn, Fabby, Greenbean, Judas, Ordyn, Gavin, Skip Mandrake, Ben, Wulf, Meh-Kola, Ishvet and Vivian.

Akita hurries to the table and says good morning to everyone. She quickly sits and savors a large cinnamon roll and chilled coffee drink courtesy of Darkwing. The excitement is boiling over inside her, "Wulf I'm going to get to meet the King of the Frost Giants. How do I look?"

Wulf winks at her, "You always look good to me. Today you are giving the look of regal with a flair of adventure. You look perfect to me."

Akita touches his hand, "Okay, gotta go now."

She hops up and heads out to the Courtyard. When she gets to the door the Lommas open the large doors for her, and she is greeted by a large group of Giants. All with pale blue to silvery skin. They tower over her but are not menacing in the least. They seem to exude a joyful quality. There is a path down the middle of the group that leads to where King Iglis and Darkwing are. Akita makes her way towards them, nodding and saying hello to the Giants she makes eye contact with on the way there.

At the end of the path King Iglis is on a stone throne that the Lommas undoubtedly made for him and Darkwing is standing in front. Akita steps beside Darkwing and puts her hand around his waist. He returns the gesture and begins to introduce her to the King, "King Iglis, this is Lady Akita Blackwing, champion of Dragons and Wyverns, Slayer of Dark Wizards. Akita this is King Iglis Frozenbolt of the Frost Giant Tribe and slayer of Kraksis, the fiercest of Titans."

Akita lets go of Darkwing and bows before the King, "It is my pleasure to meet you King

Iglis, Princess Gianna has regaled me with stories of you and her mother."

King Iglis leans forward, "She has brought back some amazing stories of your exploits also. I thoroughly enjoyed the one about you destroying the Dark Wizard. There is no reason for us to be so formal. You can just call me Iggy like my wife does. They will be here later in the afternoon. She is making sure that everyone gets through the portal with the Earth Amulet."

Akita smiles, "Is there anything that you need before you leave this world that we can help you to get?"

King Inglis shakes his head, "No, I believe that we have everything. We need only your company until we leave. Mr. Darkwing would you like to show Lady Akita your gift?"

Darkwing turns to Akita and opens his vest to reveal a clear blue amulet and a silver chain. The amulet is glowing faintly with whisps of frost emanating from it. Darkwing reaches up and takes the amulet in his palm so that Akita can see it more clearly, "Isn't it great! King Iglis made it for me. He had heard about what happened with the last Frost Amulet I had and thought a deserved a proper one. This one he assures me does not have any piece of a Dragon soul trapped in it."

Akita stares at it in awe, "It is beautiful."

King Iglis chuckles, "Don't worry Lady Akita, we have not for gotten you either." The King picks up a small ring from the arm of his throne. It looks so small between the tips of his fingers, but as it gets closer, Akita can see that it is a bangle.

"This is for you from my wife Queen Afa. It is imbued with the might of the Earth Amulet. Someone with your magical talents will be able to move the earth and create all kinds of stone and earthen objects."

Akita takes the Bangle from King Iglis, "Thank you Iggy! This is great. I will cherish it forever and it will be passed down in my family as a great treasure."

The King stands and bows to Akita, "You honor me and my family Lady Akita. If you will please excuse me, I must meet with some of my old Dragon friends before we depart."

Akita turns to Darkwing and shows him the bangle. They both begin walking back towards the Temple doors and into the Hall. They are eager to show the treasures that King Iglis has bestowed upon them.

The day goes by with many tears falling to the ground and even more smiles and funny stories being passed around. Akita and the team meet so many new Dragons that they are unable to even keep their names straight. The last of the Giants appear from a portal just after lunch and Queen Afa and Princess Gianna are the last to step through. The team introduce themselves to them and they all dine together.

As the sun starts to set, everyone begins to get anxious about the impending goodbyes. Akita is wringing her hands and can feel her heart beating more quickly than usual. Ishvet and Vivian spend most of their time speaking with Thoraxian and Onix . Darkwing takes one last flight on Granite. General Olek stays close to Addrit while meeting some of the newer Dragons with Meh-Kola. Greenbean, Ordyn, and Quinn train one last time with Shemera in the gardens. Mandrake and Elsbeth are atop the Temple with several Frost Giants. They are all enthralled while

Mandrake tells stories of Omoth and the kingdom he hails from. Ben, Judas, and Gavin along with Zold, Blitz, and Skip sit around a huge bonfire enjoying each other's company. Lastly, Wulf and Dojo fly above the Temple with Choren awaiting Annut to call them back.

As the moon rises and the sun disappears below the tall forest trees, Annut calls to all the occupants of the Temple, "Friends, it is time for us to depart. Queen Afa and King Iglis will open the portal on the roof of the Temple. Everyone makes their way there. Our friends will be there to see us off."

Everyone makes their way to the top of the temple and those that were flying land on the edges. The King and Queen are in position. They use the Frost and Earth Amulet to open a portal to the Dragon sanctuary. The huge portal lights up the night sky and the light reflects off the lower hanging clouds. It would be so pretty if it wasn't so sad. The Frost Giants step through first to make room on the roof for the Dragons. Only King Iglis, Queen Afa, and Princess Gianna remain at the edges of the portal.

Dragon after Dragon begins to fly through the portal. Akita is overwhelmed by the sight and turns into Wulf's arms. He holds her tight as she begins to sob. Annut walks over and nuzzles Akita's back, "Akita it is time. Let me see you one last time."

Akita slowly turns in Wulf's arms the lunges out and hugs Annut's snout, "I can't let you go! No! I just won't do it."

Annut purrs in Akita's arms, "I will always cherish our friendship little one. I love you beyond all the stars in the sky." With that she pulls away from Akita's hug and moves to the portal. She takes one look back then steps through.

Thoraxian follows behind her then all the young Dragons. Most of them are nuzzling the one they were bonded with before they step through. Fenix, Onix, and Aphorea are at the end of the procession and watch as the last Dragon disappears beyond the threshold. Princess Gianna steps to the middle of the portal and then turns to all the wet faces. Hers is just as wet, "Thank all of you for treating me as part of your family while I was with you. I will miss you eternally. Lady Akita you will always be my little sister. Goodbye and farewell."

King Iglis and Queen Afa step beside Princess Gianna and wave goodbye to everyone. Once they step through the portal it snaps shut. Suddenly it is pitch black atop the Temple and eerily quiet. After their eyes adjust, they can see that Warrior, Hunter, Draco, Ransom, and Allura have joined them on the roof.

Akita turns to all of them, "I am so grateful to have all of you in my life and if any of you think for even a second that you are going to leave me, I will turn you to ash." She laughs a little then opens her arms wide to indicate that she wants a hug. "I am only kidding, but not really. Get in here, I need a hug."

Vivian and Ishvet step into her arms and give her a strong hug that seems to last for a few minutes. They step aside and Darkwing and Quinn fill their places. Two by two everyone has their turn giving love and adoration to their team mother. Meh-Kola flies up and licks Akita's cheek then blinks away. Akita then goes to all the Wyverns and hugs their necks and hugs the Dragons snouts of Fenix and Onix. She is exhausted after such an emotional night. Her and Wulf go down the step from the roof that led into the Main Hall and see all the Lommas waiting for them. They are all lined up in rows and one Lomma is in front of them all. It is the one Lomma that spoke to Akita aloud when they first met. She walks up to Akita and gives her a woven blanket, "Akita it is also our time to go. Without the magic of the Dragons in the temple we will fade back to our realm. We wanted to leave you with a token of our affection before we go. We have loved being able to serve all of you. Please tell Ghod that we enjoyed creating all the crazy ideas in his head. It stretched us to our limit."

Akita reaches out and takes the woven blanket into her arms. When she takes the full weight of it, the Lommas disappear. It startles her for a second then she feels Wulf's hand on her shoulder, "What did they give you?"

Akita looks down at the blanket, "I don't know. Help me to spread it out."

Wulf grabs one side and Akita the other. They step away from each other and unfold the blanket. As they pull it tight Vivian raises her hand and creates a glowing orb so that the blanket is completely illuminated. Akita gasps at the intricate weaving. At the top is a depiction of her riding on Annut, then lower is Thoraxian and Aphorea then below them is all the Dragonlings and finally at the bottom of them are all the Wyverns with the whole team standing below on the edge of the blanket. Each stitch is so small that everyone is very detailed. It is a glorious tapestry.

Akita turns to the others, "Isn't it beautiful? I know what I'll be sleeping under tonight. Everyone, rest up. We make our way home tomorrow morning."

CHAPTER 25

HAPPY BIRTHDAY

Akita fusses with her outfit in her changing room while Meh-Kola lounges in a chair in the corner of the room. She can't seem to get the shoulders of the top she is wearing to lay just right when she buttons the waistcoat. Meh-Kola watches and giggles to herself, "Akita it looks just fine. One would be happy to wear an outfit as pretty as yours."

Akita huffs, "Thank you, but the shoulders of this blouse seem to puff out when I button up the vest."

"One thinks it is just your imagination. One thinks you are just too nervous to meet your godson for the first time."

Akita spins around, "Well you could be right. I'm also just so terribly excited. Plus, I haven't seen Ishvet and Vivian for a year now."

Meh-Kola hops off the chair and flies up to the dresser, "One believes it will be like no time has passed. One is curious to see the little one though. One hopes he is a spitting image of his father. One thinks it might be too funny if the little one had his mother's long blonde hair."

Akita pauses for a second and imagines a little Ishvet with long blonde hair. It frightens her and she shakes the image from her mind, "Oh my that would be a sight. As far as I know, when a Dragonkin and a Human have a child, they always are born as a Dragonkin."

Meh-Kola begins licking her paw and in-between licks she states in a matter-of-fact way, "I once met an Orc and a Dwarf that had a child, it ended up with short legs, long arms, green skin, and pointed ears on a very large head. It was hideous. So, one hopes Vivian and Ishvet's baby is much prettier."

Again, Akita pictures what Meh-Kola has described, "Poor child. He must trip over his hands all the time."

Meh-Kola blinks back to the chair, "Did the Sending Stone message say what time they would arrive?"

Akita looks out the window up at the sun, "It should be anytime, I have instructed the royal trumpeters to alert the Keep when they are within sight."

Meh-Kola curls up on the chair, "Ah good, One might have a cat nap before they arrive."

Akita laughs, "You sleep more than any cat I have ever known and you're not even a cat. You go ahead and take a nap and I am going to head down to the kitchen to check on the food for the birthday party."

She pulls her vest down one last time and heads down to the kitchen to meet with Quinn. Even though Quinn isn't in charge of the kitchen anymore, she insisted that she be allowed to cook the birthday cake for little Talon. It must seem funny to the kitchen staff to see the Captain of the Wyvern riders baking a cake and making cinnamon rolls.

Akita walks into the Kitchen and sees Quinn icing the warm, fresh out of the oven cinnamon rolls. Several other cooks are preparing the main meal of roasted chicken, cooked carrots, mashed potatoes, garden salad, and butter rolls. The Kitchen smells wonderful.

"Quinn, do you need help with anything? Icing the cinnamon rolls or the cake, or maybe tasting something?" A mischievous look flashes over Akita's face.

Quinn doesn't notice Akita's face and plainly states, "No, I'm almost done."

Akita blows a raspberry at Quinn, "Your no fun. I wanted to taste something. Oh, well. They'll be here anytime so we better get a move on."

Quinn grabs a towel and wipes off her hands, then reaches down and pulls out a cinnamon roll and hands it to Akita, "I knew you would be down, so I had one ready for you."

Akita's eyes light up and she quickly sinks her teeth into the cinnamon roll. She looks over to Quinn, who is amused by the scene, "Yummy! Thank you!" Her words can hardly be deciphered because of her mouth being full of cinnamon roll.

An apron flies in front of Akita and lands in a basket. Akita looks over and sees Quinn headed to the door that leads to the gardens. She swallows the last of the cinnamon roll and follows her out the door. Quinn takes a seat on a wooden bench, "Akita, can you believe it's been over a year and a half since we fought King Carthon and the Dragons left?"

Akita sits down beside her on the bench and puts an arm around her shoulders, "I try so hard not to remember those times. I try to remember all the goods that came from that period in our lives. Look at you. You are the Captain of the Wyvern Warriors. You met a handsome man, who happens to be my General Olek, and have gotten married. Soon you'll be having little ones running around."

Quinn whips her head around sharply when Akita mentions a child, "Who's having a child? Certainly not me anytime soon. I already saw how that took the fire out of Storm when her and Gavin had a child. It's too bad that they can't be here for the party."

Akita nods her head, "Yes, I miss all three of them so much. Plus, I can't get enough of my niece Zoey. She's already six months old and precious as a diamond. She's going to be a handful when she starts flying around the Keep and is talking."

Quinn has a deep-in-thought look on her face, "Where was it that they went?"

Akita looks off into the distance, "They were taking Blitz to the Dark Forest to be with his family for a while and hopefully to find a mate. Also, on the way they were going to stop by O'Malley Keep to see Jacklyn and Ben. They are just about done rebuilding the Keep and the fleet. According to Jacklyn's last message they had refitted The Sea Horse and were getting ready to take their first sail on it. Grace would have loved seeing her sail again."

Quinn lets out a deep breath, "Yeah, she would have. I think it is great that Jacklyn is giving Ben a chance to head up her Keep Guard. That boy, well I mean man now, has been through so much. Well, the cake is just about done so I'm going to go finish that. I'll meet you in the Dining Hall after they arrive." She gets up and heads back into the Kitchen.

Akita gets up and walks down the path that leads to the courtyard and goes through the iron gates. She walks over towards the stable and then turns left the go to Ghod's Smithy. She sees him pounding away on the anvil. He looks up and sees her and stops mid swing, "Akita! I was wondering when you might stop by. I have the presents you requested right here."

Akita steps across the threshold to the shop and watches as Ghod picks up a large wooden box and sits it on the anvil. He smiles through his mask at her and only his teeth can be seen protruding through the mouth hole, "Let's see, first we have this box for Ishvet." He hands her an ornate box that is about a foot square and about eight inches tall. She takes it and opens the hinged lid. A soft glow radiates from inside and lights up the jeweled bronzy skin of her face.

"Ghod it is magnificent!" She grabs the object inside and lifts it up, "It's light as a feather. Where did you get the jewels for this crown?"

Ghod chuckles, "The Dwarves left me some special trinkets after they finished the Keep. I had been saving them for just a piece like this. They say that they are one of the rarest stones in all of Alahora. Mythmots, they call them. They will glow this brilliant blue color forever."

Akita places it back in the ornate box and puts the box down on a nearby workbench, "And Vivian's matches Ishvet's?"

Ghod hands her the next box that is the same size as the previous one, "Yup, both alike but hers has a special crest from Elderwolf Keep in the silver and gold work."

Akita opens the box, and the same light illuminates her face, "Oh yeah, I see it there in the front. It's beautiful! They are going to love these. And for little Talon?"

"Well, we kept that a surprise from even you." Ghod walks over to a large cabinet and opens the door. When the door opens a small creature flies out and lands on his shoulder. Akita jumps back then laughs at herself. Ghod reaches up and hold his hand out, the little creature crawls onto his hand and rubs its head against his thumb, "A little Pseudo Dragon for Talon."

Akita's eyes light up and she reaches out and pets the little creature. She is amazed by its beautiful coloring. It is a dark purple color over most of its little body with bright orange eyes and faint green stripes across it's back. Its underbelly is white, and its wing webbing is almost black. It rubs against her hand, "I wish Sage was here so I could find out its name."

Ghod Chuckles again, "Dojo and Wulf already found all that out when they went to the Secret Grove and asked him if he wanted to be bonded with Talon. His name is Oliver and apparently, he is very excited to meet Talon. I'll bring the crowns with me when I make my way to the Dining Hall. You can take Oliver with you now. He just ate a few crickets so he will be fine for a while. He'll be happy to see the Keep since he's only been in the shop since Wulf and Dojo brought him from the Grove."

Akita turns her shoulder to Oliver, and he flies over from Ghod's hand. He rubs against her neck then curls up for the ride. She is so happy that Talon will have a little companion like she and Wulf have. She hurries out into the Courtyard so he can see everything around him.

Just as she passes the Stables Wulf lands beside her with Dojo on one shoulder and Sage on the other. He smiles at her nervously, "Hi love, I see you found our surprise. I hope you are not too mad at me for keeping it from you."

Akita bares her teeth and playfully growls, "I was only for an instant, then I saw little Oliver here and was instantly happy again. I'm so happy that he decided to leave the Grove and bond with Talon."

Sage perks up, "Lady he says that he is happy too and he can't wait until Talon can hear his voice."

Akita nods to Sage, "Thank you Sage, I was wondering what he was thinking."

Wulf laughs, "Phew, I'm glad you took that well. Dojo says he can't wait until the boy and Oliver meet. They should be here anytime, right?"

Akita looks up to the sky, yes, and I asked that the horns be played when they were close. I haven't heard anything yet."

Onix speaks into Akita's mind, "They are close Akita. I can hear my sister. I will fly up and greet them."

Just then the horns sound off and Onix flies out from the hillside to the Northeast. Akita gets excited and begins to jump up and down. Oliver begins to prance on her shoulder and Sage flies over to her other shoulder. Dojo stands at attention on Wulf's shoulder. He is scanning the sky. Wulf steps beside Akita and looks up to the northeast to find the first glint of Griffon armor.

Onix flies directly for Fenix and swings into a parallel position beside her. They both share memories in each other's heads while they fly down to the Courtyard. Vivian and Ishvet both greet her as she arrives. The Armored Griffons move to the back of the convoy to make room for Fenix.

Ishvet and Vivian are astonished as Blackwing comes into view. The trees and gardens are all coming back to their former glory. All the final details are finished on the Keep and looks like all the workshops and vendors are up and running. Before they get within half a mile, a crowd is gathering in the peripherals of the Courtyard. It seems as though everyone is waiting for them to land.

Vivian gives the command to the Armored Griffon Riders to land behind the Keep at the entrance to the Wyvern stables. They break away from the group in sync and head for the hillside. Ishvet and Vivian are on Fenix's back with Talon between them. Fenix has already informed them that she will drop them off and then fly to Annut's cave to have some time with her sister.

In almost one fluid motion Fenix lands in the Courtyard and Ishvet and Vivian climb off with

Talon. The next moment, Fenix is back in the air flying away with Onix. Akita gets to Ishvet first and wraps him in a giant hug. Wulf hugs Vivian and Talon. They pull back and switch positions. Talon seems so happy and leaps into Akita's arms. She is more than happy to oblige him and cradles him like she would her own.

Several others come up and give their hugs and greetings. The Twins are next along with General Olek. Behind them are Darkwing and Skip. Meh-Kola blinks onto Ordyn's shoulder as he steps up for his hug from Vivian. Vivian startles for a second then realizes that it is Meh-Kola. She mimics Meh-Kol's speech, "One shouldn't pop in on One or One may get a thrashing from One by mistake."

Meh-Kola chuckles, "One missed you too Vivian. Now where is One's new Godson? One needs to make sure that he is not ugly like One's friend's baby."

Akita calls to Meh-Kola, "Meh-Kola, he is over here, and he is perfect. No reason for you to fret."

Akita props up the little Dragonkin boy for all to see. He is handsome like Ishvet with detailed brow ridges and a smooth snout. His skin is light blue with speckles of dark blue. His eyes are golden and fiery. The only odd thing is that for a one-year-old he is as big as a three-year-old. It is taking all of Akita's strength to hold him up. Akita looks over to Ishvet, "What are you feeding this boy? He's as big as a Giants baby!"

Ishvet laughs and looks over to Vivian, "It seems he got more of the Dragon line of my family then the Human line of Viv's. He is growing way faster than we thought he might."

Vivian exasperates, "Oh my, you don't even know the half of it. I have to ask the seamsters to make him new clothes every week. At this rate he will be as tall as Ordyn by the age of twelve."

Everyone looks over at Ordyn and he looks scared for a second. Then he raises his arms and shrugs his shoulders. They all start laughing knowing that Ordyn didn't hear what Vivian said. Then they turn their attention back Talon. Akita starts walking towards the Keep's main doors and the crowd begins to disperse.

Akita takes him inside and immediately turns to the right. On the wall in front of them is the tapestry that the Lommas made for her with all the Dragons and Wyverns and even small depictions of the team. Akita points out Vivian and Ishvet to Talon. When she points to them Talon says mama and poppa and when Akita points to herself riding on Annut, Talon quickly says Grandma. Akita inadvertently growls then stops herself. She begins to hear giggling behind her. She turns around and sees Vivian with a hand over her mouth trying to keep the laughing quiet. Akita kind of grunts and turns her nose up at Vivian, "Okay which one of you taught him to say that?

Vivian shakes her head and then slyly points to Ishvet. Ishvet smiles a toothy Dragonkin smile, "Okay Talon you can stop pretending now. You got her good."

Akita looks confused for a second and turns towards Talon, "Did Daddy teach you to call me Grandma?"

Talon, who is standing on the floor now looks up and smiles, "Yes Lady Akita, Daddy did tell me to say it."

Akita practically falls over and Wulf catches her, "Wait what did he just say?" She looks over to Ishvet and the realization comes to her that not only is his growth accelerated but his intellect as well.

All Wulf can do to keep from laughing is stand up Akita and say, "Well, what do ya know. This is going to be an interesting visit."

Akita turn to face him and smacks him on the chest playfully, "You just going to stand there and let him call your High Dutchess, Grandma?" Then she starts laughing.

Talon grabs Akita's hand and looks up at her, "Don't worry Lady Akita, I won't call you that anymore. Dad thought it would be funny."

She leans over and whispers in his ear, "It was funny, but we won't let them know that. We are going to have to think of a way to get your daddy back. You with me?"

Talon's face lights up and he nods his head and starts to giggle. Akita nods her head to him also and then stands up and takes him into the Grand Hall. She points out the Dragons in the stained glass and has him look up and see the murals on the ceiling. She lets him sit on the ornate throne at the back of the room. He seems intrigued by all the new sights.

Next, they take the corridor from the Grand Hall to the Main Dining Hall, and everyone starts cheering as they walk in. Ghod walks up to them as they enter. Before Ishvet, Vivian, and Talon landed he went out to Akita and got all the Pseudo Dragons and took them into the Dining Hall. Now he has Oliver in his hands and is presenting him to Talon.

Oliver jumps from Ghods hands and lands directly in front of Talon. He cocks his head to the left and right a few times looking up at Talon. Talon gets on his knees in front of Oliver and Talon holds out his hand. Oliver scurries over and rubs his head on Talon's hand. Talon's eyes light up and he looks up to Vivian and Ishvet, "Wow! He's talking in my head. His name is Oliver, and he is my new guardian. He wants to know if it is okay if he keeps me."

Vivian slightly laughs, "Of course he can keep you. I'm just a little jealous, Talon. Only really special people in this world get to bond with a Pseudo Dragon. Now, you both will have to take care of each other."

Talon nods his head over exaggeratedly, "Oh Yes!"

Ishvet looks over to Ghod, "What are you trying to do to me buddy? You're going to turn him into a Mini-Akita. He already won't leave Fenix alone, and he wants to have Wyverns at the Keep, now he has a little Dragon all his own." Ishvet puts a hand on his forehead and pulls it down his face to show his disbelief.

Akita grabs Ishvet in an open hug, "Don't blame me. I didn't choose this gift for him. That was Grandpa Wulf and Uncle Darkwing that hatched the plan so to speak."

Ishvet looks around, "Where is that tough old Ice Wizard at anyway."

From behind Ordyn, Darkwing can be heard, "Oh I'm here. Just as Icy as ever. Ordyn will you please move so I can see the boy of the hour."

Ordyn steps to the side and moves behind Aphorea, "Oh I'm sorry, sometimes I don't see you little guys." Then he starts belly laughing.

Darkwing wiggles his finger and flicks his wrist, and a snowball flies from his hand, and it hits Ordyn square in the snout. Darkwing starts laughing, "Do you see me now?"

Ordyn stops laughing and looks at the snow on the end of his snout and his eyes start to cross,

"Well if I don't see you at least I can say I feel your cold presence. All I can say now is thank you, my snout was getting rather warm with all these people standing around."

Ghod whips around until he is face to face with Darkwing, "Don't you even think about throwing a snowball at me. Us Half-Orcs are immune to such things, and it would melt a foot before it got to me."

Darkwing pauses for a second, "Oh really? We may have to test that later tonight in the Courtyard. Unless the other half of you is chicken."

Ghod grumbles something under his breath then walks over to the table and sits down, "I thought there was going to be food at this party?"

Akita laughs, "Okay guys enough kidding for now. Let's get Talon and Oliver at the head table so we can start this party.

After everyone is seated at the tables, Quinn has the kitchen staff serve the meal. There is a low roar of several side conversations going on at many tables. Akita and Wulf are seated directly across from Ishvet and Vivian. Vivian thanks Wulf for the special gift that he got Talon. Wulf is as humble as ever. He states that it is actually Oliver that should be thanked because he left the safety of the Grove to bond with Talon.

Talon could care less about their conversations and spends his time playing with Oliver at the table and feeding him pieces of roast chicken. The only time he stops what he is doing is when Akita mentions cake to the table. As soon as the dishes from dinner are cleared away, Quinn motions to the Kitchen to have the cake brought out.

Two strong, young lads bring out the cake on a sturdy board. The cake seems to be about three feet tall and two feet wide at the base. It is iced in an ombre of Dark blue at the bottom to a light blue on the top tier. There are scenes of mountains and valleys painted in buttercream around the bottom tier and birds in flight depicted on the middle tier. On the top tier are clouds made of spun sugar that billow around and down the sides.

Once the cake is sat in front of Talon, Mandrake and Darkwing take a position on either side. With a flourish of his hands, Darkwing sculpts three mini–Pseudo Dragons. Mandrake uses his magical talents to animate the blue ice sculptures. They flap their wings and mimic roaring. One by one they fly around the cake and Talon. Oliver believes he has some competition for Talon's affection and tries snapping at the life-like sculptures as they fly by him.

Mandrake laughs as he has the sculptures land on each tier of the cake, and they leave tiny Pseudo Dragon footprints in the icing. Each one climbs down and stops in front of Talon. Mandrake has them individually take a bow and Darkwing has them turn into a pile of snowflakes.

Talon bursts into gleeful laughter. "I want to learn how to do that. That was great."

Mandrake steps up to Talon, "I would gladly teach you, but alas, if you take after your father or your mother, it may not be a talent you can learn. We will have to see as you get older where your talents lie."

Ishvet looks at the boy then to Mandrake, "Yes, we are waiting to see what abilities he might develop. We know there is something special about him, but just don't know exactly what it is."

Vivian adds, "I think we have time to let it play out a little more. We don't need to rush into anything."

Akita laughs, "Well I wouldn't wait too long at the rate this boy is growing. Speaking of which, I thought maybe you both could accompany Wulf, Darkwing, and me to the War Room for a moment. Mandrake will you keep an eye on the little one."

Mandrake nods his head, and the others get up from the table and head to the corridor then up the stairs to the War Room. Ishvet notices the small changes that the Dwarves made to the stone style and the lantern sconces as they proceed to the War Room. Once they get to the room, Vivian and Ishvet are completely taken aback by the table in the midst of the room. It is intricately carved as a map of Alahora. There is so much detail that they believe for a moment that it is an illusion.

Ishvet turns to Akita, "Wow, they have really improved this room. it's a far cry from the late nights we poured over parchments looking for a way to defeat the Cloud Giants."

Vivian runs her hand over the textured wood of the table and then touches the spot where

Elderwolf Keep is carved, "This is amazing. Its detail is so true to the actual Keep."

Akita smiles, "Yes, they are the best craftsmen that I have ever seen. Please don't tell Ghod I said that."

On a lectern at the side of the room are two ornately carved boxes. Darkwing goes over and picks up the box on the left and Wulf walks over and picks up the box on the right. They both take the boxes to Vivian and Ishvet.

Ishvet looks perplexed and is looking at Vivian, "What are these? It's not our birthday's."

Vivian looks over to Akita, "Okay, High Duchess Akita Blackwing-Wari, what have you cooked up this time?"

Akita laughs a little through a sly slanted smile, "Well… It is not just me this time." She motions to Wulf and Darkwing to open the boxes, "These were made by Ghod by request from a group of us."

Vivian sees the light blue glow escape the box as Darkwing opens it, "That's such a pretty light, and oh my, that is a gorgeous crown." She looks over to the box that Wulf is opening in front of Ishvet, "Wow there's even a matching one."

Ishvet reaches into the box and runs his finger along the top of the crown, "I'll have to tell Ghod that he did an excellent job in making these, but who are they for?"

Akita clears her throat, "Well they are for the both of you. On Vivian's you will notice the crest of House Elderwolf."

Vivian's jaw drops and she picks up the crown and looks at the crest, "It is my crest! But why?"

Akita walks over in between both Ishvet and Vivian, "A few months ago there was a secret meeting of all the leaders of Alahora. Before you give me that look either one of you, we intentionally did not invite you. That was because the meeting was about you. Madam Suzie brought to our attention some crucial information about your role in the unification of this continent and your son's eventual role in the war in Omoth. She was given a vision by her patron God about the future of Alahora. In this vision, she saw the two of you alongside Talon leading the charge against the Dark Tyrant of Omoth. She informed us that the patron God hinted that we must unify the continent before we could leave it to fight against the oppression in Omoth."

Vivian and Ishvet look at each other with fear in their eyes and then to both Wulf and Darkwing. Darkwing and Wulf nod in agreement to Akita's explanation. Then they take the crowns back from them and put them in the box. Ishvet and Vivian are still quite confused when Akita slightly nudges them to walk out of the War Room and down the corridor.

They all walk by the Dining Hall and see that it is empty now. This confuses them even more and a little concern creeps into their minds about the location of Talon. Akita ushers them past the doorway and turns them towards the Throne Room. Once they are in the door, they see everyone is gathered in two groups on either side of the aisle. All their friends are there and even people they do not know. Many are dressed very regally.

Akita plants Vivian and Ishvet in front of the steps to the throne and has them face the crowd. She climbs the steps and amplifies her voice, "I am so glad we could all come together today. We have been planning this for months now and we are grateful that this could occur on Talon's birthday. In our leadership meeting we concluded that the continent of Alahora needed strong and wise guardianship. Something that would go beyond the pact of the Keeps. Also, along with the information that Madam Suzie provided, we knew that our guardians had to be Lady Vivian Elderwolf and Sir Ishvet Bluescale. Madam Suzie would you please come up and tell everyone what your patron conveyed to you."

From out of the crowd, Madam Suzie appears and walks straight for Vivian and Ishvet. She nods to them and smiles then takes their hands, "My patron God of Insight, Savras showed me a vision of Vivian and Ishvet uniting Alahora under a single crown, however it was not for them to rule, only to be caretakers of the soon to be King of Alahora. That would be the birthday boy Talon. They will guide him and give him the education that he needs along with what wisdom and experience we other leaders can impart. He will be our King when he reaches maturity. According to Mandrake, that should be sometime next week." Madame Suzie looks around at the confused faces and starts to laugh.

Mandrake and Vicar speak in unison, "That boy is growing like a weed."

Madam Suzie recomposes herself, "Now we will crown both Ishvet and Vivian as the

Guardians of the Realm here at Blackwing Keep with the acknowledgement and permission of all the leaders of the regions of Alahora. They have all signed The Pact of the Keeps that Akita has. We will be stronger together as always."

Akita steps closer and tells Ishvet and Vivian to step up to the Throne. Ordyn comes in and moves the one throne over and Wulf and Darkwing carry another to sit beside it. Vivan and Ishvet take their seats and Akita places the crowns on their heads. Quinn brings out Talon and lets him go and hop on Vivian's lap.

Ishvet pats Vivian on the leg and then stands up and walks to the steps, "I'll speak for both of us because as you can imagine Viv is kinda choked up right now. We are humbled by all of you and your trust in us to raise Talon in a way that exemplifies what Alahora stands for. As parents we can only try to steer our children on the right path, and if anyone has ever met a Dragonkin child they will tell what a chore that is. Anyway, we will take on this responsibility with all seriousness and we will rely on any help and wisdom that may come. With that said, I believe we still have cake to eat. I can see Ghod in the back there with his huge fork giving the motion to wrap it up."

The afternoon turns into night and the night turns into late night. The birthday boy and his Pseudo Dragon have been put to bed and all that remains in the Dining Room is the team of misfits that turned heroes. Large amounts of ale and wine has been consumed and each story that is told becomes grander than the last. Ishvet reminisces about his adventures with Rani before he meets Akita and Darkwing. Wulf tells tales about how he met Dojo and the trouble they got into in Omoth. Vivian tells a really exaggerated story of how she beat the Basilisk in the fields under Annut's cave.

Every once in a while, Onix and Fenix would ask questions in the storyteller's mind to get clarification. They were almost in disbelief of the wild adventures that the team had been on. They listened intently from outside the Keep wall as Aphorea told stories of the Titan wars and the Uprising of the Giants. Even Ghod had stories that caused everyone to have a fit of belly laughs.

At one point in the night, Ishvet asked for Akita to give an update to everyone. Akita begins with Jacklyn, "Well it has been a good year and a half since we defeated King Carthon. Jacklyn went back to O'Malley Keep and started to rebuild. She asked Ben to go with her in the hopes that he would eventually have enough training to be the head of her Keep guard. So far, he is doing a great job and has turned into a fine young man. Let's see, Madam Suzie has taken quite well to running Cliffshade Keep and Cliffside. They have a council of elders. They have rebuilt a portion of the Keep but have decided to make it a little less grand to reflect their values.

Darkwing here, has been back at Darkwing Keep, and has been busy raising a new clutch of Roc Owls. He comes to visit me and Wulf every month. Mandrake and Vicar help me to stay sane in the Keep as my best friends and advisors. Especially now that Shamash has retired and is off traveling the countryside. At least that's what he says. I think he is hiding in Annut's cave and Ixen is bringing him food."

Ixen sits up in her chair, "I'm not bringing him food. I haven't seen him."

Akita laughs, "I guess I didn't really think that he would go off on his own. Anyway, as everyone knows, Ixen is the head of all things healing here and has even started a school of sorts for low level healers in the surrounding towns. Quinn is now the Captain of the Wyvern Riders. She spends most of her time in the underground stables and her free time with her new husband, General Olek. Isn't that right, Quinn?"

Quinn blushes a little if you can tell when a Demonan blushes, "When you put it like that it sounds as though I don't have a life. I still train with Void when he's around and I make the occasional cake."

Akita smiles and nods, "Yes, thank you. I do hope that you have a little one to make a cake for soon." She then turns to Olek, "You know you are not getting any younger."

General Olek slinks in his chair then throws his hands up, "You might as well tell her Quinn. She's never going to leave us alone about it."

Quinn looks down to her lap, "Okay, I was saving this for another day when not so much had happened. And no, Akita, I am not pregnant. Olek and I have decided to adopt a child from Prayla.

Her name is Dani, and her parents were killed in King Carthon's attack. She is nine and cute as a button."

Akita about falls out of her chair. Luckily, she grabs Wulf's arm and steadies herself, "What? Why is this the first that I'm hearing of this? We are going to need another celebration and you're going to have to make another cake."

Quinn smiles, "Okay we can talk about the details later, go on with your updates."

Akita nods her head and still has a smile from ear to ear, "Where was I? Ghod, you haven't really done anything out of the normal have you? So, you all know what he has been up to, hammer this, eat that, scare me, hammer, and eat again."

Ghod shakes his head, "No, I kept the surprise from you about Oliver. That should count for something. Now if you'll excuse me, I'm going to see if they left anything out in the kitchen for me to snack on."

Akita shakes her head and rolls her eyes, "Then there is Judas, who now spends most of his day in Windu's old Palace in Oceanfalls. He has been elected their Regent. His whole family has moved in with him and he is having a great time.

It's a shame he couldn't be here today. His last letter stated that they were having difficulties with some of Windu's curiosities, whatever that means."

Meh-Kola blinks onto Akita's lap, "One will tell what One has been up too. One single handedly eradicated the Assassin's Guild with the help of Greenbean and Fabby. One pointed them in the right direction, and they took care of the rest. One is now the Chief of Tactics for Blackwing Keep." Meh-Kola then blinks off of Akita's lap over to the fireplace to stretch and warm at the hearth.

Akita slightly growls in a playful way, "Before that, I was getting ready to tell you about Gavin and Blitz but to talk about them I will first have to tell you about Storm. Storm has gotten back to her old happy and thoughtful self. She was kinda lost after the demon was ripped out of her. Fortunately for her, Visham and Gavin were around. Actually, all four of them have formed quite a bond, Blitz included. Especially now that her and Gavin have a precious little one, my niece Zoey. So, she is off with Gavin, Blitz, Visham, and Zoey to the Dark Forest to help Blitz find his kin and hopefully find a mate.

Greenbean and Fabby have been helping to root any last followers of the Dark Wizards and any assassins or bandits. They will be back tomorrow to see all of us. Void makes his rounds from city to city helping people and teaching magic. He is a lot less about the money these days. I think we rubbed off on him. Let's see, am I forgetting anyone?"

Words rush into her mind, "Akita don't forget how Hunter and me helped train the new Wyverns for fighting in the air."

Drako speaks up, "I'm sure Ransom and I helped also. Plus, we found the new Wyverns from the South Coast."

Akita laughs, "Yes, I am to inform you all at how instrumental Hunter, Warrior, Drako, and Ransom were in the establishment of the Wyvern Army. Plus, we are friends with several new Wyverns that some of you haven't met. I'll take you to the stable tomorrow if we wake before noon."

Wulf yawns next to Akita, "Yep I think it's about that time for me."

Ordyn stands up and says with his deep smooth voice, "Wait, Akita didn't mention me. I have great news. Does anyone want to hear it?"

Akita looks surprised for a second, "Oh, I am so sorry Ordyn. Of course, we want to hear your news. I know you and Skip have been hard at work training the soldiers of the Keep and helping with the Wyvern Riders. What did you want to share?

Ordyn walks over to behind Aphorea, "Surprise, we are having a baby!"

Everybody's head whips around and stares at Aphorea and Ordyn in shock. Akita's eyes get as big as apples, "Oh dear lord, we are going to have to build on to Blackwing Keep."

About the Authors

Theo and I met playing Xbox a little more than ten years ago. We have played several different games together. I'm a Dragon fanatic and love the fantasy worlds created in the books that I have read for years. Theo is a cat lover and very creative. He keeps us laughing and entertained when we party chat. I wanted to write a book and create our own world using the characters we developed in the video games we played and the characters that our friends made. Over two years' time we pieced together our ideas into what is now our first book, Blackwing Keep: Dark Wizards Demise. I could not have gotten this far without my friend and Co-author Theo Moon. Now that we have that foundation, we were able to complete our second book in less than four months, Darkwing Keep: Return of the Cloud Giants. Now we are excited to bring you the Third book in the "Pact of the Keeps Series", Cliffshade Keep: Dark Resurgence.

CHARACTER DESCRIPTIONS

PRIMARY CHARACTERS

AKITA BLACKWING

Description: Demonan Female, age 42 in human years (Young for a Demonan), 6ft 2in height, she has a lean muscular build, long dark brunette hair, copper flecked red skin, ears are slightly pointed, she has fiery golden eyes, two deep red horns that start at the forehead and sweep back above her ears then come to a vertical point. She has two wings attached to just above her shoulder blades, the top of her wings rise to slightly above her head and the tips of her wings end at the nape of her knees, they are similar in color to the rest of her body and resemble large bat wings. She has a 4ft tail starting at her tailbone and ending with an arrowhead shape at the tip, fully controllable.

Status: Akita Blackwing is the last living heir of the Blackwing Family, after her Uncle the High Duke Edmond Blackwing died, Akita became High Duchess of Blackwing Keep. She is a strong Fire and Fear Warlock, with some poison spells. Her fear spells intimidate enemies into thinking they are in major danger from much bigger forces than they actually see in front of them. The fire spells are, fire balls, fire tornadoes, fire columns, fire bolts, and smoldering spells. She has many curse spells that inflict pain and syphon the life essence of the foe. She has raised two Wyverns from pups that she found in her travels, they are named Hunter and Warrior. They are her main mounts.

Fab Ulous

Description: Human Male, age 35, 5ft 9in height, short curly blond hair, lean build. Nickname is Fabby, given to him by Akita. He has an unusual sense of style, wearing bright colors, the shirts have frilly necklines and pants are usually tight. His boots are the finest leather and knee-high.

Status: Traveling companion of Greenbean. Unique Cleric who heals and deals damage. His spells include calming, deep healing, as well as javelin of light that sears as it penetrates the foe, burning light, and a blinding light.

GAVIN BROKINHORN

Description: Demonan Male, age 35 in human years (Young for a Demonan), 6ft 3in height, dark red skin with slight metallic bronze sheen. His horns sweep back and curl to the front. He has deep yellow-colored eyes. The edges of his wings look a little tattered. He has a 4ft long tail that starts at his tailbone, it ends in a half arrow at the tip. Gavin is wearing the typical leather hunter's garb with a bow, quiver, and long dagger at his hip.

Status: Gavin grew up in Prayla on his mother and father's farm. He is a Hunter/Ranger, proficient with a Bow and Short Swords. He uses Earth Magic to manipulate plants, earth, and stone around him. He has the ability to befriend and aid the animals of the world. He is stealthy, being able to sneak through forests and Keeps, with a unique invisibility spell that he can use on himself and others. His best friend and traveling companion is a giant fox, named Blitz.

GHOD

Description: Half Orc Male, age 45, 5ft 11in height, his face is a mystery as he is always wearing a mask. He is extremely muscular from his years as a blacksmith. His skin is a light shade of green with dark green eyes. His upper and lower eye teeth are fangs that protrude over his lips.

Status: He is a Half Orc that was raised by Dwarves that found him as an infant in the forest. Growing up he perfected the Dwarven Blacksmithing talents, he is proficient as a Greatsword fighter. He makes his money specializing in Weapons and Armor smithing, with a special talent in enchanting any item with magic. He can be a nasty old grump but once you have earned his respect and friendship, he is a decent old grump.

GRACE O'MALLEY

Description: Human Female, age 40, 5ft 11in, fiery red hair, bright green eyes, lean build. She tends to wear frilly tops, tight leggings, with thigh-high boots and a pirate hat.

Status: She is known as the Pirate Queen of Alahora. She trained as a Rogue and Assassin. She is originally from Darkforest, but when the opportunity came to buy Aquara Keep from Akita's Uncle, she bought it. She has a pirate's galleon called the Seahorse with a full crew for her Keep and ship. She has a reputation for being murderous and cruel, but how much is rumor or real, no one knows.

GREENBEAN

Description: Half Orc, age 45, 6ft height. She has long blonde hair she keeps up in a ponytail, bright blue eyes, with a lighter touch of green skin. She is muscular. She likes to dress in a plain tunic with a dark leather vest, pants, and thigh-high boots.

Status: Greenbean was born a Dwarf, at the age of 30, a Wizard she was fighting turned into a Half Orc, however she killed the Wizard before he could change her back, so she is stuck as a Half Orc. She is known as an exceptional Greatsword Fighter, fighting instructor, and a sword for hire. She owns a Café and Inn in Salthall, that specializes in an exotic coffee made from green coffee beans. This coffee is addictive to some, but it also has energizing qualities. She is Akita's and Fab Ulous' best friend.

ISHVET BLUESCALE

Description: Half Human-Half Dragonkin Male, age 32, 6ft 5in height. He has deep blue scales with golden eyes, a tall toned muscular body, he has a medium-sized muzzle with sharp protruding teeth, his eye ridges are spiked with small horns, and he doesn't have any horns or ridges on the top of his head.

Status: Sir Ishvet Bluescale was Knighted by his Human Father King Edmond Carthon III and has been traveling the country in search of the Dark Wizards that indirectly killed his mother, Ashonia. He is an exceptional Greatsword Fighter. He met Skrymir Darkwing in his pursuit of the Dark Wizards. Skrymir was able to enchant his Sword that is now known as Bitter Bite. He has joined forces with Akita Blackwing to destroy the Dark Wizards of Alahora. His best friend is his mount Rani, she is a Lamassu, which is pretty much a large flying Lion. He recently learned that his Mother was a Bahamut Dragonkin and that she passed on some type of power to him. He calls it the 'Blue Streak' ability; it causes him to glow blue and move at extreme speed while not able to be hurt.

MANDRAKE BLACKBREW

Description: Dragonkin Male, age 40, 6ft 5in height, with a bird of prey like sleek head, intelligent face, with red eyes, blue scaled with a light silver sheen. He is muscular with broad shoulders. He has four-and-a-half-foot-long Dragon-like wings that are mostly aesthetic and could possibly be used to fly if absolutely needed.

Status: Mandrake is from the continent of Omoth. He and his brother came to Alahora to find his parents' murderer. He is a Wizard of Ice magic, using icy bolts, ice walls, freezing rain, and ice floors, combined this with lightning magic and a little wind magic. He can also levitate items and animate ice sculptures. He has the ability to enchant horses with ice wings for flight. He is Vicar Blackbrew's twin brother. Both are in the service of Akita Blackwing as Advisors.

OLEK THROR

Description: Half Orc Male, age 35, 6ft 5in height, darker green skin with blue eyes and long strawberry blonde hair and a trimmed goatee. He is muscular. As with all Half Orc's his upper and lower eye teeth protrude over his lips.

Status: He is an officer in the Blackwing army. During an attack on Prayla, his skill as a leader was noticed by Akita, and His post in Prayla was moved to Blackwing Keep to groom him to take over for the aging General Ambrose.

Currently, he is heading the division of soldiers fighting the Dark Wizards.

ORDYN BAISIN

__Description__: Bahamut Dragonkin Male, age 300, 8ft height, with a sleek horned head, deep violet eyes, metallic black scales, and black Dragon wings which were granted to him by Bahamut. He dwarfs the other Dragonkin's with his broad stature.

__Status__: Ordyn was a Human man who worked for the Kings and Queens of the realm. He was a devout follower of Bahamut until the day he died. Bahamut resurrected him as a Winged Dragonkin for his dedication in life. He went on to marry a female Dragonkin and have children. After his change, he went back to working for the Royal Family of Oscain. During one of his last assignments for royalty, he received a message that his family had been massacred. He is a Master Greatsword Fighter, whose main objective for the last one hundred years has been to hunt down Dark Wizards and Evil that killed his family. By chance, he has met Akita Blackwing and is now assisting with the demise of the Dark Wizards and their minions.

ROGUE

Description: Meso-Drow Elf Male, age 150 in human years, 6ft 2in height. He has dark skin, a black curly mane of hair, golden eyes, and a tattooed face. He has a sleek muscular build, that allows him to sneak through small spaces and climb up out of site when needed.

Status: Rogue's real name is not known to anyone. He is a Rogue and Assassin in the Darkforest area of Astya. He has been retired for ten-plus years but enjoys aiding Akita in her many endeavors. He was successful in his old life as a master thief and stealthy assassin, but this could come back to haunt him. He has two sisters, Midge and Roguette who live with him on his farm, where he raises cattle and his two pets Wyverns Drako and Ransom.

SHAMASH

Description: Dragonkin Male, age 35, 6ft 9in height. He has a wide face with a short horn around his head and a beard of horns on his chin, red eyes, and grey scales. He is tall and muscular with broad shoulders. Shamash wears a tunic and pants with a traditional Clerics cloak.

Status: Shamash has been in the employ of Blackwing Keep for about ten years under Akita's uncle, High Duke Edmond Blackwing. He runs everything in the Keep that is not military. He remains a strong advisor to Akita now that she has taken over the rule of the Keep. He is a healing Cleric, with calming spells, light spells, and pain-relieving spells. He has a sister Ixenvorlux who is also a healing Cleric.

SKRYMIR DARKWING

Description: Human Male, age 102 (60 years spent in ice), 6ft height. Shoulder-length black hair, braided beard, and ice blue eyes. He has a muscular lean build.

Status: Lord Skrymir Darkwing was just a common farmer when the Cloud Giants came for the Frost Amulet that was a family heirloom given to his great-great-grandfather. After using the Frost Amulet against some Cloud Giants, he ran and hid in a cave, however because he could not remove the amulet and it froze him solid for over sixty years. When he was freed from the ice, he discovers that he had ice and Blue Fire magic. He can produce ice forms intuitively and can conjure Blue Flames that can heat and illuminate. The special type of ice that he makes is very hard to melt and some can regenerate. The flame will only consume materials if he wills it. Now he has a Keep atop the Voskaola Mountains, an aviary of Owl Roc's (Giant Owls), he has known Ishvet and Akita for many years. Darkwing is assisting them in the pursuit of the Dark Wizards.

VICAR BLACKBREW

Description: Dragonkin Male, age 40, 6ft 5in height, with a bird of prey like sleek head, intelligent faces, with red eyes, blue scaled with a light silver sheen. He is muscular with broad shoulders. He has four-and-a-half-foot-long Dragon-like wings that are mostly aesthetic and could possibly be used to fly if absolutely needed.

Status: Vicar is from the continent of Omoth. He and his brother came to Alahora to find his parents' murderer. He is a Cleric, who uses calming spells, deep healing, deep mending, removes pain, induces sleep, creates illuminating light and blinding light. He is known to preside over funerals and weddings. He is Mandrake Blackbrew's twin brother. Both are in the service of Akita Blackwing as Advisors.

VIVIAN ELDERWOLF

__Description__: Human Female, age 34, 5ft 6in height, long blond hair that she keeps up all the time. She has blue eyes and high cheekbones. Her body is very muscular compared to most women her age and height.

__Status__: Vivian is the daughter of Earl Jarkon Elderwolf, ruler of Stonia. She is a Pledged Paladin of great skill, trained by the famous Paladins of Oscain. She can produce shields of pure light, use light to damage targets, and sense Dark Magic. She uses a Mace and Shield fighting style. She wears full plate armor when fighting, otherwise she dresses in very loose comfortable clothing. She met Ghod several years ago and went with him on a mission to collect forging materials. He asked her to aid Akita Blackwing in her fight against the Dark Wizards. On her way to meet Akita, she was attacked by a Basilisk and almost died. Annut saved her life, and she was able to join the team.

WULF WARI

Description: Demonan Male, age 45 in human years (Young for a Demonan), 6ft 5in height. He has a lean muscular build, shoulder-length dark brunette hair, silver-flecked red skin, ears are slightly pointed, he has bright orange eyes, two deep red horns that start at the forehead and sweep back above his ears then curve down around his lower ear. He has two wings attached to just above his shoulder blades, the top of his wings rise to slightly above his head and the tips of his wings end at the nape of his knees, they are similar in color to the rest of his body and resemble large bat wings. he has a four-and-a-half-foot tail starting at his tailbone and ending with a hooked half arrow shape at the tip, fully controllable.

Status: Wulf Wari is a traveler from Omoth, who found himself held captive by Evad Chaos the Dark Wizard. If the team had not rescued him, he would probably have died inside of the Leviathan. He came in search of a new pet and found so much more. He uses Illusion spells to confuse the enemy. He can use anything around him in a fight, mirror image, invisibility, a distraction spell, as well as fear, stun, and the fire spells.

SECONDARY CHARACTERS

AHHA

Description: Dwarven Male, age 130 (19 in human years), 5ft 1in height. Ahha has a red mop of hair with a red mustache and a red beard down to mid-chest. He has bright green eyes and a sleek muscular for a Dwarf. He is dressed in simple but serviceable armor head to toe. He carries a simple but well-made sword and blade.

Status: He is a traditional Pledged Paladin, who decided to set out with his friends on adventures. He wanted to spend some years seeing his world before settling down to a normal life within the clan.

IXENVORLUX

Description: Dragonkin Female, age 30, 6ft 5in height. Her scales are a deep yellow with red eyes. Her head is like a cobra hood around a sleek face. She is lean and muscular. She prefers to dress in traditional Cleric robes.

Status: She is a healing Cleric, with calming spells, light spells, and pain-relieving spells. Her brother is Shamash, who is also a healing Cleric. She has traveled to Blackwing Keep assisting Shamash in the running of the keep and to be a healer for the Keep as Akita and team fight the Dark Wizards.

JESSA REDMANE

Description: Human Female, age 34, 5ft 10in height. A tall, muscular female, who is scantily clad in barely enough clothes to cover her body, with colorful tattoos on her sides and back. She has brown eyes, and shoulder-length red hair, with braids most days.

Status: Jessa was orphaned at a young age. She learned to hunt for herself, she would watch soldiers training and mimic their movements, teaching herself how to protect herself. She had a chance of meeting with Akita Blackwing while Akita was fighting some bandits. Akita was impressed with her story and told her that one day she would summon her to Blackwing Keep if she should want a position in the army. It would be after Akita finished her pilgrimage in Warlock training.

JUDAS SWIFT

Description: Halfling Male, age 30, 3ft 5in height. He has a red mop of hair, green eyes, and is lean in stature. He dresses like a Rogue, in a flat floppy hat, a tunic, a leather vest, leather pants, and knee-high boots.

Status: Judas is a Rogue employed as a special messenger and errand-runner for the High Duke Edmond and now Akita Blackwing. Halflings are known to be fast naturally but there is something special about Judas, as he can run a five-day trip in half the time.

KING WINDU

Description: Dwarf Male, age 150, 5ft height. He has dark brown eyes, with his onyx black hair and beard are meticulously groomed. He is quite overweight and wears a Sultan's desert robe with gold embroidery and green accents. Gold rings adorn each of his ten fingers, and an ornate jeweled broach hangs from a thick gold chain to the middle of his chest.

Status: King Windu was raised a Dwarven Fighter which is kind of rare for Dwarves. He struck out on his own at a young age and was curious about the world around him. He had studied artifacts growing up and decided to find them. As time went on, he gained wealth, loyal artifact hunters and over the years he found his way to Oceanfalls, where he decided to take over as King in a coup. He has successfully ruled for many years and is known to have a vault full of relics, artifacts and what he calls collectables. He sometimes employs Dark Wizards, Rogues, and Assassins to gain what he wants most.

MAGRATH BATTLEBREAKER

Description: Half Orc Female, age 40, 5ft 10in height. A tall, shapely female with long dark hair and bright green eyes. She wears leather tunic, leather vest, leather pants and thigh-high leather boots, with specially made silver gauntlets.

Status: She is a Greatsword Fighter, who is the last survivor of her battle group against a band of trolls. Her current husband, Ouch, saved her from certain death and they decided to travel and live great adventures rather than fight battles for the sake of battling. While adventuring, she and her husband met Akita Blackwing and took her up on adventurous employment.

MEH-KOLA

Description: Fenton Female, age unknown, she has a cat-like body mostly covered in short dark gray fur with vertical black stripes. She has a scaled region that starts at her neck and travels to the tip of her tail. Meh-Kola has two bat-like wings that are attached above the shoulder blades of her front legs. Her tail is covered in scales and resembles a Dragons tail with tiny horns running the length of it. She has very sharp retractable claws on all four paws.

Status: Meh-Kola is from Omoth, little is known of her back story. She is an Assassin and Thief for hire. She has a very different way of speaking. She refers to herself as "One" which is the traditional Fenton way. She has a very special ability to "Blink" through seemingly solid objects. However, she must only see light on the other side of the obstacle that she is going through. Her razor-sharp claws can cut through almost any material. These abilities are uncommon for a Fenton. Meh-Kola met Vicar and Mandrake Blackbrew on the continent of Omoth many years ago and befriended them. She met Rogue through the Assassins Guild in Alahora. She has recently been invited to be a part of the team from Blackwing Keep that is pursuing the Dark Wizards.

MIDGE

Description: Halfling Female, age 40, 3ft 4in height. She has blonde hair and brown eyes and a slight build. She wears natural forest color clothing to better blend into the forest.

Status: She is a Hunter/Ranger, with earth magic, that is proficient with a bow and dagger. Her brother is Rogue, the man of mystery. When he goes out on a mission she often worries as to if she will see him again. They have a little sister named Roguette who has followed in Rogue's footsteps.

OUCH BATTLEBREAKER

Description: Dwarf Male, age 147, 4ft 11in height. He is a typical-looking dwarf, short and stocky. His dirty blonde beard hangs to the bottom edge of his chest, and mustache is wider than his face and turns upward at the ends.

Status: His name is Gozic Battlebreaker, but he earned the nickname ouch because in training he would always holler "Ouch" when he was hit. Ouch has a very quirky sense of humor. He was raised as a Pledged Paladin, but going against clan tradition, he trained himself to be a Devout Paladin like his mother, to be a healer. He met his wife, Magrath, as she collapsed after a battle, near death. Ouch saved her life on that fateful day, and they have never been apart since.

ROGUETTE

Description: Meso-Drow Elf Female, age 35 in human years (Young for Elves), 5ft 11in height. She has coppery brown eyes, long brunette hair kept in a ponytail, and slim build.

Status: She has followed in her brother's footsteps as a Rogue and Assassin. Not much is known about her, as she wants to be as mysterious as her brother.

QUINN DRAKZHUL

Description: Demonan Female, age 33, 5ft 10in height, with light red skin that has a copper glint, shoulder-length red hair, and brown eyes. She has a three-and-a-half-foot-long tail that tapers down to a barbed point. She is muscular. Her wings are like batwings that match her skin color and reach from the top of her head to behind her knees.

Status: Quinn grew up near Salthall. Her parents made her hide her Warlock abilities because she had no training and could not control them. She had heard of a Warlock in Salthall, named Void Roasten, but he would not train a youngling. He advised her to seek out Akita Blackwing for work and training, which she did. Now she works in the kitchens of Blackwing Keep, where she is free to proactively practice her spells and build her abilities up. Recently she has become smitten with Olek Thror.

SKIP BASS

Description: Meso-Drow Elf Male, age 155 in human years, 6ft 4in height. He has bright green eyes, long white hair he keeps braided, dark tanned skin, and a lean build. He typically wears green or brown shirts and pants with brown leather boots, so he can hide in the forest better.

Status: Skip is a Hunter/Ranger, with dark magic and earth magic. He is a master with a bow and long dagger. He is from Omoth and old friends of Mandrake Blackbrew and Vicar Blackbrew. He built his home and forge on the edge of the forest near the Port City of Vaile. He has been assisting the Blackbrew twins in the hunt for an Assassin.

STORM FIREHEART

Description: Meso-Drow Elf Female, age 100 in human years, 5ft 11in height. She has fire orange eyes, white hair down to her waist, that she keeps braided, and lighter tanned skin with a golden sheen. She has a lean build and likes to dress like a Rogue. Some family members wonder if she has Demonan in her blood.

Status: Storm is a Fire Wizard, which is also rare, as most Wizards are ice, wind, and lightning. As a Fire Wizard she commands fire in many aspects, hot winds and still has lightning abilities. As a Meso-Drow Elf she also has dark magic, which she only uses in extreme cases. She struck out on her own, trying to find her own way in the world about five years ago. She went to find her ancestral magic in Omoth and hasn't been heard from since.

ADDITIONAL CHARACTERS

AMBROSE STAPLES

Description: Demonan Male, age 90 in human years (Retirement age for a Demonan), 5ft 11in height. His eyes are a silvery brown, his hair is grey, his skin is light red with a silver sheen, and wings to match. He wears the uniform of the Blackwing Keep military all the time.

Status: General Ambrose worked his way up the ranks in the Blackwing Keep army from a young age. Where Shamash was and is the right hand of the Keeps ruler, General Ambrose was and is the left hand of the Keeps ruler. He is reaching retirement age and although he was skeptical if Akita Blackwing would be able to fulfill her uncles' shoes, he is quite impressed with recent activities and battles.

BEN WEAVER

Description: Human Male, age 18, 5ft 8in height. He has bright blue eyes, dark black hair, and is barely shaving. He is well built for his age. He wears the uniform of the stable hands at Blackwing Keep.

Status: Ben is an orphan that lives with his blind grandfather. He is a street urchin in Salthall until the day he witnessed flying mounts fly over his hometown. His curiosity got the best of him, he had to go see them. The moment he saw them he knew he wanted to work at Blackwing Keep and was waiting to talk to Akita Blackwing first thing in the morning. She accepted him and even found a place for the old grandfather.

BLUE & ROSE BROKINHORN

Description: Demonan Male and Female, Retirement ages, 6ft and 5ft 9in height. Typical older Demonan couple.

Status: Blue and Rose have a good-sized farm just outside of Prayla, where they raise cattle and sheep, as well as some crops. Recently, Blue has been building special pens in hopes of raising Wyverns. Their son is Gavin Brokinhorn, who has recently been working with Akita Blackwing at the Keep.

DUKE EDMOND BLACKWING

Description: Demonan Male, Deceased.

Status: High Duke Edmond Blackwing and his wife lost their entire family, except for Akita to Annut – the Fast. Her parents, siblings, and their children were all attacked as they headed back to Akita's Keep near Salthall for the summer. Akita had wandered off from the main group. Edmond and his wife then raised her as their own and the sole heir to Blackwing Keep.

DUTCH BLACK

Description: Human Male, age 25, 5ft 8in height. He has brown eyes, dishwater blonde hair, standard build. He wears tunics, pants, and slippers.

Status: Part owner of Mystical Messenger Service in Salthall. His partner is Snappy. Akita is one of their regular customers.

ELGIN BAILEY

Description: Human Male, age 50, 5ft 6in height. He has hazel eyes and greying hair, pudgy build.

Status: He is the owner of the Hungry Boar Tavern and Inn with his wife Lucille. They live in a set of rooms above the Inn, he manages the bar and patrons.

EVAD CHAOS

Description: Human Male, age 45, 4ft 10in height. He is short in stature, brown eyes, brown hair, and power hungry. He wears a cloak of the Dark Wizards and dresses in all black.

Status: He is a Leader of a Dark Wizard sect, under the Grand Master Dark Wizard. He has Goblin minions to defend his cave of treasure and potion ingredients. He has several lower Dark Wizards to do the lower tedious magic work. He has several bands of Bandits to do is killing and gather his ingredients. He is a creator of monsters, murder of Dragonkin and only one of many that are a menace to the realm.

GRETA RISAN

Description: Human Female, age 60, 5ft 5in height. She has bright green eyes, silver-grey hair, muscular form, dressed in long dress with a house apron most of the time.

Status: Greta is the Keeps House Matron. It is her responsibility to make sure the housekeepers and kitchen help keep the rooms clean and meals cooked. She has been an employee of Blackwing Keep since she was a young woman. When Akita came to live with her aunt and uncle, Greta took on the role of nanny.

Jacklyn Moondancer

Description: Moon Elf, Female, age 74, 6ft 2in. height. She has bright blue eyes, white hair and porcelain white skin, lean form, dressed in leather armor and leggings with a long slender Greatsword at her side. She can use ancient magic but is forbidden to use her Clan's more powerful magic in Alahora. She can imbue her sword with moonlight to cut through any dark magic wards. She can also take Moon Form to trick her enemies by casting a projection of herself.

Status: Jacklyn in the employ of Grace O'Malley at O'Malley Keep. Until recently she was a captain in the Keep Guard. Now she Is second in command after Grace.

King Edmond Carthon III

Description: Half Sun Elf/ Half Human Male, age 50, 6ft height Dark Brown Hair, Blue eyes, manicured beard. Tall and lean, but quite muscular.

Status: King Carthon rules the region of Astya from Cliffshade Keep. His family has ruled the east coast region for hundreds of years. He is Ishvet Bluescale's Father. However, the King wasn't present in Ishvet's life. The King is a well-known Wizard. It has been discovered that King Carthon may be tied to the Dark Wizards plaguing the lands of Alahora.

LEADER FERON

Description: Human Male, age 32, 5ft 8in height. He has brown eyes, stringy black hair, with a skinny build. He stays hidden in his Dark Wizards cloak.

Status: Leader Feron is a scholar from the town of Cliffside in Mina, and a self-proclaimed expert in Dragons. He is currently working for King Edmond Carthon on a special project.

LUCILLE BAILEY

Description: Human Female, age 48, 5ft 3in height. She keeps her hair up in a bun and is in a dress and apron every day.

Status: Lucille is Elgin's wife, and she supervises the Hungry Boar Tavern and Inn rooms, keeps the kitchen stocked and cooks most of the meals. The couple lives in a set of rooms on the third floor of the Inn.

MADAM SUZIE

**Description**: Human Female, age 50, 5ft 1in height. a handsome older woman with a colorful headwrap and an equally as colorful dress that seems to have many layers of sheer fabric.

**Status**: Knower of the unknown, temptress of fate, and brewer of concoctions. A mysterious woman with an ancient friend.

SCOTCH BROWN

**Description**: Human Male, age 25, 6ft 3in height. He is long and lanky, but strong. He has hazel eyes, short blonde hair that is always messed up, tanned skin from being in the sun a lot.

**Status**: Scotch is a stable hand that has been working at Blackwing Keep for a couple of years. At first, he thought it would be a job to get him through until he could save up to travel. Although he still wants to travel, the activities, excitement, and the awesome mounts he takes care of have made it hard for him to leave anytime soon.

SHAM RHAM

Description: Human Male, age 35, 6ft 4in height. He is tall and muscular. He has brown eyes, long strawberry blonde hair that is always pulled back or braided, he is also tan from working in the sun all the time.

Status: Sham is the lead stable hand that has been working at Blackwing Keep for over ten years. He makes sure all the mounts are fed, exercised, and cared for in every way. He has helped raise Akita's horse Nightmare, as well as Hunter and Warrior.

SNAPPY HOUND

Description: Half Wood Elf, age 24, 5ft 7in height. He is an average man, with shoulder-length black hair, brown eyes, and a bright smile. He looks more like his dad than his elven mom.

Status: Part owner of Mystical Messenger Service in Salthall. His partner is Dutch. He uses what little forest magic he has for various tasks and his natural ability with animals, with the Thunder Hawks. Akita is one of their regular customers.

DRAGONS OF ALAHORA

ANNUT — THE FAST: Female Fire Dragon, her scales are red, orange, red-orange, and dark red making her look like fire as she flies. Her horns and ridges are dark red. Recently spotted in the Prayla.

APHOREA — THE BRILLIANT: Ancient Female Ice Dragon, her scales are white. Her horns and ridges are like bright white pearls. Whereabouts unknown.

ASHONIA — THE SKY: Female Water Dragon, her scales are light blue like the sky reflected in water. Her horns and ridges are a darker shade of blue. Last seen in the region of Astya.

BUZZONTIR — THE SCARY: Male Cloud Dragon, his scales are dark grey to black. His horns and ridges are dark black with glowing cracks on the surface that mimic lightning streaking across a black sky. He has not been seen for hundreds of years.

JAXIAN — THE TSUNAMI: Ancient Male Water Dragon, his scales are a mixture of sea green, turquoise and light blues, like a clear ocean water, with turquoise horns and ridges. Vague reports put him in the area of Oscain near the Southern coast.

RETHU — THE FIERCE: Male Fire Dragon, his scales are blue like the color of sapphire with blue, royal blue and dark blue scales, his horns and ridges are royal blue. Whereabouts Unknown.

RUKUR — THE BRIGHT: Ancient Male Stone Dragon, He is gold like precious metal, but his horns and ridges are like tarnished gold. Last sighting was 45 years ago in the region of Franken.

THORAXIAN — THE SHADOW: Ancient Male Fire Dragon, his scales are dark black with a silver sheen, his horns and ridges are onyx black and shiny. He was seen in the region of Craonia.

GLOSSARY OF RACES

Races

- o Bahamut Reborn – Dragonkin biped Humanoid Dragon/Demonan Demon Humanoid

  - ▪ Transformed by the God Bahamut

  - ▪ Can be any race before transformation

  - ▪ Was granted one special ability upon transformation

  - ▪ Any Scale Colors

  - ▪ May or may not have wings

  - ▪ Rare to be Fire Breathers

  - ▪ Any class

- o Dragonkin – biped Humanoid Dragon

  - ▪ Any Scale Colors

  - ▪ Do not have wings

  - ▪ Rare to be Fire Breathers

  - ▪ Any class

- o Demonan – Demon Humanoid

  - ▪ Various shades of Red Skin

- Precious metal tints to their Skin
- Leathery Dragon like wings
- Long tapered tails
- Any Class

o Wood Elf

- Tall Elves
- Forest Magic
- Typically, Rogues, Clerics, Hunter/Rangers, Warlocks, and Wizards

o Sun Elf

- Shorter Elves
- Earth Magic
- Typically, Rogues, Clerics, Hunter/Rangers, Warlocks, and Wizards

o Meso-Drow Elf

- Tall Dark Elves
- Dark Magic

- Typically, Rogues, Clerics, Hunter/Rangers, Warlocks, and Wizards
- Half Elf/Half Human
  - Magic depends on which Elf the Parent is.
  - Strength depends on dominant characteristics from Parents.
  - Any Class
- Human
  - Standard Humans
  - Rare to be Magic Users
  - Any Class
- Dwarf
  - Short and Stocky
  - Long hair and long beards
    - Beard length will signify age and supposed wisdom.
  - Stone and Metal Experts
  - Rare to be Magic Users

- Typically, Paladins, Fighters, Greatsword Fighters

- Half-Orc

  - Half Human Orc.

  - Tall and muscular.

  - Protruding Upper and Lower Eye Teeth Fangs.

  - Typically, Fighters and Greatsword Fighters.

- Fenton – Quadruped

  - Flying Cat

  - Long Hair or Short Hair

  - Soft, Supple Bat like wings

  - Magical

    - Blink, Invisibility, Stealth and more.

GLOSSARY OF CLASSES

- ➤ Warlock
    - o Dark Magic
        - ▪ Soul Energy Drain and Projected Fear
        - ▪ Illusions – Mirror Image, Invisibility
        - ▪ Fire – Smolder, Fire Ball, Fire Blast
        - ▪ Power Words – Stun and Kill
- ➤ Wizard
    - o Ice, Lightning, and Wind Magic
        - ▪ Freezing – Chill Touch, Ray of Frost, Wall of Ice
        - ▪ Storms – Control Weather, Meteor Swarm
        - ▪ Electric - Shocking, Lightning Strikes, Chain Lightning
        - ▪ Vortex Winds
- ➤ Cleric
    - o Healing, Power Buffing, Light Damage

- Healing with Divinity Light

- Searing Light Javelin Magic Spears

- Power Buffing with Light

- Illumination

- Calming spells

➢ Hunter/Ranger

  ○ Earth Magic/Fighter with Daggers and Bow

    - Magical and Non-Magical Arrow shots experts

    - Root Traps

    - Invisibility and Stealth

    - Manipulation of Earth and Stone

    - Special Bond to Animals

➢ Rogue/Assassin

  ○ Chemistry, Fighting, Stealth

    - Shadow Cloaking

    - Dash Invisibility

    - Potion and Poison Crafting

    - Targeting Blades, Blade Flourish

- Paladin
  - Pledged
    - Light Magic to generate shields of Protection
    - Empowers team members in close proximity during battle
    - Detect/Dispel Evil, Good and Magic
    - Fighter – Shield of Faith
  - Devout
    - Light Magic to Heal the Wounded
    - Heals team members in close proximity during battle
    - Detect/Dispel Evil and Good
    - Fighter – Shield of Faith
- Greatsword Warrior
  - Heavy weapons – two handed weapons
    - No Shields
    - Brute strength
    - Inner Magic to empower their weapon abilities
  - Only encompasses the individual

➢ Keeps and Territories

- o Blackwing Keep – High Duchess Lady Akita Blackwing

  - ▪ Prayla- Prayla, Stagbreak, Salthall

- o Darkwing Keep – Lord Skrymir Darkwing

  - ▪ Voskaola Mountain, Emberfrost, Deerbreach

- o O'Malley Keep – Grace O'Malley Pirate Queen

- o Cliffside Keep – King Edmond Carthon III

  - ▪ Astya - Mina, Darkforest, Myst Marsh

- o Elderwolf Keep – Earl Jarkon Elderwolf

  - ▪ Stonia - Neg Grove, Riverhost, Dragon Rest

- o Oceanfalls Keep – King Windu

  - ▪ Craonia – Oceanfalls City, Port Tristan

www.StaplesMoonBooks.com

StaplesMoonBooks@gmail.com

www.ingramcontent.com/pod-product-compliance
Lightning Source LLC
Chambersburg PA
CBHW070147120726
47909CB00001B/19